THE DIVINE GARDENER'S HANDBOOK:

Or What To Do If Your Girlfriend Accidentally Turns Off the Sun

THE DIVINE GARDENER'S HANDBOOK:

Or What To Do If Your Girlfriend Accidentally Turns Off the Sun

ELI SNOW

SATURDAY
BOOKS
NEW YORK

This is a work of fiction. All of the names, characters, organizations, places, and events portrayed in this work are either products of the author's imagination or are used fictitiously.

First published in the United States by Saturday Books, an imprint of St. Martin's Publishing Group

EU Representative: Macmillan Publishers Ireland Ltd, 1st Floor, The Liffey Trust Centre, 117–126 Sheriff Street Upper, Dublin 1, D01 YC43

 For information, address St. Martin's Publishing Group, 120 Broadway, New York, NY 10271.

www.saturdaybooks.com

Designed by Devan Norman

Endpaper credit: rose pattern © Svetik_Kalaturs/Shutterstock
Designed edges: botanicals © Vizerskaya/Getty Images;
blue rose © Stefan Grau/Getty Images

The Library of Congress Cataloging-in-Publication Data
is available upon request.

ISBN 978-1-250-39518-4 (hardcover)
ISBN 978-1-250-39519-1 (ebook)

First Edition: 2026

10 9 8 7 6 5 4 3 2 1

CONTENT WARNINGS

DEATH, DEATH OF A PARENT (PAST),
CHILDHOOD TRAUMA, VIOLENCE

THE DIVINE GARDENER'S HANDBOOK:

Or What To Do If Your Girlfriend Accidentally Turns Off the Sun

CHAPTER 1

CYPRIN

Cyprin walked through the undercity. It had taken a long time for the city of Asperia to get to where it was today. The new had been built on the bones of the old, and there were whole forgotten worlds below ground.

Asperia was a giant megacity, the only city in the Kingdom of Verdure, and beneath it lurked a wealth of history, actual preserved buildings, and tunnels a person could walk through, instead of just stuff pressed into layers of sedimentary rock.

The bioluminescent mushroomy glow of a headlamp strapped to Cyprin's forehead was the only accompaniment to the relentless dark. The lamp used a small-scale version of the mycelial network that powered most of the city's lights, cheap and self-sustaining, perfect for creeping around. The glow was enough to render everything spectral, but not bright enough to warrant detection by any of Asperia's law-keepers.

Cyprin was headed for the black market—a place run by a rebellious organization called the Underground that existed simply because, in a city of seven billion, there were always people who wanted illegal things.

People like Cyprin.

She reached a fork in the passageways where an old vending machine flickered with staccato fluorescence. Some damn breakfast cereal jingle was stuck in her head.

"What's the taste that fuels kids all day long? Makes 'em run and play and sing this song? Mom loves, Dad loves, dog loves, kids love—Sugar Bombs!"

Cyprin took a bronze coin out of her pocket, slotted it into the ancient vending machine, and punched in a code she'd copied from toilet-door scrawl in a nightclub bathroom. A robotic arm pushed out nothing from an empty pigeonhole inside the glass. She looked furtively over her shoulder at the barren hallway behind, then squatted down to shove her hand through the collection flap. Her arm came back out with a piece of paper. The map on it was hand drawn and scraggly, but she could make out where it wanted her to go.

She wished she was at home, watching *Lust Island*, a show based on a few minutes of restored footage from the fossil record. There was something both totally prehistoric and inherently human about it. Not to mention the coconuts. But no.

Everyone had a story about the black market. There was always somebody's aunt's best friend losing their leg to a rat the size of a toy poodle. Always a co-worker with a tale about how some poor soul had turned the wrong way and been found as skeletal remains months later.

Cyprin had only come down here a handful of times. It was practically a local rite of passage to visit the black market at least once in your life, and every now and then, when a night out got out of hand, she'd be back chasing an illegal high. Today was different, though. Today she was going to commit a real crime.

"What's the taste that fuels kids all day long? Makes 'em run and play and sing this song? Mom loves, Dad loves, dog loves, kids love—Sugar Bombs!" Cyprin's voice went an octave higher as she took the right-hand path and started going down the stairwell at the end of the hall. Depth had a smell, not something she thought about on the regular, but it was there, unmistakable. Like a whiff of carrots left too long in the fridge. It wasn't a smell that inspired you to go toward it. Cyprin checked the map one more time, even turning it upside down to make absolutely sure she hadn't got it wrong. Nope. Okay.

The stairs went down in a spiral.

In Divine mythology, the undercity was synonymous with the twelve hells. All twelve had different environments, kind of like the *Lust Island* sets if you replaced the sea with boiling napalm, turned all the contestants inside out, and gave them extra eyeballs. But the layer Cyprin was wandering through wasn't yet a hell of its own—it was more a kind of purgatory, outside of the purview of the priestguard.

After the stairs, Cyprin emerged into a barren room. Who knew what kind of building she was in now. There were no signs left to identify it by. Everything had been looted. Then a noise like the movement of a ton of rats freaked her out until she realized it was the muted sounds of people bartering and chatting.

Cyprin found the black market in a large hallway. Big chunks of wall lay horizontally down the middle, which people were using as bench seating. Metal scaffolding and chicken wire held back a cave-in. Across the ceiling, strings of dull blue globes like the one attached to Cyprin's head cast just enough light to see by. The space was set up like a farmer's market, trellis tables and wheeled carts holding all manner of produce. Even (optimistically, in this damp-carrot environment) food stalls.

A crowd meandered around the space. Most were wide-eyed teens with glow-stick bracelets. Then there were the slumpers, people who sought salvage from the undercity, thin enough to fit through most cracks, muck-wrecked from delving in the deeps, probably here for their equivalent of a grocery run before they went home. Individuals with a distinct air of danger about them purchased illegal body-mods and outlawed tech. Some beige office-types were there too, giving in to various vices, but they were few and far between. And Cyprin, what category did she fit into? The criminal element?

Cyprin took a chance on a sausage roll and drowned it in sauce that shone black under the blue lights. She knew what she was looking for. She'd only been here a few times, but she'd seen it before, and it had stuck in her head. She remembered thinking at the time, *Who in their right mind would buy something like that?* Now she had an answer.

"I want to buy something that will ruin a plant and look like natural causes."

"Specific type?" The woman at the stall wore a balaclava, even down here in the dark.

"Rosebush."

"Range?"

"Range? One. One bush."

"Ruin? You want to kill it?"

Cyprin's palms itched. She thought of the roses in the Divine Gardens, so red they took her breath away, and swallowed down a lump in her throat. "No. Just maim. Something that will recover with tender care and a few months."

The woman's balaclava buckled as she smiled. "Not a problem, I have just the thing."

A buzzing jar was handed across into Cyprin's arms. Cold hard cash went the other way.

All this had started a day ago.

God's gardens were beautiful in a way that a simple word could never do justice. The leaves so lustrous they could have been polished. Petals had peeked out in saturated hues that put Cyprin in mind of fresh paints. The grass—even the damned grass looked like it had been laser cut. Planed rather than trimmed.

The gardens were nothing like the city, where Cyprin worked in one of twelve hundred apple orchards, where apples undulated like ocean waves whenever she closed her eyes, where only stale light made it down past the scrapers and the hot-sick smell of full trash cans and close bodies surrounded her—getting a job there was like getting plucked out of obscurity by one of those claw machines at a fair. It was an almost-impossibility.

But for the first time in a lifetime of trying, Cyprin had secured an interview in the Divine Gardens.

The pinnacle of horticultural research and practice happened in the Divine Gardens. And only ten thousand lucky individuals got to be a part of it. Which had sounded like a lot until Cyprin had thought about the seven billion who lived in the Divine Kingdom of Verdure, most of them with green thumbs. And until she'd remembered hardly anyone ever vacated their position in the gardens. Most went through to retirement. Some chose to keep working until they died, nodding out with the bluebells in some quiet corner. No matter how old or infirm they were by the end, the garden admin staff seemed to find ways for them to contribute. After all, the divine gardeners were like a big family. A big elite family. Okay, maybe more like a cult. A cult Cyprin desperately wanted to belong to.

God's gardens were full of purist snobs who bathed in starch and dewed instead of sweating, and for the interview, Cyprin had made herself a close approximation of them. Dark hair waxed tight to her scalp, lips precision-lined, tawny brown skin scrubbed of imperfections. She'd even donned impractical but showy all-white coveralls. But after walking in the midmorning heat to get to the garden admin center, everything was sweat-soaked.

At least the garden admin center where the interview was to be held was cool and damp, hewn out of the bedrock. Grow lights strung up in lines at ankle height constituted a major OHS hazard, and seedlings littered the floor in disposable cardboard pots.

If only Cyprin had known whom she was about to meet. How this was about to go. She would've run back to the city. And maybe avoided the black market. Maybe.

Toward the back of the admin center, two women talked at a stone desk, dressed in the white outfits of palace staff. They were everything Cyprin wanted to be. One held a watering can and had soft, round features, with stunning green eyes framed by large glasses. She was short and medium-sized, with a curly bob of brownish hair and pinkish-white skin, while the other woman was tall and eggshell-white, thin, and blond. The blond had a good sassy eyebrow-raise going, as though whole parts of her face were leaning away from the conversation.

Cyprin tried to butt in for her appointment. "Hey, excuse me?"

The short woman shushed her before returning to her conversation, and Cyprin's visions of perfect, floaty, enviable garden angels evaporated.

She tried to butt in again. "Hey, I'm here for—"

The blond's eyes were sympathetic, but the brown-haired girl was rude. "Be quiet for a moment, will you? Wait your turn."

Cyprin's glare should've withered her on the spot, but the woman just went right back to her whiny conversation.

"—I wanted gold petals for the petal-mail fitting, but there weren't enough perfect gold roses, so I've ended up with red *and* gold! That's a problem, isn't it? Do you think that's a problem? I'm worried it's going to make God look sallow!"

Cyprin committed the whole of her to angry memory. The manic corkscrew curls, cheeks the pink of rat tails. *Drip, drip*—the watering can was as emotionally off-kilter as its owner. Droplets fell from it and completely failed to hit a plant a mere finger's width away. Cyprin's eye twitched faintly.

It was hate at first sight.

"Excuse me," Cyprin said, very loudly and firmly. "I'm here for my interview."

The blond on the other side of the desk turned toward Cyprin with an unmistakable air of relief. The short lady with the brown curls tipped the watering can onto her own foot. Good Divine, what a dorkus! Cyprin had never seen such large eyes on a person, luminous and green, almost hypnotic.

"Oh! You must be Cyprin Voltag!" said the blond, the owner of the sassy eyebrow. "I'm Amanda Anstan, and this is our head gardener, Purcell Whitlock. So nice to finally meet you in the flesh."

"Fine. I'll leave you to it." Purcell smiled in a brittle way. "After all, I'm supposed to go and dress God." She looked cute but bitey, like a terrier that had suffered too many pats on the head.

A-hur-hur-hur, dress God, Cyprin mocked Purcell in the safety of her imagination, suffering the end of their exchange with a polite smile plastered on her face. These two were chatting about how tight they were with God while her whole life rested on a knife's edge. Unbelievable.

Purcell jostled her on the way out, and that was when Cyprin realized she could *smell* her, sweet and cloying like a candy shop. Cyprin had the unhinged thought that if she cracked Purcell open like a piñata, pink musk sticks would spill out. For a moment she felt every bit the predatory city rat she was trying not to be. The possibility of there being ten thousand Purcells in the gardens reared its ugly head. Cyprin pictured them as little marshmallows she would pop in her mouth one by one until she was sick. But she had to get in. She had to finally see him.

"Are you ready?" Amanda asked.

Cyprin had always thought that when this moment came the pressure would crush her into diamond. She'd driven herself half-mad practicing gardening skills anywhere she could: growing carrots from old carrot tops in her kitchen, coaxing avocado plants from stubborn pits, tweezering seeds from supermarket tomatoes to plant in a thin layer of dirt in her bathtub. She'd copied out a whole almanac on roses until its pages danced behind her eyes. She'd drafted and redrafted her resignation letter to her boss in the apple orchards an astounding seventy-three times. She was supposed to be ready.

Instead, she'd turned into soggy carbon.

Facts and spiels about herself she'd practiced so often they had formed trenches in her gray matter inexplicably vanished, just like Maverick had fourteen years ago, leaving her chasing after him ever since. The moment the interview started, all she'd been able to think about was Maverick. How much he'd let her down. How close she was to him there in the gardens. How she longed to confront him.

Even when he was not around, Maverick still managed to ruin her life.

Presently, in the deep darkness of the undercity, Cyprin hefted the buzzing jar of vicious bio bots in her hand.

The joke was on Maverick, because she was going to ruin his life right back.

CHAPTER 2

PURCELL

At the foot of the marble staircase that led up to the Divine's rooms, Purcell stopped and had a mild panic attack while holding onto the banister. This was her first day as head gardener, after the former, Miss Glint, died. Miss Glint had reached the ripe old age of ninety-three, which meant Purcell, her subordinate, had effectively been running the gardens for the last five years. But Purcell had never tended to God.

If she fumbled this new duty, God would be inadequately dressed for the ceremonies in which he made the sun rise and set, and he might get distracted and not do it properly. But *worse* than this, Purcell would be swiftly demoted and never offered the top job again.

She kept telling herself she was the best, she was the best. Purcell knew she was the best. She also knew that ten thousand knives, or at least garden trowels, waited at her back for her to make a wrong move—for her to *fail*. People already didn't like her; some of the gardeners played practical jokes on her, hiding large plastic spiders among the rhododendrons, switching the sugar out for salt at her favorite table in the cafeteria. She was the best, until she wasn't, and the longer she spent in the rarefied air at the top of Success Mountain, the hungrier her rivals grew to see her fall.

Purcell was head gardener, but she was also a collective of cells, bacteria, and electrical impulses, all of whom could benefit from a course in self-confidence. She was second-in-command to God now. She had to begin the unenviable daily task of linking fresh petal mail for him *as well as* holding responsibility for the running of the entire Divine Gardens, which God obviously couldn't do as he was busy with the sun.

Things would be less hectic if she delegated some tasks, but the problem was no one could do her job as well as she. People were unreliable chaos engines. You had to watch them, and watch yourself, and watch them watching you. A whole lot of watching and a dearth of relaxation. That's what life was.

In the rare moments where Purcell stopped to daydream, she imagined a garden full of Purcell clones, all wearing their gold lanyards of authority, each one nodding to congratulate the others on a job well done. A world devoid of jealousy and ambition, where order reigned. Maybe there'd even be time for a little romance. A little Purcell-on-Purcell action. Because, unfortunately, nobody else was good enough.

She was the best, she was the best. Purcell went up the stairs to face God.

"Good morning!" The Petaled Divine was *right there*. Looming like a thug in his own throne room. He was taller than she remembered from the few times she'd glimpsed him at ceremonies and pageants, and thin in a way that made his clothes hang off him like a scarecrow.

The bag of rose heads Purcell had collected for this occasion dropped onto the tiles, some of them rolling out to color the floor red and gold. This was a mess, and it was all the fault of that dark-eyed hopeful in the admin center. That woman had thrown Purcell off-kilter by disrupting her venting session with Amanda. Purcell scrambled to retrieve the roses, then stood up, forgetting protocol as she stared directly at God. Of course, the first thing she saw was the ragged hole in his petaled mail. Torn like it had been snagged on something, pinks and reds muddying.

"Oh, oh dear." Her gaze swung up to the Petaled Divine's face to thoughtlessly include him in the oopsie. She saw a flip of black hair. Pale olive skin that glowed as though polished. Washed-out brown eyes looked back at her from a face that should have belonged to a tired librarian. A faint smile broke out amidst the designer stubble. Purcell got all the way up to contemplating the man's craterous pores before she realized she was wearing her work glasses and had the telescopic lens flipped down over her right eye. She coughed and lifted it up and then remembered with a lurch of acute embarrassment that she wasn't supposed to be acting like this at all. Purcell almost cracked her forehead on the floor in her rush to defer to him. "Seasonal Demiurge, forgive my insolence!"

She glanced up. The Petaled Divine was sniggering. His mouth was closed, but his sides twitched in what looked like a withheld sneeze, and the sound came out anyway. A soft hand enveloped Purcell's and tugged gently but insistently until she got to her feet.

The Petaled Divine endeavored to look serious but wasn't fooling Purcell. She was being laughed at. What could be worse? Well, she'd also stared treasonously upon his holy face, an indiscretion that used to be met with the retribution of immediate death but had thankfully been downgraded in more recent generations to public penance: being shorn and anointed with cleansing oils. Her free hand went to the bob she cut with a ruler and precision shears. Her *free* hand? Purcell gasped and stepped back, winding herself on the wall.

"Calm down, please!" said the Petaled Divine, alarmed but still clearly amused. He seemed to sense he'd need to lead the conversation. "What is your name?"

Purcell risked one more blasphemous glance at him and then looked for safety in her feet.

"Your name? I assume you have one. I think I recall you from the Verdure Flower Pageant. Persal, wasn't it?" A hint of impatience crept into the Divine's voice.

"Purcell."

"Perseal?"

"*Per-sell.*"

The Divine smiled. "You seem sure about that, at least. That's a good start. A very good start, indeed." The petaled mail rustled as he turned away from her. "Would you care for some tea? I always have some here, think it might even still be hot."

"Um. Uh, Divine, I'm here to link the petal chain." Purcell lifted her eyes cautiously up over the pale, gold-grained marble. She'd never been in here. The room was sparser than she'd imagined. One of the peonies in the corner looked sick. And there, in a dirt well in the center, was the Mint Throne itself, grown into the shape of the Petaled Divine's holy ass, or so they said. It all looked rather woody. Her fingers itched to give it a trim and some fertilizer.

"This is star orange, you know," said the Divine. "They tell me it's made by harvesting cave mushrooms that only fruit once a year. It gets dried out in the dark. Photosensitive. Becomes utterly flavorless after an hour or so in the light."

Purcell followed his voice around the bulk of the throne to find him sitting on a little stool at a plain wooden table. The Petaled Divine poured, with his own holy hands, two cups of steaming tea. He looked oddly like a vulture, hunched over the teacups.

"Be a shame to let it go to waste. A sin even," he continued, oblivious to Purcell's growing horror. He finished pouring and waved a hand at a second stool.

No clause, subclause, footnote, or addendum in any rule book Purcell had ever seen covered the correct etiquette for taking tea with God. Purcell looked back longingly at the throne-room doors, still slightly ajar.

God misinterpreted, perhaps deliberately. "Oh, don't worry. No one's coming past. Believe me, I know. Take a seat. Take a breath. Take your shoes off if you want." He placed the gold Trellis Crown on the floor with a clang, then massaged his temples.

Purcell edged closer, her fingertips on the tools in her pockets, ready to quick-draw her pliers gunslinger-style in case he tried any plant-god nonsense like in the stories where he became a golden shower and harassed some poor girl.

God was a part of life, like gender and the twelve-hour workday, that she had never questioned. Human knowledge was a holed sieve that God and his magic plugged like overdone pasta. But now that he was right in front of her, her perspective was shifting. The stories couldn't all be real, could they? Surely not the one about the swan.

She perched with perfect discomfort on the stool, making as little actual butt-to-chair contact as possible, so that if it were pulled out from under her, she'd be left hovering in a squat. With the air of a cricket that had just been dropped into a frog enclosure, she eyed the steam that rose off the cup in front of her while sneaking another glimpse of the Petaled Divine.

He seemed totally at ease. Had crossed one knee over the other and was watching the sky out over the balcony as he sipped from his cup.

Purcell gave in. Her mouth was parched anyway.

"I'd like for you to call me Saul," said God.

Black spots bloomed and swarmed like flies in her vision.

"Purcell, are you all right?" The sound of his voice reached her distantly, like her ears had gone underwater. God wanted to be treated just like a regular guy? No, no, no, no. Purcell didn't even know how to treat a regular guy like a regular guy.

"I'm—I'm all right." *Twelve hells, no, she wasn't.* Right in front of her, the Petaled Divine was sitting on a stool, drinking tea. Purcell squeezed her eyes shut tightly, breathing in and out through her nose. This was all that presumptuous job candidate's fault. She'd unsettled Purcell. *Cyprin Voltag*, what a ridiculous punk name.

"Tell me, do you enjoy working here?"

"The—the roses are everything." Purcell banished her thoughts of Cyprin. That woman did not belong anywhere near the throne room, not even in thought.

"The roses are everything. What a marvelous answer. You'll have to tell me all about them when you come back tomorrow."

"But linking the petal-mail armor is a time of silent contemplation!"

The Divine huffed air out of his nose. "Says who? Your predecessor, Miss Glint, couldn't shut up about her ten cats. And she had a long, fruitful career, don't you think?"

"Well, yes, but—"

"It's settled then." A lean hand was extended, and Purcell took it, fighting a fresh swell of terror. "It's been nice to meet you, Purcell. Go on home early. Take the afternoon off, the petals can wait till tomorrow."

Take the afternoon off? What madness was this? Winking? Was he winking at her? Purcell stood, nodding vigorously instead of pressing her forehead subserviently to the floor. It had all gone wrong. No one was behaving as they did in the textbooks. Not even her.

She failed to close the doors on her way out. Everything—breathing, moving limbs, remembering social etiquette—had been switched over to manual and she was forgetting what was supposed to come next. Several chefs and a cleaner looked at her as if her sweaty dismay might be contagious.

Purcell threw open the back doors of the palace in a burst of hot air. Outside, the familiar gardens were, in her panic, rendered into a seasick confusion of competing colors. Nothing seemed the right shape, and the sunlight was giving her the visual equivalent of microphone feedback. In her mind, the mantra started up again: *I'm the best, I'm the best.* But it was starting to sound like *I'm a mess, I'm a mess.*

Purcell rushed into her house with the air of someone about to commit grand larceny. She closed the door behind her and leaned back on it, sweating. Even the light looked wrong, a bright, early-afternoon sun highlighting the dust bunnies in the corners and making everything look shabby. Grubby hand marks marred the fridge door, one of the bins in the kitchen had a tea-stained lid, and the throw rug was harboring cookie crumbs. Her home needed mood lighting, the way a good soap opera does. Without it there was no suspension of reality, no end-of-day relaxation. Just a lot of jobs that needed doing.

Purcell ignored the things that were begging to be cleaned and, with shaking hands, poured herself a glass of sugared wine. She overfilled her cup, drank the top, and then overfilled it again. God had told her to take the afternoon off. She had a feeling when he'd said it, he'd thought he was giving her a gift rather than a punishment, but it didn't matter. She'd been given an instruction from God, and she had to obey. It was okay, it was okay, she had hobbies—a hobby. There was outside gardening and there was . . . inside gardening. Houseplants.

To claw back some sense of normality, she talked to them. "—and he just sent me home! Just like that. On my first day. I don't know what to think. Ugh, and there was this awful woman in the admin center, she had eyes like black holes, and she was scowling at me as if I was something on the bottom of her shoe!"

A climbing rose at the back of the room looked suspiciously like it was trying to open the window to get away.

Purcell gestured wildly with the wineglass, spilling some on the carpet. "There's going to be twice as much work to do tomorrow. Not to mention, getting anything done with him yabbering on will be much, much harder. And I think he does intend to yabber on."

A droopy peony dropped its deadhead on the floor with a rustle of desiccated petals. It was as good as an eye roll. Purcell stared daggers at it until it visibly straightened up.

"You're right. I have to calm down. I have to get used to this. This is my life now." Purcell drank the wine down so fast it almost came out of her nose, and then repeated, "This is my life now." Her world had shifted from a responsibility for plants to a responsibility toward God, and that was hopelessly overwhelming.

She finished her first—more like third, with all the refills—glass of wine and then got a box of manure out from the laundry cupboard. Foliage rustled softly in anticipation. May as well make the plants happy. Her place would be stinky, but it was home.

The scoop went in, and she ladled horseshit into the pot of a black calla lily that tangled itself in the curtains with excitement. "Here we go, I know you love a good bit of poo."

People knew she talked to plants, but no one knew they listened to her. When she was a child, her grief counselor had worried that her chatter was an isolating coping mechanism. Her horticulture teacher thought it auspicious. And Purcell herself had seen pretty quickly that it made the other kids stop wanting to play with her, and it made adults have heated arguments above her head, so she'd gone stealth, fortunately before the plants had started moving and making sounds. Now she only interacted with plants this way at home, treating it like an ugly habit along the lines of nose picking and indulging in celebrity gossip.

"Knock, knock!" The front door opened a crack and Amanda peered in. "I can come back if you're busy?"

Purcell's face burned. "No, not at all."

"I thought I heard you talking to someone." Amanda let herself in and started nosing around the apartment, the way only a person who'd known Purcell from childhood could get away with doing. She was elfin, elegant, with a perfect flick of eyeliner that Purcell had tried for months to emulate before realizing it just got lost under the frames of her glasses.

Amanda paused to take a glass out of Purcell's kitchen cabinet, poured herself the dregs of the wine, then continued with her nosing.

"Did you get my email?" said Purcell, thinking of the scowly job candidate from the admin center again, almost against her will.

Amanda's eyebrows rose. "Your seven emails? Yes. I decided not to hire Cyprin, as you practically demanded. You know it's not very nice to turn an applicant down based on their appearance."

"She looked damp," said Purcell. The woman *had* looked damp, not unlike those supermodels who did shoots in swimming pools. And the dark sparkle in her eyes had made Purcell's intuition scream, *Here's a hungry rival.* She'd had no choice but to get rid of Cyprin Voltag.

"It was a hot day!" Amanda rolled her eyes. "I guess she did bungle a few answers. Well, you got what you wanted, Queen Nasty. Now I'll have to make time to interview someone else."

"I think that's for the best." Oh Divine! And here was another bevy of thoughts about Cyprin, butting in as rudely as the woman herself: the city grime that hung in a punk aura around her, the way she'd made no attempt to step aside in the doorway so that Purcell had to *touch* her on the way out. Such a relief she was gone for good.

"It stinks in here," said Amanda. Purcell shrugged and put the manure back in its cupboard.

"I wanted to check on you. You seemed kind of unhinged this morning. But I can see the wine is helping with that." Amanda stopped in the doorway of Purcell's bedroom, looking at the giant poster of Purcell's great-great-grandma Amma on the wall. "You've had that up for ages. You know, it's creepy, having a picture of your grandma above your bed. Why don't you take it down?"

Purcell was an orphan.

Except Amanda, all anyone ever said to her was how lucky she was to be a Whitlock, to have come from a line of ancestors who'd run the gardens, to be practically royalty, a princess of horticulture sure to be a prodigy. Thank the Divine there was someone left to continue the Whitlock line. Some shoulders to rest all that legacy on.

Life had never set Purcell up to be normal. When she was five, an adult had taken her hand to lead her away from a bier of two hundred dead flowers and one dead mother, and the grass had died in the shape of her shoes.

Amanda had always been by her side, always been her friend. But Amanda didn't know about the plants.

Purcell cleared her throat. "Great-great-grandma Amma is famous. There's a whole museum dedicated to her."

"Yeah, that doesn't answer my question." Apparently satisfied with her snooping, Amanda shifted a plant aside and sat down on Purcell's armchair, scratching at a loose seam with her fingernail.

"Purcell, you have to stop this." Amanda looked tired.

"Stop what?" Purcell glared thunder at her.

"You're like a twelfth-hell hall monitor. Stop trying to be perfect. Stop trying to be Amma Whitlock. You're not her, and you don't need to be. You know, you're always like this around the flower pageant. It makes you go all obsessed."

"It does not!" said Purcell, knowing, really, that it did.

"Oh, so you're perennially obsessed? My mistake." Amanda smiled, nastily. She loved Purcell, and Purcell knew that, but like a real sister, Amanda could not resist pulling Purcell's pigtails.

While Purcell was gathering herself for a biting comeback, Amanda's face grew serious. "Do you know what people say about you behind your back?"

That rankled. "Do they ask who my hairdresser is?"

Amanda sighed and rubbed her face. "They call you an egotistical, controlling, obsessed perfectionist. Sometimes all in the same sentence."

Purcell's mouth opened and closed a few times. She'd known people hated her, but that mostly happened quietly in the background, which was its own kind of respect. Amanda acknowledging it to her face was new, and it *hurt*.

"And what are you doing while they're calling me names? Staunchly defending me?" Purcell vibrated with anger, and some of the leaves around the room started rustling in response, threatening to expose her secrets. She had to calm down.

"Of course I defend you! If anyone is allowed to call you names, it's me, and I prefer Short Stuff and Little Piglet. Purcell, you're unpopular. But you don't have to be. If you would relax a little. If you'd stop trying to be a carbon copy of Amma—"

"Did you know she won the flower pageant fifteen times?" Popularity was irrelevant against other markers of job success.

"Purcell!"

"She shepherded these gardens through a long period of darkness. And she parented fifty-eight new varieties of rose, while flawlessly executing the role of head gardener."

Amanda rolled her eyes. "Purcell, the history books airbrush everybody's imperfections. It's an impossible standard. You can't know what she was really like. And that stuff about the sun going out in Amma's time—it's nonsense and propaganda. I know you love your family, but this is too much."

She did love her family. Almost as much as she trembled at the awful pressure of their legacy. None of them were here to pat her on the head and say, "Good job." The only way to be sure they would be proud of her was to make a bigger notch in the bedpost of history than all other Whitlocks combined.

A hanging fern by Purcell's shoulder suddenly wilted and Purcell stared at it in alarm.

Amanda got up to touch the floppy leaves.

"What happened here?"

Purcell coughed. "It must be parched."

She'd been too lax, letting this happen in front of Amanda. She had to get a handle on her emotions before Amanda figured out she could communicate with plants, Purcell heaved a sigh. "I just hope tomorrow doesn't go this badly," she said, fishing for reassurance.

"You're new to the petal mail. You and the Divine will settle into some kind of routine. Trust me."

"Thanks," said Purcell, but Amanda's attention had gone to a cupboard door on the other side of the room that was slightly ajar.

"You know, I'm sure I heard you talking to someone."

"I really wasn't."

"I have . . . friends . . . that I talk to, outside of the gardens. Maybe you do too?" said Amanda.

Purcell quaffed her wine. "We can't all be as cosmopolitan as you."

"Twelve hells, you take an afternoon off like a death sentence! Stop being so grumpy. I just want you to know that you can tell me anything. You do know that, don't you?"

"You think I'm hiding someone under my bed?"

"Not with that picture of your grandma up."

Purcell convinced Amanda to go back to work after her half glass of wine, but not before Amanda looked over her shoulder twice in the doorway, as if she thought she'd see someone holding a potted plant over their privates as they dashed from the bathroom to the bedroom.

Sometimes Purcell wanted to tell Amanda about the plants, but then she'd remember Amanda couldn't hear a secret without telling five other people. She was a central node in the garden's web of gossip; all sorts of information seemed to flow through her.

Apart from the back-of-the-skull fear that maybe this was all in her head, Purcell didn't advertise her plant-talking abilities out there in the gardens because she didn't want to give anyone ideas. Even at the top of her game, she saw the value in keeping an ace in her pocket. Success was nerve-wracking and brutally fleeting. Or so her lizard hindbrain told her, despite a lifetime—no, *generations*—of privilege.

Sooner or later, a perfect rival would come along, or Purcell would trip on her own shoelaces and fall on her face. Sometimes, she was sure both would happen at once.

Purcell went back to spooning out poo to her dependents and started mentally planning how to fit two days of work into one.

CHAPTER 3

CYPRIN

Back in the overcity, Cyprin made her way home from the black market. Small shapes scurried damply into an overflowing trash can and she crossed to the other side of the street to avoid them. Things grew colder and darker in the shadows of the scrapers. The dual moons had risen, but they were barely visible. The smaller second one was blown out, trailing fragments like breadcrumbs, and everything outside the bounds of the city had a faint sepia tone, as if only the flashy neon lights were real.

She returned to her apartment and got ready for crime. Cyprin sat at her coffee table and pulled a stocking over her head. Black boot polish ringed its eyeholes. She was wearing puppeteer clothes now, black ones that disappeared into the dark, but they'd be on fire in a trash can by the end of the night. She had no clue what kind of security measures the Divine Gardens might have, whether she'd be captured on camera . . . or just captured. This was madness, really. Desperation.

Her head was circling between the surety that she couldn't do this and the absolute knowledge that if she couldn't beg, borrow, or steal herself a role in those gardens, life would not be worth living.

She had half a mind to go and throw herself in the lake at the center of the Divine Gardens. But that was a *very* final solution. Better to spend a couple of days blind roaring drunk and *then* consider jumping in the lake. She thought about Maverick finding her face down in the water and wondered if he would even care.

After her failed interview, Cyprin had found a sheltered spot behind a cluster of azaleas so bright pink they looked like they existed outside of reality. She'd dropped to her knees, bent some stems aside gently, and vomited into the garden bed.

"Can I help you?"

The only thing worse than facing absolute defeat was having it witnessed.

A man was there, leaning his chin on a hoe in the sort of laconic way she'd only read about in storybooks, where no one did any real work and crops mysteriously transmogrified into gold overnight. Cyprin shifted back onto her heels and fluffed the grass in front of her to try to rid it of the indentations from her knees.

"You're priestguard, aren't you?" The palace priestguard wore robes in a deep shade of red with gold trim at the hems. The Divine's right hands were always magenta-clad (to make it harder to see the blood). "Surprised you even know how to hold a hoe. What, do they put just anyone to work here?" It was meant to be a jab at him, but Cyprin's throat locked up.

"You look as if you could use some help." His tone was at least friendly.

"Don't bother, I don't work here. Just on my way out."

"You had an interview, didn't you?" A lucky guess. Apart from the Divine himself, people weren't allowed in the gardens unless they worked there or wanted to work there.

"I screwed up. Lost cause."

"Don't be so sure of that."

A large gap between the man's shoes and his ill-fitting priestguard robe caught her attention. Staring at his ankles seemed weirdly improper, so Cyprin looked at his face instead. His eyes were kind. And his skin was a sallow yellowish green, no ruddiness or wrinkles from the unforgiving sun. His hair swept back in a fashionable wave. The fingers that topped his hoe were manicured. And there was no gun on him at all.

"Who are you?"

He shrugged. "A friend. Maybe even a co-worker."

"Right. I'm not in the mood for games." Cyprin stood up and brushed the crinkles out of her knees, readying to leave.

"Me too, but no one seems to ever let me off the board." The man stepped closer, and Cyprin stiffened. From its place tucked into a tool belt at his hips, he produced a red rose, offering it to her. "A memento."

Over his shoulder, the same type of flower polka-dotted a bush shaped like a lollipop. Her eyes zeroed in on the snapped cane where he had ripped—yes, ripped—it off.

"You didn't even use pruning shears. Surely that's an arrestable offense here." The flower was the most perfect thing she'd ever laid hands on, despite its mangled stem. It was an unseemly red, the spirit of blood and rubies distilled. Cyprin ran a fingertip over petals so lush and hydrated they sparkled like velvet in the sun. "I can't take this out of here. I'll be in a world of trouble."

"It won't be a problem. Come on, I'll walk you to the gates."

He looked a bit like a librarian. And he did work there. Nothing about the situation screamed danger. It just whispered weird. And really, she'd begun to feel like the only way she'd give up the flower was if someone pried it from her cold, dead hands. It was a glittering consolation prize. She wanted to look at it while she drank so much her tears turned to vodka.

"You can call me Saul," he added, as if having a name might tip the scales of trust.

"Cyprin."

"You're doing *me* a favor, really," said Saul. "I watched you on the way here, and you took the longest possible route across the gardens. It was painful. This way, we should be out in about an hour and a half." He sounded like he was trying to be jokey and put her at ease, but the words rubbed salt into all Cyprin's psychological wounds.

A gust of pleasant cool breeze passed by, solidifying the hair wax that dripped down Cyprin's temples to her chin. Then the day recommenced stifling. As the sun went half-mast, the moisture rose up into the air and made her feel like she was drowning as she walked. Unseen crickets took up song around them.

"What's life like in the city?" said Saul, suddenly. An odd question. There was only one sprawling megacity, where seven billion souls lived on top of each other in a life-and-death game of Jenga.

"Asperia?" He couldn't have come from anywhere else.

"I haven't left these gardens in years. Hardly remember what the outside world is like."

Cyprin looked around them at the bees getting lazy in the late-afternoon heat, the flower heads turned toward the sun like children watching TV. *Why would you want to?*

The Divine Gardens were situated to the north of Asperia, surrounded by a short, dense halo of farmland. A single train line connected the gardens to the city. Aside from divine gardeners heading to and fro, only wide-eyed city rats with an invite, like Cyprin, got on it.

"Oh, well, you haven't missed much. Mama Inkburn is still doing her twenty-cent buffet. Still pretending tofu is meat too, but for twenty cents nobody minds. The Ascendant Spires collapsed last week and we had a bad couple of days where the rats from there looked for other homes. There was an explosion of ratborne fever off the back of that. Most of it is just the same."

Saul stared at her like she'd just told him his mother had died. He mouthed the word *rats*, then said, hopefully, "All back to normal now?"

Cyprin looked at him sideways. "That is normal."

They skirted a decorative pond in silence. Cyprin glanced out to where she thought the light pollution from the city should be visible in the darkening sky. This place was so secluded she couldn't see a thing.

"Will you be competing in the Verdure Flower Pageant this year?" Saul asked.

"I don't think so. I haven't so far." That hoity-toity flower show. What would she bring to it? An apple? An interesting mold bloom from her shower recess?

"I think you should give it a go."

"Maybe." Why did strangers seem to have such an imperative to give life advice? It was almost always insulting. *Oh yes, I'll just pop out into the back garden for the rare orchids, or the rafflesia.* People from the Divine Gardens had no ability to empathize, they had no context. The rats and the swaying towers and the person-plugged city streets were probably just a fond memory to him. A quaint origin story. How nice.

They moved onto a gravel path Cyprin hadn't noticed before. It passed under vine-covered trellises that muffled the worst of the heat, and from there it was a pleasant stroll to the white picket of the garden gates.

They stopped there, still inside the gardens. On the other side of the gate was a short walk to the train and then a long ride back home.

Saul smiled at her and leaned on his hoe again. "Think of me as a friend, if ever you return."

The snort came up from deep within Cyprin and bypassed all attempts to control it. "I doubt I'll ever be back."

But Saul was undeterred. "Don't give up on your dreams, Cyprin."

After presenting her exit papers to the checkpoint official at the gates of the garden, she'd taken a handful of petals off the rose and shoved them in her mouth as she rode the train home. If Saul hadn't mentioned the flower pageant, she might have forgotten it entirely. But . . . No, it was days away, and she had nothing to show. She couldn't.

The winner of Best in Show in the Verdure Flower Pageant each year was entitled to an honorary position in the Divine Gardens. It was a rotating position, without the job security of a regular role. And that wasn't even the main problem. The main problem was that no one ever seemed to beat the flowers grown by the palace staff. It felt rigged. Year after year, the same people won, and they were the ones already in the gardens. It wouldn't surprise her if even God was a charlatan.

Wouldn't it be funny to expose that hypocrisy? Life would have meaning again. Sure, her dreams would be bones and char, but so would the reputation of the divine gardeners.

The need to do something about all this dragged Cyprin back into the present and, not for the first time, she looked up last year's flower-pageant winner on her tablet.

Purcell Whitlock. The person she'd met before her interview, with an attitude like a cat who'd had to wait past dinnertime. Any moral qualms that might have been building up evaporated on the spot. She'd never seen anyone so desperately overdue for a reality check.

Cyprin flicked back through previous years. Purcell had won the last five pageants. Each year managing to smile as though a surprise party had caught her on the toilet. And always with the same flowers.

On Cyprin's tablet screen, a little mousy figure in oversized glasses clutched a bouquet of roses that all looked exactly like the flower Cyprin had taken out of the gardens. The memory of their location shone like a beacon in her head. If she was right, and this Purcell character rocked up to the pageant with the same old trick, stealing those blooms from the Divine Gardens should put them on an equal footing.

Her plan was sound. She was going to thieve Purcell's roses and then sabotage what was left of the bush with the black-market bio bots.

This would win her the pageant. And if it didn't, she could enjoy the sick satisfaction of knowing the competition was unwinnable.

The door panel of her apartment buzzed, and Cyprin checked the video screen, where a person stood impatiently in double denim with almost translucently white skin, glossy red hair, and piercings on every available surface of their face, nose bulging through the fish-eye lens of the door cam. She held her breath. The intruder gave up buzzing and started knocking. "Cyprin! I know you're in there! I just did two back-to-back double shifts for you. A fucking quadruple! I slept in a chair! If you don't let me in, I'm going to tell everyone at work you're faking sick!"

Cyprin grabbed the jar off her coffee table and buried it under an orange cushion on the couch. She ripped the stocking off her head and shoved it up her left sleeve. Then she opened the door. "Moss."

Moss gave Cyprin a thorough eyeballing and screwed up their nose. "I knew it. You're not sick. You never get sick."

Cyprin smiled sheepishly. "Sick of work."

"Ha, ha, Cyprin. Not cool." Moss walked in and sat on the couch, right up against the cushion hiding the jar of chaos. They shifted uncomfortably and Cyprin felt the stress of imminent discovery take years off her life.

"Don't worry," said Moss. "I'm not staying long. I'm just doing my civic duty and making sure you aren't an undiscovered corpse. What have you been doing? And what's up with your makeup?" The way they narrowed their eyes at the end of that question made it clear it meant: *What nefarious plans have you got?*

"I'm marathoning *Lust Island.*" Cyprin made her face as unreadable as possible. "It made me cry."

"You're not and it didn't," said Moss, crossing and then uncrossing their legs, wiggling their back against the orange pillow again. Cyprin jerked, fighting the urge to lunge forward and rescue her bottle of bio bots.

Moss continued, "The last time you disappeared from work for this long was when you tried to join that professional a cappella group because you thought they had a performance booked in the Divine Gardens—" Cyprin winced. "—and, oh! This is something to do with the Divine Gardens, isn't it?"

It would have been easy to say, *Yes, I went for an interview, but I didn't get the job. I'm devastated about it and embarking on harmful and chaotic coping strategies, including, but not limited to, actual crime.* Cyprin said, "No."

Moss gave her a look of cartoonish incredulity. "I'm here. I care. Why won't you let anyone be your friend?"

That one stung. Cyprin tried to conjure a comeback, but Moss had moved on. "And what in twelve hells am I sitting on?" They reached behind the cushion and pulled out the jar. Their expression sailed quickly from *gross* to *radioactive* and they put the jar down very carefully on the coffee table. "Cyprin, what is that?"

"I'm starting a flea circus." That this was the wrong comeback at the wrong time wasn't a reason to waste it.

"You have feral bio bots in your apartment."

There was nowhere to go with this. So Cyprin fell back on the worst stereotype of all time: the sad little orphan girl. "I was going to let them go in the Divine Gardens."

"Oh. Oh, Cyprin." Moss got off the couch and Cyprin submitted to a hug, standing stiffly all the while. She would do anything to get into those gardens, anything at all. Even this. "You have to stop looking for Maverick," said Moss, gently.

Everyone in the city knew what had happened to Cyprin. It came at her when making restaurant bookings, taking exercise classes, paying for groceries. *Oh, Voltag? You were that little girl who got pulled out of a collapsed scraper by a divine gardener. True hero, that man.*

Maverick had been boning her mother for twelve months before the scraper collapsed. When he'd carried a tween Cyprin out of the wreckage, dusty and bleeding, to meet a crowd of concerned citizens, emergency workers, reporters—priestguard and Underground working together to pass bits of twisted metal and concrete chunks along a line—Maverick had puffed up his chest and said, "Her mother didn't make it, but, Divine as my witness, she'll never be alone." And they'd clapped, and cheered, and Cyprin had pictured the way her mother had looked covered in dust, curled up like she was sleeping, dead from dust inhalation, and she'd coughed, and cried, and been taken to the hospital, where she waited days and days for Maverick to come and get her.

A neighbor brought her some salvaged belongings that fit in a shoebox, and she'd told them, "It's okay, I'll open it when Maverick gets here."

Some of the nurses tried to take her to the hospital café for a change of scenery and she'd said, "Not without Maverick."

The hospital counselor suggested it might be good for her to cry, howl, anything, but she'd just stared fixedly at the corner of the room until they'd left. Asperia was a big city, and it ate the vulnerable. If Cyprin couldn't cry with Maverick, she was never going to cry again. When the hospital morgue sent up her mother's ashes in a tiny cardboard box, Cyprin stole discharge forms from the admin desk and faked Maverick's signature. On her way out she bought her first pair of knuckle-dusters from a vending machine. These days she had a collection.

She never heard from Maverick again. That no one in the Divine

Gardens had said anything about her name during the interview process was the icing on the cake.

Moss stepped back and Cyprin palmed the hot prickles out of her eyes in a way she hoped only looked like she was brushing her hair back. "I wasn't really going to do it," she said. "Just going through a rough time."

"Okay. It's okay. We all do silly things. Just take it to the authorities—no, wait, don't do that. Take it back to wherever you got it from, tell them you changed your mind."

Cyprin had ripped a whole-ass Band-Aid off her feelings for this, and she hoped it was worth it. Her eyes still stung. Her lip threatened to tremble, and she bit it until it stopped. Cyprin struggled with emotions. They snuck up on her. She often thought she was totally fine right up until she wasn't. "I'll get rid of the jar, I promise," she told Moss, choking on the words. "I'm sorry. I'd just like to be alone right now."

"Are you sure?"

"Yup, yup. Alone. Alone time. Bye." Cyprin took Moss by the shoulders and ferried them out the door.

When Moss was gone, Cyprin calmed her shit down, staring at the wall and tapping her finger against the little jar on the coffee table. The contents buzzed faintly. She almost wished she *could* return it. Plants were blameless. The roses wouldn't know what was happening to them. And if the black-market ailment was too strong, if no one on the garden staff had the smarts to figure out what was wrong in time . . . it didn't bear thinking about.

What are you going to do, Cyprin? Spend the rest of your days processing greenhouse apples? And in the end, she'd go out looking like one of them, a wizened old apple, dropping onto the soil to become fodder for the next generation—each generation standing on the backs of successive generations sounded impressive until you realized everyone composted together and no one made it out of the dirt. Sooner or later, you had to ask yourself what it was all for. In the gardens it had felt like she was finally about to be someone of importance. A person Maverick couldn't ignore.

With a violent exhalation, she got up, grabbed the jar, and breezed out of her apartment. Walking as if there was a strong wind behind her, that was the way. Doing and not thinking.

Ten thousand people worked in those gardens. When she won her place, she couldn't be the only fraud.

CHAPTER 4

CYPRIN

Asperia was busy all through the night, and no one gave Cyprin a second glance. She had the jar of bio bots swaddled like a baby in an old T-shirt, but it was still making suspicious noises. When she cut through a mall where the Underground were setting up a temporary tent city for people displaced by a recent scraper demolition, an operative winked at her and her hands started sweating.

After that, walking with the wind behind her became meandering aimlessly and then chickening out completely. Without really knowing how, she ended up outside the hive of fluorescence that was Mama Inkburn's Buffet. It was amazing how often this happened, especially if she was drunk or distraught. Mama Inkburn must have had cognitive distorters fitted in her advertising somewhere.

Cyprin arrived at the counter like a bit of driftwood washed in on the tide. She took a peek under the wrapped T-shirt. A few specks lay still at the bottom of the jar now, little soot grains. Were the bio bots running out of air in there, or did they just have very brief lifespans?

"Costume party?" Mama Inkburn was a large woman, with porridge-pale skin and a beehive of gray hair. She was always at the restaurant. Except for one time, when Cyprin had spotted her in the factory district. She'd followed, out of curiosity—from an embarrassingly close distance, because Cyprin wasn't any kind of superspy—and Mama Inkburn had entered an AI repair factory.

There were only a few of these in the city. Asperia wasn't capable of making its own sentient AI—somewhere in history they'd lost the knowledge and no one could find it again—but slumpers dredged old robots out of the undercity occasionally. They were usually clanking and gibbering, and needed somewhere to go and be repaired. Verdure had talented robotics technicians who could at least make the kind of functional but flimsy repairs that would let an AI recover enough to help itself. They'd never cracked sentience, though, and the AIs themselves seemed to have some kind of built-in rule against making more of their kind.

Inside the factory, Mama Inkburn had taken up a seat in front of a robot. Mama Inkburn's charge was missing a face, but it had a magnificent head of blond hair. As Cyprin watched, Mama Inkburn spread a colorless blank face over her knee: a rubbery, jellyfish, nightmare thing. She took out a little paint set and started painting a complexion on it. While she painted, she talked to the robot. Cyprin had heard of people doing work like this. Volunteers who donated clothes, painted skin, even told stories to the robots, talking softly to socialize them, calm them down, bring them back to themselves. It was one of those things people always said they'd do if they had the time or money. Cyprin had never gotten around to it.

Sometimes Cyprin thought Mama Inkburn must *be* a robot to be on duty at all hours, but then, if a robot had horrible blue haloes of eye shadow like that it would probably be time for it to go back to the factory. It occurred to Cyprin what an uncharitable thought this was, given the boot polish she'd put around her own eyes.

"Something funny?" said Mama Inkburn.

Cyprin pulled the stocking off her head. "Just thinking what a treat I must look."

Mama Inkburn shrugged and waved a jiggly arm at the rest of the room. "No judgment here."

A couple of body-mod addicts sat in the corner, their toughness ameliorated by the jolly pink-and-yellow booth seating. A group of schoolchildren still in uniform, up way past their bedtimes, played chess on the floor under a table. The usual lineup stood around the buffet, everything from cardiganed grandmothers with tissues and knitting needles up their sleeves to the slender and creepily pale slumpers, decked out in their underground spoils, some of them still with headlamps on from their adventures in the city under the city.

The purple neon heart on the wall was more of a religious icon than anything to do with the Petaled Divine. He might have people by the hearts and minds, but Mama Inkburn had them by the stomachs, and that was far more powerful.

When Cyprin's eyes wandered back to Mama Inkburn the woman winked at her. "I think your makeup looks quite stylish," she said, which could only be a joke; Cyprin looked like a sad raccoon. Then came the punch line. "About a thousand years ago, coloring the whole eye socket like that was all the rage."

Cyprin laughed. Mama Inkburn did not.

Oh, she was serious. "An old AI tell you that?" asked Cyprin, immediately cursing herself for giving away that she'd spied on Mama Inkburn at the AI repair warehouse.

Mama Inkburn failed to react. "You want to order something?"

"Just a Noodle Soda, please."

The can appeared almost immediately, advertising a cartoon swirl of noodles in a pink bowl.

"You're all skin and bones, love. Ought to take a turn at the buffet. Twenty cents."

"Maybe next time."

Mama Inkburn scrutinized Cyprin over the top of the counter and Cyprin thought she was about to be the recipient of another unwanted sales pitch.

After a moment, Mama Inkburn spoke. "It's going to be all right, love."

A puce-colored bowl, cracked and oxidized with use, was pushed across the counter.

"I told you, no—"

"It's on the house. Go, fill up at the buffet. Sometimes people fall through the cracks in this city. But not when they're in my diner." Mama Inkburn made an upset clicking sound with her tongue. "Things are bad. Haven't seen so many people in need since just before the last rose-borne apocalypse."

That last part didn't make sense, but Cyprin waved it away as creative blaspheming, like when people said, "Haven't seen a cold snap this bad since the Divine's balls dropped," which both referred to a fortnight of frost about twenty-five years ago and blamed the weather conditions on their deity's rough, squeaky puberty. Cyprin was shocked into compliance. She'd never seen Mama Inkburn give so much as a discount to anyone, though the prices were rock-bottom enough that perhaps Mama Inkburn was giving discounts to everyone, all the time.

With the faintly buzzing jar tucked under one arm, Cyprin approached the buffet, where a gray rainbow of bubbling soups let out appetizing smells that belied their appearance. Now and then liquid popped in a minigeyser. Driven by mysterious convection currents, unidentifiable chunks rose to the surface and then sunk back down again.

Sometimes people fall through the cracks in this city. So, she looked pitiable. Fair. She served herself a few scoops of the mushroom-and-tofu soup, which could always be relied on, and then sat at an empty table, drinking it straight from the bowl. The jar buzzed at her elbow. Nearby, a baby screamed, and its mother rocked it gently back to sleep. Cyprin stared at the woman's bob-cut hair and slowly reached up to touch her own. A man at a neighboring table put his boots up on a chair and Cyprin glanced down at her own identical pair. A slumper's dirty, cracked nails made Cyprin fold her fingers into fists. Everything got kind of uniform with too many people and not enough space. But, worse than that, everyone here looked like they had worked a month of Mondays. That same look greeted Cyprin from every reflective surface.

Cyprin liked to think of herself as unique, but in a city like this, the universal human experience tended to get more concentrated, like grapes in a barrel. And no matter where you went, what you did, how you thought, you were still a part of the uniformity of that barrel. It was hopeless. But then, that was probably what arrogant, self-important gardeners like Purcell wanted everybody to think. *Damn it.*

None of this was about Purcell, but seeing the shocked look on her face when Cyprin turned up at the flower pageant with prizewinning roses was going to be a highlight. It was extra motivation.

Cyprin stood up, picked up the jar of bio bots, and pulled the stocking back over her head. She nodded to Mama Inkburn on the way out.

Less than an hour later, Cyprin was on a train to the gardens, rehearsing what she'd say if she got caught. *I was upset about the interview . . . I wanted to see the gardens one more time . . . don't worry, I was never going to go into the palace.*

The train carriages were all white and all plastic, hosed down three times a day. Cyprin's hands pressed boot polish into the seat before she realized it was happening. She looked nervously around, but there were only an old lady with some grocery bags who had fallen asleep and a slumper recumbent on the bench seating, studying a map of spider-webbed lines: the overcity and the undercity. The jar hummed. This definitely ranked in the top 1 percent of Cyprin's terrible ideas. Right up there with the time she'd had her hair permed. She stared out the window, which actually meant looking at the light reflection from the inside of the carriage, where a hellaciously shifty mirror Cyprin squeezed a swaddled, buzzing jar like it held her life savings.

Cyprin was the only person to get off at the Divine Gardens stop. She gathered her belongings with the furtiveness of a shoplifter, and for one heart-attack moment the jar threatened to slip. She made an involuntary sound of panic as she caught it.

As soon as she was off, the train departed back toward the sprawl of Asperia. This station was practically in a paddock. Outside the tiled platform there was nothing but grass and a little gravel road that joined up with an asphalt one connecting the city to the Spring Palace.

It was bright, far too bright for a wannabe criminal. Past the smog of the city, the stars shone like stage lights down onto the countryside. Some of the plants by the road looked like heads in an audience, disappointed by Cyprin's lackluster comedy routine. Cyprin moved from signpost to bush, edging closer to the Divine Gardens.

The checkpoint office outside the gates of the gardens was dark and unoccupied, but Cyprin peered into the window anyway in case someone was in there with infrared goggles. When no one was, she went for the fence.

The fence around the gardens was a white-picket thing that aimed for prettiness rather than security. Cyprin hopped over it and then froze, waiting for the lights and sirens. There was nothing. What was to stop people from doing this all the time? The fear of Divine retribution? Corporal punishment if caught? It didn't seem enough of a deterrent. She was missing something. Had to be. Unless people were just too wrapped up in their own lives to come out here? Or too respectful? No. There would be security.

She looked harder. Over to her left, under a gazebo, was a group of priestguard. Cyprin did her best to fade into the undergrowth as she watched them. One was reading a newspaper by flashlight. The other two were smoking cigarettes. The sights of their energy weapons painted little colored dots on the ground at their feet. The way they were milling around and chatting loudly told her that they viewed their roles here as purely ceremonial and did not actually expect anyone to be creeping around the gardens à la Cyprin. Hah. But still. This was real. This was *too* real, and so was the risk of getting caught. Cyprin glanced back at the fence, feeling a brief but powerful urge to flee. But she would look even more conspicuous vaulting back. No, she'd made it this far, and that was a gift. She waited until the priestguard had turned away from her, then darted across the green with her jar of chaos held tightly in one hand.

Cyprin slowly retraced the path she had taken with Saul. She didn't dare put on her headlamp, creeping from bush to tree to ornamental pond. Random coughs and the odd beam of light let her know she wasn't alone.

The viny pathway looked cobwebbed in the night. Cyprin passed the decorative pond she'd walked around with the priestguard man. It felt like following a treasure map, and just around a hip-high hedge was the spot marked X.

The rosebush had its many flower faces turned up toward the moonlight. Some of the newer blooms had closed slightly for the night. Even in darkness, it was spectacular: the red petals were so bright they still showed up in shades of black cherry in the gloom. She snipped off a handful of roses, cutting the stems where they left the trunk, taking the flowers from all over the bush so no one area looked too patchy. The only way anyone would realize there had been foul play was if they kept a running count of the blooms on this bush, one out of many hundreds of thousands in the gardens.

Or, of course, if Purcell inspected it too closely tomorrow morning when selecting her pick of the crop for the flower show. But Cyprin's little gift would take care of those risks. Once she'd unleashed the bio bots, nobody would be getting too close to this plant. She only wished she could see Purcell's face when she discovered it. If only Cyprin's mother could see her now, if only Maverick could—her eyes prickled again, like a sudden attack of hay fever, and she squeezed them shut until they behaved.

Cyprin held the jar up to her face. She couldn't see the particles buzzing around, but she could feel them. She gave the top an experimental twist. Her hands shook. Of course the lid would be stuck now. It was a sign! Was it a sign? No, no, it wasn't. She lifted a knee up to get the most out of her abs and wrenched the screw top open. She tipped the jar upside down over the middle of the rosebush and tapped the bottom of it, imagining all those little specks falling out, 'cause she sure as shit couldn't see them in the dark. And then it was done, irreversibly.

Despite no signs of pursuit, Cyprin ran away from the scene of the crime. This just meant she had to wait a while at the train station. She was warming herself over a bonfire in a bin when the train arrived, the boot polish streaked in two long lines down her face and the satchel full of roses a glorious secret at her back.

CHAPTER 5

PURCELL

Bio bots buzzed around the rosebush with a rattle of static. Plumes of red and green wafted off like smoke as parts of the plant atomized, rising in the morning stillness. It looked like it had been holed by tiny cannonballs—the flowers, the leaves, the stems and woody little trunk, nothing was left unscathed. The basket fell from the crook of Purcell's arm. She let the pruning shears follow it, narrowly missing her foot.

It was a misty predawn, the morning of the Verdure Flower Pageant. Hardly anyone was up except for the decorators and caterers in the Foliage Concourse, setting up for the event. Purcell had been getting ready to be named Best in Show for the sixth time in a row with these, her favorite flowers in the gardens, which were now turning into a fine spray of organic matter before her very eyes.

She was the only person who knew about this existential threat, a garden-eating nightmare that had appeared like the first blush before a plague. This couldn't really be happening. It was a bad dream.

Any moment now, Purcell would wake up in a cold sweat and be oh-so grateful that this wasn't real. But she raised the alarm just in case it was.

"Code black," she said into her walkie-talkie, using the emergency channel that would make ten thousand other units sing out and wake their owners. "Code black." Her voice sounded like the voice of a stranger.

Sweet Divine, what was she supposed to do? Her fingers reached out toward the roses she'd been about to pick, trembling. She snatched them back before they made contact. No telling what would happen if she touched it. The whole plant might turn to dust, or Purcell herself might be irreparably contaminated. No, she couldn't touch it, couldn't comfort it, couldn't do anything for the poor thing.

"Code . . . did you say 'code black'?" said the walkie-talkie. It was Amanda, on a private channel. Her role as administrator meant that she'd be expected to coordinate the emergency response. If she'd just woken up, Purcell couldn't tell. She sounded more like she'd arrived in a war zone.

"A swarm of rogue bio bots on plant fourteen-five-six-three," said Purcell. "I don't know if others are affected. I can't leave the spot I'm standing in, I'm alone and protocol states I have to wait and watch until a containment team arrives."

Bio bots were a natural phenomenon. The ones that littered the air in Verdure were dormant, but those outside of the kingdom hungrily converted plant biomass into energy that, in the way of all life, they used to move and make more of themselves.

The latest research suggested they were some kind of AI hiccup, though who really knew; they'd been around since forever. The rogue bio bots resisted harnessing and seemed to come and go like viruses, despite several comprehensive programs to co-opt their function into something useful or else corral them and break them down. By the grace of the Divine, the bio bots in Verdure were always docile. There had never been an aggressive swarm reported here. Until today.

Purcell had heard about the region of Immersea to the south, where all the arable land had been ravaged. And everyone, *everyone* had heard about Norla City to the east, where a glitch in one of the bio bots had led the self-replicating swarm to switch fuel from plant matter to human flesh. But it was a sideshow, a horror movie. These things did not happen in Purcell's life. They did not happen in Purcell's gardens.

"I'm sending out a containment team now. I—Hold on. It's taking me a while to convince them this is real," said Amanda.

The radio crackled with the same kind of static that seemed to be going on in Purcell's head. When she looked around, she thought the whole landscape was atomizing, but that was in her head too. She sat down, tried not to faint, and waited for help to arrive. Every minute seemed enough time for civilizations to rise and fall.

The containment team arrived in under ten minutes, sirens wailing, wheels ripping across the perfect lawn in a way that made Purcell's eyes water. By the time they'd erected a plastic bubble over the rosebush, a third of it was gone. What remained looked like a toothpick dipped in acid. Despite the encroaching start of the flower festival, Purcell sat on the grass with her head in her hands, watching the hazmat suits pick over the plants nearby for any signs of cross-contamination. A half hour later, an engineering team arrived, setting up an analysis tile on the outside of the plastic dome and checking where the dome met the earth to ensure a complete seal. They all seemed very competent. Deep beneath the horror, Purcell found herself appreciating their efficiency.

For a team that had only ever practiced this in a series of fire drills, they were doing remarkably well.

It was midmorning by the time the flurry of hazard containment finally slowed, and Purcell could feel the beginnings of a sunburn prickling her nose. If she didn't hurry, she was going to miss the judging entirely. But nothing mattered if the whole garden was about to be eaten into dust.

Purcell rushed to her feet as one of the engineers approached her. The man looked peaky, like he'd stuck his finger in an electrical socket or, well, like he'd woken up to the worst news of his life, which was fair. His hair was corkscrewed and fanned, and he'd mismatched the buttons on his lab coat so that one side of it hung lower than the other.

"Head Gardener?" he said.

"How bad is it?"

"We got lucky." Sweat still dripped down the engineer's temples. "Something's wrong with these bots. Their programming is making them eat plant cells, but the moment they do, they're dying. They're faulty. Once all of them have had something to eat, they'll die off and we can take the barrier down."

"No other plants were affected?" Purcell felt relief, but it was the relief of going to the doctor thinking you're terminal and finding out you only need to cut off a limb. Her roses. Her favorite roses.

"That's the funny thing," said the engineer, and Purcell gave him the stink eye because nothing, absolutely nothing about this was funny. "You'd think with all this garden around they'd have got to the outskirts first. But nope, just these roses. I gotta tell you, I'm going straight home to have a stiff drink after this."

"I know the Divine is nearing the end of his life cycle. Could . . . could that have something to do with this?" Despite having actually met

God, Purcell's grasp of theology was wobbly. She only cared about her plants.

The engineer shook his head. "Divines come and go, it's natural. We don't get any changes in the environment when they die and are reborn. This must have been something else. We'll do a full investigation."

Sabotage, then! Of course this was unnatural! She squinted at the remains of her prize rosebush, suspicion rising. "Do you have this situation in hand?"

"Yes, ma'am."

"If you'll excuse me, I'm required at the flower pageant."

It wasn't true. She wasn't required to be there, but no one was about to say that to a five-time prizewinner.

Still trembling with adrenaline, Purcell brushed the worst of the grass off the seat of her pants and began walking home. As soon as she was out of anyone's immediate line of sight, the walk turned into a run.

All the flowers shifted to face the door when Purcell swung it open. Their leaves shivered as she walked through the house, radiating anxiety. She had hardly enough time to think, let alone get changed, so the morning's grass-stained, sweat-soaked uniform had to stay on. Purcell wet her face in the bathroom. Leaning over the sink, she looked herself in the eye. Mirror Purcell gave a flint-hard stare back.

No mistaking it now: someone was out to get her. To fuck with her in particular. Amanda had told her nobody liked her. She bet a whole bunch of gardeners were itching to ruin her day. Was it—Could it be the Divine himself? Could this be a test? Were head gardeners tested? That idea had a strange sort of pull to it. But it didn't matter. Whether it was him or someone who was jealous of her repeated success at the pageant, they weren't going to best Purcell.

Nobody was. Not today, not ever, because if someone could best her, then they'd be besting the Whitlock line. She'd be letting her ancestors down, and that burden was enough to knock the air from her lungs. It was time to get out the big guns.

On the nightstand by the window in Purcell's bedroom, a tiny hothouse steamed. It was shaped like an ornate birdcage, with glass between the golden bars and a padlock on the door. Purcell shook her pillowcase, and a key fell onto the floor. She opened the lock, and a cloud of condensate burst outward to reveal rich green leaves covered in a fuzz of tiny moisture-trapping hairs and . . . a flower. Technically it was Amma's flower, a Whitlock family heirloom that was admittedly a lot more interesting than a hand-me-down ring or collection of porcelain dogs. Purcell still remembered the day her mother had given it into her care. By that point, her mother's arms had been too withered to lift the thing in its steamy golden cage, but her eyes had indicated it to Purcell, and she'd said something along the lines of *This belongs to you now, you are our future.* Or maybe the words had been even more portentous than that. Maybe she'd said, *Purcell, I have to unburden myself of this earth-shattering secret, listen carefully.* Purcell could never remember the right kinds of things about her time with her mother. That scene had only stuck in her mind because she'd tried to pick the terrarium up with her five-year-old noodle arms and had dropped it on her own toes. The potential unfairness of entering Amma's flower into the pageant crossed Purcell's mind briefly, but she dismissed it. She felt instinctively that in cases of a Whitlock versus the world, all the other Whitlocks would give their ghostly approval to using any means necessary to get first prize. She glanced up at the poster of Amma above her bed, tornado-green eyes, curly hair as unruly as vines. Hells, Amma probably would have loved to watch her spite-fueled rise to six-time pageant-winner.

Moving with the precision of an expert, Purcell took a pair of scissors out of her bedside drawer and sprayed them down with a bottle of ethanol. While they were drying, she took out a pair of tongs. She maneuvered the tongs carefully into the hothouse. Once they were in place, the scissors went in too. Steady as a surgeon, Purcell cut the bloom and retrieved it. She left the little hothouse steaming and bolted out of the house, tongs in hand, bloom in tongs, heading for the palace.

CHAPTER 6

CYPRIN

Cyprin had never been to the Verdure Flower Pageant before.

She'd worn her best faux-leather jacket for the occasion: the teal one with the skull on the back. There would be no more wearing white, pretending to be pristine and boring. She was only going to be Cyprin from now on.

Entry was by invite only unless you were participating in the flower competition. When Cyprin reached the palace doors, her work boots and knuckle rings standing out among all the suits and ball gowns, the doorman laughed. The laugh turned into more of a choke when she opened her satchel and proudly showed him the roses, wrapped safely in rice paper. Deep satisfaction stretched and yawned within her. Shoving this in Purcell's righteous little face was going to feel so damned good.

And then she was inside the big white marble cavity. It was a surprise to know the world held this much marble. Every height and corner had been cleaned to within an inch of its life. Carpets and frescoes and potted plants were in abundance, but it looked more like a museum than a home. Where were the old slippers, newspapers, toast crusts? The Great Petaled Divine did live in the palace, didn't he? Lived here and, presumably, went to the toilet here, showered, ate boiled eggs and toast.

The concept of God on the toilet nearly did her head in. Funny, she'd always assumed, deep down, that the Divine was just a man in a ceremonial position. Gods couldn't be real, not in a world where people worked all their daylight hours for the privilege of just living to work another day. It had to be another trick, like the rigged pageant and the concept of mental-health days. She'd meant it as an amusing thought, but for some reason, that made Cyprin angry. If God couldn't even enjoy his own palace, what hope was there for everybody else?

A plateful of sausages on sticks sailed past and Cyprin wrinkled her nose. She'd intended to make the most of the food, drink, and spectacle of the pageant, but now that she was actually here, she found she couldn't stomach it. Waiters squeezed by her wielding dairy products, bartenders cracked real eggs and mixed the whites into frothy drinks. Cyprin made a disgusted face at all the chipmunk cheeks she passed, the chocolate truffles going into mouths, the drinks swirling past teeth and tongues. The Foliage Concourse was filled with colorful people, most of them in attire that would have cost her a lifetime of wages. Where had they all come from? The penthouse floors of apartments, the richer hinterlands close by the Divine Gardens? What did these people do for a living? Were they property tycoons, CEOs, drug lords? And how was it they felt comfortable overindulging like this when so many in Asperia had so very little? She thought she understood: If your neighbors aren't actually dying, why share with them? Why not exact a price from them instead? This was always what the Underground said about the Divine Kingdom and its neighbors. But it seemed it wasn't just happening between nations; it was happening internally as well.

Cyprin was busy rubbernecking when she crashed into someone.

"Oh, hells! Sorry, sorry!" Cyprin's arms were steadying the person before she had time to register who they were.

Her hands retracted like offended sea anemones.

"What are you doing here?" said Purcell.

Cyprin raised an eyebrow, scanning Purcell for flowers. "Same thing you're doing here, I suspect."

One of Purcell's hands moved hurriedly behind her back, concealing whatever she held. Her big googly eyes roamed unabashedly over Cyprin, and Cyprin just smirked, because her roses were tucked away in the satchel.

It should've ended there. They were barely even acquaintances. Any normal person would've acknowledged that with a nod and walked away, but Purcell lifted her chin, squaring up for a fight. "Show me your flowers," she demanded.

Oh, Cyprin already hated her, for her life of privilege and obvious sour attitude, but something about the way Purcell seemed ready to throw blind punches at the world had Cyprin struggling to keep the grin off her face. "No," said Cyprin, her smile fully blooming.

"Show me!" said Purcell again, more petulantly.

Purcell could probably count the number of times someone had said no to her on one hand. Cyprin cocked her head to the side and said, "No," again, with more emphasis. She was not about to let Purcell inspect the stolen flowers up close.

It looked like Purcell was trying to solve a math problem. Then she actually stamped one of her tiny feet, which made Cyprin's heartbeat turn irregular.

"I have had a terrible day," Purcell moaned, and Cyprin immediately imagined her as someone who overshared in the grocery-store checkout line.

Cyprin stood in open-mouthed fascination as Purcell kept on going. "Twelve hells of a morning. My—my favorite flowers—my flowers, and I think my nose is sunburnt. I didn't have time to change my outfit and it's sticking to my back. And I'm so hungry! I didn't have time to—I missed morning tea."

"Oh wow, not morning tea!" said Cyprin, reveling when this was met with more of Purcell's obliviousness.

"If Amma could only see me now, she'd be so disappointed." Purcell's shoulders drooped as she said this.

Cyprin had no clue who Amma was, but she felt strangely invested. "About you missing morning tea?"

"About me turning up late to the pageant with a last-minute flower choice and a sweaty work uniform!"

The surge of glee made Cyprin want to do a little victory dance. So Purcell had a second-rate flower then? Where was it? Cyprin shuffled to the left to try to catch a glimpse.

Purcell's body turned with Cyprin. "Why am I still talking to you?"

Cyprin couldn't shake the damn grin off her face, she was enraptured. "I don't know," she said, kind of hoping it would never stop.

"You won't win," snapped Purcell suddenly, as though this was a natural progression of their conversation.

Cyprin raised an eyebrow. "I think I will. Over you, at least." There had to be a ton of other good entries that Cyprin had failed to sabotage. But somehow victory over Purcell meant more to her than it should.

"Win over me, or win me over?" Purcell seemed discombobulated, not really paying attention to what she was saying, but the air grew hot and taut between them anyway, and Cyprin forgot what arms and legs were for, for a second.

Without a further word, Purcell turned on her heels, deftly transferring whatever she had in her hand—her hidden flower—to the front of her body where Cyprin couldn't see it. Cyprin watched her stalk off into the crowd in the direction of a champagne pyramid, feeling strangely effervescent.

It took a moment to shake off the interaction and pick out a table in the judging arena.

Creeping ivy hung suspended from a wood trellis overhead, disguising the high ceilings of the palace and making the judging area feel more private, though it was open on all sides and no doubt a crowd would gather. Cyprin unrolled her roses from their tissue paper, and they tumbled out, bloodred and vibrant, ready to conquer. Everything else aside, these flowers deserved to be seen.

Had Maverick ever been in here? Was he here now? Truth be told, she didn't know what she felt about him. The man had fueled a lifelong obsession for the Divine Gardens. An insatiable urge to discover what was so good about this place that he'd never come back. To prove herself worthy of his love and at the same time evade all affection so that no one else could abandon her like that ever again. She'd written letters addressed to the Spring Palace that had probably ended up in the dead end of a mail room. All of them had gone unanswered. Cyprin didn't know which possibility was worse: that he was an asshole who'd ghosted her or that he'd died. One of her hands started shaking and she pressed it into the table with her other hand until it stopped.

Boredom closed its milky eyelid over the world as Cyprin waited. Seemingly in stop-motion, the tables filled up with people and flowers. Cyprin gauged her competition.

An older lady with not a single laugh line on her face arranged a pile of cute fluffy Hoya Rebecca blooms. Whimsically, she wore a matching costume of pink tulle that contrasted nicely against the sternness of her expression.

The spindly petals and weird cone-like protrusions of black bat flowers sat on a table to Cyprin's right. Their owner had just left them unattended as if they weren't irreplaceable and worth a small fortune, and Cyprin's fingertips twitched with an urge to pilfer one. So many of the flowers here were straight out of fables. It felt strange to be among them, wonderful and horrible at the same time—wonderful that she could experience this beauty firsthand, horrible that the pageant was only accessible to people who could come up with perishingly rare and expensive blooms.

Someone had brought in a stinking-corpse lily. They'd tried to position themselves close to a window, but every time Cyprin turned her head that way, she gagged. The corpse lily's owner caught Cyprin staring, and the cutthroat gleam in their eyes had Cyprin imagining them threatening their plants every morning.

Most entrants were sizing Cyprin up with a sour look on their faces. She was clearly the only person here who bought their clothes from chain stores and had the wiry toughness that came with working long hours of hard labor for a living. Cyprin took sick enjoyment as scowls turned to widened eyes when her competitors laid eyes on her flowers. Then they looked back at her, reappraising her as a threat. Delicious.

A few brown spots and curled leaves plagued her competition. Nothing was a match for the brutal perfection of Cyprin's flowers.

She was going to win.

Frustratingly, the other attendees did not include Purcell, who must still be out there downing cocktails. If she didn't get here soon, she'd be late, which was no good. Cyprin wanted Purcell to witness this victory.

She draped herself over her own display as she waited, forehead to table, careful to make sure she wasn't crushing any petals. The crowd hushed into silence for a moment, or maybe Cyprin was drifting off. Then they roared with sudden applause.

Cyprin picked her head up off the table. God had arrived. She turned to the gap in the circle of tables where a phalanx of magenta-clad priest-guard flanked the tall, gold presence of the Divine, like tugboats around a cruise ship. And . . . and where the fuck was Purcell?

A late entrant rushed into the room, cutting in front of the actual Divine, unkempt and hectic, maybe also a tad tipsy. There she was, the five-time champion of the Verdure Flower Pageant: Purcell Whitlock, looking dramatically disheveled, as though she'd run here through a windstorm.

What—What was that flower? If the thing Purcell had put down on her display table could even be called that. It was the vibrant shades of a sunset, and somehow seemed to be emitting its own light. Diamond-shaped petals dwindled to curling tips. Delicate fuzzy down adorned its serrated leaves. Cyprin realized she'd stopped breathing. Why had Purcell shown up every other year with the roses? Had she been holding back? It was glorious nonsense. After so much struggle, Cyprin was going to lose, and couldn't even be mad. She'd never seen anything like Purcell's flower before. It was astoundingly gorgeous. Cyprin was struck with the sudden need to reevaluate Purcell as an opponent. Comparing Purcell's flower to the others was like comparing stones to statues.

Purcell's head snapped up and she glared at the roses on Cyprin's table as if they'd personally offended her. No way she'd recognized them. Roses were roses. You couldn't tell they were yours unless they were growing on your tree, right? Cyprin met Purcell's luminous green eyes and found a well of shrewd intelligence there. If she didn't know, she at least suspected.

Cyprin fixed a vacuous look on her face and did her best to pretend that she hadn't just fallen a little for Purcell despite the fact that Purcell was a complete villain, winning five prior pageants by exhibiting the Divine Gardens' flowers as her own. Cyprin would get away with this or die trying, and if Purcell tried to claim these roses didn't belong to her, Cyprin was going to lie through her teeth. After all, no one could tell these were roses from the Divine Gardens, could they? *Could they?* The worry of possible oversight made Cyprin itch. She rolled up her sleeves and scratched her elbows, casting her eyes around the room to get away from the handcuffs and iron bars of Purcell's gaze.

The Great Petaled Divine shuffled past Cyprin's table, getting ready for the judging. Cyprin had never seen the Divine before. You weren't *supposed* to see the Divine, not directly, but she looked now. What was the harm? They didn't kill people for it these days. She might never get another chance, and she had to do something drastic to burn Purcell's face out of her brain.

It was like glimpsing a fancy bird through the bars of a cage. The priestguard rotated around the Divine as he moved forward, keeping their eyes fixed on the crowd gathering in the judging arena. What Cyprin noticed first was the golden Trellis Crown. It must have been a good two feet high, with a honeycombed lattice as thick as fingers and gold roses the size of fists, and Cyprin wondered if the Divine had to do neck exercises in order to wear it. There was so much gold on him: gold rings, a golden crown, a big gold foil thing over his shoulders like a survival blanket, where the emergency was a need to display wealth. It didn't seem right for a vegetation deity, and it made the Divine's skin look very anemic, but it was impressive.

Cyprin looked at his face.

The Great Petaled Divine looked at Cyprin's face.

She smiled. He smiled back.

The Divine was the man who had walked Cyprin out of the gardens, who had given her the rose. That was such an impossible thought she began to fear she might really be dreaming. She was going to wake up any moment and realize her interview was actually today. Cyprin started hyperventilating in anticipation of disaster.

The judging of the flower pageant began quietly, far away from Cyprin's display. Her nerves were on fire. It was almost impossible not to look at Purcell—even if Cyprin shut her eyes, she could still *feel* Purcell glaring. Cyprin's heart thumped in her chest with the force of a thousand coffees, her hands clasped behind her back so that no one would see them dripping sweat. She tried for restraint, but about every five seconds snuck another look at the Divine. Hope was dangerous. Cyprin had heard people say that before, but she'd never understood it the way she did today.

The Divine approached Cyprin's table, complimenting the man next to her on his begonias for what felt like a million years. Then the reflected light from his golden cape fell across Cyprin's rose display.

"It's you," said Cyprin quietly, finally averting her eyes like she was supposed to under the watchful gaze of the Divine's retinue of priests. She was experiencing a treacherous sense of elation. God was a person she'd met before. More than that, he'd encouraged her to enter this pageant.

"It is me." He seemed pleased Cyprin had recognized him, or maybe that she'd done so in an acceptably vague way. "My, these roses are lovely."

God picked one up, his hand hovering over the bunch for a moment before selecting the rose with the longest stem. He twirled it, and it left her field of vision.

Cyprin felt like she'd been handed an armful of fizzing bombs and then left standing. The anticipation was terrible. If her heart went any faster, it was going to fly out of her chest. With her head still respectfully lowered, she peeked at the Petaled Divine as he scrutinized the other entrants' offerings, Cyprin's rose still clutched in his hand. Purcell's gaze haunted the side of Cyprin's face, but Cyprin refused to look at her.

The Divine was the laconic priestguard who'd walked Cyprin off the palace grounds after her failed interview. She wanted to doubt herself. But there were those kindly librarian eyes, those shapely ankles peeping out among the gold of his robes. And he'd said, *It is me.* He'd admitted it. Wait, what if this wasn't a positive thing? Had he recognized the roses? Was she about to be arrested? The way he was drifting around the room certainly didn't sing of impending arrest, but this was God. If he wanted to get Cyprin, he could do it anytime, anyplace. Whether or not he was a real deity was beside the point. He was the most powerful person in Verdure. The gravity of what Cyprin had done finally hit, and she realized that she might just have ruined her life over Maverick.

Maverick, who didn't care at all.

The Divine finished his rounds, and the room fell into an expectant hush, except for a woman in the crowd behind Cyprin who was loudly speculating that Purcell's flower was the clear pick of the bunch. Without looking up, Cyprin could imagine Purcell shivering like an expectant puppy, and it made her feel sick. That Purcell's flower genuinely deserved to win wasn't the problem. If Cyprin's world were as full of resources and opportunity, she might even be happy for Purcell. But it wasn't, and therein lay the rub. There wasn't a single level playing field anywhere in this kingdom, and that was pure bullshit.

The Divine cleared his throat, and the priestguard opened up the little cage of protection around him to give space to his announcement. "What a wonderful display of horticultural prowess. You should all be very proud of yourselves. But, as they say, there can only be one winner. This year's award of Best in Show goes to the most ingenious entry I have seen in a long time. Congratulations, and I look forward to seeing you among the staff on the palace grounds, Cyprin Voltag!"

A loud, scraping bang made Cyprin jump and look up to see that Purcell's table had fallen over on its side. The entrants beside Purcell scrambled to help right it. Purcell's cheeks glowed pink with embarrassment.

"Cyprin?" The Divine offered Cyprin the gold lanyard that she'd wear to work in the Divine Gardens, every day for the next year. Holy hells, he was giving the prize to her! *The* gold lanyard. Yep. Yes. The one she saw every night in her dreams.

Cyprin forgot herself, forgot everything. The dark hole in her heart, always pushing, cold and demanding, was gone. She felt only weightlessness. She was breaking, this was breaking her. Hardly one to cry even in private, she found herself crying openly in public now, a proper ugly cry where her nose made clogged-drain sounds and the rest of her face screwed up like a juiced lemon. She'd spent her whole life trying to get to this point, fighting for a place in the gardens like her survival depended on it. Relief and fear swirled in a sick cocktail inside her.

Cyprin's hands did not seem to be under any direct control, but she managed to wind the gold lanyard around them anyway. It was slightly cold to the touch, made of fine metal instead of fabric. Cyprin had ascended.

She had ascended to motherfucking greatness.

She looked directly into the Divine's eyes. They had the dappled clarity of black tea.

When all six priests tackled Cyprin to the floor for her blasphemous gaze, it was totally worth it.

CHAPTER 7

PURCELL

Purcell's eyes settled back on the familiar petals. Now, this was truly nightmarish. The roses she had seen disintegrating in the gardens were across the room from her. Looking perfectly well put together. Looking perfect. Perfection incarnate. Twelve roses arranged in a fan shape. Petals the color of a dying star, the fragile, pillowy softness of a dewdrop. Not even the tiny hokey demons in the theater of her subconscious could cook up something this dreadful. This was real, and Purcell's roses had just won the pageant, in the hands of somebody else. In the hands of Cyprin Voltag.

Getting rid of Cyprin should have been as simple as asking Amanda to reject her candidacy. But clearly it was not. Purcell should have blacklisted Cyprin from the gardens and laid caltrops in the road leading up to the palace. She should have employed tactical nukes.

Now she had to watch *her* lanyard swinging around Cyprin's neck as Cyprin paid penance.

Purcell's fingertips drifted to the razor-sharp edge of her bob as

Cyprin got stripped in the middle of the judging arena. One of the priests had fetched a pair of gold-plated clippers, or perhaps he always carried them around with them in his pocket, enterprisingly. Another brandished a bottle of oil, seemingly from nowhere. Purcell wondered what kind of oil they used. Was it olive oil, like you'd use for salad dressing? No, that didn't seem right.

Public penance for looking at the Divine did not happen every day. For starters, the Divine never left the palace grounds, so that limited the number of people who could look at him. And despite their stiff reputation, the priestguard didn't really get evangelical about the whole penance thing anymore. Purcell had seen them catch people looking at the Divine during previous pageants and let it slide. The only times they flew off the handle was if somebody tried to take photographs of him, or for egregious staring, but the latter she'd never seen anyone do before Cyprin. It was a once-every-few-years kind of occurrence. This would make the news.

Purcell hustled for a place among the spectators, then watched as Cyprin knelt, naked and perfectly still, a small giddy smile on Cyprin's lips, hunks of her dark hair falling to the floor. The room was full of rubberneckers, but the only sound was the buzz of the clippers. The skull on the back of Cyprin's discarded jacket laughed at the ceiling.

The priests chanted rhythmic gibberish as one of them poured the oil over Cyprin's bald head. It was a thin stream—any slower and they'd be doing it drip by drip. It seemed to go on forever, cascading down the back of Cyprin's neck, over her shoulders, into her eyes that had squeezed shut. The damn smile remained on Cyprin's annoying face, like she didn't care at all, like she was celebrating victory in her head. The oil coated Cyprin in a glistening layer that seemed almost like honey, sticking to the fine downy hairs of her naked, perfect body.

Purcell tugged at the neckline of her coveralls. It was hot. Wasn't it hot in here?

Finally, finally, the last drop of oil gave up the ghost and left the bottle. The priest squeaked the cork back in, and before the priestguard could step back, Cyprin laughed and shook her head like a dog, causing the priests nearest to her to clutch at their oil-spattered robes in horror.

Cyprin stood up and rolled her shoulders. Her neck cracked like a gunshot in the silence. The hard lines of a body that worked long hours and spent little time around indulgent food shone slick with oil. Her nakedness was all the more striking among the overdressed festivalgoers. It was the least penitent penance Purcell had ever witnessed. Eyes as sharp and unreadable as an insect's surveyed the crowd. Oh no, Cyprin was magnificent.

Purcell risked a quick glance at God to see if he was similarly affected. He was standing a little apart from his priests, as if to signify he disapproved of the barbaric practices that were being carried out in his name. And he was—like a gentleman—not staring at Cyprin's ass. His eyes did flicker to her face, though, and his previous air of constant amusement was gone. There was something else there. Desire? Veneration? Hope? But what could a god possibly see in a criminal, other than a nice set of—Penance complete, Cyprin was handed a plain brown shift to put on. She didn't wait for further instructions, just grabbed her stolen roses, slung her bag over her back, and made her way out, head held high, the gold lanyard sparkling around her neck. As Cyprin passed God, Purcell saw her wink at him. If the priests noticed, they didn't give anything away. Repeating a punishment so soon would be a descent into farce, anyway.

Purcell had to respect Cyprin for going to such lengths to get what she wanted. *Respect, but not enable.* Being hot wasn't an excuse to get away with high crimes. Now that the excitement was over, it was time to sort out this nasty business with the stolen flowers and incorrectly bestowed prize.

Purcell approached God with her eyes fixed carefully on the floor.

She spoke to the Divine's shoes, which were golden and polished. They reflected a weird potato Purcell back, forehead bulging, eyes small and angry. "I was wondering if I might—"

"All judging decisions are final, Purcell. I wouldn't have expected this from you." He was looming, glowering. The Divine was clearly not in the mood to hear her out.

Purcell tried several other opening sentences in her mind, but none of them made it as far as her mouth.

"Purcell?" said Saul when she failed to move out of his way.

Her mouth actually made the shape of words she for sure shouldn't be saying to God. Then she said, "Yes, I understand."

But she did not understand.

She was furious.

Purcell stepped to the side and God moved on, his priestguard gathering around him like an oncoming storm. This was too much excitement for one day, for everyone. She resolved to approach him again in the morning when it was just the two of them and the petal mail. When he'd heard about Cyprin's crimes against nature, he'd have to do something about it. Fire Cyprin from the gardens at the very least. Fire her from a cannon, preferably.

Back home, Purcell filled her kitchen sink with water and put her heirloom flower in along with a sprinkling of sugar. It looked a bit wilty now, but the colors were still spectacular, like a fire in her sink. Her flower might not have won any prizes, but at least she could enjoy it for a few days.

Part of her couldn't believe that the bio bots, the pageant, and watching Cyprin's penance happened in the same day. It had been so much pressure, so much routine change—so much hot, naked rival!—she felt like a different person. Anger at being unfairly usurped had given way to the strange feeling that she'd had the most interesting day of her life. Exhausting too. It occurred to Purcell maybe every day that featured Cyprin in it could be as interesting and exhausting. What a terrifying thought. A one-year tenure was far too long to put up with Cyprin Voltag's chaotic presence in the gardens. Hells, one day felt like it had aged Purcell ten years. She would speak to the Divine about it, first thing in the morning.

But then, the thought of never having another day as exciting as this one was a little terrifying too.

The urge to go and whine about unfairness and sexy criminals to God was still there, but Purcell set it down for the moment. She showered and wrapped a pink towel around her hair, feeling grateful she still had hair to wrap a towel around. She buttoned her flannelette pajamas and popped on her slippers with the fluffy rabbit ears on the toes. The house felt quiet and empty after the buzz of the flower pageant. Calm. Soothing. Purcell slumped down into her armchair with a cup of tea and the surrounding plants leaned over her like weeping willows.

"You guys, I'm fine, I promise. It was just a rough day."

Purcell sighed and closed her eyes, and the image of Cyprin naked—Purcell's eyes flew open again. "I just need to watch TV for a while. I'm sorry, I know the light from the screen makes you grumpy."

A fat shrub rustled in the corner.

"Sorry, I'll turn the volume down."

Here she was, back in the familiar environment of home, with all her creature comforts. It was going to be all right.

Purcell switched the TV on, and it was like the universe was conspiring against her. Flicking through the channels she found *Lust Island*, *Undercover Executive: Special Dating Edition*, and a movie called *My Sapphic Sweetheart*. She changed hurriedly onto the fishing channel. Sweet Divine, what a relief. There was nothing more monotonous and dependable than the fishing channel. It was perfect. Purcell settled farther into her chair.

". . . and that's it folks! There's a tug on my line! I've been out here for days hoping to catch one and give you all a glimpse of this elusive fish," said the TV. The picture showed a man in a flannel shirt and rubber coveralls, waist-deep in a stream, somewhere in the agricultural hinterlands around the Divine Gardens.

Purcell took a fortifying sip of tea. Her nerves were steadying already. The ticking muscle in her eyelid dissipated.

On the TV, the man's line went taut, he hauled on it, and up came a spiky silver giant, thrashing around, dripping water. "Would you look at that! What a superb specimen. Cyprinus Cyprinidae, common name Cyprin." Purcell managed to swallow her mouthful of tea. She rubbed her eyes as if they were going to make a tuning adjustment to her ears. "And what a cyprin! I've never seen one so impressive! Get a load of those shiny scales, the fine lines of its—"

Purcell turned the TV off. It was going to be a long night; she could feel it in her bones.

CHAPTER 8

CYPRIN

A big globule of oil rode Cyprin's nose like a slippery slide and then launched onto the floor, exploding across very familiar gray tiles. She looked up at the purple neon heart on the wall in front of her. Mama Inkburn waved her over to the bar.

Her head was swirling with flowers, lanyards, angry priests, smoldering rivals, and God in his bright gold uniform.

Cyprin shuffled onto a barstool and tried to wipe the oil out of her eyes. Mama Inkburn handed her a dishrag, and, after a moment spent contemplating how dirty it was, Cyprin blotted her face with it. She couldn't remember how she'd gotten here, but that was a common story in Mama Inkburn's diner. If you walked around the city stressed and not paying attention, this was where you ended up.

"You look like you've seen the Divine," Mama Inkburn's eyes almost disappeared in smile lines.

"Hah, yes, very funny. I did, you know." Cyprin ran a hand over the baby hedgehog fuzz that covered her scalp. Her tidy bob was back on the palace floor somewhere, as was her clothing. She itched at the roughspun hemp shift that was sending drafts up her nethers. But it was worth it, it was so worth it.

"I have a present for you," she said to Mama Inkburn. For some reason they had let her leave with her satchel of roses, which was perfect, because she wanted to give something back to the city that had sustained and crushed her for her whole life. She held the roses out to Mama Inkburn. "A thank-you for giving me free dinner the other night."

Mama Inkburn wiped her hands on her pants and reached out for the flowers. "What pretty things." She ran her thumb gently over a thorny stem, smiling faintly. "And deceptively dangerous. Glad you cut these ones before they cut you." Mama Inkburn seemed touched that Cyprin had thought of her, and Cyprin felt warm and fuzzy inside. "I'll find a glass for them."

Cyprin watched as the roses went into a cup clouded with hard-water residue and chipped with overuse. They stuck out like a handful of diamonds in dirt.

"Got any champagne?" said Cyprin, knowing full well that Mama Inkburn never served liquor.

"We have sham-pagne? Sparkling-apple flavor."

"I can't think of anything more appropriate."

Goodbye trash cans, goodbye scrapers, goodbye wind-tunnel streets, goodbye long shadows, and artificial light, and people pressed together like sardines. Hello sunshine, and grass, and flowers, and long, hot showers. Cyprin arrived back in her apartment like she was floating on the wings of a dream and immediately prepared to leave. She wanted to make sure she got to her new job on time—no, not on time, *early*—with everything she needed to move into a new apartment on-site among the other palace gardeners. Entry to the gardens was by invite only, but she had the gold lanyard. She was going to show up and be undeniable.

She couldn't wait to see Purcell's reaction to her arrival; that marshmallow-scented bitch was going to turn herself inside out.

Cyprin did up her laces, slipped on some amethyst knuckle-dusters, and kicked her suitcase out behind her in a jolly way so it was ready to roll along on its little wheels. She dropped her key card on the coffee table—wouldn't be needing that anymore—and started tunelessly whistling something related to curly fries as she opened the apartment door.

Moss stood there, caught in freeze-frame, their hand poised over the buzzer. Cyprin almost brained them, not looking where she was going.

"What are you doing here?" Moss was an unwanted intrusion. Their presence always brought Cyprin back to reality, and she didn't want that. Not now.

In answer, Moss grabbed her by the shoulders and walked her backward into the apartment. "Do you know what I just saw on TV?"

"Justin started dating himself on *Lust Island*?" This was too much to hope for.

Moss's face went slack with incredulity. "You! Paying penance after winning the flower pageant!"

"Must have been someone who looked like me," said Cyprin. She tried on her proprietary death stare, but Moss was immune.

Moss ran a finger across Cyprin's forehead like they were checking for dust on a mantelpiece. It came back slick and perfumey with oil. "Oh really? And I suppose I should get my eyesight checked, because those roses I saw you with must have been apples?"

The glitter of the last few hours started to look like dirt, when refracted through Moss's perspective. Cyprin smiled, joylessly, the muscles pulling back like a slingshot. "Now you get it."

"And what's this?" said Moss. Cyprin's wheely suitcase sat at her feet like a murderer lingering at a crime scene. "Are you leaving for the gardens *right now*? Are you *never* coming back to work?"

Cyprin shrugged. "I sent my resignation." Awkward farewells were best done secondhand. That's what emails were for.

"You can't—I—" Moss had always seemed self-assured, and caustic, yes, but in an entertaining way. Now their face resembled cracked porcelain. "I thought you were my friend."

There was an accusation in that. Cyprin always went on about them not being friends, but it had become a running joke between them. Hadn't it? "Wait—What? I didn't do anything to you."

"You're abandoning me! And making me lie for you. First at work, now maybe to the priestguard. *What did you do with those bio bots, Cyprin?*"

What did she do, indeed. So many things were justifiable in your own head. She had not been expecting to have to pitch any of it to Moss. "It's not like I asked you to go grocery shopping for me or to clean my apartment! All you have to do is nothing—it's the opposite of an ask!" While avoiding Moss's gaze Cyprin noticed Moss's hands were dirt-stained, cracked, and callused . . . and she felt a little bad.

"I should have known better," said Moss. "You're always out for you, you never think about anyone else. Maybe I should do the same. How about this: come back to work or I'll turn you in to the priestguard myself and tell them what I know."

Oof. Moss was so quick to resort to betrayal. That was exactly how life in the city was. So many people living on top of people. You put yourself first or got crushed. Cyprin tried persuasion. "How does ratting me out help anyone? I'll just get thrown in jail."

Moss's face turned red with anger. "I'm trying to make you see reason! If you come back to the apples, they'll have to give the pageant prize to someone else, and no one will ever figure out what you did. There's too much scrutiny in the spotlight, Cyprin."

"You're just sore about doing my shifts!"

"I *am* sore about doing your shifts!" The volume went up on Moss's voice. "I've worked a hundred and sixty hours in the last fortnight, and do you know why? Because I care about you keeping your job and I care about the apples! What happens after your year is up, huh? You think you'll just slot right in where you left off? What's the grand plan?"

"I'm never coming back." Cyprin was just realizing the truth of that as she said it.

Moss stared at her, waiting for her to retract the words, but she didn't. She couldn't. She hadn't meant to say it, but it was done now and walking it back felt cheap.

"Crab mentality," Cyprin muttered.

"I'm sorry, what?"

"None of us will ever make it out of the bucket if the rest always pull them back down." She'd overheard Maverick saying this on the phone once, and she hadn't understood it at the time, she'd just thought it sounded cool. Now she got it.

There was shocked silence, during which Cyprin's stomach rumbled very inappropriately in a Pavlovian response to the mention of crab.

"Is that what you think of me?" said Moss. "Is that what you think of the apples, the city, *everything* that isn't the Divine Gardens? We're all a big bucket of chum?"

Cyprin wasn't sure how she could possibly make this any worse. "You have to let me get out," she said. She couldn't stay for anybody. Nobody would stay for her.

"Get out? You're not getting out of anything, you're getting into something. It's a country club up there, full of rich, narcissistic airheads. You're going to hate it."

"Please."

"Cyprin. He's not there, and if he is, he doesn't deserve you. There are people right here who care about you. *I'm* right here, Cyprin."

The future forked out in front of her: one shining path where she'd get roaring drunk with Moss, admit they were friends, retract her resignation, and find a really good therapist. Another darker one where she'd go to any lengths to find Maverick and make him feel just a fraction of what she'd felt for the last fourteen years. Maybe she'd rise up the ranks in the gardens and ignore him. Maybe she'd spread vile rumors behind his back.

Cyprin chose violence. "The whole thing *is* a crab bucket. If you had your fingertips on the rim I would never, ever pull you down. *That's* what it means to be friends. Hells, that's what it means to respect someone as a fellow person."

"Cyprin!"

But Cyprin was already on her way out of her apartment again. "Do what you have to, Moss." She was resolved now; she was going to walk away with the toughness of a hero turning their back on a big explosion. Though in this instance, the explosion was her life.

In the elevator, she mashed the close-doors button, and Moss just stood there, arms folded, looking at her with pity until the doors slowly slid shut between them.

❧ ❧ ❧

On the way into the gardens, Cyprin tried to resurrect the good vibes again. The gold lanyard was hers, and she deserved it. She deserved it for all the hours spent laboring over apples, she deserved it for all the nonsense Maverick had put her through, she *did not* deserve it for the roses she had shown at the pageant, but she deserved it *adjacently* and that had to count for something. What did Moss know? Their dreams were too small. Their thirst for revenge was too . . . nonthirsty.

The checkpoint officer waved her through, and secondary fears kicked in as she approached the garden gates. It was hardly dawn, stupidly early to come out here. She should have waited for instructions from the garden staff. Shouldn't have just marched on her own with all her earthly possessions. What was she going to do? Wander around the gardens with her suitcase? Should she call someone? She should call someone.

"Hello again." A figure peeled away from the viny trellis that arced over the gates.

It was the Divine, back in his priestguard robes, looking handsomely exhausted, as though he'd spent all night wrestling every single hair into place. Her heart gave a little start at seeing him after he'd helped her—God had helped her!—at the pageant. He didn't look like a god; it wasn't like he was levitating. But some questions you didn't ask, because if you did, the sky invariably fell on your head. It was probably a culturally accepted fiction like the world's financial system being based on something real or everyone who works hard getting what they deserve.

Cyprin pasted a smile over her shock. "I wasn't expecting to see you here."

"Why not?" Saul had rolled up the cuffs of his sleeves and trousers this time to make the size discrepancy of his uniform look more deliberate. His hair was such a fashionable wave Cyprin had the urge to pin a tiny plastic surfer in it. "These are my gardens."

"Shouldn't you have underlings doing this sort of thing for you?"

"Oh, yes. They're probably busy trying to figure out what the protocol is for an outsider winning the flower pageant."

"So, what happens now?"

God smiled weakly. "It's been years since anyone outside of these gardens won. My fault, I'm afraid, I took too long to exercise my power in that arena. I don't think they'll know what to do with you. But if I set you up with a house and a uniform, they'll all think one of them did it, and you should be able to get started without any problems."

"Don't make me feel so welcome." The gold lanyard was supposed to change everything, but here she was being treated like a mistake again.

"I am sorry about your hair. The priests can be quite overzealous sometimes," said Saul.

Cyprin shrugged; hair grew back. Becoming a divine gardener was a once-in-a-lifetime chance. "I'm here now. And I think I like it short."

"Let me take your bags."

"Oh! Thank you."

She trailed after him in awestruck silence for a while as she entered the Divine Gardens for only the fourth time in her life (and the third official time). They passed a pond where giant goldfish bobbed and bubbled, went through a display that buzzed with lavender.

Cyprin was watching a couple of turf-tenders aerating the grass with what looked like long-handled salad forks when Saul dived behind a large bush shaped into a miniature Spring Palace and beckoned to her, frantically. What in twelve hells was going on? Cyprin launched forward onto her stomach in her rush to hide, ribs complaining. She brushed grass off her luggage and then rounded on God. "Are you sneaking around in your own gardens?"

She'd expected denial, but Saul smiled wickedly. "I am. You wouldn't believe what goes on here."

His voice had gone deep and quiet and . . . and it was not a good idea to get a crush on God. "Your 'kids' cutting class and smoking behind the garden shed?"

"Oh, it's much, much worse than that."

"What? Hiding murders in the compost? Smuggling drugs in the fertilizer? You gonna deal me in?" If there were secrets here, she wanted to wield them like weapons.

The Divine picked a leaf out of his hair and examined it. "You know, I think I might."

Something treacherous was happening in the gardens. Perhaps . . . perhaps Maverick's silence had been an attempt to protect Cyprin from such things. For one golden moment she tried to use that to nail her feelings back into their coffin. But it didn't work. When her mind conjured up illegal poker-playing rings and money-laundering rackets, it was Maverick's face that appeared amidst the swirls of secondhand smoke.

Without any further incidents of diving into bushes to escape garden staff, they reached a hillside spotted with housing, overlooking the gray stillness of Lake Pensive. Saul moved through the streets like he owned them . . . which he did. And Cyprin got a crick in her neck from whipping her head left and right at every home they passed. Each was a rustic little cottage, where the rusticity had a designer vibe to it, as if the builder had smashed a few roof tiles for the look of the thing and painted the front doors with a patchy brush. There was even lichen on some of the keystones, so healthy and green it looked as though someone had been spritzing it with water in the mornings. The whole picture brought to mind the word *heritage* rather than *old*. One house had a window box full of pink flowers, another had a window full of cat. Bicycles were tied up out the front of a few places, and at one point Cyprin smudged a chalked hopscotch grid in the middle of the road. It was such a stark contrast to the graffitied walls, rat gangs, and shoulder-to-shoulder crush of the city that it made her queasy to think about it.

Ten thousand homes made up this picturesque town. Saul unlocked the door of a little cottage house in a sandwich of little cottages.

She looked sideways at him. "And you what? Just went and took the key?"

Saul shrugged. "My gardens." Twelve hells, the privilege!

Cyprin had never lived this close to the ground or this far from her neighbors. It was weird. She stepped over the threshold and practically passed out from joy. There were three rooms. *Three rooms!* Not just the usual multipurpose one. She walked through them as God dealt with her luggage. Kitchen and lounge, bathroom, bedroom. All clean and well-appointed. No scraper sway, no smell of mold. And the noise! Her ears were ringing with the lack of it. She lay down and made a snow angel on the plush rug.

God cracked open a beer. "Your fridge is fully stocked. There's a touchscreen menu inside the door in case you want to order something."

Cyprin propped herself up by her elbows. "Why do I feel like you've already put things on my tab?" There had to be a catch. Wasn't there always a catch?

God sniffed the effervescence off the top of the bottle. "They don't let me have beer, you know. It's not pious enough, or something."

It was way too early in the morning for beer. It was the first day of the rest of her life. "Throw me one."

Cyprin got off the floor and sunk into a couch built with the overstuff of a teddy bear. She caught the beer one-handed and opened it with her teeth.

"I see you have some interesting skills." Saul sat down beside her, and a treacherous thrill ran through Cyprin's body at their proximity.

The curtains were open, and Cyprin and God looked out on an astounding view of the lake, with the island in the center: the birthplace of God, the navel of the world. She was surprised they were allowed to even look at it; she'd heard the priestguard killed people for trying to go there. Outside the window, a bluebird chased a dragonfly, clicking wildly.

"I stole those roses from you," said Cyprin. God already seemed to be doing the wrong thing. That was, if God doing a thing didn't make it right by default. She wanted him to know: To conspire with her.

"I'd hoped you would," said God. He cleared his throat. "Cyprin. I'm going to ask you to do some things for me. Take some risks."

Of course. Nothing was ever free. The child in her that insisted on revering Maverick was disappointed that the world of the Divine Gardens was as transactional as the one she'd just left. But Cyprin stifled the sadness and sought to turn the situation to her advantage. Two could play at this game. "I want permanent tenure. And I want to be head gardener." Cyprin was thinking of Purcell—of Purcell's face if God just handed the head-gardener title over to Cyprin. Of the sheer dark joy of turning all the unfairness of the rigged system back on Purcell.

God laughed. "Well, you don't mess around. I'll see what I can do. I am sure, at the very least, that you can win the pageant again next year."

A crease appeared between Cyprin's brows as she considered that statement. Just because it was in her favor didn't make it any more fair. But she'd been asking for favors, and this was how the world worked. God plainly had an agenda, like everyone else. Speaking of agendas—

"If I wanted to find someone here—an old friend—how would I do it?" Cyprin said it in a carefully breezy way, though her heart felt like it was being choked.

"Oh, I can make inquiries. What's their name?"

"Maverick. Maverick Trelowny." Even saying his name out loud did something bad to her insides, as if a little piece of her went rotten every time.

God looked right between her eyes like he could see the child she used to be, sitting there with her arms wrapped around her knees while bloodred thoughts of unhinged vengeance danced about her. He looked entirely indifferent. "Consider it done, Cyprin."

God finished the rest of his beer and went to rinse his mouth out with water like a teenager expecting his parents to catch him when he got home. "I must take my leave. There's somewhere I need to be. It's not easy for me to get out like this. If you can find a way to come and see me, you should."

"You're not gonna tell me what a den of iniquity I've walked into?"

"Soon. Time is shorter than I'd like. You'll be very useful to me, Cyprin. You can move freely around here." He headed for the door.

"Wait, what am I supposed to do now?"

God smiled diamonds. "Whatever you want."

CHAPTER 9

PURCELL

Purcell yawned so hard her eyes rolled back in her head. Her body felt dull and heavy, as if the missed hours of sleep had tacked onto her like weights. She stabbed an unnecessary hole in the petal she was linking and had to take it off and start again with another one.

"Late night?" A hint of humor in the Divine's voice was tempered with something darker. Evidently, he was still annoyed with Purcell from the flower pageant. She didn't know why; it wasn't like *she'd* done anything wrong.

Well, it didn't matter that he was annoyed. He needed to hear what had gone on in his gardens yesterday, under his very nose. "I didn't sleep very well," said Purcell. "Not after the act of sabotage in the gardens." And the deliciously hateful dream where Cyprin had turned up at her house with a wink, holding the stolen roses as a gift—one of a tirade of recent dreams featuring Cyprin, ever since Purcell had first laid eyes on the woman.

God's face was all mild interest. "Ah, yes, we had an unfortunate biobot infection on one of the rosebushes, I heard. Exciting times."

"Unfortunate? Somebody planted them there!"

God shuffled back to look down his nose at her. "I don't recall hearing anything to that effect."

But Purcell wasn't about to miss her chance. "The same person who then showed up at the pageant—"

"Careful, Purcell."

"—with roses from *our* garden."

What was happening? He should be incensed! He should be calling on the guards to pay Cyprin a visit, that is if Cyprin wasn't already on her way to the palace gardens. Then they could stop her at the gates, strip her of her position, maybe give her a night in the dungeons (the very thought of Cyprin in chains gave Purcell sweaty palms), and after that, they would restore the rightful honor of Best in Show to Purcell—

"Tell me, what would you have done with the prize?" The Divine tugged the edge of the petal mail away from Purcell and she was forced to give him her full attention.

She put her tools down on the floor. "I have a dedicated shelf at home where I—"

"Where you stash it with all the others." God looked like he was confirming something with himself, and it wasn't in Purcell's favor.

She scrambled to get through to him. "Winning isn't about the gold lanyard. It's about knowing I'm the best, *proving* I'm the best."

Saul rubbed his hands over his eyes. If she was being unkind, she might think he'd had trouble sleeping too. "Purcell Whitlock. You are the head gardener. You *are* the best. Yesterday you weren't Best in Show, but you can't win everything all the time. Consider this: you've proved yourself time and time again. You don't need to anymore. Standing back costs you nothing and gives others an opportunity to shine."

Purcell's insides twisted like snakes. "But, then I—"

"You already have a position here. One that is unassailable, I might add. You can't win your way into these gardens, but others can, if we give them the opportunity. Don't you think we should give them the opportunity?" God's face was stern and teacherly, waiting for her to give him the right answer.

"She stole those roses!" Purcell knew those flowers like old friends. She'd have recognized them anywhere. Why didn't he care?

God's eyes flashed. "This is very immature of you. You lost to the better competitor yesterday. But you did not *need* to win, Purcell. Sit with your feelings and you'll come to understand that. Try to adopt a more gracious attitude to defeat."

"But she destroyed the rosebush—"

"More conjecture, born from jealousy. It was a small bio-bot storm, exactly like the ones seen elsewhere in the world. Pure bad luck that it happened here. Listen, if the plant still lives, we will rehabilitate it. If it has died, we will replace it. It's just a plant."

Those last four words settled like tombstones between them.

Purcell started packing up her tools. She couldn't be there anymore, not with God belittling her. She knew some people thought her seriousness about plants was silly, but it was also *everything*.

God laughed. "What are you doing? You haven't finished the petal mail yet."

But Purcell was already storming out the door.

Run! Whenever her stress levels got too high, everything in her head narrowed down to one instruction: *Run*. With the wind in her ears, her problems would coil out behind her and there would come a brief moment in which she felt free. Until she stopped, of course, and everything came careening back.

Just a plant. Just a pageant. Unimportant. Let someone else win. The whole world was overwhelming static. The whites of the palace blurred into the greens of the palace gardens, and Purcell ran. Her tools had fallen out of their pouch and were scattered back behind her.

The lake was only going to stop her in the same way that a sand trap stops a runaway truck. Purcell cannonballed into the water and went under.

She'd been expecting it to be lukewarm—blood-like, with the trapped heat of a thousand sunny days—but it wasn't. The shock of the cold seized her lungs like a pair of hands and squeezed. Purcell's vision went dark for a moment, or maybe it was a swirl of silt from the lake bed. Deeper, deeper. She sunk down and hovered, suspended in the peaceful press of water. Her clothes billowed around her like spectral wrappings. Nothing but the *da-dum, da-dum* of her heartbeat in her ears.

As the heat of her anger slowly sapped out into the cold water, she acknowledged maybe God was right.

The rosebush Purcell had used to win five pageants in a row had been cared for and tended to by Purcell, sure, but it had been in the gardens long before she had been born. As much as she'd come to think of those roses as hers, they weren't. Not really. And the flower she'd brought to stand in for the roses at the pageant had come from her great-great-grandmother's stock, so that wasn't really hers either. She had merely been the caretaker. She hadn't created anything of her own. Neither had Cyprin.

She bounded off the bottom with a kick and a burst of bubbles.

Purcell's head emerged from the water and a nearby duck took off in alarm. She gasped and gulped in air, disturbing the mist that swirled in an eddy around her. She looked up, and then further up at the dormant volcano that rose out from the center of the lake. It made her feel small, the way she needed to at times like this.

Oh, yes, she could see it now. Her flower and Cyprin's had been plausibly matched at the pageant. The running and the lake had helped clear things up.

It didn't matter which of them won the pageant, because neither of them deserved to. She thought she understood now why God had scolded her.

He was pushing her to become more.

When she created a flower of her own to show, there was no way God would award Cyprin instead of her. Or anyone.

A gust of wind blew wrinkles over the water. With it came a spark of neon blue, and Purcell startled, momentarily fearing someone was firing on her with an energy weapon.

A petal settled onto the surface of the water, incandescent as a blue flame. It shimmered in the way of a hologram, and then dissolved like fairy floss. Purcell looked up to the densely forested cone in the middle of the lake. No one ever set foot on that island. Here, in the middle of a lake, in the middle of a garden cultivated to an insane degree of control and perfection, was a little piece of wild, untouched land. No one knew what was up there—it was considered the birthplace of the Great Petaled Divine and exploration was expressly forbidden, punishable by death. But there was something on that mountain.

Something pageant winning.

After she'd dried off and put on some clean work clothes, Purcell pulled The Box from under her bed. It held everything of her family history that did not belong to the public record. She was going to make her own way forward, but not without every possible advantage she could wring from the other Whitlocks. She started with Amma's diaries, opening one up at random.

". . . found the perfect ratio of tea to milk: 4:1 . . ." Nope, that wasn't any good. "Ceely brought me some sick flowers to look over, but they weren't very unwell. I think she did it just to see me. She was wearing that pink sweater with the top button undone, and I find my thoughts wandering often to what she is like underneath it—" Purcell snapped that one shut. Nothing but uncomfortable personal stuff in there, and she had already read every scientific paper Amma had ever published. Looked through every old lab book on file.

She'd never seen anything that adequately explained Amma's accomplishments. This left Purcell with the unsettling impression that Amma was hiding the key to her success, guarding it from the world and her unworthy descendants. Purcell put the diaries back, pulling out a pink envelope containing a letter her mother had left her, and a photograph. She read the letter maybe once a year when she was feeling particularly maudlin, looking between the lines for signs of affection that weren't there, because her mother had been an eminently practical, to-the-point kind of person. Today seemed like the right kind of day for it.

The photograph came out first. In it, Purcell's mother smiled and spread her arms wide in a field of sunflowers. She was wearing her gardener whites, with rubber bands to cinch the wrists because she was already showing signs of the wasting disease that would take her life a few years later. Purcell touched her own face. She looked so like her mother that her own reflection in a mirror was too much sometimes. Purcell was only a few years younger than her mother had been when she began to decline.

She unfolded the letter and mumbled the words out loud to herself. "'Purcell, you're so young it must feel like you have all the time in the world. That is how I felt when your grandmother started getting sick, and how she felt when her mother grew sick before her. The time will disappear from you all too quickly.

"'Know this: Amma, with all that she'd achieved, fighting darkness, creating roses, even with all that she knew, she didn't waste a moment looking for a cure. I remember when my own mother told me that, I didn't believe it. I went through all Amma's research to see for myself, but your great-great-grandmother stopped working when the doctors told her she was terminal. She took Ceely and they went and lived by the sea until the end. I often felt like she'd cursed us. She was too big, flew too close to the sun. Amma was the first one to face the wasting sickness. Then your great-grandmother, then your grandmother. Then me. I have no hope that it will spare you. Do big things with the time you have. Make us all proud.'"

Purcell often stopped there, but today she read on. "'I leave you Amma's heirloom flower, my savings, and my porcelain-dog collection. Take especial care of the bulldog shepherdess. She brought me much comfort.'"

Purcell's eyes went to the linen closet where the porcelain dogs lived. That was one of the worst things a person could do to you: die tragically and leave you their ugly collectibles to hoard for all time.

She brought forth the bulldog shepherdess and placed it on her bedside table next to Amma's hothouse. It was as awful as she remembered, big-headed and jowly, with an iridescent dress. She picked lint off its ear before heading back to salvage what was left of the workday, thinking about a mother who would leave a porcelain monstrosity instead of an I-love-you, and a famous great-great-grandmother who took her secrets with her to the grave. There was no help from them. No help from anyone at all.

Purcell stood on the edge of Lake Pensive in a sensible black one-piece bathing suit. She strapped on her goggles. She couldn't remember why she'd entered this swimming competition, but it seemed important. She glanced left and right and saw no competitors; only Amanda was there, blowing the whistle to mark the start.

Purcell dived into the water and Cyprin rose like a monster from the depths of the lake, wearing a bikini made from marshmallows. Purcell's arms and legs churned harder and she veered to avoid Cyprin but then lost sight of her. She stopped, treading water, trying to see her opponent, and Cyprin's strong hands seized Purcell's ankles, dragging her under. Drowning her.

Purcell's predawn alarm went off and her hand shot out to quiet it, the image of Cyprin grinning underwater fading away. But things on her bedside table were not quite as expected. The sharp tinkle of something eminently breakable had her scrambling. She twanged off her pink silk eye mask, already imagining Amma's hothouse in pieces, but it was still there, steaming gently, a new flower already budding inside. Purcell's hand fluttered over her heart like she'd seen someone almost drop a baby. She leaned over the side of the bed.

On the floor, half rolled under the mattress, the porcelain bulldog shepherdess lay in three pieces and several tiny, toe-curling shards. The first thing Purcell felt was deep relief. The second was guilt.

Well, no one could blame her for throwing it out now. Even if it was *maybe* repairable, nobody needed to know.

She hopped over the broken remains and went to get a dustpan and brush. When she came back to clean it up, she saw some envelopes poking out of the bulldog's bottom half. Five of them, each one labeled with a Whitlock name: AMMA, GLORIA (her great-grandmother), VIOLA (her grandmother), ESME (her mother) . . . and PURCELL. She opened Amma's first. It was full of hair.

It was too early in the day to have touched a dead person's hair. Purcell went and washed her hands, then changed her clothes for good measure, coming back armed with tweezers. *Gross, gross, gross. What kind of deranged keepsakes*—She was horrified this had been in her house the whole time. Keeping people's hair seemed like a suitably weird old-person's thing to do, though it was difficult to logic it away like that since none of them had made it to forty. Purcell used the edge of the tweezers to open the envelope with her name on it. Yep, more hair. Kept tidily together with a rubber band. But this one had a slip of paper in it too. Purcell shook the contents out onto the floor and flipped the paper over with the tweezers.

She read it once silently, and then again out loud, because she didn't believe what she was reading. "'Purcell. I don't know if I ever want you to find this. It won't do you any good. It didn't do me any good either. Burn the hair if you want to, and forget you ever read this. But, if you do decide to look for answers, I want you to know: I chose to have you in the traditional way of the Whitlock line, but I did not know what Amma did to herself—to us, until it was too late. I'm sorry. I love you. It was always hard for me to love you, because of who you are, but I do love you. Esme.'"

The *I love you* echoed through her. Her mother had said it, had put it in writing that Purcell could reread and revisit. Purcell had memories of her saying it—rarely—but over time she'd started to think she must have been making them up. That was unexpected and wonderful. But the other parts—*the traditional way of the Whitlock line, what Amma did, who you are*—were entirely disturbing. The handwriting was spidery, from a time when her mother must have been already losing motor control. What was this? A deathbed confession? Purcell's appointment with the petal mail was looming, but she did not check the time. She picked up all the hair barehanded, shoved it in her pajama pocket, and went straight to the garden's genetics lab. The porcelain crunched underfoot on her way out; she had forgotten it was there.

❧ ❧ ❧

Ominous messages should not be allowed to appear before five in the morning. Purcell wasn't in full control of her faculties, bits and pieces were slotting together like a game of Tetris and she couldn't stop them.

The traditional way of the Whitlock line. A chill in her bones thought it knew what that meant—But they wouldn't! The only thing that could save her now was the sequencer. Purcell's access card let her into the plant genetics lab out of hours.

The plant lab was underneath the palace grounds, a level above the admin center, carved out of cool stone and filled with buzzing machines and an abundance of specimens sliced between glass slides or cryofrozen in little numbered tubes. The lights came on when Purcell entered. Obsessively safety conscious under normal circumstances, she did not stop to don a lab coat. She did not put on gloves or safety glasses. Her rabbit slippers stamped across the linoleum floor, the little rubber nubbins on their soles saving her from skidding. She used both hands to take somebody else's plant samples out of the direct sequencer, dropping them unceremoniously across a benchtop. She put a strand of each family member's hair in their own sample slot and closed the lid.

The machine made a mechanical buzzing noise that would usually make her scrutinize the cleaning and maintenance records, but this time she just prayed. Not to the man upstairs, who was probably waiting quite impatiently for her petal-mail visit, but to the universe at large. To any and everything that might be listening and could help her. *Please don't let this be what I think it is.*

Dried-seed packets in the cold storage of the seed library rattled anxiously. A fridge door sprung open when genetically enhanced seedlings outgrew the space inside. Purcell shushed them. The direct sequencer beeped, and its green light came on to indicate the run had finished. She read the results. Her heart sunk.

Purcell had always wanted to be Amma, but not like this. Amma had abused her background in biotechnology by cloning herself, starting a family tradition of cloning that had encompassed Purcell's mother, grandmother, and great-grandmother too.

Purcell was Amma.

It was so shocking she almost didn't see the secondary finding: Purcell and all the other Whitlocks were part plant.

❧ ❧ ❧

Habit moved Purcell cursorily through the steps to tidy up the lab. Pure autopilot pushed her home and got her dressed for work, though she walked over the shards of the porcelain dog again as she left. A long scream was happening on the inside. It started like the first whistle of a boiling kettle and then moved on through tsunami-warning range. Somewhere in the middle of her early-morning ritual, the scream surprised her by cutting out and leaving silence in her head. Soft and muffled as socked feet. And then into the silence, the thoughts came.

Purcell thumbed away tears of panic as she collected rose heads for the petal-mail fitting. She was running a half hour late for work, for the first time ever in her life—hah, or was it? When she thought about *her* life, was she supposed to include her mother's too? Her grandma's? Amma's? Amma, she was Amma, she *was* Amma. *She was Amma*, and she was her great-grandmother, and her grandmother, and she was her mother. Her mother. *She was her own mother.* She had raised herself! She was a by-product of her own crappy parenting. She was mad at herself! She was dwarfed by her own accomplishments! But they weren't really hers—it had been another iteration of her. It wasn't the same, was it? Not to mention cloning was outlawed. The city had tried it for years on animals to boost food production, but all that had achieved was a series of sickly, deformed creatures: six-legged sheep and cows that coughed all night. The outcry of public disgust had been enough to nip that in the bud, but apparently not for Amma.

It was not okay that she was an Amma clone, although some deeply awful part of Purcell could understand how that had happened. If Purcell had been as successful as Amma, struck down in her prime by some wasting disease, wouldn't she have looked for a way to continue? This brought up a dreadful uncertainty, though: which came first, the cloning or the disease?

It was *maybe* okay that she was part plant. But this was highly dependent on what kind of plant Amma had spliced them with. It would be totally undignified to be part mulberry. Mulberries were the plant equivalent of a certain type of kid she remembered from school who ate glue and laughed excessively at fart jokes. A camellia could be all right; they were aesthetically pleasing, though their flowers didn't last long. Or . . . or a rose. Complicated, thorny, and quite, quite beautiful.

She thought of Amma's hothouse flower. The porcelain dog, the flower—perhaps her mother had laid it all out for her. Shockingly late for God's petal mail now, she rushed back home, clipped a leaf off, and returned to the lab.

Purcell sequenced her own hair and part of the leaf. But it wasn't a match. She ran her hair sample against the entire DNA database of the gardens and found nothing. She could spend forever trying to figure out which plant Amma spliced them with, burning up her limited time. And for what? Knowing wouldn't change what had been done to her. Purcell ground her teeth together. She was number one in this world when it came to plant knowledge, and she still didn't know how a plant could have given her the powers she seemed to have over other plants, the ability to communicate with them. She imagined a malicious edge to using her powers now, like a ghostly Amma laughed every time Purcell talked to a shrub.

Combining plant and human DNA was an impossibility, she should have just sickened and died as an embryo. Amma must have been devilishly clever. But how was that fair? Purcell *was* Amma.

CHAPTER 10

CYPRIN

Cyprin bit into a strawberry. It couldn't taste as good as it looked, the big, shiny red ones never did, they—Oh. It did.

"We don't eat the produce, dear."

"Sorry! I, uh, sorry." Cyprin went back to plucking and inspecting strawberries, putting them in a small basket. It made sense that they'd started her in the chef's garden, collecting for the kitchens. It would be hard to fuck that up. A glorified pair of pruning shears, she wasn't even allowed to lay the manure. But she was still grinning. She'd won her way in. No one was disputing that. The absolute bottom rung of the ladder was still miles better than the floor.

Her supervisor was eighty-seven and it seemed her only purpose was to order Cyprin around, which she did with the sprightly vigor of a twenty-year-old. Sitting under a paper parasol, wearing oversized sunglasses, she looked more like a fashion critic at the front row of a show than a soon-to-be-retired gardener. "The leeks next, and then the potatoes," she called to Cyprin.

"Righty-o, righty-o."

"On the hovercart and then into the kitchens by eight, so that the night shift has it for the following morning."

Cyprin mouthed the words, having already heard them a number of times. Her hips ached from being stuck in a crouch and her shoulders and neck burned from picking fruit and vegetables. But she was in the Divine Gardens. It was the best feeling in the world.

A shadow stretched over her, and someone cleared their throat, making a squeaky sound, nothing like her supervisor's voice. Cyprin's spine stiffened.

"I thought I'd see how you were getting on," said Purcell. For some reason her hair was wet and smelled funny, like she'd taken a swim in a bird bath.

Cyprin glanced back to see her supervisor sitting very upright with a frozen expression of horror on her face. No one seemed to like Purcell. That was not surprising.

"Well, now you've seen," said Cyprin, as cordially as she could manage. "Boss," she added, because she was not sure how you were supposed to address a head gardener.

Purcell's expression writhed in distaste. "Just Purcell will do."

The head gardener got down on her haunches to inspect the way Cyprin had been snipping off strawberries. Cyprin was equal parts offended and amazed that Purcell would go to such lengths to annoy someone who should be to head gardener as an acorn was to a whole-ass tree.

Purcell's lips twitched in a smirk as she searched through Cyprin's basket of harvested fruit. She picked out a couple of berries, a hair lighter than the others, and tossed them on the ground. "They won't ripen after you pick them," Purcell said, her tone so self-satisfied Cyprin wanted to smoosh her face into the basket and show her just how ripe the strawberries were.

Cyprin picked up one of the rejects, perfect and red, and shoved it under Purcell's nose. "What's wrong with this one?" she complained.

Purcell seemed to grow a few inches taller, utterly assured of her own superiority. "Maybe that's ripe by city standards, but you're in the Divine Gardens now." Her tone made it clear: *You're in my gardens and I can mess with you as much as I want to.*

"Try harder, okay?"

And then the head gardener got up and walked away, while Cyprin was still steaming.

Try harder? *Try harder?* This was petty revenge for the stolen rose, it had to be. Purcell was going to make Cyprin's life as difficult as possible, and Cyprin had no way to combat that, because Purcell was the head gardener and the only person above her was God. Wait—God. God was on Cyprin's side, wasn't he? He could fix this, if Cyprin ingratiated herself to him.

Cyprin finished with the strawberries. Interminably squatting between a bed of leeks and a little potato field, she glanced up at the palace. The Divine would be somewhere in there, doing his thing. He'd asked her to come find him, and she'd seen it as the next challenge to overcome. A test, to see whether she was worthy of his favor and his secrets. She did not intend to disappoint.

With the memory of Purcell's gorgeous, scowling face fueling her, Cyprin would rocket into the Divine's good graces and leave Purcell eating dust.

After the Divine had left Cyprin to settle in, she had checked into the admin building to make her presence known. She'd asked for a list of Mavericks first, because you never knew how easy a thing might be without trying, but Amanda had flatly refused and looked at Cyprin as if she suspected her of being a rabid fangirl. Cyprin diverted to ask about the Divine's schedule, pleading religion, which turned out to be a much more defensible position, and so she'd been allowed to see the whiteboard where the Divine's daily activities were recorded for possible conflicts with the gardening schedule.

"I could grow potatoes faster than you're digging them up," said Cyprin's supervisor.

Cyprin groaned and cracked her knuckles, picked up her trowel and picked up the pace. She had to be in the kitchens with this produce by eight. What would the Divine be doing then? Cyprin consulted the scrap of paper in her pocket covertly, where she'd scribbled his movements down. Eight until ten today was blocked out for "matters of state," whatever that was. Apart from religious ceremonies, the schedule was vague. So, what was she going to do? Hide out in a closet for two hours and then go snooping to find the Divine? She had more panache than that. *Find a reason to be there.*

Cyprin and her hovercart full of vegetables wandered into the palace.

With enough capacity to host events like the flower pageant, the kitchens were cavernous. Parts of them were hives of activity while other sections were quiet. A lone man scrubbed dirty dishes in a way that suggested his arm would keep moving even if you removed his brain. A bunch of pastry chefs on ladders were carefully placing the upper tiers on a cake that could have rivaled Asperia's scrapers—for the Divine? For practice? Who knew. Buttercream roses spilled over its sides and Cyprin had to work very hard to quell a sudden urge to poke her fingers in it. This place was a fantastical wealth of excess, and unappreciative complainers like Purcell did not deserve any of it, even if Purcell did look like she fit here with her hair like wild vines and her evergreen eyes.

Cyprin found the most active part of the kitchens, where vegetables were being julienned and pots full of water were brought to a boil by industrious red-faced people wearing outfits even more starched and white than her own. Absurd, the palace's obsession with having staff wear white. Cyprin's knees were currently tempered with green and brown, and quite a few of the chefs sported splatters in crime-scene red.

Cyprin approached the guy with the cleanest uniform and the least sweat on his brow. The way he was leaning back with his elbows on a sink, an unlit cigarette behind one ear, was a dead giveaway too. "Hey, you. You the head chef?"

"Yeah." He looked her up and down in a way that said, *I saw you naked at the flower pageant.*

"Here's your vegetables." Cyprin resisted the urge to throw a potato at him and parked the floating trolley. It settled slowly to the floor. "Got any spare wine?" She wanted to make him do something for her.

"That was some show you put on at the flower pageant. I was working the floor, saw the whole thing."

Oh, here we go. Cyprin gave him her best death stare. "Two. I'll be taking two bottles of wine. And snacks. Any cheese and biscuits?"

The man snorted. He had the kind of goatee that looked like an accident. Cyprin waved a hand at it. "Shouldn't you be covering that thing? What if a hair gets into the pudding?"

The head chef touched his chin reflexively. "You know, we have bets going about how long it's going to be before you get stripped and shaved again. Youngbloods like you always take a while to learn the ropes."

He was disgusting, but she'd dealt with worse. "I'll have to get myself a Velcro suit."

"Hoo, that's the spirit." The head chef clapped Cyprin on the shoulder and she jumped like she'd been touched by a live wire. "All right, let's see about those requests. In the bag?"

"Going in the satchel, yeah." She was getting away with all kinds of things these days. She unslung her satchel from her shoulder and handed it over. It came back with high-quality snacks.

Cyprin left the kitchens, walked through the vaulted areas of the ground floor, and headed up a set of marble stairs. There were hardly any guards inside the palace, it seemed, but two stood at the top of the staircase. She prickled with sweat.

When she got up to them, the guards didn't ask anything or cross their weapons over in front of her. Cyprin probably looked right at home in her white gardener's suit. There was every chance she could walk by without raising any kind of suspicion. She started overexplaining anyway. "I need to check all the plants on the second floor in case they need replacing."

"All right, go on through."

She passed the guards with one nervous look back. They were staring down the stairs again, disinterested. Ahead was a hallway filled with closed doors. One by one she began throwing them open.

This place was a fun house, each door opening into its own little world. Cyprin found an empty room painted to look like you were standing in the sky, and another where a handful of priestguard steamed themselves under towels (Cyprin left that one very quickly).

She cleared the level and went up another set of stairs without encountering any more guards. The palace seemed woefully underdefended. Ripe for Cyprin's misdemeanors. Or maybe that's what they wanted her to think. She started scanning the walls for hidden cameras, but if they were there, they were . . . hidden.

Cyprin went up another floor, and another, and another. This felt more familiar. The sense of height under her feet, the narrowness of the corridors. She opened—wow—the Mint Throne Room. Went in and looked around. Fought a desperate urge to perch on the throne for a moment, then lost the fight and sat down. There was a nice view out the open balcony. Stars twinkled. She tapped her fingers against the branches that formed the armrests. Had Purcell ever dared to sit

in God's seat? By dint of molecular residue, was she touching Purcell's butt right now? She got up and brushed the seat of her pants off, just in case.

It was a quarter past ten. Cyprin wondered where she was in this tower, and whether the Divine's room would be at the very top. He was probably heavily guarded, surveilled, and booby-trapped. But for some reason, that thought was not enough of a deterrent. Some people laughed in the face of danger, but Cyprin . . . forgot about it? It wasn't quite bravery—it was the flip side of being the kind of person who bought ten jars of cinnamon because she could never remember what was in her cupboard. Danger didn't exist when she couldn't directly see it, and neither did cinnamon.

She opened the next door, and there was God. Lying in bed beneath a canopy of green velvet with reading glasses and a novel. Under the soft light of the bedside lamp he didn't look so sickly anymore; he looked in his element. God tipped the glasses down his nose and smiled like he'd been expecting her. "Ah, Cyprin."

She reached into her satchel. "I brought wine."

"So you did."

Cyprin nosed around his expansive bedroom. The bed was an eight-poster and he looked like a little boy in it. A nearby bookcase boasted a mind-boggling collection of hardcore romance. The day's petal mail had been thrown over a nearby chair. It looked bafflingly short. Fancy candelabras set off a warm glow. A giant mosaic of the gardens covered one wall. A series of shelves held glass jars with exotic teas in them. He had his own balcony, overlooking the stars and—way out there—the lake and its forbidden holy island shone under the moonlight. When Cyprin looked back, the Divine was scrutinizing her. She scrutinized him too, ran some internal calculations, then went to shut the bedroom door. For good or ill, whatever happened between her and God was going to happen between her and God alone.

"I take it you didn't bring wineglasses," said the Divine.

"I thought we could drink out of the bottle." She hadn't thought this through.

"A novel idea." He put his book down, marking the page, then stepped out of bed, muttering, "So many firsts at the end of my life," which was way too ominous for the end of a workday.

God wore beige silk pajamas. Cyprin stared at his bare feet. Suddenly, all of this felt startlingly intimate. She was a nobody, in the Divine's bedroom. She was Cyprin, in a man's bedroom. The discomfort paled against the opportunity. She could leverage God's good will, manipulate him. She was going to be head gardener one day, even if it killed her.

She thought through a few ways she might bring up Maverick again, but daddy issues didn't seem like an ideal icebreaker, so instead, Cyprin smiled and waved the wine bottle. "Come on. Tell me your worst conspiracy theories."

"Oh, if only that's all they were." God's polite, tidy exhaustion still made it clear he thought the gardens were so fucked they were both in danger. Cyprin tried to glimpse a hint of rot under all the silk and velvet in the room, but it was nothing but picturesque to her.

They sat on the floor of the Divine's balcony, the cheese beside them, swinging their legs between the marble columns of the railing, the Divine holding onto them like they were the bars of a cage. Far, far below, the gardens were empty, the white marble walkways glistening through them like veins.

"When I was a boy, I really thought I *was* God. I winked at budding roses, nonsense like that." Saul was talking to the night sky, getting lost in his own recollections, not even looking at Cyprin. She liked it better that way and wondered if he'd already worked that out about her.

"The gardens are a very beautiful prison," said Saul. "So beautiful it took me more than thirty years to understand I was trapped."

"Trapped?" If someone had given her five hundred guesses, she never would have come to that conclusion. Could someone really be trapped if they had pajamas that shiny and a ten-step skin-care regime?

"Well, not completely trapped," Saul admitted. "So long as I perform the role of the Petaled Divine, there's wiggle room for sleuthing. If I take it too far, my calendar fills up, meals get worse, and a hundred other mild inconveniences nudge me gently but firmly back into the mold I am supposed to occupy. The more I break that mold, the bigger the pushback. As it stands, I've only put a foot beyond the front gates. I'd sworn no one had seen me, but it earned me six weeks of limp asparagus and a rock under my mattress. I have to be careful."

Oh, *trapped*. It made more sense now. It was a gentlemanly kind of trapped, like being trapped in conversation or ensnared by a good book. When Cyprin thought of being trapped she pictured rats, so desperate from hunger that they would walk right under a snappy metal bar. She'd seen them chew through their own tails just to get free.

But Saul really believed what he was saying. Everyone was limited by their own scope of experiences. Purcell, for instance, probably thought having a hangnail was the worst kind of pain ever. Cyprin wondered what Purcell would do if she got dropped off in the undercity and had to fight her way out through hairless tails and mold. She had an undercurrent of darkness to her; she might do something surprising and emerge triumphant wearing a cloak made of rats. Wait, why was Cyprin still thinking about Purcell? Cyprin dragged her focus back to God and adjusted her face from dumbfounded skepticism to deep concern so that he wouldn't be put off from talking.

"There *is* eternal spring," said Saul. "Visiting dignitaries from neighboring kingdoms all thank me for my Divine providence, bemoaning the finicky state of crops and blights and seasons. War. The scales that balance the fate of nations go up and down outside our kingdom, but

Verdure is a magical cornucopia, the food never seems to run out. I have nothing to do with that. Sooner or later, I'll get to the bottom of it."

"Wait," said Cyprin, as the penny finally dropped. "You're saying you're not God?" It felt ridiculous putting that into words, like she was a kid who'd asked their mother, *So you're not really the tooth fairy?*

Saul smiled at her, weakly. "I was raised to be God, but I am *not* God. I don't *do* anything. The sun and plants don't answer to me, I just take credit for those things, as I've been taught to."

"But where did you come from? Did they kidnap you while you were flipping burgers in the city? How does this happen?" *How do I get in on it?* The world was going down the drain in a gurgle of unfairness, but at least Cyprin was seeing that. Really, all this was just confirming her own worst suspicions.

"I don't know. I must have been very young when they took me. I've tried to picture my parents, but all I can come up with is a priestguard tutor. He raised me as a child, taught me how to be God. When I turned twelve, the lessons stopped, and I was left to sit the Mint Throne by myself. So, there you have it. I'm not God. It's all a sham. I'm sorry—this must be difficult for you to hear." God sounded almost bored.

Cyprin had to rub her eyes to make sure they weren't falling out. But she wasn't really surprised Saul was a regular guy, only that he was admitting to it. If Cyprin was a fake Divine, admitting it would be the last thing she'd do. She'd be too busy dozing in her silk pajamas. "But I mean, even if you're not God, you sit the Mint Throne. Can't you call the priestguard out?"

"I've tried. I really am a prisoner," said Saul. It seemed to Cyprin that for a moment he looked fondly back at his plush room, undermining the whole prisoner thing. "I am working on it. Finding out who is involved, how far this extends. I have to work faster, though, because my life cycle is almost at its end. That's why I was hoping you would help me."

"Your what?" said Cyprin.

Saul looked like he'd smelled something awful. "Divines age to forty-two, and then we wither and cycle again into infancy—or so the story goes. I think the priestguard use poison."

"How old are you now?"

"I turn forty-two in three weeks."

Cyprin put the mouth of the wine bottle in her own, tipped it up, and tapped on the hollow bottom, glugging down the dregs. She felt like she'd stepped into water and realized it wasn't shallow enough to stand in.

"I've never told anyone this before," said Saul.

Something was happening in Cyprin's head that she didn't like. The treachery of it all was sinking in. It was one thing to secretly believe that God wasn't real, but quite another to have the man himself admit it to her face. To hear him say he wasn't just fake but expendable and slated to die soon. All this struggle to get to the top, just to find out life in the stratosphere was equally as unfair. The game of life was rigged from top to bottom. She wanted to scream.

"All I ever wanted was to be a gardener here. To be head. Head gardener," she said. Which wasn't true.

All I ever wanted was to be loved.

"You are a gardener here, and there may be the opportunity to rise to head gardener. If you help me, I'll find a way to ensure you stay, win the pageant again next year. Don't you want that anymore?"

Cyprin popped the cork out of the second bottle of wine and they both watched it sail over the balcony and plummet below.

"What I want." Cyprin said it slowly; the shape of it had always been there, inside her, but she'd never given words to it. She'd never thought to. "What I want is to see it all burn down." She took a sip of wine, then passed the bottle to God. She was imagining the glorious power of erasing everything off the face of the map and starting from scratch. The only way to truly make life fair.

God nodded, though he looked slightly unsettled by her answer. "Let's see what 'it' is before we do that."

The contents of the second wine bottle disappeared, and then the sky began to lighten. Their conversation trickled into a comfortable silence. Cyprin found herself looking at God's feet again. They were feet that had never worked a day in their lives and were no strangers to the complimentary pedicures that must come with the job of being Divine.

God moved his little finger to touch Cyprin's on the cold marble between them, and she tensed and stared out at the world like she was going to bore a hole into it. Being touched hijacked her attention, focusing it on the point of contact in a way that wasn't entirely pleasant. It made her feel too perceived. He went to move his hand away, but she hooked his finger with her own. Something about Saul's vulnerability made her chest ache. He was rich, pampered innocence. He was the center of the world's biggest scam. The way he looked at her was like a puppy waiting to be called inside.

She could use him to get everything she'd ever wanted in life.

"I don't think I've ever touched anyone before. Not that I can remember, anyway. Maybe when I was a child—" he began, haltingly.

"I don't like touching people," said Cyprin.

"Oh."

"But I'll make an exception for you, here, now." She tightened the grip of her pinky finger around his. Yes, she could use him to make her dreams come true, leverage the parts of him that were lonely, but if she caught anyone else doing the same thing, they were dead.

Someone knocked at the door, if you could call it a knock. It sounded more like thugs were about to break it down. Cyprin ripped her hand away from God and swiveled. They had talked all night.

“Oh, no.” God wiped an exhausted hand over his face.

“What?”

“I’m late for the petal-mail fitting. That’ll be Purcell.”

CHAPTER 11

PURCELL

Purcell had to tell God about Amma. If anybody knew what to do, it would be him.

But God wasn't in the Mint Throne Room. Nor was he breakfasting in the Peach Sitting Room. She'd missed her appointment time and he'd wandered off somewhere. Typical.

Purcell paced the top corridors of the palace and was about to actually start pulling her hair out when she heard voices in God's bedroom. She knocked—nay, pounded—on the door. Eventually God deigned to open it.

"Aah, Pur-cell. You left me with cold ankles. The petal mail hardly covered my knees." The Divine was trying to get her on the back foot, but she only had eyes for Cyprin, sitting on the side of *his actual bed*, stuffing things into a satchel with the apparent calm of someone who was exactly where they were meant to be. Cyprin had decided to crawl out of Purcell's dreams and make her real life a nightmare. *This couldn't be happening.*

"What is she doing here?" Purcell didn't even try to hide the incredulity in her voice. She felt like she'd opened a regular car and found five hundred clowns in it. The thoughts about Amma that had been building and multiplying and chasing their own tails in her head crashed like a dropped jigsaw puzzle.

"Oh?" God looked back over his shoulder as if he was surprised to see Cyprin there. "Pur-cell, this is our newest recruit, Cyprin Voltag."

So, they were doing regular, everyday introductions now? In God's bedroom? On cue, Cyprin crossed the room, acting like they hadn't already met. A bony hand was thrust toward Purcell. There was nothing friendly in Cyprin's expression. "A private blessing—part of the pageant prize," she explained.

Purcell's gaze flickered to the rumpled sheets on the bed. Was there one indentation or two? Surely not! Saul should have dignified, mature tastes that did not include Cyprin. And Cyprin! Shouldn't she want someone closer to her age? Someone like Purcell? Part of her brain said, *A blessing, is that what they're calling it these days?* The rest was hurriedly flicking through rules and manuals to test the truth of what Cyprin was saying. But it had been such a long time since an outsider had won the pageant. She couldn't recall.

Purcell said, "We've already met." But in a daze, she took Cyprin's hand and shook it. The sudden physical contact induced heart palpitations.

Cyprin snatched her hand back several moments before it was socially appropriate, wiping it on her pants like she'd touched something nasty, and the butterflies tentatively flapping in Purcell's stomach fainted as if they were in a killing jar.

"You'll be wanting to work on the petal mail," God prompted. Purcell's head spun. She'd forgotten he was in the room.

"Yes, I, uh, had something I wanted to ask you too."

"Very well," said God. "Cyprin, I—I'll see you around."

That was not how you talked to a penitent subject. That was how you asked the cute girl in school if you could hold her books. Purcell scowled and oh! She was jealous of *God*. That was probably more than enough to send her to one of the twelve hells, assuming he didn't send her to rake leaves in the back gardens first. This was her job, her god, her gardens. Cyprin's very presence threatened to throw all of it into disarray, and that could not be allowed.

Purcell hovered in the doorway and Cyprin slid by her, squashing against the doorframe so as to avoid bodily contact. Thanks to Amma, Cyprin wasn't Purcell's biggest problem anymore, but she *was* a hateful, hateful creature. And her attractiveness? Well, that was hateful too. As Purcell descended into another sexy-rival thought spiral, Cyprin disappeared, leaving only Purcell and God.

God stared at Purcell's elbows, and Purcell realized she had her hands on her hips. She dropped them. This was an unpleasant development to be sure, but it didn't need to alter Purcell's trajectory. It couldn't. Cyprin was a distraction, that was all. If Purcell wanted to right this upside-down world, she was just going to have to force Cyprin out of her thoughts.

Given time, Purcell would be rid of the image of Cyprin in God's bedroom, the image of Cyprin oiled and naked at the flower pageant, her shoulders like little cannonballs, her sharp chin held sky-high, her breasts like—

God cleared his throat.

Purcell couldn't bring up being an Amma clone right now. Cyprin had derailed everything all over again. "The petal mail!" said Purcell, desperately.

God seemed to agree. "The petal mail! Yes, let us alight to the Mint Throne Room. I feel the need for a change of scene."

In the Mint Throne Room, Purcell knit fresh petals together with gold links while God yawned and massaged his temples. It was clear to her that both of them needed a spell of quiet reflection. And why was the Divine so tired? It wasn't that early. Really, a deity should know better than to—An image popped into Purcell's head, of Cyprin tying her shoelaces in God's bedroom. A feeling went with it, about God stealing her girl. Which was absurd. Cyprin was hardly even a girl, she was toxic waste in human form.

"I was thinking about what you said yesterday," said Purcell, desperate to change the channel in her own mind.

"Ah, yes?"

"You were right. I didn't deserve to win the pageant."

"That's not quite what I—"

"I've reflected on it, and I think I need to get out in the world and make something for myself. Domesticate my own flower. Like my great-great-grandmother used to do for these gardens. Did you know a third of our roses owe their genealogy to her?" An alarm blared in Purcell's brain again, bigger and louder than all the usual ones. *Run. RUN.* She had to get away, before a heaping pile of family history and hot rivals avalanched her into oblivion. It wasn't enough this time to run out into the gardens or into the lake. Purcell wanted to run from her skin, her hair, her voice, everything that was Amma's. But that was impossible—and what about the things she'd done in her own lifetime? Did those achievements belong to Amma? Purcell had a different body, a different name, if nothing else. She wasn't ready to give up on the idea of making her mark in the gardens. Looking for the flower that must have produced that glowing blue petal at the lake seemed like the perfect excuse for her to both run away *and* make her own legacy. Two birds, one stone.

The Divine seemed more awake. "Purcell, this is great news. If you want to take a few weeks to pursue this, a month, I'll see if I can organize someone to step in and cover the petal mail in the meantime. After all, research and development are an important part of what we do in these gardens. It's been too long since anyone has taken an interest."

"You—You'd do that for me?" It seemed too easy.

"Absolutely. You should have at it. I'll make the arrangements."

A blue flash—a dissolving spectral petal—lit up Purcell's mind. "I'd like to start my search on the island in the middle of Lake Pensive." She knew the island was prohibited but God did seem in an agreeable mood this morning, which made sense if he'd just—No. *Stop it, Purcell.*

"The birthplace of my line." The Divine had a faraway look in his eyes.

"So the myths go." Purcell said it without thinking. It earned her A Look.

"Purcell, that's positively blasphemous!"

"I, I, I—I'm sorry. I'm not myself today." *Ha. Ha ha.* She was Amma.

The Divine hitched up the hem of the petal mail, which Purcell had just completed, and headed toward the balcony of the throne room. Purcell followed along like an apologetic duckling. He leaned his elbows on the balcony rail, and she grimaced. He treated the petal mail as if it were just another part of his body. It was bruising already.

The island was a gray-green lump in the distance.

"You know," said the Divine, "I haven't thought about it in years. It's simply out there, every day, a part of the scenery."

Purcell worried for a moment that he was going to subject her to a retelling of his creation myth. But he didn't.

"You cannot go to that island, Purcell. The priestguard have killed people for trying and I—I can't stop them." God's tone was firm. His eyes were still kindly.

"I understand. I'll choose somewhere else." Purcell had never disobeyed a direct order in her life. But then, she'd never faced a rival like Cyprin.

Inside her a dark fire ignited, burning unclean fuel.

CHAPTER 12

CYPRIN

It was hardly even the second day since Cyprin had got into the gardens, and the golden mist of happiness that had settled over her postpageant had been holed by the Divine's assertion that he was not truly God. Why had he told her of all people? Why had he recruited *her*? Was it just because she'd been in the gardens for her interview at the right time? And now she knew about the grand conspiracy, what was she supposed to do about it? Saul had asked for help but not specified what he wanted her to do. Sit and wait for further instructions apparently. Maybe it was enough for him that he'd passed on his big secret before . . . before his own priestguard killed him. Ugh, now she was looking at everyone funny, analyzing priestguard's every butt-scratch and sneeze for hints of who might be pulling all the strings. Surely not all of them. Most of the priestguard walked about hardly looking where they were going, like they'd been in the same routine for years. Running the world couldn't be that bland, could it?

wasn't a dry eye among them. This fantasy went on: when she turned up to do the next batch of turnips, her supervisor smiled and said, *You're too good for this. We've moved you up, and now you're in charge of the pansies. Oh, and did you prefer if I curtsey or bow?* Purcell fell to her knees before her, saying, *Teach me, oh great master!*

Cyprin was out under the light of the dual moons with a shovel and her tool belt when she realized she didn't have any plants with which to build the sculptural marvel gathering form behind her eyes. But no matter. This was a garden full of plants. Who'd miss a few? It wasn't even stealing this time, it was relocating. Cyprin took some metal wiring from a trellis of honeysuckle, carefully unwinding the honeysuckle and looping it around a nearby tree. Plucked a few lush greens: some monstera, fiddle-leaf fig, and decorative moss, leaving behind craters in the dirt. Then she sampled one of every type of red flower in the gardens that she could find.

By midnight, she was putting the finishing touches on an arrangement that, from a distance, looked strikingly like a mosaic of a red rose. It was only when you got closer that you could see it was a living sculpture: a flower made of many flowers, embedded in the circular garden bed like a fancy rug.

Cyprin froze and switched her headlamp off as the glare of a flashlight approached. But she'd already been seen. Amanda stopped a distance away. People talked about "good" distances and "polite" distances—well, this one was "cold." Cyprin wiggled a few fingers in uncertain greeting, but Amanda turned and disappeared like a ghost.

Was *she* in on the whole God conspiracy? No—Amanda was head of admin; if she was in on it that meant Purcell, her superior, had to be in on it too, and Cyprin had seen the permanent air of anxiety that followed

Purcell like a black cloud. Purcell would crumble if anyone told her a secret.

God's confession had tainted everything in the gardens, making Cyprin paranoid.

She tried to stop worrying and went home to catch a few hours of sleep.

The sunshine through the bedroom window woke Cyprin up gently. She smiled before opening her eyes and did one of those big stretches she'd laughed at people for doing in wellness classes. Her limbs didn't even stick out past the edges of the bed, it was glorious. She got up and cooked (actual!) eggs and whistled the *Lust Island* theme tune (breaking off to make weird noises for the violin parts) while waiting for her toast to finish.

Cyprin swaggered back out into the gardens, ready to be appreciated. A crowd had gathered around the plot she'd guerrilla-gardened in, admiring her handiwork, and indeed, there were a few misty eyes and some people taking notes. This was exactly as she had imagined. Elated, Cyprin strode forth to receive her accolades.

"It's better to ask for forgiveness than permission, right?" She said it with just the right amount of lighthearted charm. A hundred sets of eyes lifted away from the sculpture to Cyprin. Cyprin's pits got sweaty when she realized Purcell was among them, like a mole rat in a colony of mole rats.

Purcell smirked. "I'm glad you agree." Something in her face had changed. Her eyes shone, Chihuahua-level feral.

Cyprin turned slightly to address her crowd of adoring fans, but her eyes never quite left Purcell. If Purcell disappeared from her periphery, Cyprin was sure she'd be getting teeth around the ankles at about the same time. That was the vibe. "I'm glad you're glad that I agree," said Cyprin, slightly losing it.

"I was thinking of calling it Whitlock's Triumph," said Purcell, and for some reason the words came out bitter.

The penny dropped.

Purcell was claiming it for herself.

This was punishment for the flower pageant.

"But I did it. This is my flower arrangement." Cyprin swung around to look at Amanda standing in the crowd, and by some miracle nothing yappy bit her ankles. "I did it. You saw me."

Amanda pushed her way forward and laid a hand on Purcell's shoulder. "Purcell!" Thank goodness, what a relief. Cyprin was going to be rescued from that unfortunate but highly deserved bid for revenge. "Purcell made this sculpture last night. I saw her on my way home," said Amanda.

The two of them stared, squint-eyed, at Cyprin. Oh, it was like that, was it?

"Well done, Purcell," said a voice from the crowd. A smatter of polite clapping broke out, followed by a few questions that Purcell responded to with bald-faced lies. *Oh, yes, I chose the carnations for the texture of their frilled edges, and my use of moss balls to suggest dew on the leaves was quite inspired, wasn't it?*

Cyprin stood there, flabbergasted. She might as well have been a mannequin that was wheeled out and forgotten. Why didn't Purcell let Cyprin take credit and then punish her? Surely that was a more direct route to revenge? This seemed out of character. Instead of whining or pompously pulling rank, Purcell had dealt a hand of cards and sat down to play.

Purcell grinned, but dark rings lurked beneath her eyes, suggesting she hadn't slept well. It was as if some part of her had sunk, like the person who looked out of Purcell's eyes wasn't sitting on a high horse anymore, but a throne deep in the twelfth hell.

Cyprin shivered. It was unsettling. It was also, frankly, very hot, which disturbed her even more. Instead of protesting her ownership of the display, like Purcell had done fruitlessly at the pageant, Cyprin inclined her head and walked off to trim carrots. But this wasn't over. Far from it. The next floral sculpture she made would be a raised middle finger or a nude self-portrait. Let Purcell claim that.

Cyprin could concede a battle because she knew what it took to win a war.

CHAPTER 13

PURCELL

Back in the safety of her house, Purcell was so mad she was huffing every ten seconds. The sheer number of rules Cyprin had broken by building that sculpture was totally uncountable (there were nine). And the worst part was, Purcell had been so unsettled over Amma's secrets that she had *let Cyprin get away with it.* This had been a golden opportunity to get Cyprin booted out of the gardens and she had let it slip through her fingers. It was almost like she wanted Cyprin to stay.

Purcell stood over her toilet, holding the flush down. Torn-up scraps of the Amma poster that used to live above her bed circled the bowl and she felt righteous as she watched Amma's image drown. She blamed Amma for this. Even long dead, Amma was reaching through the years to ruin Purcell's life, distracting her horribly so that Purcell could no longer handle a rival like Cyprin. With Amma's face gone, Purcell brushed her teeth. Then she went to bed.

An hour later, after she'd felt the need to look up how many people had died by getting tangled in their bedsheets (809 last year), she gave up and switched the lights back on.

The next few nights were not an improvement. In the wake of so much sleeplessness, Purcell's petal-mail appointments became affairs of small talk and silence. There was careful avoidance of contentious topics like misbegotten prizes, destroyed rosebushes, grandmothers, forbidden sacred sites, and hot girls in God's bedroom.

She paid careful attention to the duty roster in order to avoid Cyprin.

But Cyprin proved unavoidable.

There was Cyprin, jostling her in line to get the last apple muffin in the staff café. There was Cyprin, working where Purcell had not expected to see her because Cyprin had apparently volunteered to check petunia petals for early signs of wilting. There was Cyprin at the back of the staff movie theater on the opening night of a new blockbuster, laughing so hard Purcell couldn't hear the dialogue. And the most unexpected one, Cyprin loping gangly at the back of a social runners' group as Purcell passed by on her way to the palace early in the morning. Purcell had to check her glasses after that.

It got worse. One day, Purcell saw Cyprin working as a turf-tender when she should not be, but when Purcell seized her by the shoulders and the woman turned around it was *not* Cyprin at all. Another time, Purcell startled at the sound of Cyprin's cackle, but it was a bird in a nearby tree.

Purcell was at the start of a second unsuccessful week of Cyprin avoidance when something in her broke, and she began to consult the rosters to *find* Cyprin. They were crossing paths anyway, so it might as well be on her terms. She trailed Cyprin to the palace post office, where Cyprin had a bunch of letters to return to sender. She watched Cyprin hiding behind a pillar watching God cross the lower floors of the palace with his retinue of priests—what a creep! Who did that?

But all this Cyprin obsession was not enough to turn Purcell from her purpose. Purcell made sure she spent time dutifully considering possible locations for novel flora around the Kingdom of Verdure, but it had all been done before. In this overpopulated area of the world, there wasn't much left that wasn't either farmland or high-rises. Maybe if she tried really hard, she might discover a new species of rhizome in the soil somewhere and bend it to her will. Absolutely a worthwhile contribution to the field of horticulture. She should be happy with that.

But Purcell knew what she'd seen in that lake. Knew where it must have come from. Perhaps if she just approached the Divine in the right way?

It was with this purpose that she found herself at the Solar Closing Ceremony on a midweek evening. She really, truly wasn't attending because she'd heard Cyprin was going to be there, with her long legs and slouchy shoulders.

Purcell was not a regular attendee of religious ceremonies. They happened, much like her favorite cereal happened to show up with her groceries, and a complex set of electrical circumstances happened to put a picture on her TV screen. As far as she saw it, the best way to honor other people's hard work was to completely ignore them and get on with being good at the small subset of the world her mind labeled as hers. She knew the Divine made the sun rise and set, knew he made the environment more hospitable to plants, but she didn't spend any time thinking about how he did it, or attending ceremonies. Even though they were held right in the gardens.

The twilight courtyard and the almost musical murmuring of the priests were pretty, but her purpose was to corral God afterward and ask him her question (again). Purcell tended to be bullet-like in her pursuits. Hopefully he'd be more amenable at this time of day. God was not a morning person.

She hung back, separate from the crowd, as the Great Petaled Divine got up on his golden podium, arrayed in gray silks. His reflection hung elongated on the still surface of the pond in front of him, a mirror image of the volcano in the lake throwing its long, gray reflection over the water.

A small crowd hemmed the pond and the Divine in a semicircle. Against her will, Purcell spotted Cyprin. Cyprin's makeup was perfection, her gardener whites unstained. She was absolutely, undeniably playacting at being pious. *Getting the Divine's blessing*, ha! At first, Purcell had been confused to find Cyprin in the Divine's bedchamber. She hadn't known what to think. But when the initial shock had settled, it had become all too clear. Cyprin was prepared to work any angle to get ahead.

Steal flowers, make unsanctioned sculptures, flirt with God, turn up to ceremonies pretending at piousness. An imagined target burned on Purcell's back. Oh, she knew what this was. But how would she get the Divine to see it without looking jealous? That was the real challenge. No, no. *Focus*. Purcell was here about her island and the flower she knew must be up there awaiting discovery. Giving Cyprin attention was just adding fuel to the fire. And it was one of those fires you get from pouring gasoline down an anthill and lighting a match—it was already underneath everything, and it was going to burn for days and days. She risked a look at Cyprin, who was appreciating her own reflection in the decorative pond with a slight smirk on her face. Purcell wanted to bite the wry twist of Cyprin's lips, kiss the profanities out of her mouth.

God ended the ceremony and moved off on his own for a moment, looking out on his handiwork as the shadows deepened and the dual moons shone brightly. This was it. This was the perfect time to talk to him.

Purcell started skirting the pond toward God. Across the other side of the water, Cyprin matched her pace, heading the same direction. Cyprin was taller, her legs were longer. She was going to get there first! She was—Purcell collided with a priest, landing jarringly on her tailbone as the priest slipped into the pond. She squealed in embarrassed panic. A lot of the crowd focused their attention on Purcell now as she yelped apologies and helped the bedraggled priest haul himself out of the water. He glared daggers at Purcell and then went squelching off into the night with his robes clinging nastily, and Purcell looked up to see Cyprin already toe-to-toe with God, the two of them all tall, chiseled perfection, the king and queen of Purcell's own personal hell.

Purcell was too far away to hear what they were saying. Somewhere mid-conversation, Cyprin's eyes strayed, not quite reaching the blasphemous heights of God's eyes, but looking at his chin, or his mouth—was she staring at his mouth? The sting of jealousy knocked the wind out of Purcell. Around them, the priestguard began closing in.

Cyprin and God seemed oblivious to the approaching danger. Cyprin's hand moved like she was going to touch the Divine's hand, and as if drawn by magnets, his hand moved too. In the old days, Cyprin would have already condemned herself to death for this. But Purcell didn't want to see that. Not even when it was somebody as richly deserving as Cyprin.

Cyprin pulled away before her hand made contact and Purcell sighed in relief. The priests were almost on Cyprin now. As Purcell watched, Cyprin swaggered back, grabbed a fistful of the front of her coveralls, and pulled. The sound of Velcro ripping echoed across the silent plaza.

One of the priests barked a laugh, then immediately looked guilty. Cyprin dropped to her knees, waiting for the oil and the haircut. It seemed suspiciously like the dark fuzz on Cyprin's head was at the stage where it could use a little tidying up. Purcell fought down a swell of astonishment, desire, and anger. That infuriating small smile was on Cyprin's face again. The priests started with the oil and the crowd was transfixed and entertained, Purcell along with them. Droplets of oil spilled from around Cyprin's knees into the pond where they floated on the surface as little circles of gold.

Purcell remembered to blink when a midge flew into her eye. Her jaw hurt from hanging open and she knew, she just knew, that she'd be seeing Cyprin in her breakfast cereal again in the morning.

People were laughing, but Purcell didn't mistake Cyprin's actions for a joke. Cyprin was here to stay, and she was desperate enough to make anything happen. Cyprin cocked her head to the side to acknowledge Purcell and grinned, triumphantly. *This is what I'm prepared to do to get what I want. What lengths will you go to?*

Purcell read her loud and clear.

That was when she decided she was going to go to the island in the middle of the lake.

Without permission.

CHAPTER 14

SAUL

Two weeks. Saul had less than two weeks left before his "life cycle" was at an end and the priestguard replaced him with someone younger and more pliable. And he had not yet managed a plan to avoid this.

He trailed petal mail into the third-floor conference room.

"All stand and avert eyes for the Great Petaled Divine, the metal that became plant that became Person Divine: Seasonal Demiurge, Protector of the Realm, Ruler of Verdure, the Kingdom of God."

A priestguard attendant ushered Saul through to a raised dais at the back of the room, where he sat down on an elaborately carved wooden chair. A table was slotted over the top of his legs so that he could eat, TV-dinner style.

This was a diplomatic dinner hosting delegations from Verdure's southern and eastern neighbors. Baskets full of showy produce—husky ears of corn, giant-ass pumpkins, and bunches of absurdly purple grapes—formed the centerpiece of a triangular table in the middle of the room. On the south side sat representatives from the southern region of Immersea, thin and upset, gray-clad in the ceremonial colors that represented their only successful endeavor to date: mining rocks. Bio bots ate their crops quicker than they could grow them, but they did okay. Verdure bought their lovely marble and sent a few things the other way.

On the east side of the table were reps from Norla, which clung to the eastern border of Verdure. They were a little scary, dressed in titanium-mesh suits with hard-plex faceplates even here, in relative safety. Where they lived, bio bots ate people. Verdure gave them medical aid and bolstered their workforce, and in return they made weapons for the priest-guard, had engineered quite a few of the recent strains of flu-vax and, of course, gave Verdure bags and bags of money.

The west side of the triangular table was symbolically empty. West of Verdure was the sea: gray and acidic, prone to scouring winds and yellowish salt-isotope buildup, and nevertheless full of tasty things that often went pop when you dredged them up into the light.

This Saul knew: the other countries were as children to Verdure. Their numbers were too small and too dependent on Verdure's resources to mount any kind of rebellion, nor did Verdure want to conquer the nothing that they had. This was the world: rocks and ice, storms so violent they could suck the breath right out of your lungs, dark places where the axial tilt was so unfavorable even lichen wouldn't settle there. And Verdure. Warmth, light, life. A safe haven from bio bots and all the rest. When Saul overheard things like this, he expected the delegates to ask to be allowed to join Verdure. To beg. But they never did. It was clear they would rather be free and hungry than owned by Verdure. Saul envied them that choice.

God could look at whomever he wanted, so he stared at all of them. Right now, the first course had just come out, and the table was filled with an ASMR nightmare of cutlery against plates. Delegates from both sides ate like it was a competition and threw wine down their throats with hasty abandon. It did not escape Saul's notice that one or two of them put bread rolls up their sleeves for later.

Four courses down, and a priestguard attendant *ding, ding, ding*ed a fork against an empty glass. Things were rough out there, or so Saul gathered. They no longer scheduled his address before people ate.

Saul said, "I am life and death and life again. I am the metal that became carbon."

The reps gave the response. "The seed that cycles forever." They always side-eyed each other at this point, and Saul was sure they didn't believe in him. They just said whatever they had to in order to get the deals done and go home without starving. Saul was jealous. He said whatever he had to too, but he had no home to go to. Nothing but this bone-white palace. Nothing but these lies.

By the time the sixteenth course was distributed, at least one delegate had passed out face down on the table, along with a couple of maybes who were either unconscious or licking the Jell-O off their plates for an extended period of time. There was plenty of conversation to eavesdrop, but it was all stale: bio bots, bio bots, bio bots, people getting eaten, crops getting eaten, somebody's grandma's hat dissolving right off her head. Horrible, yes, but once you'd heard about the thousandth tragedy the empathy dried up, your eyes glazed over, and you started to give it the same level of interest as the bottom of your shoe.

Saul wondered what Cyprin was doing now. He hoped she was comfortable in her new house. Perhaps he ought to bring her some extra pillows, just to be sure. That wouldn't be inappropriate, would it?

The Divine's flute player got tired and was subbed out for someone with a xylophone. A rash of red-clad priestguard began gathering in the doorway, like a clogged artery. It was almost time for Saul to head to bed, which suited him completely. All the excitement Cyprin had brought to his week had drained him. And the last fifty pages of *Erin Gets with Hugh* waited on his nightstand.

Normal routines begged, but these days they felt like cling film over a more dangerous reality.

Hardly anywhere seemed safe anymore. Not now there weren't even two weeks left before he was murdered by his own subjects.

Sometimes he thought he ought to really inhabit the role of God and threaten them all with Divine retribution and death, see how many he could take out before they ended him. Other times he thought he would sell himself out to the first person who promised to smuggle him out of the palace.

Titanium mesh made a nice *shoof* sound as a rep from Norla tripped over his own drunken feet and skidded to the floor by the base of Saul's podium. Saul looked to the priestguard in alarm, but the rep was already picking himself up. "Blink twice if you need help," the rep whispered, and then he dared to look directly at Saul.

Saul felt instinctively that he shouldn't trust this, but he was ragged with hope and helplessness. Against his better instincts, he started blinking like someone had blown sand in his eyes. Some of the priestguard in the doorway took that as their cue, rushing into the room to grip Saul quite firmly by the elbows. Others were helping the Norla rep straighten his clothing, or they had seized him. Saul didn't get to see properly as they led him off to bed. It had happened right under the noses of the priestguard. Had they heard it? Were they punishing the reps from Norla right now? Or had they missed it and the Norla reps were regrouping, planning how they would get Saul out? His head spun with possibilities.

Saul snapped his book shut and stared at the billowy velvet canopy above the bed. "Together beyond the grave," he muttered. "Preposterous ending." Fifty pages had not been enough to calm him down and transport him out of the world he was trapped in.

Less than two weeks. He had less than two weeks left.

The bedside lamp went out and he was too hot, and then too cold. The usual solution of covering only his feet wasn't bearing fruit, and every time he closed his eyes, he saw the delegate from Norla shining in silver armor, asking if he needed help. No one had ever asked Saul if he needed help before. It seemed like, *maybe*, Cyprin was the sort of person who would, but no. That was wishful thinking. Cyprin was using him.

Did the reps know enough about the layout of the palace to find their way around? It seemed unlikely. Perhaps, even now, the priestguard were apprehending them. Maybe they'd been put in cells before the end of the dinner. Or they could be lost in a second-level bathhouse, looking for him.

The lamp went back on again and Saul pulled on his stolen priestguard robes. He didn't know exactly where the foreign delegates were housed, but he knew it wasn't anywhere he'd been before, and he had visited a lot of rooms in the palace. One of the sub-basement floors, then. Below the level of the staff library. That made sense. The farthest point they could be placed away from his bedchamber without leaving the palace grounds.

Saul had to get to them first in case they made things difficult for him.

Saul reached basement-level three in a frenzy of panic. He threw open the first door he came across with the total impunity he believed came with his priestguard outfit and walked right into a priestguard meeting.

Everyone fell silent, including an older priestguard man pointing to a chart on the wall where the gardens were divided into numbered sections. Saul scanned their faces, anxiously hoping none of them had seen him up close before. But these were the night-duty dregs. Only one of them looked familiar: Gary, a big man with dark, thinning hair, skin that looked boiled, and a permanent twist of concern on his face. Gary had seen Saul skulking around in his priestguard reds before.

"Did you get lost?" said Gary. "You're the new guy, right? What was your name?"

"Roman," said Saul. The real Roman, his priestguard tutor who'd raised and then abandoned him, owed Saul an identity.

"Roman?" The priestguard at the front of the room lowered his pointer from the chart and looked like he was trying to remember where he'd put something.

"Where are you supposed to be?" asked Gary.

A trickle of sweat made its way down Saul's temple. "The delegation from Norla City?"

"I'll take you to them." Gary glanced to the front of the room for permission, and the older priestguard nodded.

As they descended to another level, Saul said, "Thank you. What were you all doing in there?"

"Oh, top-secret stuff"—Saul missed a step and almost tumbled down the stairs—"divvying up the midnight-to-five AM shift in the gardens. They'll draw straws for who gets to stand closest to the admin center. Amanda brings an extra hot chocolate out on her way home."

A set of metal doors greeted them at the end of the hall. "Staff elevator," said Gary. "You'll find the reps on level minus five. I'll unlock it for you."

Saul stepped in. "Why is this button red?" The buttons for levels minus one to minus fifteen were a calm and luminous yellow, but below them, set apart, was a red square for minus sixteen.

"Oh, that's the bottom of the palace. Storerooms and such," said Gary. "Off-limits. You know, can't have anyone pilfering supplies."

Saul pressed the button for level minus five. A lurching feeling gripped his stomach as the elevator descended, or maybe it was just a growing sense of dread.

He might never get this chance again—which was something you could say about the Norla City rep's offer to help him, but *also* about the opportunity to see what was at the very bottom of the palace. And—and if the reps couldn't help him, if they only brought attention to his frequent escapades, perhaps going to see them was the wrong decision.

Saul pressed the red button for the bottom floor. He could come back for the reps after he'd had a look down there.

More often than not, snooping revealed the great beige underbelly of an organization whose day-to-day workings were as boring as watching grass grow—and Saul had done just that once, back when he wanted to see if he could have any influence over it, so he knew exactly how boring that was. There were juicy secrets to be found, for sure, but the Garys of the world did not know them. This was a harmless little detour.

❧ ❧ ❧

The elevator came to a smooth stop at level minus sixteen. The doors opened. The floors outside were rainbow tiled. A mural of happy trees smiled over the walls.

This was not a storeroom. This was a place Saul recognized.

A smell like crayons made the years drop away as he stepped out onto the rainbow floor. The lights were different; they warmed the skin like the sun. *Five more minutes, Roman, please!* Saul's voice seemed to echo back to him like time had tied itself in a knot.

Down the hall, a left, and—There it was. One of the trees painted on the wall was grinning with a mouthful of teeth. The green paint had dried in dribbles under its eaves, and he ran his fingers over the bumps. Saul had been allowed to paint one every year.

He knew why this area was off-limits. This was where he'd grown up. This was where they'd taught him to be God.

Farther down the rainbow road was, yes, Room 108 where he'd learned his scriptures, and Room 109 where he'd been taught deportment and practiced moving without tearing the petal mail. Room 106 housed the austere single bed and footlocker Roman had used. Saul's fingers grasped the door handle, rattled it, but it was locked. In his mind's eye the interior was exactly as his mentor had left it, no cobwebs or dust. Just a metal hanger rail with a row of red tracksuits on it—one for every day of the week—a poster describing correct posture, and a measuring tape curled up like a yellow snake in a corner of the room, used to chart Saul's growth.

Saul walked on. Here was Room 101 where he had slept with a rat stuffy called Gus that he'd found dropped in the hallway. The ceiling had plastic stars on it, and he'd counted them each night before going to sleep. Thirty-seven big ones and five little ones. Saul put his palm against the door. The loneliest boy in the world. How he wished he could reach through time and comfort that child.

The sepia tones cleared, and Saul wiped his eyes on the sleeve of his priestguard robe. This was enough. It was late, and there was nothing new to find. He had lived it all already.

But a strange sound drew him farther down the hall. Doors 115 onward were a mystery to him. He'd always thought of them as supply closets, or something equally boring, and one of them was certainly a sick bay. But supplies didn't cry.

"Hello? Is someone out there?" said Door 121.

Was this his replacement? Saul gasped and pressed his ear against the wood. The sound stopped immediately.

A deep voice behind him said, "Who are you, and what are you doing here?"

The shock jolted Saul all the way to his toes. He'd been listening so intently that he hadn't registered anyone coming up behind him. He raised his palms and got ready to bullshit, starting early with, "I'm Roman."

Saul turned around. The man before him had skin that was a bronzy olive, and was older with a tidy gray beard. He wore a red tracksuit instead of traditional priestguard robes, and he looked like he'd stepped straight out of a photograph, his hair losing color on the way.

"No. *I'm* Roman," said the man. "And I know very well who you are."

The priestguard robes pooled at Saul's feet like wizard robes. He felt like a child again. Saul's first instinct was to apologize for being bad, for breaking the rules. He choked it down. When he'd finished gasping, he said, "Is there a child in that room?"

Roman placed a hand on Saul's shoulder. It was just as weighty as Saul remembered. "It's not safe for you here. We have to get you back to your chambers." Roman's eyes sparkled with emotion. "You've grown up well."

Saul was too shocked to say anything.

"Come," said Roman, and he took Saul by the elbow and led him away from the door. Saul kept glancing back over his shoulder until they went round a corner and into the elevator.

It was a long way up to Saul's bedchamber. "There was a child—" Saul tried several times, but Roman just pressed a finger to his lips and said, "Ears everywhere."

Saul was sweating in anticipation when Roman threw open the door of his bedroom and led them in. But instead of talking, Roman put his hands on his hips and looked around the room with an air of . . . pride?

"You've done very well for yourself, son," Roman said eventually, and Saul had the sinking sense that this was *it*, he was never going to see Roman again. He was never going to get more than a "congrats for faking your way to the top of the heap" from Roman. Did Roman even care that Saul was slated to die in a matter of days?

Saul sat on the side of the bed and put his face in his hands. His heart was hammering so hard he felt dizzy. "What happens now?" Roman was going to make Saul behave again, Roman was going to punish Saul for wandering and impersonating a priestguard. The Norla reps were going to save Saul, they were going to kidnap him, they were going to kill him and use his body to start a revolution.

Roman's joints creaked as he crouched down and put his hands on Saul's knees, the way he used to when Saul was little. "You stay here. Sit tight. Be good."

The *be good* at the end was a ghastly kind of familiar. It pinned Saul like a butterfly.

"Okay," said Saul, and he was twelve again, sitting alone on the Mint Throne for the first time, crying so hard a janitor mopping the floors outside had run to get help. Roman had returned looking flustered but not unempathetic, someone who'd carefully raised a fledgling bird and tried to set it into the wild, but it kept coming back. He'd cupped Saul's knees with his hands, just like this, and said, *Don't do this again.*

Satisfied, Roman stood up, adjusted the collar of his red tracksuit, and headed for the door.

"Wait!"

Roman paused.

"Will I ever see you again?" Zip Saul open and there'd be a lonely child sitting right there on the side of the bed.

"For your sake, I hope not," said Roman. And then he was gone.

These costumes, these damned costumes. Saul was always pretending. He unbuttoned his high neckline and gasped for air.

He was half slumped on the bed, gulping from a carafe of water, when he noticed he wasn't alone. Saul stiffened, and Amanda stepped out of the shadows on the balcony.

"What do you want?" Saul knew who she was. Everyone in the gardens did. But you didn't just pay God a social visit. Either she was already part of the grand conspiracy that tied him to this place, or she'd spotted him as both priestguard and God and was here for leverage.

"I want to help you." Amanda was always with Purcell, as if they'd grown out of the same garden bed. For a moment it was difficult for Saul to think of her as someone not to be trusted, just for that reason. But she was here alone in his bedroom after hours, and only people who wanted to use him seemed to do that.

Saul laughed, the sound high and unhinged. "You want to help yourself," he said.

Amanda had her hands clasped together in front of her, a perfectly poised professional. If she was hungry for power, she was great at hiding it. "Why can't it be both?"

"Because everyone is just using me." Saul realized when the words came out that he was only beginning to understand that himself. "Everyone." *Even Cyprin.*

"I know what you want," said Amanda. "And I can help you get it."

Saul laughed again and loosened the cuffs on his sleeves. They were strangling him. "What do I want?"

"The truth."

Truth, beauty, love, religion. Freedom. Just a bunch of ideas. You could think about them but never actually hold them. "And how would *you* give me that?"

Amanda smiled with easy confidence. Authority. "Join the Underground, and come with me, tonight. You know you're in danger from the priestguard. The time to act is now. We can accomplish so much together."

"Who are the Underground?" said Saul, and Amanda did not manage to hide the look of pity that flashed across her face. *Ah, yes, I'm just naïve little Saul. Go on and lie fantastically to me, I can't tell the truth from the lies anyway.*

"Freedom fighters. We oppose your regime."

"And you'd liberate me from this palace?"

"I can't do that. Your position here is far too advantageous. You'd have to return, keep up appearances. But we might help each other. Consider the things we could achieve—"

"No, thank you," said Saul.

"You don't trust me." Amanda didn't seem overly surprised.

"I don't trust anyone." Not after Roman. Never again.

"You trust Cyprin."

"I suppose that's true," said Saul. But it wasn't. He didn't *need* to trust Cyprin, because he knew what she wanted, and he could help her get it.

A shiftiness came into Amanda's eyes as she switched tactics. "All right, listen. There's something very important on the island in Lake Pensive."

"Important how?" Saul began to fear some escalation and glanced toward the priestguard call button by his door.

"I can't tell you here." Amanda's voice was firm, reasonable, but the sharpness of her eyes spoke of a growing impatience.

"Oh, so this is a ploy to get me to go with you?"

"Send Cyprin to the Underground. Tell her to ask about Lake Pensive. Let her decide whether we should be trusted."

Everyone had their own scheme. Everyone wanted him to do something for them. Saul pinched the bridge of his nose. "I'll consider it. Now, please, I'd like to be alone."

"I don't think you've ever wanted to be alone," said Amanda. And then she left.

Ah yes, know what someone wants, and you can control them.

Saul opened one of his books, but his arms shook, and his sweaty fingers made the ink run and the pages grow soft, so he gave it up. There were no stars to count on this ceiling, but he stared at it anyway. Time distorted and the night felt both fast and slow. Saul went through his tea collection and readied the best ones to bring with him when the Norla reps arrived. Then he sat at his balcony and counted the real stars as they faded out.

Nobody came, and he couldn't have said why.

In Saul's closeted world, he didn't have a hope of guessing the motives of those around him.

CHAPTER 15

CYPRIN

Cyprin twirled her noodles with a fork while the *Lust Island* palm trees swayed on the TV, and Justin tried to pretend like he was comfortable in a pink bikini two sizes too small that nevertheless looked fully worth it. It was a good episode. He had only one rose to give out, and both Benjamin and Tizac were totally debasing themselves for it. Speaking of people who would totally debase themselves over a rose, Purcell was definitely in that camp. Her behavior last night at the Closing Ceremony had been proof enough of that. Cyprin slurped down a noodle and replayed the moment Purcell had knocked one of the priestguard into a pond. The delicious look of shock on Purcell's face when she realized what she'd done in her haste to ruin things for Cyprin. It felt like winning.

A knock sounded at Cyprin's door. Tucking the bowl of noodles into the crook of one elbow, she opened it.

"I'm in a meeting with the Seventh Earl of East Immersea and his retinue." The Divine pushed past her, letting himself in. There were bags under his eyes; he looked exhausted.

"I can see that." Cyprin wound more noodles around her chopsticks and closed the door with her hip.

"In reality, they all imbibed too much at dinner last night, and the only things meeting are their eyelids, but they'll find their contracts signed by tomorrow and all will be well." Saul kicked his shoes off, sitting down on Cyprin's couch, and she handed him the beer she'd just opened. She didn't have another one but gave the bottle to him anyway.

"Twelve hells, what is this?" A little sparkle came back into his eyes.

"*Lust Island*," said Cyprin, perching on the arm of the couch. "Well, I say 'island' but it's an artificial set."

"Why is nobody wearing any clothes?"

"Lust works in mysterious ways." Cyprin watched the way God's slender toes moved over the carpet. Wanting to *own* him so that he could never abandon her was the same as wanting him, wasn't it?

"I was just wondering if you'd managed to ask around about Maverick?" She tried to keep her tone casual despite the burning in her heart.

God stared open-mouthed at the tanned bodies on the TV for a moment longer and then wrenched himself away. "How is it that you know him, again?"

"Oh, he, ah . . . he ruined my childhood by vanishing on me." The words were flippant, but the way her voice broke was not.

Now Saul did glance at her, an ancient darkness in his eyes. "I'm so sorry, Cyprin. He's dead."

"Dead?" This didn't feel like grieving. It felt like a weight had been lifted, like a big, difficult thing had been taken off the tick-list of life. She tried to hold back the smile that threatened.

God was still looking at her in that ancient, fragile way. "I need you to do something for me, Cyprin."

"Something . . . reciprocal?" His proximity, his physical presence, body heat, all made her nervous.

"I need you to go into the city and ask around about the island in Lake Pensive. I want rumors, blasphemous stories, everything. In particular, I'd like to know what the Underground have to say about it." Cyprin had not been expecting this, and that made her realize she had instead been expecting something romantic. She felt both disappointed and relieved.

"How do you know about the Underground?" She'd been convinced he wasn't worldly in any way.

"You agree to do this, and tomorrow morning, when I announce Purcell's sabbatical, you will be made interim head gardener."

"I'll be—what!?" This was all happening too quickly. Maverick was dead and she was being made head gardener. Was there even any point to being head gardener if Maverick wasn't around to hate it? Well, at least Purcell would.

"Cyprin," said Saul, sternly, "I only have ten days left. We must act now."

Cyprin barely heard him. She was going to be head gardener. One in seven billion. Fraudulent head gardener. The best of the best in title only. She knew by the drop in her stomach and the flutter of her nerves that she didn't deserve it. Would it even be the regular role, or was she just going to be errand girl for the Divine? The latter didn't seem like a job with career longevity, or for that matter, life longevity. But he was offering her the title, and Cyprin wasn't going to let fears or morals get in the way. Why was she so lightheaded and queasy?

The power he offered, the way he looked at her like she really mattered—she'd never been so desperate to make someone like her.

Oh, wait, once. Maverick. Maverick, who was dead. She stifled a giggle just thinking about it and couldn't have said why. The meaninglessness of wanting to shove her existence in the face of a person who wasn't there anymore? The disbelief that the man who had been the grain of sand to her pearl was really gone from the world? Disbelief? Wait, was that one of the stages of grieving?

Maverick had been so cool, his gardener whites seemed to resist the muck of the city. He'd been the only person Cyprin had ever met who'd worn aviators indoors. To an eleven-and-a-half year old, that was true elegance. Peak fashion. And she'd tried so hard to make him like her. At first, he'd just patted her on the head and disengaged from her as quickly as possible. Even the kids at school had treated her like an over-excited puppy; she was always too much. But somewhere along the line, Maverick's attitude had changed, and he'd started to play games with her. Cyprin wasn't that child anymore, but it still gave her secondhand embarrassment to think of it now. Games like: How long can Cyprin sit in a chair without moving? How long can Cyprin stare at a wall without blinking? How long can Cyprin go without talking? When her mother found her face down on the lounge-room rug after a game of How Long Can Cyprin Go Without Breathing? she'd yelled at Maverick until she'd lost her voice, and he hadn't come back to their apartment for seven long days. Cyprin remembered begging her to let Maverick return.

Please, please, it wasn't his fault, it was all me, I wanted to hold my breath. He told me it was a bad idea, but I didn't listen. He's so cool, he's so cool, he's so cool. You have to let him back; his toothbrush is still in our bathroom and his purple underpants are here too—how do I know about that? Well, I'm sorry about the washing. It's all purple now.

Maverick had always been a douchebag, but a familiar douchebag. He'd been *her* douchebag. It had been almost a crush, an obsession to be everything to the man without any clear idea of the implications. And hadn't that worked out well.

It was a good thing this wasn't a direct repeat, that she wanted Saul to like her for entirely selfish purposes—*career ones*, ones that didn't have anything to do with the way Saul kept reaching for her, checking himself at the last moment, his fingers hovering over her upper arm, lower back, back of her hand, like a ghost touch.

"Cyprin, are you all right?" God studied her face in a way that made her feel far too seen.

"Fine. I, just—How am I going to become head gardener? I'm barely *a* gardener here."

God sipped his drink for rather too long. He was stalling. "There is a historical precedent for the Divine to choose his own head gardener. But that right hasn't been invoked since, ha, well, incidentally, Purcell's great-great-grandmother, Amma Whitlock, was selected almost a hundred and thirty years ago. I expect there will be some backlash."

Of course it had been a Whitlock. Purcell's family stink was all over the gardens. A nasty thought occurred. "A backlash? From the ten thousand other people who were in line before me?"

"I have no doubt you're capable—"

"Of defending myself against ten thousand acts of jealous revenge?" Probably all as whiny and vindictive as Purcell.

"And I have absolute faith in the way you—"

"Buckets of water over the doorways, superglue in my shoes, rat tails left on my pillow. I'll never be able to trust a meal, never be able to so much as walk out of my house without looking over my shoulder. You don't understand. These people have the all-consuming, murderous ambition of ballerinas, and you want to make me the prima."

The look the Divine gave her seemed ancient again, not in the way of a God, but in the way of a man who had never been in control of his own life. "This is what you wanted, Cyprin. And this is how we make a difference."

Her noodles were growing cold on her lap. "This is how we burn it all down." The potential unfairness and danger of letting God make her head gardener seemed almost justified if she could use the position to tear the whole corrupt institution apart.

"This is how we *unravel* it," said Saul, pointedly.

Head gardener. She was going to be head gardener. Even if it killed her. Even if it killed *everyone*.

"How much longer does this program go on for?" God's eyes had strayed back to the TV.

"I think another forty-five minutes."

"Do you have any more noodles?"

Cyprin didn't, but as she handed her bowl over to God, she didn't tell him. She watched his eyes reflect the TV screen as he slurped her noodles down and her chest burned uncomfortably with the urge to be his everything.

God needed her, and she was not going to let him down.

"Do you have any cash for takeaways?" Cyprin's mother had been working late one night, and she and Maverick ordered noodles. Or, rather, Maverick had ordered them, along with a bottle of wine, from a five-star shop in the city center. He'd been sprawled across one of their armchairs like a bored jarl, a rug around his shoulders giving the look of a fur cloak. He always leaned on things like he was doing them a favor.

"I have some money, but it's for books," Cyprin had told him. It was only years later that it occurred to her it couldn't have been coincidental that Maverick "forgot" his wallet the same day Cyprin's mother gave her a wad of cash for the back-to-school sales. Faux coincidence. Fauxincidence.

"What's cooler? Noodles or books?" Maverick had said. To which Cyprin had screamed, "Noodles!" until he threw a cushion at her, and she'd been quite sure that she was in love.

She didn't want to impress Maverick anymore.

She wanted to impress Saul.

CHAPTER 16

PURCELL

Purcell couldn't believe what she was hearing. She'd been apprehensive enough about God announcing her temporary absence, but to know she was going to be replaced by Cyprin! Cyprin, whose image tap-danced on the inside of her skull at all hours now. Cyprin, whose chaos could make the mildest day feel burning hot. Cyprin, whose dark eyes and long limbs haunted her dreams. Several other candidates were *much* more suited to the role. In fact, putting 9,999 names in a hat and drawing one out would yield a better result. That Cyprin had been chosen was appalling. It was gross negligence. She glared around the plaza where the gardeners had all gathered for the official announcement, trying to see where Cyprin was now. She'd be there gloating, no doubt.

A big crowd had turned out, and who could blame them. It wasn't every day you got a new head gardener, and how many times had God appointed one himself? Never, oh, wait—hardly ever. A corner of Purcell's mind recalled that if you looked back far enough in her family history, a Whitlock had achieved almost everything that could be achieved in these gardens. She still felt a sick sense of pride over that, even as she itched to get away, away, away. The gardens had been her safe place, but Amma had lit them on fire and Cyprin was lounging by the wreckage toasting marshmallows.

There was Cyprin now, leaning against a pillar in the courtyard with her arms crossed and a smug look on her face. Ugh, she had legs for days and effected a good designer lean, like some kind of celebrity. If Cyprin wasn't so inherently evil, Purcell would've been stumbling over her words trying to ask for a coffee date. Purcell put her hands on her hips, and then she was walking over there, feeling lightheaded with anger.

"Hey, watch it!" Cyprin tried to back away, but she had nowhere to go. Purcell came up so close, the toes of her shoes touched Cyprin's shoes.

"What did you do?" Purcell demanded, holding onto her anger with desperate, clammy fingers. "What did you give God for this?"

"I'm trying to listen to the announcement, could you not?" said Cyprin. Even affronted, her body language was always so slouchy, giving an impression of "cool" and "disinterested." It was a distorted mirror of Purcell's straight-backed "prefect at the ready" posture, and Purcell could tell it took just as much effort for Cyprin to create the illusion of not caring. That was interesting.

Purcell was struck with the irresistible urge to crack Cyprin's facade.

She tried to block Cyprin's view to the podium where God was standing, but Cyprin was a head and shoulders taller, and it was a lost cause.

Somewhere behind Purcell, God cleared his throat, and the microphone whined. "I'm pleased to welcome you all here today for a special purpose."

"I'm going to sit at your desk," Cyprin whispered, "and chew on the ends of all your pens." She seemed to be trying to break Purcell's composure too.

The thought of Cyprin with a pen in her mouth made something wobbly happen to Purcell's legs, but Purcell stood firm and said, "I'm going to dip them all in poison before I leave!" Which—oh dear!—was not giving "God's perfectly composed right hand" at all.

"In about ten minutes, I'm going to have to ask you to address me as Head Gardener." Cyprin's smile was almost more of a snarl, and she was leaning forward, looming over Purcell, her hot breath in Purcell's face.

Purcell tried to look unruffled. "*Interim* Head Gardener," she spat, feeling warm in all the wrong places. Cyprin was almost in kissing distance, and there was something wrong with Purcell that she was even thinking about that.

God droned on, "—Our beloved head gardener, Purcell, is going on a much-needed research vacation, and—Oh, there she is over there! With Cyprin as well! It's so nice to see the spirit of collaboration alive and well in our gardens!"

Having been spotlighted by God's words, Purcell turned to face the podium and did her best to pretend she hadn't just been threatening her rival with death and kisses. All the other gardeners were looking at them now.

God said, "I officially announce our newest recruit, Cyprin Voltag, as Interim Head Gardener. I know she will do a fabulous job." He was sweating in the morning sun.

God seemed quite stressed, actually. That gave Purcell pause for about zero point two seconds and then was followed by the thought, *Well, he should be stressed. He's bypassed every sane choice in the gardens to hire a cruel, conniving city creature with a pretty face.*

The Divine was walking back into the palace now, or stalking, more accurately, wearing stress like a cape of authority and purpose. Purcell had to reach him, but Cyprin was staring like she could see through Purcell's clothes to the second-rate mismatched underwear Purcell had on. Purcell bared her teeth at Cyprin and tried to tear herself away. Cyprin stuck her foot out in a last-minute effort to trip Purcell up, but Purcell's center of gravity was too low and it didn't work. Finally free, Purcell scurried after the Divine, elbowing her way through the crowd.

She caught up with him just inside the doors, in the middle of the Foliage Concourse that was, for the moment, an undecorated white tunnel.

Not now, Purcell, was written all over his face when he stopped and turned, but he did stop. Purcell's anger at Cyprin and fear of God in a bad mood warred with one another, and she found herself standing there, jaw working but no words coming out.

"You shouldn't have picked her, she's not worthy—" Purcell started.

God cut her off with a hand gesture. "You speak to me of worthiness? How many generations in the gardens has your line had? Ten? More? Have you any idea of the privilege—" He stopped himself.

Privilege? Her privilege was a curse. In that moment, Purcell was struck by an enormous urge to dump Amma's transgressions on him, but he didn't look well-disposed to receive it. In fact, he looked quite like he was going to fire the next person who spoke to him, which Purcell would never want, she—

"I quit." The words came from deep inside her, where the resentment boiled like lava. These were *her* gardens, *her* routines, *her* life, and all of it had been upset by God awarding Cyprin top prize at the pageant.

God sighed raggedly and ran a shaking hand over his sweaty brow. "I don't accept your resignation."

"You can't do that!" Just because she hadn't meant to say it, didn't mean she wanted to take it back.

"I'm God," said Saul, rather bitterly. "I can do anything I want."

"That isn't fair! Nothing's been fair since I took this job! Is this another test? They never told me to expect tests!" Purcell was creating a scene in the palace hallway now, but she couldn't stop. A couple of chefs stuck their heads out of the kitchens to see what was going on, but, spotting the head gardener and God having a row, quickly disappeared.

"You can't quit," said Saul. "You're on sabbatical. Take some time, Purcell. You're tired. Come back refreshed." God had this way of looking ancient sometimes, and frail. She felt a flash of worry for him.

He walked away before she could gather herself for a counterattack. Purcell felt a nervous breakdown coming on. She'd just threatened to quit the gardens—*her* gardens. What madness was that?

Cyprin.

Cyprin had brought it on. That woman was like a virus, getting into every cell, making things hot and dysfunctional. But Purcell couldn't run the risk of having her life derailed any further—her legacy was too important for that. Like having a very bad fever, she saw no option but to remove herself from polite society and let things run their course. She was going to leave—go on sabbatical like God so wanted—and explore the forbidden mountain.

Purcell would have walked right to the lake and gone on to the mountain were it not for the expectation that she'd attend the night's festivities: a party to mark the start of her sabbatical and Cyprin's appointment as interim head gardener.

She did not want to go. But she had a reputation to uphold, so in the evening, Purcell put on her gardener whites and her best fake smile and went back to the palace.

The decorations were weird. It took her a second to process that the red streamers hanging from the ceiling in the foliage concourse were not about her demise as head gardener but about God's impending renewal. She'd completely forgotten that was happening this year.

Clear balloons were filled with red sequins that sloshed about like blood. New tapestries lined the walls, alternating between showing a withered flower that represented the old Divine and a green shoot bursting from the soil for his reincarnation. That had always struck Purcell as strange, another part of Divine mythology her brain glossed over. Seeing it now, in the light of her departure on sabbatical, it disturbed her. Was this why God had seemed stressed lately?

Her mind brushed up against religion and rejected it entirely. Purcell believed in growth algorithms and cataloguing soil microbiomes. God's supposed power over the sun, his ever-cycling life—*her* plant magic—didn't fit with this view of the world. She mostly tried to ignore the things that didn't fit, just concerning herself with the running of the gardens, but here, now, she admitted that what she really believed was that magic was science. Advanced, or unknown, but science all the same.

What did that mean for God's renewal?

Purcell turned her head, distracted by the sound of rowdy laughter, and saw Cyprin, standing on a damn chair, surrounded by a circle of sycophants. She forgot entirely what she was thinking about and crept closer, listening in.

"And we'll have Taco Tuesdays, where everybody gets the afternoon off!" Cyprin shouted, a drink sloshing in her hand and her cheeks glowing with good cheer.

The crowd hooted in agreement.

Cyprin was making new rules for the gardens. Drunk, at a party. Purcell saw red. She stalked forward, intending violence, but Amanda grabbed her arm, stopping her at the back of the crowd.

"Let her have her moment," said Amanda.

"Why?"

"Because you'll be back before you know it, and a few weeks aren't going to change much."

Amanda was absolutely wrong. A few *minutes* of listening to this horseshit was enough to haunt Purcell for a lifetime.

"They love her," Purcell grumbled, and it was true. Cyprin, a shunned outsider just a few hours ago, had the crowd eating out of her hands. They had never eaten out of Purcell's hands, and Purcell had spent a lifetime preparing to be head gardener, not five minutes of positive affirmations in the bathroom mirror or whatever nonsense Cyprin was into.

Amanda frowned. "Is that what this is about? Purcell, I told you, you should ease up. *This* is what easing up looks like." She gestured to Cyprin, who was now promising everyone could have a flower named after themselves. "Look, it's harmless."

"You're meant to be on my side!" Purcell shouted, and a few heads turned to stare at her. Including Cyprin's.

"Oh, Purcell!" Cyprin sketched a facetious bow and then stepped down off her chair, cutting through the crowd. "The *former* head gardener graces us with her presence!"

The crowd parted for Cyprin, all leering at Purcell. Cyprin walked right up to Purcell, smiling triumphantly. "Any last words?"

Purcell grabbed Cyprin's arm and marched them out of the palace. For some reason, Cyprin actually let her. The garden staff moved into the doorway, watching, scandalized, as they headed across the lawn.

When they were far enough that no one could hear their words, Purcell sighed and said, "I'm begging you."

"Begging me to what?" Cyprin's fingers curled and Purcell realized she was wearing knuckle-dusters. They looked like they were made from bubble gum, but Purcell did not want to test that theory out. Did Cyprin think Purcell had dragged her out here to *brawl*? Did Cyprin *want* to brawl?

Purcell cast her eyes up at the two moons, wishing she could fly off and live up there, alone. "Don't make me say it again."

Cyprin shoved her knuckle-dusted hands into her pockets. "Oh, but I'd like to. Beg me."

The bite to Cyprin's words had Purcell spellbound. She found herself leaning forward, toward Cyprin's slightly parted lips. Astoundingly, Cyprin began to lean in too—this was going a very different way to how Purcell had thought it would.

Purcell took a shallow, panicked breath and her words came out in a rush. "I'm begging you not to wreck the gardens in my absence."

It killed the moment instantly.

Cyprin's eyebrows lifted like a preparation for a gut-wrench suplex. "That's what you think I'm going to do?" She snorted. "At least God has trust in me."

Amanda was right, Purcell should have left this alone.

Purcell said the most hurtful thing she could think of, knowing nothing really about Cyprin except that Cyprin seemed to like God. "God will be a twelve-year-old soon!" This was not only verging on blasphemous, as the Petaled Divine was supposedly wise and godly at any age, but it sent a stab of fear into Purcell's belly. Purcell did not like change. She tried telling herself that this was *all* really just about not liking change. But it felt bigger than that.

Cyprin sobered immediately. "I have to get back to work."

"Work?" *What?* The shift in gears had Purcell suddenly suspicious that Cyprin knew more than she was letting on. She was in cahoots with God, that much was clear. What had he told her? Purcell was suddenly desperate to know.

Cyprin started walking away. Purcell asked the grass to stop Cyprin and some of it rose and tripped her. Purcell ran to help her up.

"What the fuck?" said Cyprin, shying away from the offered hand. "How did you do that? Did you weaponize the garden's bio bots?"

Purcell's mouth worked emptily. She'd never considered that the messages passing between her and the plants might be carried by ambient bio bots. The idea was plausible. The bio bots were an enduring mystery. No one knew what they were for, and the ones in Verdure hung in the air like dust, invisible but for small glints of reflected light at sunset. Purcell never really thought about them, but she bet bio bots would be on the mind of whoever had infected the prizewinning roses. Any fond feelings she may or may not have been desperately trying to ignore were lost with that thought. She wanted to shout accusations, but that would achieve nothing, because she'd already tried it, and God did not believe her. No one did.

"You're drunk!" she managed to snap, implying Cyprin had tripped on nothing.

"Well, obviously," Cyprin got up off the ground on her own.

Before Cyprin could leave, Purcell got out what she wanted to say, free of antagonism this time. "Is God all right?"

Cyprin looked taken aback, and of course she should be—Purcell was acknowledging that Cyprin, an all-round awful person and total beginner to the world of the gardens, knew more about God than Purcell. She wanted badly to take it back, but it was true. So.

Cyprin smiled widely, but her eyes glittered with pain. "He's fine. Why wouldn't he be?"

Purcell did not have the stomach for any more partying after that and left the palace to hurry back to her apartment.

First thing in the morning, she foisted her potted plants on her neighbors, then cleaned out the perishables in her fridge by guiltily eating a lot of them. More specimen containers and tools than any normal person would want to carry up a mountain were shoved in a backpack. A foldable tent was strapped to the side of the same pack. Enough food to last about a week somehow fit too. Medical supplies. Ropes and climbing gear. Purcell was the sort of person who would pack ski gear on a summer holiday.

It was time to beat the crap out of Amma in the most direct way available. Time for a rise so meteoric, no one ever spoke Amma's—or Cyprin's—name again. And how long did she have to do it? Not long enough. Purcell had no time to waste before she started wasting.

Before she knew it, she was halfway down the green, laboring under the weight of her enormous backpack. Eyes on the prize: the peak of the mountain, shrouded in cloud.

At the shore of the lake, she looked back over her shoulder at the gardens she'd known and loved so much they were almost an extension of her own body. It felt like she was leaving her baby with a stranger. No, not a stranger. You didn't know what you'd get with a stranger. This was worse. Cyprin was a teenage babysitter who was going to lock the child in a cupboard while she ate pizza and snogged her boyfriend on the couch. Thoughts of Cyprin and God together came with savage jealousy and Purcell ground her teeth.

Well, God didn't want to listen to Purcell. So, the only way to combat Cyprin's influence was to let it colonize the gardens. Let God have her. One of those "be careful what you wish for" scenarios. Cyprin was going to mess up the petal mail, get on God's nerves, and run the gardens wrong. But at least Purcell didn't have to be here while it happened. She had her own goals to pursue. No doubt they'd be falling all over her when she got back.

One last thing to do before she left. Purcell needed to tell Amanda what she'd found out about Amma—needed someone to understand that crushing burden of a secret. The problem was, she couldn't seem to get the words out.

Amanda breathed through her fingers because her head was in her hands. "Purcell, what are you still doing here?"

Purcell wandered farther into the cool, plant-filled sanctuary of the admin center. "I just, I, every time I try to leave, I—I've never left the gardens before, okay?"

"And you want me to . . . ?"

"Talk to me until I can leave?" There was a hopeful lilt to Purcell's voice.

"We did this an hour ago. You came in here wearing the same all-purpose-terrain suit, with your stacked sample cases, your backpack with the sippy tube, your socks up to your—your knees! I have never seen anyone so ready to go out into the wilds. And do you know what? There aren't really any wilds in Verdure anymore! You'll run into a convenience store even if it's against your will! If you need shelter from the elements there will be a hotel. The worst predator you'll find out there will be somebody's stray cat."

"I hear they can be vicious. Do you think I should pack sardines, to distract them?" Purcell put her things down and began inspecting the seedlings. She'd been in here a lot recently, going straight through to her desk in the back to organize the gardeners' schedules. She hadn't stopped to smell the roses, or, in this case, scrutinize the seedlings. Now seemed like a great time.

Amanda was watching her. "I'm going to take that as a joke, because if it isn't, you really are beyond anyone's help. Just go, Purcell. This is a wonderful opportunity for you. A wonderful bit of *life experience*, and believe me, you need that."

Amanda had been born in the gardens too, though she was less married to her job and more worldly than Purcell, going into Asperia on weekends for shopping and culture. She was Purcell's rock, a much-needed reality check, and could spot and disarm an anxiety spiral from a thousand paces. The latter was accompanied by a definite eye roll, but she still did it, all the same. Purcell was grateful for her, and she was listening to her, until Amanda said, "There might be another reason why you don't want to leave the gardens. Don't take this the wrong way, but I've seen how you look at Cyprin, and I think—Look, there's an easier and, and more direct way of dealing with tension like that than running away from it."

Purcell was incensed. "I am *not* running away from Cyprin!"

Amanda had her "I pity Purcell" face on, which was adding insult to injury. "Purcell, I know when you're in the middle of something you can't see the woods for the trees. I'm just asking you to consider that maybe the reason you're so reluctant to leave the gardens is because you have unfinished business. Unfinished business with Cyprin. She pushes and challenges you, and I think that's a really good thing. You should shoot your shot before you go. You'll feel better if you do."

Purcell's mouth hung open for a moment, then her eyes narrowed. "There are far more important things at play than anything to do with Cyprin."

Amanda leaned across the desk and fixed Purcell in her crosshairs. "Like what? What is going on with you, Purcell?"

Shit. Now there was no way around this. "There's—I, uh, there's something I need to tell you, but it's going to sound insane. I don't know how to say it, I, ah—"

Amanda stood up straighter, her expression lighter. "It's all right. I already know."

"You know?" Purcell was wracked with thoughts of panicked exposure. Amanda had known about Cyprin, which was mortifying enough, but how could she possibly know about the plant-talking, or about Amma?

Amanda said, "I mean, look, you just wilted that little petunia. Yes, and now I'm pointing that out, it's straightening up again, but don't go pretending it didn't happen. Purcell, you have some kind of power over plants. You're special."

"I'm special?" If only Amanda knew how truly nonunique Purcell really was. Purcell was on the cusp of blurting her secrets about Amma, but the way Amanda had dredged up her secret crush on Cyprin and her plant-talking abilities was off. Real friends didn't go full CSI on you.

"Yes, you're special," Amanda continued, her face a perfect picture of concern. "And you're wasted here. You know, we've known each other forever, and I love you so much. I want—I want you to be more than you can be here. These gardens have you stifled. I have friends, in the city, who would appreciate you properly. Friends who would use your abilities to make the world better."

Amanda had an agenda. Purcell's so-called best friend had sniffed out her secret and wanted to use her. A plant by her left ankle turned yellow. "You've told people my secret? I haven't even told *you* my secret!"

Amanda lifted her hands off the table. "I haven't told anyone, I swear. But why is it a secret, Purcell? Why would you keep that to yourself unless you were sure the priestguard were going to misuse you? I'm your best friend, why didn't you tell me?" Amanda's expression was one of high anxiety now, but was she anxious that she'd done something bad or that she was getting told off for it?

"Why didn't you tell me you already knew?" Some best friend. All this time, had Amanda been by her side just to be close to her plant powers, or the latest descendant of the famous Whitlocks? Purcell couldn't tell her about Amma now.

In a world full of clone grandmas, bad best friends, and faltering gods, it felt like the only clean thing left was the certainty that Cyprin was out to get her.

Purcell's insides vibrated with rage, and a pot full of seeds and dirt on the desk in front of Amanda exploded like a land mine. Both of them jumped backward.

"Purcell, please! I didn't tell anyone. I don't want to hurt you, not ever." Amanda eyed the broken pieces of the terra-cotta pot as she said this.

"How can I ever trust you again?"

"Purcell, come on. You're blowing this out of proportion. Why do you get to be mad? You're the one who was keeping secrets from me!"

"Am I, really?" snapped Purcell. "Who are these friends of yours, then, the ones I could be helpful to?"

Amanda's face twisted. "I can't tell you."

Purcell's eyebrows rose. "Can't, or won't?" Hot tears—yep, definitely tears—ran down her cheeks.

"Purcell, you're taking this the wrong way—"

A greedy rush of growth happened as the seedlings fed off Purcell's indignation. She let the feelings grow until she could no longer contain them. Until they burst out of her body and fed the plants. The room exploded into dirt and cardboard and pottery shards. Green leaves flapped like wings. Flowers burst in fireworks of pollen. She reveled in it. This destruction that had come from within her. How would Amma feel if Purcell used this inherited power to tear the whole palace down?

While Amanda dived for cover, Purcell turned on her heels and walked out, head held high.

All the times Amanda had been a snarky plus-one for her at parties. All the moments she'd said something reassuring when Purcell was in an anxiety spiral. The way they laughed at the ever-worsening production quality of *Lust Island*. Had all of that been a lie? Every smile? Every compliment?

Well, screw Amanda.

Screw all of them.

Screw Amma, screw God, and especially, screw Cyprin. They were all just weights holding Purcell down, and she didn't have the time for that. She didn't have the lifespan. She was better off alone.

CHAPTER 17

CYPRIN

Cyprin was in the undercity, seeking out the Underground on God's behalf. It was worrying behavior. Very worrying. She was feeling things too similar to what she'd felt for Maverick, and that did not mean anything good.

". . . *If it's not choc-a-block with choc-o-late, then it's third-rate, and we won't wait!*" Deep down in the dark, there always seemed to be a food-related jingle in Cyprin's head. Something about the darkness begged to be sung at in a commercially cheerful way.

She'd entered the undercity via a trick panel at the back of the change-rooms in a basement department store. And now Cyprin was back at the very same vending machine as the last time or, certainly, one very much like it.

Cyprin entered a code into the vending machine's selection panel. She heard rattling behind its facade and muffled voices. *Nice one, guys. If I was one of the priestguard, you'd be busted.* A camera on a flexible line fed out through the bottom flap of the machine. It came up so close to her face she was surprised it could see anything other than her nose.

She'd found the code for the map to the Underground on a poster's tear-off tab on a pub wall. She didn't know if it was legit. And even if it was, now that they were seeing her in her white gardener's uniform, they might think twice about letting her talk to them. She should've changed, but too late now.

The silent judgment of the camera eye gave her the heebie-jeebies. "Yeah, all right, I work in the gardens. So what? I'm not going to narc on anyone, just give me the map to the Underground."

The camera retracted. More noises came from behind the vending machine, some clanks and what seemed like a heated argument. A slip of paper appeared and dropped into the collection area. Cyprin stuck her hand in and pulled out a map.

"This had better be genuine," she said, loudly. "If you send me around in circles, I swear to God"—*God, ha*—"I'll feed you to the rats myself." A toothless threat. If Cyprin actually saw any rats she'd run a mile.

The vending machine remained deadly silent.

"Right, okay," Cyprin held the square of paper closer to her headlamp and turned it a couple of different angles, trying to at least pretend to herself that she wasn't terrible at navigating. Shining her headlamp onto the ground highlighted the dank muck creeping up the cuffs of her trousers. White was the entirely wrong color to wear down here.

The vending machine sat at a fork in the passage. The cold carrot scent of stale undercity air beckoned from both directions. Cyprin headed left. She was pretty sure she was supposed to head left.

She'd been to a few lectures from the Underground, up top when she was a rebellious teenager. But even though she was a rebellious adult now, she'd never been down to see the real organization. Had never felt the need to be part of an organized rebellion. She preferred the singular disorganized one that went on in the confines of her own head.

She skidded on a film of slime and managed to catch her balance. Really, it was disgusting. Did they have to hunker down in the basement of the world, practically the sewer? Now that Cyprin knew God was orchestrating his own kind of rebellion and did not give a crap about opponents to his regime, the secrecy of the Underground and the black market felt silly. What would happen if they brought everything up and out into the open? Would the priestguard come for them? A handful of cops? Pitted against how many? The Underground was popular. They'd never helped Cyprin directly, but she'd seen them fumigating buildings, making food drops. Everyone had seen them doing their civic duty. Despite their reputation for shady political maneuvering, the bones of the organization were good. If push came to shove, regular people might choose to help the Underground right back.

Funny, she'd never thought of it that way before. The hierarchies of society had always seemed so absolute and unassailable. Now it reeked of the hollow threats in cautionary tales for children: don't step on the cracks, or you'll break your mother's back; if you get out of bed at night the monsters will eat you; if you keep doing that, you'll go blind. That kind of stuff only worked for as long as you were gullible enough to believe in it.

Cyprin power walked past a stretch of decrepit restaurants. Scenes like these made up the worst of the undercity, as far as she was concerned. Moldering heaps of unidentifiable goo were somehow tolerable. But nothing struck fear in the heart quite like an empty candy store or supermarket, or . . . baby store. That shit was a straight line into the Twilight Zone.

A scraping sound was coming from an old ice-cream parlor, and she stuck her head through the remaining half door, just to make sure the sound wasn't from some flesh-hungry nightmare creature with rapier-like claws. Up the back, past a glass display where stainless-steel tubs showcased black residue with alarmingly intact cherries on top, a mixer continued its lazy figure-eight path through a bowl that was now paper thin.

Mentally, Cyprin added that to the worst things that could happen to you. There were the rats, the getting lost or trapped until you turned into bones, and then there was the remnant AI. Power was off down here, but some of them ran on their own almost inexhaustible nuclear fuel or self-renewing batteries. Trapped and alone, the lucky ones were rescued and reprogrammed by slumpers. The unlucky ones went mad, fixating on tasks, inventing new ones, getting stuck in endless feedback loops. Cyprin had heard of a barber's chair where an enterprising slumper had thought to get his hair cut and had ended up with quite a lot off the top. Quite a lot indeed. She left the mixer, relieved that it didn't have eyes or ears, and continued on her way.

Cyprin rounded a bend and went down so, so many stairs. By the end of it, her quads were reduced to screaming jelly and she had to lean against a slime-ridden wall to catch her breath. She wondered what God would be like if she brought him into the undercity. It was almost impossible to imagine his silks and clean skin in these sewery halls, but she could just about do it. She pictured him cracking jokes about the sludge and carrot smell and telling stories in the dark. For someone who knew jack shit about real life, he seemed remarkably calm and collected. Confident. Comfortable in his own body. His body? No, she wasn't thinking about that.

Cyprin rounded another corner, and someone threw a bag over her head.

CHAPTER 18

CYPRIN

Cyprin couldn't see anything, but she had the sense that the room was filled with people looking at her. It had to be the Underground. The darkness huffed and shuffled. The carrot smell—Actually, after a while, her brain had tuned out the carrot smell. All she could smell right now was someone's bad deodorant. She was in true jeopardy.

"I think we started off on the wrong foot," said Cyprin. "Come to think of it, maybe I don't even need to be here. I'm supposed to be at some meeting at the palace, and as soon as they realize I'm not there, they'll be looking for me. It might be best if you just untie me, and I'll keep my eyes closed until you leave—"

In a stressful situation, Cyprin's mouth ran on its own. More often than not, this made things worse. Right now, she thought she could sense the room growing angry at her. "You know, I—I've got the worst song stuck in my head. You might know it, it's that one from the ad with the tap-dancing cows and the river of chocolate. *If it's not choc-a-block with choc-o-late—*"

A sharp, prickling sensation happened at the crook of Cyprin's arm. "Oh! Are you—Is that—Are you drugging me!?"

Now the darkness did talk. "Who sent you?"

"Saul, the Great Petaled Divine, he—ah, oh, shit, I feel funny. What did you give me?"

The darkness around her tittered with the sounds of many people.

"And who are you?" said the voice in front of her.

"Cyprin Voltag, the head gardener, well, the interim head gardener . . ." She trailed off, trying to hold the words in. With just a little push she'd be telling them about the times she was bullied as a kid, her collection of hovercraft models, the way she had to try on every pair of aviators she came across, hoping to find the same ones Maverick had.

"Head gardener, with a mission direct from God," said the voice. "Wonderful."

"He's not really God"—*oh, fuck*—"he's just a man who's been tricked into pretending. He wants to know what's on the island in Lake Pensive, whether you've heard any rumors about it. He's trying to find out who's pulling his strings and the *why* of everything. Why there's eternal spring, why there has to be a Divine. He thinks the island has something to do with all that." This was much, much worse than her usual rambling. They'd better not ask her about anything to do with her bank account or how many hours a week she spent watching *Lust Island.*

"Excuse me for a moment, Head Gardener." The voice moved away and went into a conference of whispered voices that Cyprin couldn't quite make out. God—God could not have foreseen this. He'd seemed so careful with his secrets, He couldn't have told them to her just to have her blab to the Underground.

"It's really cold—Is it really cold in here?" Cyprin shivered.

A blanket was thrown over her shoulders and she started to feel less like she was about to be murdered. But only a little less.

"It's the truth serum, messes with temperature regulation," said a voice by her ear.

"Great. Just great."

They left Cyprin sitting there for what felt like an eon. Whatever drug they'd given her was sparking off a rave in her head. Her eyelids lit up with an internal aurora borealis. "I don't—I don't wanna bother anyone, but I really do have somewhere to be. If you could just drop me back at the vending machine, that'd be really cool."

The movement of a tide of unseen people happened again and the original voice addressed Cyprin. It was a well-rounded news-anchor-y voice that made her think about *Lust Island* commercials. She hoped she wasn't about to tell them that.

"We believe that the sacred island is home to some kind of terraforming technology that regulates the local environment. Two of our operatives were killed trying to go there and verify, but I imagine a divine gardener like you would have no problems," said the news anchor.

"Well, great, great. We have a common cause! You can let me go, then. I'll go there and report right back, or at least send you a letter?" She was desperate to get out. No way she was going to die down here.

"Cyprin, was it? I'm sorry, Cyprin, but first we're going to need you to bring us the Petaled Divine."

"Well, I won't. I'll tell you I'm going to do it and then I—Oh damn."

Hands unbuttoned Cyprin's uniform to the waist and what felt like a cattle prod was shoved into her stomach and then immediately removed. For a torture technique it was bafflingly abrupt. "Ow! Hey, what was that for? I'm already telling you everything!" A numbness spread across her torso.

"We've installed an explosive with a delayed timer. You have twenty-four hours to bring us the Divine."

"*What? You what?!*" They'd turned her into a homemade bomb. What the fuck. What the actual fuck.

"It's just an incentive. We know you'll come through for us, Cyprin. And to be clear, we want both you and the Divine to continue to hold your positions in the gardens. Nothing much has to change for you. You'll just be serving new masters. People, not priests. You should feel good about that."

"Threatening to blow me up is serving the people? You sick fucks—"

"The good of the many above the good of the few," said the voice. Several others echoed the phrase.

Cyprin copped what felt like a nail gun to the temple, the swirling lights behind her eyes concentrating to a pinpoint, and then she was out.

The glow from the vending machine lit up Cyprin's eyelids and she opened one eye tentatively, as if flipping aside a curtain to check for unwanted neighbors, before committing to being fully awake. One of her arms was going numb underneath her and she was covered in muck and filth. But she was untied. She was free. As free as someone could be with explosives in their abdomen. Oh, shit.

Cyprin sat up and wrestled off the top half of her coveralls, finding a tiny red bullseye on her stomach, no bigger than a mosquito bite. She pressed at it, feeling for the telltale lump of an incendiary device, then realized she might set it off this way. She stopped, got gingerly to her feet, and hammered on the vending machine. "Terrorists! You're a bunch of fucking terrorists!"

Cyprin shook the machine, then kicked it. One of the lights flickered off inside. No voices or signs of movement on the other side anymore. In all likelihood the people who had handed her the map had fled. Giving up on that avenue, she leaned back against the glass and sunk to the floor. *Think!* She had to think. Cyprin rubbed her fists into her eyes. Thinking is what she should have done when God told her to go speak to the Underground. Did he think at all, or did he just look like he was thinking, with his books and his fancy teas? This was the same as it had been with Maverick and here she was passing out on the floor because God had asked her to hold her breath too long.

Cyprin wiped the sweat off her face. It trickled down so easily now that she had no hair. Being mad at God didn't help anything. Relying on other people was always pointless. She had to decide for herself what she'd do next. She was the one down here in the dark with the rats. She was the one with the bomb in her stomach.

She wasn't going to hand Saul over to the Underground. God had enough to worry about already. Maybe if she hadn't known him, she might have been tempted. But she cared about him, even if it wasn't in her best interest. What a bad time to have a heart.

So she'd go to the island, find God what he needed. And then . . . blow up? Cease to be? No, no, she wasn't that noble. Wasn't noble at all. She would trade that same information back to the Underground. It wouldn't be what they'd asked for, but it was something that they wanted. They'd see her usefulness and hold off.

Cyprin stood up and brushed some of the muck off her bottom, mostly spreading it like a finger painting. She'd never been so humiliated, frightened, or absolutely determined to get herself out of a mess.

There had better be something incredible on that island.

"Cyprin! I'd—No one knew where you were!" God's face was all concern. He had his hands hovering over her shoulders like he wanted to touch her.

"I got you a present." Cyprin shut the doors of the Mint Throne Room and opened her satchel. She'd done quite a few things on her way back from the undercity, including shopping for some essential items and stopping off home for a shower and some toast. It was amazing how little her hands shook now. She hesitated, her arm halfway into the bag. "I'm head gardener now, right? I'm meant to be here for the petal fitting?"

"When you didn't show up this morning, I feared you had changed your mind."

"So, you organized for someone else to do it?" Horror crept into her voice. She couldn't shake the feeling that God had required a blood sacrifice, and she had unknowingly agreed to it, like the times Maverick had directed her to call in sick from school and then cough into the phone to his boss so that he could hang out in the city all day while she sat alone in her mother's apartment.

"No, I—That is to say, I pretended we'd pre-agreed you weren't attending this morning's petal fitting, and I hoped for the best," said Saul, his eyes roving over her as if searching for injuries.

"Good." Cyprin pulled a pile of clothing out of her satchel and thrust it at God.

"What's this?"

"The petal mail. A plastic replica, anyway. They sell them in all the markets." She'd bought it out of practicality, but . . . it had felt nice buying Saul a present too.

God shook the fake petal mail out. It was still a little crumpled. He looked over it, at Cyprin. "Why are you wearing sunglasses indoors?"

Cyprin, still hopped up on truth serum, said nothing. She was terrified she might blurt out that she was in an uncontrollable state of limerence over him, just like she'd been with Maverick.

God's eyebrows shot up. "Oh! Is this something to do with the errand I sent you on?"

"Ye-es." Cyprin ground her teeth together in an effort not to say more.

God put on the fake petal mail. The cuffs were a little short. It was very obviously a fake. "No one will be the wiser," he said, inspecting the plastic petals on one forearm.

"Purcell will," said Cyprin. As if speaking Purcell's name conjured her, Cyprin caught a faint scent of marshmallow on the air, perhaps lingering from Purcell's last time in here, and her heart lurched.

"Purcell left the gardens this morning."

Cyprin put on a smile. "Cool, time to change the locks."

God gave her a quick look of disapproval, and then moved on. "Did you go to the Underground? What did you find out?"

"They think there's a terraforming machine on your island."

God's eyebrows raised and the Trellis Crown wobbled perilously. "Oh, they do, do they? So, the real source of godly power isn't God, but something on that island. Thank—Well, thank *me* that I didn't let Purcell go there."

Cyprin experienced a flash, like a sudden headache, where she saw Purcell, stubborn and defiant, marching up the side of the mountain in the lake. But that couldn't happen, could it? Purcell was a Goody Two-shoes, through and through. She'd never break any rules.

"I'm going to go myself, today, to check it out." Standing still for this long in front of God while she had a bomb in her stomach had her sweating. She needed to get this show on the road.

"Today?" The pleasant expression on God's face faltered.

"Yeah. You've got the petal mail now, so I figure I can go. Like you said, no one will be the wiser."

God plastered on a big, nervous smile. "You're in such a hurry! Perhaps we should talk this over a little more, make plans together? Don't you want to enjoy some time as head gardener first?"

Cyprin tilted her head. "You seem off. Is everything all right?"

"I could say the same of you," said God, and the mirth evaporated from his eyes.

She was almost offended. "I'm following the plan, aren't I?—*Your* plan. To find out the why of it all before your own priestguard kill you, remember?" Absentmindedly, Cyprin's hand went to her stomach where the little mosquito bite, evidence of her capture, pulsed and stung. She'd thought about demanding to know if he'd had any idea of how dangerous seeing the Underground would be for her, but she had the feeling that bringing him into the loop would just make him want to march down there and hand himself over. No matter the danger she was in, she really didn't want that.

"I suppose I was hoping we could spend some time together before we get ourselves into a world of trouble. Smell the roses, while we still can." God looked wistful.

He cared about her; Cyprin could see it in the way his body language was always open to her, the way he searched her face like he was doing a crossword. Maybe he even loved her. Ha, as if she was any good at telling when somebody loved her. Suddenly her whole body felt like an open wound that she was rolling in salt. "It's never going to happen," said Cyprin, bluntly. "I don't do romance. And we're like broccoli and strawberries: we shouldn't even be in the same plot." *You're head gardener now. You've got what you want. Better end it now, before he realizes you are too much and cuts you off.*

Better end it before you sacrifice yourself for him, like you're kind of already doing.

Saul's mouth hung open. "I didn't say—"

But Cyprin wasn't finished. She didn't know if this was the drugs talking, or if she was using them as an excuse, but every word out of her mouth made her feel like she had switched places with Maverick. "You should be careful of who you trust, Saul. I could have ruined you if I wanted."

"What? By exposing me as a false god? It doesn't work that way; the system would eat you. Believe me, I know."

"No, by manipulating you for my own ends. I might still." She managed a shrug, as if it didn't pain her to say that. But God was hopelessly naïve, and time was running out. He needed to learn. "You trust too easily."

His shoulders slumped and Cyprin felt his hurt like a gut punch. Damn it, she cared about him so fucking much, even if it wasn't a healthy kind of caring.

"Cyprin, I don't understand where this is coming from. I just wanted—I just wanted to know you, that's all. I know—I know you were using me, to get into the gardens, to move up the ranks, but I thought we were—"

"You thought we were *what*?" snapped Cyprin. It hurt that he'd said she was using him, but she couldn't freaking lie right now, so she couldn't refute that.

Saul was stunned into silence. This was like kicking a puppy. But she'd relied on Saul too much. When push came to shove, Cyprin felt vulnerable and exposed, just like she had been with Maverick. The only person she could really trust was herself, and sometimes not even that. It was time to go out to that mountain in the lake and find whatever the Underground thought was there, to trade the information back to them for her life and then never, ever do any favors for anyone ever again.

"I have to go," said Cyprin. "I'll bring back answers soon."

"I guess I'll hold the fort, then." God looked like a sun-bleached thing, colorless in his coat of plastic rainbow petals, internally collapsing. He really had been getting attached to her. Or at least the idea of her. Maybe he'd cry until his eyes were bruised, like she had done when Maverick didn't show up at the hospital. Maybe he'd write tragic acrostic poems.

Cyprin managed to summon some saliva from wherever it had all mysteriously gone. "Good. Goodbye." She gulped hard, and then fled the room.

She was gonna die. She was gonna die and she was breaking hearts on her way out. This was the exact opposite of what you were supposed to do with your last hours. She should've been telling him what he meant to her, hells, maybe even telling Purcell, but instead she'd just metaphorically slapped God in the face and now she was going alone up a mountain to find dark secrets and trade them to the worst people in the world. Cyprin reached up to rub her eyes under the sunglasses, and her hand came back wet with tears.

CHAPTER 19

PURCELL

Purcell washed up on the shore of the island in the middle of the lake. No one had seen her, she was sure of it. She'd kept her glasses on, because she was almost blind without them, but they were fogged up with her breath and she had to windshield-wiper them with her fingers. She drank an energy drink as the volcanic sand stained her feet black. Her calves were cramping, and her skin was cold rubber.

She was a husk of herself, really. All her insides had burned out suffering betrayal after betrayal, but she felt oddly clean now. She knew where she stood in the world, and it was alone. She was going up this mountain to find her flower and when she came back down successful, they'd all be too intimidated to cross her. And there was only a hair's difference between intimidation and respect.

The mountain peak was haloed by cloud like a man with a tonsure. As she looked up at it, something in Purcell's stomach became dizzy with the perceived height. She'd always known it was big, but it hadn't seemed *this* big from the gardens. She'd been thinking it would be an hour's trek up, maybe two or three if you factored in the collection of interesting specimens. But this looked serious. So did the jungle just past the black shoreline she stood on.

She split open her waterproof bag, put her safari suit and hiking boots back on, and pulled her socks up to her thighs. It was time to be brave and create her legacy. It was time to kick ass. As Purcell walked into the jungle, the vines cinched aside like curtains to let her pass.

CHAPTER 20

CYPRIN

Amanda said, "What are you doing here?" which wasn't how Cyprin felt a head gardener ought to be addressed.

Given their last interaction, it was tempting to indulge in a little nastiness, but every single pot in the room seemed broken. Amanda was sweeping dirt into a little hill by the desk, and it looked like she'd been crying. In another pile on the floor was a tangle of quite large plants. Cyprin squinted at them, sure she'd seen them as little seedlings only a few days before.

Cyprin hung in the doorway, the beaded curtains getting seriously close and personal, and countered with "What happened here?"

"A sudden gust of wind," said Amanda, which was completely absurd; they were below ground.

But Cyprin was an old hat at using absurdity to deflect from emotion. She'd once told Moss that she'd stepped on the prongs of a rake and the stick had flung up and hit her between the eyes, and that's why they were watering. At the time they had been in the bathroom of a cocktail bar. Cyprin still thought it was funny.

"I hate when that happens," she told Amanda, deadpan.

Amanda straightened up and regained some composure. "What can I help you with?"

That was more like it. "Purcell has an office back here somewhere. I would like to sit my ass on her chair and rifle through all her things."

She was expecting some kind of pushback, but Amanda just gestured to the stone hallway behind her desk. "Be my guest."

As Cyprin started walking, Amanda quipped, "You know, you two really are obsessed with each other."

Purcell's chair and desk were hilariously oversized, the surest sign of little-dog syndrome; the littlest, yappiest ones always thought they were enormous. Cyprin sat down with relish and folded her legs up under her. She took a minute to conjure up Purcell's face, the sudden telescopic depth to her eyes when she realized Cyprin was up to something, the way Purcell pursed her plump little lips in response to an insult. Beautiful. She contemplated the mountainous stacks of paper on Purcell's desk.

The morning had been a complete train wreck of bombs in the stomach and disappointing God. Cyprin could still picture his wobbly face as she said those nasty things to him, and it made her feel like month-old milk, even though it had been the only way out for both of them.

She had twenty-four hours to sort shit out with the Underground, to their satisfaction, or they were going to end her career for her, in the form of making her go pop. Hells, she might get caught and executed for going out onto God's forbidden mountain. Which was exactly why she had to take five and sit in Purcell's chair: being head gardener was a bucket-list item.

A bronze plaque shone on the desk with Purcell's name on it. Cyprin found a permanent marker in the desk drawer and changed the *u* in Purcell and the *o* in Whitlock, and then laughed for two whole minutes at *Parcell Whitlack*. Purcell would be absolutely incensed at this, and that was how Cyprin liked her best. Purcell was a silly little house cat, but if you pushed her buttons in just the right way, she rose to the challenge and became wild and unpredictable.

There was an in tray, and Cyprin set about drawing smiley faces and flowers in the margins of a couple of reports before incidentally settling down to read one. A coalition of mulch-makers were pleading their case for permission to create and distribute their mulch mixtures without having to wait for a final sign-off from Purcell. Several of them had more than thirty years' experience on the job.

Cyprin put it neatly to one side and picked up the next report. A group of turf-tenders were grumbling that Purcell had taken their radio. Okay. The next one, dated six months ago: a scientist in charge of rose research was asking, very politely, if there was a particular reason why Purcell felt the need to assess her work daily, because it slowed her down. It was the clearest case of self-sabotage Cyprin had ever seen. Purcell was going about life on the highest difficulty setting because she did not trust anyone to be competent. She was trying to do everyone's jobs. No wonder she looked so overwhelmed all the time. No wonder everyone hated her marshmallow-scented, big-eyed, curly-haired sanctimoniousness.

"Amanda!"

Amanda did not come in, so Cyprin went out. In the messed-up foyer of the admin center, she waved a handful of papers. "Are they all like this?"

Amanda dropped another fragment of broken pottery in the trash and sighed. "Purcell's approach was very hands on."

"Is that what *you'd* say if this were a murder, and Purcell had just been caught strangling the victim?" said Cyprin. She put five reports down on the admin desk. "I want you to tell these people I've approved their requests. I'm going back in to look at the others."

Amanda dutifully made her way over to thumb through the reports. "Purcell's not going to like this."

"Great," said Cyprin. "Even better."

It wasn't long before she had cleared out the rest of the in tray. She didn't find the job nearly as difficult as Purcell made it out to be.

By the time Cyprin decided to leave Purcell's office, she was feeling quite sentimental. Having such a clear-cut enemy made her feel so alive, so consequential. She hadn't had a crush on anyone like this in ages, certainly not on someone of equal abilities, with shared interests, who, had the circumstances been otherwise, might have even been a healthy choice. It was nice to know she had that in her. You know, before she exploded.

But now it was high time to go.

Bucket-list item ticked just in case, Cyprin headed out to the island in the middle of Lake Pensive. Time to save herself. Time to hustle.

Cyprin peeled her wet suit off on the island's shore and put away the multi-tool that she had at the ready. It had been a peaceful stroll across the gardens. And an uneventful, if bracing, swim across the water. She'd thought the island itself would make up for all that with any number of fun-but-lethal traps and puzzles. She'd been expecting to have to cut a hole in an energy field, take out some guards, anything. It was almost disappointing that there was only a monstrous pimple of volcanic rock and dirt, shrouded in greenery and cricket song.

She had a bodysuit on, designed to hide her heat signature from any watching cameras or drones. Now that she could see there weren't any, she was regretting it. Cyprin plucked at the damp fabric that was giving her an atomic wedgie.

She'd half expected the plants here to be as fake as the petal mail the Divine was wearing. Or a holographic setup, hiding the metallic underbelly of the island and the massive terraforming machine that the Underground thought she'd find. But what looked very convincingly like a real jungle was before her, rising and disappearing in the clouds. Cyprin had prepared for a lot of things, but not for this. Not for an actual mountain. Not for a real live jungle. There were probably spiders in there the size of her hand, or ants for whom her bodysuit would appear as an interesting but entirely surmountable challenge. Cyprin pushed down her feelings of unpreparedness and inadequacy—easy to do when she had a genuine bomb in her stomach. That was incredibly focusing. A few spiders? *Pssshh.* So long as they didn't explode.

She strode right into the jungle. This had about the same effect as a fly walking into flypaper. Cyprin thrashed around a lot and didn't make any progress. The plants were thick as thieves, leaning drunkenly on each other. Some brambly number unfairly sporting thorns underpinned the taller plants, vines roped over everything with more diabolical knots than a troupe of Boy Scouts could create. The only way Cyprin could get through was to lean her body weight forward and step, and lean, and step, all the while with elbows up to defend her face. It was draining and frustrating.

It seemed unfair that there was this much chaotic growth within eyesight of the most manicured gardens in the world. Some serious oversight there. At this rate she was going to be a small mushroom cloud on the side of the mountain when the Underground detonated her before she had time to do anything. Still, no alternatives presented themselves. There had to be something hidden in the undergrowth, and she had to find it or she was going to be strawberry jam and a mild seismic reading in a handful of hours.

She'd just got on her hands and knees to crawl through a rabbit tunnel in the brambles when she heard someone calling out for help.

"Help. . . . Help." The voice had a desultory element to it, as if its owner had read somewhere in a survival manual that you were supposed to do this but wasn't expecting actual results.

Cyprin, as a rule, did not walk toward danger unless it came in a cocktail glass, but she recognized the voice and could not resist basking in some schadenfreude. With a lot of effort, broken branches, and fallen leaves, she managed to stand up, head turning like a radar dish.

The voice gave her a direction to go in, and she went. Cyprin burst through the undergrowth with a crash and a grunt and emerged in a little clearing where the only way farther up the mountain was to scale a short rock wall.

Purcell was clinging to the rock face halfway up, with a mess of ropes and crampons all around her. She'd got to around shoulder height. And, holy guacamole, the outfit she was wearing made her look like a cross between a cheerleader and a safari guide, which was far too close to a recent fantasy Cyprin had been having.

"You're kidding me," said Cyprin, trying to look tough with her arms crossed while she grinned.

Purcell turned around very slowly and carefully, her foot dislodging a rain of shale that scattered downhill around Cyprin. "What are *you* doing here? Did you follow me?"

"Oh, I've got better things to do than follow you, believe me," said Cyprin. She'd been smiling at the scene, but her smile faded. Purcell was here and she was going to get badly underfoot, like a cat in a kitchen. "What's wrong with you? Why don't you jump down?"

"I can't. I—I'm stuck. And you didn't tell me why you're here. You should be out there being head gardener. You *are* head gardener now." At that last bit, Purcell's face screwed up like she'd just sucked a lemon.

Cyprin had to respect the short turnaround time from sheepishness to accusation. And the acknowledgment of her new position was like a warm bath. "Yes, I am head gardener. I just sorted out all your mess. Approved all those requests on your desk—you're a nightmare."

"You what? You're ruining everything!" The anger! If Purcell wasn't glued to the rock face, she would surely be launching herself at Cyprin.

"I'm here on a mission from God." Cyprin smiled, mercilessly. "And you're here defying his orders."

"I'm on a mission too." Purcell's fingers slipped and she squealed.

"You're not." Cyprin drew closer, arms crossed, not committed to helping yet.

One big jump and a haul up top, and Purcell would be over the worst of it. Cyprin contemplated climbing past her, just to prove a point.

"What are you wearing? I can see your . . . your everything." Purcell was ogling, no mistaking it. She had the best eyes for ogling. And for that matter, the best feet for stamping, and the best squeaky little voice for yelling.

Cyprin shrugged, quite satisfied with the level of shameless eyeing she was getting. "You've seen it before."

"Somehow it's worse with that fabric *clinging* everywhere."

It was a fair point. She treated Purcell to a wasplike stare. "Do you want help, or not? Because it's sounding like you don't, and you know, I'd like to get on with my day." The offer of help came out almost against Cyprin's will, but hey, if Purcell never made it off this mountain, she'd never get to discover everything Cyprin had done in her office.

"Yes, please. If you could get up top and lower me a rope? Here, you can have some of my equipment if you didn't bring your own."

Cyprin came right up to the rock wall. She was close enough to smell Purcell now, and Purcell's marshmallow scent smacked her in the face. Maybe Purcell ate them every day. Just shoved them in that little mouth by the fistful. "Jump and I'll catch you." Cyprin spread her arms out wide. She was going to help, but she didn't have to be nice about it.

Purcell's mouth flattened into a thin, angry line. "You're making fun of me. And anyway, even though you've been out there in the gardens, ruining my life, I'm not going down. I'm going up."

"It looks like you're not going anywhere."

Having an audience seemed to be just the kick in the ass Purcell needed. She turned back to face the rock wall and scrambled up it with all the grace of a hamster, stubby arms and legs wheeling.

"Purcell! Just go back and I won't tell anyone I saw you here!"

But Purcell was already stomping up the grassy rise toward the next clump of trees, acting like she couldn't hear.

"Purcell!" The last thing Cyprin needed was that stuck-up do-gooder getting in the way. The clock was ticking in her abdomen, and she didn't need any more distractions. With a huff of irritation, Cyprin took the miniature cliff in two frog-legged strides. She jogged up the grass and Purcell upped her scurry speed, disappearing into the next section of jungle.

Cyprin crashed in after Purcell, putting on her most serious voice. "You're here to find new flowers, aren't you? That research project God said you were on? Trust me, you don't know what you're walking into. Go home, Purcell. I mean it. Find flowers somewhere else."

Somehow Purcell managed to go faster without running, like a professional walker hitting full stride. They were in the thick of the undergrowth now, and the overgrowth seemed to be leaning in all around them too. Cyprin was getting slapped by every vine and leaf, but for some reason nothing touched Purcell. Still, with twigs in Cyprin's bodysuit and cuts across her arms and face, she managed to get close enough to snag the back of Purcell's shirt. Purcell spun around, her cheeks pinking in anger.

"You want it all for yourself, don't you? The pageant, God, my fucking job! And now you're out here following me because I've got a lead on something else that you want! How can you be so entitled?"

It was like conversing with a swarm of bees. Cyprin let go of Purcell's shirt. She looked for words but, shockingly, couldn't find any, which turned out to be fine, because Purcell wasn't finished.

"I'll give you one chance, Cyprin. Let me have this. Turn around, leave the island. I don't even want to win the pageant anymore. The gold lanyard is yours. And you can keep my job. Hells, I'll even tell everyone that sculpture in the gardens was really yours." Purcell's face contorted with sudden fervor. "I want to develop a new species. I want to do something bigger than me. Create something that will outlive me. Take all the rest, I don't care. But if you take this, I promise you all-out war."

The vines closest to Purcell had become live noodles. The ends of their runners swayed from side to side like little heads preparing to strike, and then they reared up, pointing directly at Cyprin. Maybe the island did have some defense mechanisms after all. It had certainly noticed them now. Or noticed Cyprin anyway, which seemed unfair. She wasn't the one yelling.

Cyprin lifted her hands in a gesture of surrender. "I'm sorry. I can't do that. I have to be here. It's nothing personal, I swear."

A visible wrestling match happened behind Purcell's eyes. Purcell was so exasperated Cyprin thought the woman might fly at her in a petite, marshmallow-scented rage. And she was close enough to lick, which probably—definitely—wasn't a good idea.

Purcell turned beet red and walked away, and inexplicably, the plants around Cyprin, the ones that had felt claustrophobically close before, genuinely did close in, wrapping around her like chains, standing on all sides like woody bars. She was stuck there, in a jail made of trees.

CHAPTER 21

SAUL

Saul's time was running out, and he could not rely on Cyprin. He had done this to himself. Manipulating Cyprin, wanting Cyprin to like him—he'd tried to do two incompatible things and had failed at both. He had a pang about the lie he'd told her. Maverick's death. The truth was, he had no idea who Maverick was and had done nothing to find out. But he knew all about the never-closing wounds left by missing persons. If someone had told him the same thing about his parents, had manufactured closure for him, his life might have changed. Been better.

But now Cyprin was heading off up the mountain and he had no idea if she was doing it for him or herself. If she found something up there that could break the world, would she bring it back and use it to save him? Or would she burn the city down with it?

He supposed it didn't matter.

His life was in his own hands, as it had always been. And he was finally going to do something with it.

Saul swept into the staff library, where Gary was thumbing through a book on fashion, his back turned to the door.

"I'll need that key again," said Saul.

Gary turned around. "Oh, hi, Roman. I'm sorry, someone really ought to have sorted a key out for you by now. I don't think I can lend you—"

Saul raised the energy weapon. Its nose shook. "The key, Gary."

Gary's mouth made a hard line, but he unclipped a key from a bunch hanging around his waist and handed it over. When he was about to drop it into Saul's outstretched hand, he reached his other hand out for the gun instead, and Saul flinched, but not quickly enough. Gary flicked a little lever. "You'll want the safety off," he said.

Saul's hand closed around the key. The nose of the gun lowered. "Why are you helping me?"

"There are kids down there," said Gary. "Most of them have never seen the light of day. If I did something about that, they'd know it was me. Hells, they'd probably even catch me just thinking about it. But you . . . maybe you could do something."

Not just a kid. *Kids.* This was worse than he'd expected.

"You're with the Underground?" said Saul.

"No, you are." They stared at each other for a moment. "Aren't you?"

Saul straightened up. "I'm the Great Petaled Divine." He turned and stalked out of the room before he could think better of this whole enterprise, and his priestguard robes swished behind him in an acceptably dramatic way.

Saul went down the elevator again. The doors were still there, but they weren't locked anymore. He opened Room 106, Roman's old room, and it was filled floor to ceiling with boxes. He tore one open and found . . . toothpaste?

Saul went into his old room, discovering more boxes, this time packed with toilet paper. He kicked a stack of them in frustration, and they fell over. A bit of orange fluff on the floor caught his eye, and he bent down and rescued a stuffed toy from under the crush of cardboard. It was a hamburger, with legs and arms and eyes, and it looked well loved. It had never belonged to Saul. He would remember something like that. All he'd had was Gus the rat.

So there *had* been a child down here—multiple children, according to Gary. Replacement divines? And where had they gone? Saul slid down the wall, the burger doll clutched to his chest. The world was getting bigger, and he was shrinking. Shrinking to the size of an ant. His heel caught on the edge of a raised square on the floor.

Saul got onto his hands and knees, his left hand squashing the burger doll's face into the floor. He eyeballed the edges of a square panel. Some kind of trapdoor? Or just a patched bit of linoleum? It was so flush with the floor you almost couldn't tell it was there. When he pressed down on it, there was a little give, so little it might have been his imagination. He tried to prize the edge up with his fingers, but only broke a few fingernails with the effort. If it was a hatch, it wasn't designed to be opened from this side.

Saul beat the shit out of that patch of floor. He began by firing the energy weapon at it, which fried the overlay of linoleum but wasn't enough to cut through the steel below. In the end, he sledgehammered it with the butt of his gun until the warm metal folded inward. Sparse rungs led downward, into the utter, utter dark. Saul left the damaged gun behind and climbed in.

At the bottom was a small tiled room. A plain metal chair faced a mirrored wall. A cup full of coffee dregs and drowned cigarette butts smelled so like Roman that Saul's fingers twitched like he was five years old and hadn't yet realized Roman would never hold his hand.

Saul walked up to the mirrored wall and pressed his forehead against it.

Through the smoked-out glass he could see a warehousey space honeycombed with dozens of cubicles, open at the top but walled off from each other. Inside the cubicles, children of various ages wore petal mail and big tippy crowns. Saul couldn't hear what any of them were saying, but he could recognize the gestures of the Salutation Ceremony.

There was a door from here to there, and a set of corrugated iron stairs that led downward. Saul made his way down.

A dream. He was in a dream. None of this could possibly be real. He kept missing steps and almost falling. He should turn around now, go back out, find Amanda, and tell the Underground everything, and maybe, just maybe, he'd survive. But the burger toy had made it back into his hand again somehow, and Saul kept walking down.

At the bottom was a dim hallway. Saul let himself into the first door he passed. The room was a blank brown square. A child not much more than a toddler was in there, all tousled hair and snot nose, and they climbed up onto the bed on the far side of the room as if height was some manner of defense.

"How dare you raise your eyes to me!" the kid screamed. "I am your God!"

"I'm not here to hurt you," said Saul. "I'm going to get you out of here."

"Get on your knees and beg my forgiveness, blasphemer!" But the end of that sentence lost power as the child spotted the fluffy burger doll in Saul's hand.

Saul edged closer and then knelt down by the side of the bed and offered up the toy. "Would you like to take care of this for me?"

"You will pay for this insolence—Really?" Sticky little hands snatched the toy away.

"Come on," said Saul. "Follow me." He went out and opened the next door down.

This child was older—ten, maybe.

"You're not Roman!"

"Roman sent me in his stead. I'm Saul. And this is—" He looked down at the small child beside him.

"The Great Petaled Divine."

Both children stared nails at each other.

"I am the Great Petaled Divine," said the older child.

Saul's heart was flipping around like a fish. "We're all the Great Petaled Divine. Come on, everyone with me."

He opened another door.

"Forehead to the floor, reckless nonbelievers!" said a buck-toothed boy who'd ripped the corners of his petal mail to shreds.

A tense moment happened where the kids all eyeballed each other. "Quickly now," said Saul.

He managed quite well until he had a train of thirty or so of them and could no longer account for the one or two who must have slipped away.

Thick smoke began to curl around Saul's ankles and rise. Some of the children started crying. Priestguard appeared at either end of the hall.

Of course he was never going to make it. He should have known better by now and retired all the bouts of reckless optimism.

"I'm unarmed," said Saul. He raised his hands, he got onto his knees, and he felt not the sting of defeat but the sick pride of finally having been brave enough to do something.

The priestguard threw a hood over his head, held his arms securely behind his back, and pushed him back into the elevator. Saul was dragged upstairs and then bundled into the throne room.

And then . . . and then nothing.

It seemed impossible that there should be no consequences after that, but he supposed they had let him go all the other times. Though *let him go* was generous—they had put him back in his cage. All those poor children down there, little Petaled Divines, fated to follow in his footsteps, or worse. What happened to the surplus Divines, the ones who weren't needed?

Saul changed into and out of his priestguard robes, tempted to make a break for it, but what if that was what they wanted? An anonymous moving target running across the palace grounds? No, they could come for him on his terms.

Saul was sipping tea in the Mint Throne Room when he heard a polite knock at the doors. He sat up stiffly, a cup halfway to his face. "Just a moment."

This was his rarest leaf. Grown only in the climate-controlled greenhouses of Asperia, only one in a thousand Holy Hemlock plants made it to maturity. Unlike other varieties of hemlock, this one wasn't poisonous, but it did have a mild psychotropic effect, making the user unnaturally calm, regardless of circumstance. The tea itself was a pale yellow and smelled like mouse wee. But it didn't taste too bad. A little spicy and rooty. It had been a good choice. The shakes had stopped after his second cup. After his third, he'd felt nothing but clarity.

His birthday and the end of the Divine life cycle were still a handful of days away, but his time was done. Saul had known this day would come. Really, the end had been coming his whole life, the countdown going faster every time he questioned the way things were, every time he snooped around or didn't put on a convincing enough performance as God. But the day he'd named Cyprin as head gardener, he'd felt himself overstepping an invisible line, and he'd known it was only a matter of time before They came for him. Tonight, he'd doomed himself with this failed rescue operation.

Saul put his tea down again carefully, stood up, and adjusted the fake plastic petal mail Cyprin had bought for him. It was the only gift he'd ever been given. He wondered if she'd realized that. He picked the gold Trellis Crown up from its resting place on the floor and positioned it on his head. Outside, the dual moons were right there, as if taking a peek into his throne room.

He hoped Cyprin would never come back. That seemed like a possibility after their last interaction, though, deep down, he knew it was a remote one.

No, she would return with whatever she found on the mountain, and They'd be waiting for her. Perhaps They'd be waiting too obviously, and she'd spot Them in time to do . . . something.

He couldn't save Cyprin. She would have to do that herself.

It was time to live life on his own terms for one fleeting moment.

Saul opened the throne-room doors. "Hello, Roman."

Roman leaned against the wall in the hallway, his arms crossed and a hard look on his face. Something in it softened when he saw Saul. At Roman's signal, a team of six priestguard put down their handheld battering ram and left. Saul stepped aside to let Roman into the throne room, and Roman closed the doors.

"I was hoping it wouldn't come to this." Roman still wore his customary priestguard-colored tracksuit. One of the sleeves showed signs of fray, and Saul wondered if it had been the same tracksuit all these years. "I've been watching you, you know. You seemed to have a pretty good life: a couple of hobbies, a girl who cared about you."

It didn't escape Saul's notice that Roman was talking in the past tense, and the horror must have shown on his face, because Roman said, "I'm going to give you a choice, son. And I want you to think carefully about it. I'll give you the whole truth, right here, right now, and that's where it all ends. Or you make me a promise that you'll forget about the things you saw today, the things you've learned, and we'll both go on like this never happened. They'll kill you in your sleep when you turn forty-two. It'll be painless. You won't even know." A note of desperation entered Roman's eyes. "Please."

Saul had been ready to give it all up plenty of times before. What did the truth matter anyway if it only bought more emptiness? Another few days of comfort and a gentle exit tempted him. But Roman seemed to mistake Saul's introspection for hesitation, and added, fatally, "I put so much time and effort into you. Into making you the Divine. Why would you waste any of that?"

All those children down there, queued up to repeat the same sad life that Saul had. The Seed that Cycles Forever, ha. It wasn't far wrong. He couldn't get back his own years of loneliness, but maybe he could do something to stop the same thing happening to those kids if he understood why this was happening, what it was all for.

Saul said, "I want the truth." He'd been wrong about freedom. It wasn't only about space. It was about time as well, and no matter where Saul went, who he pretended to be, a part of him was trapped in the past with a man in a red tracksuit who never had a kind word for him, never had a hand to hold. "What happened to my parents?"

Roman regarded him with a look of mingled pride and pity. His eyes might have been watering a little when he broke Saul's gaze and looked out over the balcony. "You know, it's a fantastic view you have. You can almost see the whole gardens from here."

"My parents," said Saul.

"You never had a mother. Not really. It was a donor egg, deidentified. You were a lab baby."

Saul breathed out, and it was like letting go of a breath he'd held for more than thirty years.

"And my father?"

"Donor sperm . . . from me."

"*You're* my father?" The world filled with black dots. Saul stumbled and held onto the back of the throne.

"I was a conduit," said Roman. "For you, and the other gods."

"The others?" Saul echoed, but his words had no bearing on what was being said; the narrative was a runaway train now.

Roman turned, concern written all over his face. "I am the head of the priestguard, and when my time is over, my second-in-command will succeed me to father a new generation of Divines. The priestguard were founded after the first of us discovered the terraforming object on the mountain. We created the cyclical system of Divines to hide the terraforming object, and in turn we shield the Divines. It's a selfless duty, for the Kingdom, to keep safe what is rightfully ours. The Divine moves through me. Through me the seed cycles endlessly."

"No," said Saul. "No."

"I taught you the ways of the Divine. I hold the reigns of Verdure's economy. I keep the iron fist of the priestguard strong. Do you understand, Saul?"

Saul pushed away from the throne, stumbled again, walked drunkenly out toward the balcony. The calming tea wasn't enough, not for this. He didn't know whether he was seeking air or escape, and maybe it didn't matter. It was the same thing.

"You have been my greatest triumph. You sat the throne at twelve and gave us thirty years of peaceful rule," said Roman.

"Rule? I don't rule anything—this is a prison!" Saul stopped backing away.

"I love you, my son." His eyes looked genuine, but then, they always had.

"You don't know what love is. You never touched me, never comforted me!" Saul rushed forward and embraced Roman, squeezed until he heard Roman wheeze. It was a hug and an attack all at once. It was love and violence.

They were out on the balcony, and Saul wasn't heavy, but he was tall. Roman struggled in the wrap of Saul's arms, and they teetered, so close to the balcony railing. The polished marble squeaked desperately underfoot, and the stars wheeled above them.

Saul held his father.

There was a rush of air and then silence.

CHAPTER 22

PURCELL

Purcell stood with her hands on her hips and surveyed the last few feet of mountain. It was a clear, cool afternoon, with the sun sinking low on the horizon. She could breathe freely now that she was alone.

The words *awkward* and *unrequited* had no business in Purcell's love life. She preferred *intimidating* and *aloof.* Purcell wanted Cyprin but was *not* going to pursue her. She was not even going to think about Cyprin again, it was all beneath her (Cyprin beneath her? Aaahh!), and those rocks to the left certainly didn't look anything like Cyprin's behind in that ridiculous jumpsuit.

Purcell took her time going up the final slope, weaving between cold muddy pools and stepping carefully over mossy earth. Her emotions began to settle, and she slowly got back into the calm, methodical state that was Purcell Working with Plants.

On a table-shaped slab of igneous rock, she arranged her specimen collection tools and jars in size order and then according to function.

She was going to find and collect the iridescent blue flower she'd seen a sign of in the lake, oh, she was, she was. But she wasn't about to ignore everything else. And Cyprin was safely detained; there had been no sign of her for hours. With any luck the plants had scared her off and she was skulking back to the palace to play at being head gardener.

Purcell hummed as she scraped a bit of moss into a jar. With the total absorption of a kid making sandcastles, she pottered around, collecting specimens. Here an interesting cutting of alpine herbs, there some lichen or a tiny purple flower underfoot. Purcell's specimen collection jars clicked together to form an unstable tower in her arms. This was exactly what she needed. This was where the world shifted into place and all the ugly betrayals—Amma, God, Amanda, Cyprin—faded out of the foreground.

Slowly, Purcell's meandering led her up to the top of the mountain. A blue glow reflected off her shoes, the same alarming shade as an energy weapon or a very hot flame. The jars she'd been carrying went down on the ground, and she raised her head, shielding her eyes with an elbow.

The mountain peak held an old crater about the size of a football field. Right in the middle of the dimple left by the mouth of the old volcano was a glowing blue rose. It had its head cocked to the sky. Only a single flower. The scent it gave off was the sickly sweet of rotting fruit. The air above it shimmered like an oil slick. Strange sounds emanated from the plant, a distorted symphony.

Purcell had known in her bones that there was something like this up there. Triumph crackled through her. Her mind was vividly conjuring the future gardens studded with the flower's descendants. Possible names for it like Purcell's Glory or Purcell's Perfection. It would be almost unfair to show a specimen like this at the flower pageant, but maybe she would have a display area separate from the judging arena, where people could come and congratulate her on the find. With a flower like this, no one would ever mention Amma's name again.

Purcell went to get her equipment. It took so long to lug up the special climate-controlled case that the sun was a faint yolky memory by the time she got back to the rose. But she'd seen the way its petal had dissolved in the lake, and she wasn't taking any chances.

She dug around in the soil under the plant, but the root system seemed to go on forever. The flower itself was mature, though, a luminous marvel, chock-full of healthy, viable seeds.

Purcell took time lining up her tools, making everything orderly, calm. It did trouble her that there was only a single bloom. To remove it for her own personal needs seemed a little like sacrilege. But needs must, and, as God himself had said, flowers grow again.

The blue rose hummed with a sound like faraway singing. Purcell took out her clippers. They flashed in the bioluminescent light.

She made the cut.

The world dropped into darkness.

CHAPTER 23

CYPRIN

As soon as Cyprin pulled the vines off, they wound around some other part of her. Scooting around one tree left another inexplicably in her path. After this, the concept of sentient plants was going to haunt her in the wee hours of every night. Even if these ones *were* engineered to protect the island, it was going to change the way she looked at daisies and legumes for the rest of her life. No more salads, that was for sure. Everything would have to be cut up and cooked.

The plants put up a solid fight. She had to climb over a brace of trees that clasped branches together like players in a rugby scrum. At the top, a large and stinky flower spat stinging pollen in her face. One enterprising vine had even tied her shoelaces together, as she found out when she faceplanted into the ground. Cyprin snapped stems with her bare hands, kicked trunks, even bit leaves to get free.

Finally, finally, she made it past the worst of it, and the jungle opened out to an alpine environment. A few little shrubs tore at her ankles, but they didn't have much luck stopping her. Cyprin looked up at a clear night sky and, shadowed against it, the mountain peak. A small blue glow alighted on her arm, and she smacked at it, feeling guilty when it dropped and sputtered out on the ground. Then the sky was full of them, tiny fireflies on fragile wings. It was lovely. One of them went up Cyprin's nose and she coughed until it landed wetly in the palm of her hand. A blanket of creeping thyme stopped savaging her boots, its blooms stuttering with a sudden flash of purple as it hurried to join the light show. The land around her lit up into a neon fairyland, with the intensity of a thousand pachinko machines.

It was impossible that she'd never noticed this, even during her brief time in the gardens. It was the kind of light that would make you put foil over the windows. Cyprin looked back toward the gardens, but the view was obscured by the mountain's constant halo of clouds.

The light show colored Cyprin in shades of confetti. This was all lovely and everything, but right now, up there somewhere, Purcell was probably sticking her finger in a terraforming machine that was about to suck her in bone by bone like a leaf mulcher. Someone had to save her from herself. Nobody understood that quite like Cyprin.

Cyprin, who had turned her whole life into a monument to pointless revenge. Cyprin, whose desperation to impress first Maverick and then Saul had done nothing but land her in hot water. She'd thought she'd been in control with Saul, that she was impressing him purely for her own gain, but somewhere along the way she had slipped and grown to care for him—maybe not the *right* way but in the only way Cyprin knew.

She didn't know what manner of thing had fueled Purcell's win-or-die campaign, but it must have been a doozy. Real juicy trauma could wind you up like a mechanical toy so that you spent your whole life shooting off in a direction you had no say in.

Sore, hungry, tired, and very angry, Cyprin kept on heading up the mountain. The peak wasn't far away now, but thanks to the plants delaying her, neither was her impending explosion. She had whatever was left of tonight and that was it. *Tick, tick.*

An old crater took up the peak of the mountain, the lip cragged with sheared-off obsidian. Cyprin struggled up the side of it and stopped. Down in the dusty bowl before her, a celestial blue glow drew her eye.

This was no terraforming machine. It was a flower. The most incredible flower she had ever seen. The first thought she had was *God is real.* For a moment, there wasn't space for any other thoughts. Saul's face, with its kindly librarian eyes, smiled across her consciousness. Did he really make the sun rise in the morning? Had he known this was up here? Had he sent her to make her believe? But no, that didn't seem right. Not after he'd gone to such lengths to explain his predicament, to explain that he wasn't God, he was just Saul. So, this was a machine that didn't look like a machine, then?

A false God, a fake sacred site with a weird artifact in it, strange shadow people pulling all the strings, a freedom-fighting organization just as likely to help an old lady cross the street as put a bomb in Cyprin's stomach. It was almost enough to make her want to go back to the apples. At least apples were just apples.

The sky above the mountain hazed in the oil slick colors of a very localized aurora. The air was thick and smelled faintly of cherry liqueur. The distant sound of music seemed to float in and out, as if peeling back the world here would reveal a heavenly choir. Cyprin was supposed to report this back to Saul and the Underground, but she wasn't sure how. She couldn't take back a story. They'd never believe this. She'd have to take pictures, maybe a sample? But touching the blue rose felt wrong. No, she'd just get close enough to have a good look.

She was over the rim of the crater and walking down when a rocky shadow resolved itself into Purcell. This raised considerable annoyance but did not raise any alarms. Despite Purcell's meddlesome nature, Cyprin was kind of glad to see her again. It meant that she didn't have to maybe explode alone. A machine with a big red button, sure, Purcell would wreak havoc with something like that, but this was a plant. Plants were Purcell's life. She wouldn't do anything to harm it . . . would she?

The blades in Purcell's hand flashed in the glowing air. Cyprin tipped into a run. "Purcell! Purcell, wait! You don't know what—"

The clippers clacked.

The sounds of the airborne choir cut out. The lights of the other flowers, the fireflies, the glowing air, winked out block by block like a power-grid failure, and the ghostly blue flower in Purcell's hand turned into a lifeless stem as its petals phased out of existence one by one.

Drawn by strings of horror, Cyprin turned slowly and looked out over the ring of clouds. The city was visible from the lip of the crater. In the distance, the bright boil of Asperia flared impossibly brilliant, then went out. Blue afterimages haunted her vision. A sudden noise in the silence scared Cyprin until she realized it was her own breath, hyperventilating. Even the sky was dark. No sign of the stars, and the dual moons that usually hung over the land had gone missing. She waited for the lights to come back on. And waited and waited. For a moment she was even able to convince herself she'd gone suddenly blind.

"Cyprin? I can't see anything," said Purcell.

Cyprin had never heard her name sound so watery with uncertainty. A tremor of fear and rage shook her. Purcell bumbling up here, messing with things just because they existed, had doomed Cyprin to a very short existence indeed. She was going to go out with a bang—Ha. People always said that like it was a positive thing.

"Cyprin, I think I've done something bad," Purcell bleated in the dark.

Cyprin's legs folded under her, and she sat down exactly where she'd been standing. Whatever *this* was, her heart told her it had nothing to do with priests and politics and the Underground. Purcell had destroyed it, and with it, any hope of Cyprin's salvation. Although maybe, maybe, if Cyprin had got to it first, she would have destroyed it too. Maybe they'd both sealed its fate the moment they stepped onto this island. But she wasn't feeling charitable enough for that thought yet. This was all Purcell's fault.

"Cyprin?" There was the muffled thud of a stubbed toe. Purcell was trying to make her way over blind.

"Put it back!" Cyprin called out. "Can't you put it back?"

"I've tried."

"It's a machine, isn't it?"

"What? No. It's a flower, and I've killed it." A tremor shook Purcell's voice. Well, at least she was showing remorse.

Had the city really gone dark out there? If that were true, it would be chaos. People lost in their own apartment buildings, trapped underground, wandering the streets blindly until the sun came up. Would the sun come up? Images of Saul clutching his chest and keeling over as Purcell cut the rose's stem danced through Cyprin's thoughts. No, no it wasn't going to happen like that. Saul was just a man. Terraforming object, the Underground had said. Nothing to do with the sun. The lights, they . . . they were just part of the ecosystem. All the city lights ran on mycelial networks. When Purcell had snipped the flower off it must have done something to the plant life. Though . . . though that didn't explain where the moons and stars had gone. The air felt colder too. Maybe it had always been the flower that was in control of the environment here. It might have been old tech like the bio bots. It might have been something else entirely.

Purcell's clammy hand whacked Cyprin in the side of the ear, then scrabbled to hold on. "The moons and stars are gone, did you notice that? There was a rumor that a long period of darkness happened in my great-great-grandma Amma's time. She saved the roses during it, and—do you think this could be the same thing? She should've left me a guide! Why didn't she leave me a guide? *I* would have left me a guide!"

Purcell kept on rambling, but Cyprin was barely listening. They were going to have to get down from the mountain in the full dark, and—oh fuck—the bomb in Cyprin's stomach was going to explode for sure. Cyprin rolled away from Purcell's grip and got to her feet.

Purcell clutched at her arm. "If we can get down to my bag, I've got a battery-operated flashlight in there, and if that doesn't work, some matches."

"There's no we. I'm going to go and tell the Divine about this. You do whatever you want." She should've let Saul in on everything. Who did she think she was, trying to protect him? Cyprin couldn't even protect herself.

There was absolutely nothing to see by. Cyprin staggered a few steps and then tripped over.

"Oh, thank you, thank you," said Purcell, somewhere off to Cyprin's left.

"Are you talking to yourself?" That was all she needed, Purcell going batty.

"The plants are . . . pushing me in the direction I ought to go."

In Cyprin's head, two plus two added up to make seventeen. "That was *you* back there, making the jungle attack me!"

"I don't *make* them do anything. I just . . . have a knack for talking to plants, and sometimes they like to help out. Don't tell anyone, okay?"

"*What? How?* Is it biotech? It's biotech, isn't it! I knew you made the grass trip me up at that party!" Why did Purcell deserve plant magic on top of everything else? It was hideously unfair.

Purcell fell uncharacteristically silent. The sudden clink of stones suggested she was walking away. *Fine. Whatever.*

Cyprin scanned the darkness for anything to orient herself by. Her eyes had already begun adding an illusory overlay of random colors and shapes. It wasn't good. She got on hands and knees and began crawling over the moss and rough stones. At this rate it was going to be a long time before she got down off this mountain. She'd probably explode on the way. And what did that matter? Her chances of finding the Underground and being able to give them a story they found useful were slim to none if all the lights had gone out. The undercity would be terrifying . . . well, more terrifying than usual.

Purcell's flashlight shone right in Cyprin's eyes. "I'm not leaving you here. You have to come with me."

"Oh, you were fine with leaving me in your tree cage earlier!" Cyprin was fuming, but her head moved to follow the beam of light as the flashlight swung away.

"I would have come back for you when I was finished. You really think I'd leave you here to die?" The telescopic lens over Purcell's right eye made her look chameleonesque. Her attention had a subtle undercurrent to it that made Cyprin feel like Purcell really gave a shit. Instead of being pinned, Cyprin felt *seen*, which was new. She wondered if this was what Purcell's plants felt like when they were being studied or cared for.

"I don't know." A lie. Cyprin had been so sure Purcell would leave her.

"For your information, I wouldn't leave anyone to die. But especially you. You're a worthy opponent. If you hadn't entered the flower pageant, I'd still be going through the motions. Winning without trying. Every day, waking up and growing things without growing myself." Purcell's face was glowing, ecstatic, off on an almost-religious tirade of self-aggrandizement.

All positive feelings for Purcell evaporated into thin air. It was unwise to antagonize her only hope of getting down off the mountain. Cyprin did it anyway. "I'm a self-improvement tool, am I? The plucky kid from the city who made you get off your laurels and actually do something for a minute, huh? Showed you your own greatness, did I? Your wasted potential?"

"I'm glad you agree." Purcell's face, shadowed behind the flashlight like she was about to tell a ghost story, showed no hint of irony. Either she meant it or Cyprin should never, ever play poker with her.

Cyprin managed to tear her eyes away from Purcell. "Whatever, let's go," she said.

Purcell offered a hand, gleaming sweaty in the glare of the flashlight. Cyprin's stomach twisted as she thought about taking it.

"I am not holding your hand."

"Suit yourself." Purcell walked off, and the shrubs around her feet gently nudged her away from rocks and debris. Cyprin stomped along close behind with nothing helping her at all, rolling her ankle a couple of times and getting bogged in deep patches of mud. It was dark. It was so dark, in a way that it never was in the city. The stars and moons being gone didn't disturb her nearly as much as the lack of light pollution. Even in the darkest parts of the city, there was always something: the standby light of a TV, the glow of a phone or cigarette butt. Even the undercity had its vending machines and the unblinking lights of dormant AIs.

After ten minutes or so of following Purcell, Cyprin's heart rate had slowed enough that she no longer felt like she had swallowed a bird. Now that the fear had gone down, the anger was rising. And Purcell—Purcell was picking her way down the mountain, a ditzy forest fairy, the plants holding her hands and pointing out the safest way. Purcell, who seemed to act as though she had a birthright to the position of head gardener, Purcell who had a special affinity with plants and the total conviction that she had earned everything herself. Purcell who was so undeniably hot and mean. It all gave Cyprin a sick feeling, as if she'd overeaten chocolate cake. She had to say something about Purcell's insufferable privilege, about her hotness, anything. But that would only make things worse. She had to stick close to Purcell, because Purcell had the light, and not because Purcell's peachy little behind looked like a snack. Best stay quiet so that they could get this over with as quickly and painlessly as possible.

"I know you killed my roses," said Purcell, smugly, striding ahead. She didn't even look back over her shoulder.

Cyprin's blood boiled. She fought down an urge to bite. "They weren't your roses. They belonged to the gardens. And last I heard they weren't dead, not completely."

Purcell thanked a tree branch for sweeping some loose rocks out of the way. It didn't escape Cyprin's notice that the same tree flung the rocks back into her path. Why the fuck were they helping Purcell?

"That didn't give you the right to steal them," said Purcell.

Which was fair, actually. Or so close to being fair that it looked like the same thing. Cyprin was almost prepared to shut up and simmer down, when Purcell said, "I knew I did the right thing when I told Amanda not to hire you."

"I'm sorry—what?" Cyprin had heard perfectly well, but she wanted to see if hearing it twice would make her twice as furious. That little shit. Cyprin wanted to twist Purcell's arm until she squealed.

Purcell stopped and turned around. "I told Amanda not to hire you, after *you* turned up for your interview looking like you'd done your makeup with your eyes closed."

The leaves of the plants nearest to Purcell rustled like laughing schoolyard bullies.

Cyprin lost it. All the pressure, all the feelings that had been building inside her since she'd got to the gardens snapped like a high-tensile wire. "I'm gonna kill you."

To Cyprin's surprise, Purcell smirked and said, "Go ahead and try," in that mad-Chihuahua, slightly toxic, slightly attractive manner she seemed to have taken on recently. God, Cyprin wanted to kiss Purcell open-eyed and hating. Forget cliché, lovey-dovey emotions—there was nothing more real than the ones that nipped and chafed, and Purcell was an endless fount of those.

Cyprin ran at Purcell with absolutely no clue what she was going to do when she made contact. She wasn't the violent type; it was usually enough to just look like she could be, with her punk outfits and knuckle-dusters. But this was different. Something in Cyprin had an urge to see Purcell in the dirt. She had an itch for the kind of protoviolence that made five-year-olds push other five-year-olds over on the playground. Purcell had been handed everything she could've ever wanted in life and still found fault with it. She was the kind of person who would go to a dinner party empty-handed and then complain about the food. Cyprin thundered toward her.

Purcell started to look nervous, which was satisfying, but then a large-trunked tree pivoted into Cyprin's path at the last moment, and she hit it nose-first, seeing stars.

At first she thought she might have exploded, but then her blurred vision resolved into Purcell looking concerned, offering tissues from some obscure pocket of her pack to shove up Cyprin's bloodied nostrils.

Cyprin said, "Thank you." And then she grabbed Purcell's hand and yanked her onto the ground.

They rolled together in the dirt.

Cyprin was much ganglier than Purcell. She wrapped her limbs around Purcell and rolled them both away from the trees and into the open, where there was only the stony ground and a patch of moss that tickled Cyprin's forearm like a goldfish trying to bite. Purcell in her arms felt strangely right, like there were two ways this could go: one that involved choking Purcell until she tapped out and another where Cyprin kissed up all her little snarls.

She pinned Purcell to the ground and leaned over her. Cyprin's aversion to touch didn't seem to apply to Purcell. Normally she didn't like the intense feeling of being perceived that came with physical contact, but maybe what she disliked was being perceived *wrongly*. This was a communion of demons, and Purcell got that just fine. Cyprin growled, "Oh, your plants can't save you now."

Suddenly, Purcell's big watery eyes looked terrified in the light of the flashlight. Really, truly terrified. Cyprin had been about to snap her teeth in Purcell's face, but she hesitated. Purcell was clearly wet-her-pants-level scared. Cyprin had meant to rough her up a little, but this was too much. Was Cyprin really scary enough to—

With no warning, Purcell surged up and kissed her. Those soft lips, the weirdly comforting marshmallow scent, everything was like a warm bath. Cyprin ate it up for a second before she realized what she was doing.

Cyprin sprang back.

Purcell started babbling, pushing her glasses up her nose so thoroughly Cyprin was worried they were going to leave an imprint on her skull. "I misjudged!"

"Misjudged what—" Cyprin's reaction had been automatic, and she was still processing what happened. Purcell had *kissed* her. As the adrenaline subsided, it dawned on her. "Wait. You like me?" This came as a shock. She was too used to her crushes being one-sided. Oh, she'd thought Purcell was ogling her earlier, but the truth was she invented things like that. She hadn't thought it could be real. That the attraction went both ways.

"Oh, no, no I—" Purcell was backpedaling like a professional cyclist.

"You think I'm a likeable person." A slow smile crept across Cyprin's face. She was thoroughly enjoying this, but also was deflecting to humor. Making fun of someone else's feelings was a defense mechanism. If everyone was laughing their feelings off all the time, there'd be no more acute disappointments.

Purcell tried on an anger that didn't reach her eyes. "You? You ruined my life, you—"

"Then why did you just try to kiss me?" The grin froze on Cyprin's face as she forcibly kept it there. Her heart was thundering. This was a joke. So why did she feel so nervous?

"I, I, don't know I—it was an accident!" Purcell's flustered denials were . . . weirdly endearing. She might be a shit, but she was fucking adorable. And she definitely liked Cyprin. No one had ever blushed and stammered like this in front of Cyprin before.

"Oh, an accident!" This was hilarious, but behind that was another feeling. Someone thought she was worth liking. Purcell, *Purcell* thought she was worth liking.

And maybe Saul had thought so too, before she'd broken his heart.

"Let's make a truce," Purcell said, and had her lips been that distracting before? "We'll go together to see the Divine. Suspend hostilities for the moment. It's only fair."

"So, when did you first catch feelings?" Cyprin tried to keep it casual as the pure terror of being liked lit up her veins.

"I didn't—I told you it was a mistake!" Purcell's voice went raspy.

"I bet it was at the pageant, wasn't it?" Cyprin's brain began conjuring a fantasy wherein Purcell fell head over heels the moment she'd lost first prize.

"I'm not talking about this." Purcell brushed dirt off her arms and started walking.

Cyprin skipped to catch up. "Do you write my name in your diary over and over with little love hearts on top of the *i*'s?" This was unexpectedly delicious, and she was going to revel in it, twisting it in her chest like a knife.

"I will not dignify that with a response." Purcell was breathing far harder than the walk warranted. She seemed flustered.

"Do you fill them in with a pink glitter pen?"

"Just shut up," said Purcell.

Cyprin grinned and tipped into a daydream where she and Purcell skipped across a field of marshmallows together. The edges of her eyes prickled with unexpected tears.

For the rest of the trip back down the mountain, Purcell was angry and silent, especially after Cyprin hummed the theme tune of *Lust Island* behind her back. But as time went by, Cyprin's thoughts kept tipping from cozy fantasy into cold panic. Fears of rejection began to twine around each other like snakes in her head. She always stressed out when anyone showed the faintest sign of caring about her, romantically or otherwise.

In the silence, there was nothing to stop the particulars of their situation presenting themselves like a lecture she couldn't get away from. The Divine, the Underground, they had been right. There *had* been something on this mountain, something tied to the Kingdom of Verdure's unnatural prosperity. And Purcell had broken it. Purcell with her apparent magical powers. Cyprin felt a sense of responsibility to report all this back to God, and a sense of self-preservation was telling her to report it back to the Underground as well.

But a dark part of her was excited to see what would happen next. Things couldn't go back to normal after this, and that was a relief. She was too much like Maverick now—it could only be a mercy if the whole world burned down with her in it.

Purcell liked her, but it didn't matter. Even before the Underground had put a bomb in her stomach, Cyprin had been rigged to self-destruct. There was nothing left that she wanted to preserve.

Viva la revolución, baby. Burn it all down.

They emerged from the inky nightmare of the lake after a long struggle in which Purcell insisted on carrying what was left of the rose across, holding it out of the water in one awkwardly raised hand. Purcell had given up keeping the rose in her bulky, hermetically sealed container, a small mercy. She'd just wrapped it in plastic to keep any loose seeds in with the stem and held it tightly in her sweaty little hand. It had dried up like it had already spent a hundred years pressed between pages, its petals gone. Cyprin didn't know what Purcell planned to do with it. It wasn't much to show anybody. Perhaps she thought she was going to grow it in a little pot somewhere.

In the gardens, they found people responding to the chaos of sudden darkness. Tiki torches were being punched into the grass and lit on fire. More priestguard than Cyprin had ever seen were arrayed like red dominoes across the lawns, close enough to each other that if you pushed one over you might start a cascade. They looked ready for war.

The palace windows flickered with soft candlelight. Without moons or stars, the sky seemed close enough to touch and gave off the unsettling illusion that it was getting closer.

Purcell checked over the flower, making sure what was left of it was dry and undamaged. Cyprin shivered off excess water and put her pack down on the shoreline. Well, the kiss had been grand, but it was time to stop playing nice. Time to make sure Purcell didn't get to speak to the Divine first. Without further ado, Cyprin sprinted for the palace.

"We agreed we'd go together!" Purcell's cupped hands made the sound carry strangely behind her. And then there was only the pound of Cyprin's feet on the ground and the *whum* of blood through her ears. She was trying to head to the palace as the crow flies, but there was too much stuff in the way. Cyprin leapt over an ornamental hedge. Dodged a couple of priestguard. One foot sploshed in a fishpond and she apologized to the shocked koi. The torches blurred past her in a cacophony of light and shadow, grass, flowers, and fire kaleidoscoping together.

But Purcell had a surprising turn of speed on her. She drew level with Cyprin, shook her head like an angry horse, and then peeled off, heading in the wrong direction. Purcell knew the Divine Gardens much, much more intimately than Cyprin, who could barely find the palace and the vegetable garden without getting lost. Cyprin jogged a couple of uncertain steps, then decided following was an obvious trap. She fixed the palace in the center of her vision and picked up the pace again.

A group of palace attendants in their customary white uniforms stared at Cyprin as she burst into the building, puffing and steaming in her ridiculous stealth suit. But she was recognizable enough, with her shaved head and death stare, and none of them tried to stop her when she ran up the stairs.

Candles had replaced all the lights from the mycelial network, and they made the stairs flicker in a way that suggested they were moving. Cyprin's wet feet slipped a few times, and she had to give in and hold onto the banister.

She got all the way up to God's hallway (which seemed to take more flights than she remembered), rehearsing what she was going to say. How she was going to drop Purcell in it and convince the Divine that he needed to cooperate with the Underground—needed to find *them* in this shitshow too. She'd been determined not to hand Saul over to them, but that was before the sky went dark and before so many hours had passed with a bomb in her stomach. Maybe Saul would even *want* to work with them, and he could come with Cyprin, and the Underground would be so pleased they'd take their bomb back. *Without anyone getting hurt.*

If only he really was God, then he could miracle the bomb out of her stomach and the moons back into the sky. Cyprin's foot skidded on some water in the hall. Wet little pockmarks tracked all the way along the corridor and into the Divine's throne room, where the big bronze doors were left ajar. She could hear voices inside, mumbling. Purcell had got there first.

CHAPTER 24

PURCELL

Purcell eased the throne-room doors open and cleared her throat to make herself known. Kissing Cyprin had been foolish, misguided. She couldn't let it stop her from doing what was right and royally screwing Cyprin over.

Drippy candles stood in mushroom clusters on the floor, flickering in a way that suggested Purcell had just walked into an anteroom of one of the twelve hells. The Divine was there, alone, sitting on the Mint Throne with his back to her, apparently mesmerized by the fathomless darkness beyond the balcony. At the sound of her he stood and turned. It wasn't Saul.

"Who are you?" This man's manicured eyebrows formed a downward slant toward his nose that made him look somehow both angry and surprised. Maybe he was. The resemblance to Saul was uncanny. If they'd stood together, she might have thought them brothers. But she would never mistake one for the other. Just like the roses in the gardens, they had their tells.

It didn't make sense. She'd known the Divine's life cycle was nearly over, but a fading Divine was always replaced by a child.

Purcell found her voice. "I'm head gardener." Well, damn it, she still was, wasn't she? "Purcell Whitlock."

"Ah yes, I remember," the pretender lied. "Downcast your eyes, Purcell."

Purcell looked at her feet, and the marble flickered, reflecting the candle flames. What in twelve hells was going on here?

"Thank you," said Saul's replacement. "Now, I'm going to have to call my priests in and have you pay penance, you know this. But as you are my head gardener, I take it you would not come in here unscheduled, eyes wandering, for anything less than an emergency, so I am prepared to hear you out first."

"Thank you, Divine."

"Forgive me, Seasonal Demiurge," prompted the new Divine.

"Forgive me . . . Seasonal Demiurge." Purcell got down on her knees and put her forehead to the floor, recalling the first time she did so, the smile in Saul's eyes as he'd laughed at her and offered her tea. *Where was he?* She wished that Cyprin was with her, that she hadn't rushed to face this alone.

Anything less than an emergency of world-ending proportions would have stopped Purcell right there. But the moons, the stars, and all the lights were gone, and she had the dried corpse of the most amazing flower she had ever seen in her pocket. She strongly suspected things were going to get worse. The moment she thought it, the myths of the Petaled Divine, the sacred mountain, the ethereal flower, and Cyprin's assertion that they'd disturbed some ancient terraforming technology collided, and she thought, *Oh no, the sun isn't going to come up tomorrow.*

This must have been the same as the rumored period of darkness during Amma's time. She was Amma, and she was repeating Amma's life exactly. It was frustrating—it was absolutely sickening, and she had no idea how to stop it. Had Amma gone onto the island and cut the rose? If she had, why hadn't she tried to prevent her descendants from making the same mistake? And how had Amma undone the darkness?

Purcell's palms dragged sweat across the floor as she sat up onto her knees. She stared fixedly at a marble tile in front of her. "I think that our eternal spring is about to be over." The words felt heavier than metal slabs. It was her fault. But it was also Amma's fault for making her into this monstrous product of ambition and vanity.

"Excuse me?" The new Divine sounded genuinely convinced that he'd misheard, even though Purcell was a mere two feet away. He was kindly offering an open invitation to retract her statement without consequence. It was more than she had a right to hope for . . . but it wasn't enough. Purcell forged ahead, frightened and determined.

"There . . . there was a flower blooming, on the peak of the mountain in Lake Pensive. *You* sent Cyprin up there because you thought she'd find terraforming equipment, but what we found was something else. It did something to the sky, and the electricity . . . the, the city went dark too. I think . . . I think maybe the sun isn't going to rise in the morning." Purcell risked a look up at the false Divine to gauge his reaction. If he didn't understand, or didn't want to, this would be high blasphemy. She might die for it. But a grown man, taking over a role like this . . . some part of him had to wonder what had happened to his predecessor.

What had happened to Saul?

A moment of fluttery-eyed panic came over him before he fixed the mask of authority back on. "You can relax, Purcell. I make the sun rise in the morning." His voice was stilted. "These . . . these, thoughts of yours are unhelpful. I suggest you go home and forget about them."

He was letting her off the hook again. But that wasn't what she needed; she needed help! "Divine, I—" Purcell stood up and looked directly into his face again.

The new Divine was standing close to the wall, his fingers hovering over a call button that would summon a retinue of priests. The eyebrows weren't angry now, they were scared. "Go home, Head Gardener, and return only when you are ready for the silent introspection of the petal mail."

Purcell gulped. Her feet took a little convincing, but eventually she stumbled out through the throne-room doors. In the hallway outside she collided with Cyprin. Cyprin, who was still steaming from her run, or perhaps from the heat generated by her annoyance that Purcell had reached the throne room first. Cyprin, who had no right to look that good after two swims, a run, and a trek across a mountain. Twelve hells, and Purcell had tried to kiss Cyprin—she *had* kissed Cyprin, which was a mistake, but also wasn't. And wow, she was relieved not to be alone.

"Don't go in there, it isn't him," said Purcell, trying hard not to look too directly at Cyprin's bodysuit.

"What are you talking about, it isn't him?" Cyprin brushed Purcell aside to open the throne room door a crack. Using both hands to keep the doors quiet, she closed them again, her face frozen in a kind of agony. "It isn't him."

"I told you."

"Holy crap," muttered Cyprin. "Did I miss the end of the Divine's life cycle? Have the priestguard killed Saul? Is this how it's supposed to happen?"

"What are you talking about? No! No. This is bad, but it's something different."

"Maybe we can still reason with this guy?" Cyprin was clutching at panicked straws.

Purcell shook her head again, so emphatically that her ears rang. "I just tried. I almost didn't make it out of there." Something a lot bigger than them was happening, and Purcell was beginning to realize that though she'd given a lot of her life to the gardens, she did not want to lose her life to them.

It seemed like Cyprin's body was present, but her mind was somewhere else. Maybe trying to row up shit creek without a paddle. "We gotta go find Saul—the Divine, I mean."

Purcell wasn't much of a history buff, but she knew enough to know what had happened to all the old kings and warlords when new ones were appointed. Knew what happened to yellowed leaves at the end of the growing season. The Divine was dead.

"Find out *what happened to* him" was Purcell's way of saying it, without actually saying it.

Cyprin's eyes did that uncanny thing where they seemed darker and meaner. In that moment, Purcell thought she saw exactly what Saul had meant to Cyprin, and jealousy gripped her like heartburn. She pictured the two of them together, both lean, tall, and charismatic, and it made a terrible sense.

"We have to find him," Cyprin said, firmly.

Purcell chose to bypass that particular sticking point. The betrayals—the sense of danger—had shocked Purcell out of being all-in for the gardens. Now she just wanted to escape. She said, "We need to get out of here and find a historian in the city—do you know of any? This darkness happened in my great-great-grandma Amma's time too, she'd have left some kind of message. I know she would have."

Cyprin pinned her with a look, something lost and wavering in there. "I'm not leaving the gardens without Saul. You want me to be your tour guide in the city? Well, first you have to use your big head-gardener balls to help me find Saul. Then we can all go together."

"Clout," said Purcell, darkly. "I think you mean clout."

When Cyprin shook her head in impatience and started heading back down the staircase, Purcell was hit by a blinding sense of panic.

There had to be other options for help. There was Amanda (if she swallowed her pride and talked to her again) and the other gardeners—they might be more acquaintances than friends, but they were still under Purcell's management, weren't they? They'd have to help her, or listen to her, or something. They couldn't all betray her, could they? There was no—absolutely no—reason for her to rely on Cyprin. Cyprin had been the one following *her* to the gardens, to the pageant, to the palace, and up the mountain, for Divine's sake! (Wait, did that mean Cyprin liked her back?)

But Cyprin had three things to recommend her right now. One: She was nearby. Two: The Divine had been replaced, and aside from Cyprin, Purcell didn't know who could be trusted. And finally, Cyprin already knew what had happened on the mountain, and the thought of trying to explain that to somebody else was entirely unappealing. In conclusion, Purcell was not going to be alone in this scary dark world for a second, even if that meant she had to team up with the worst person ever to exist.

"What are you doing? It looks like you're talking to yourself." Cyprin was waiting for Purcell at the bottom of the stairs. She flattened herself against the wall exaggeratedly as a group of priestguard with strap-on riot gear *hut-hut*'ed past.

"I was just trying to think of a better plan," said Purcell, honestly.

"And did you?"

"No."

Cyprin nodded vaguely as she scanned the floor below for more priestguard. Coast clear, she strode out, beckoning for Purcell to follow. "I'd love to go home and change this damn outfit, but I think we should keep going, y'know?"

Nerves Purcell didn't even know she had were unraveling. She took a long, unsanctioned look at Cyprin's bodysuit and her face burned.

"You coming, or you want to take a picture first?" said Cyprin.

CHAPTER 25

CYPRIN

"Where are we even going?" whined Purcell.

"The admin center, of course." It was the beating heart of the gardens; everything went in or out through there. If anyone knew where Saul was, that seemed a likely place to start.

To Cyprin's surprise, Purcell stopped dead. "No. No, no. Not there." She looked a bit scared and a lot embarrassed. Which was absurd. Purcell and Amanda came as a double set, like bargain-basement Barbies.

"What's your problem? Your evil twin lives there, you should be happy."

"My—" Purcell's eyes said, *How dare you*. "I can't. We had a falling out."

"Over what? No, Purcell, don't tell me she wore the same outfit as you to a party!" Unfortunately, Cyprin was all too familiar with falling out with friends, but she made light of it anyway.

"It wasn't—" Purcell made an obvious effort to downgrade the petulance in her voice, but it didn't quite work. "I can't go back there, okay?"

Cyprin looked at her. Really looked. Purcell's luminous green eyes were watery and bagged, her hair damp and matted. She looked like she needed to be wrapped in blankets and given hot chocolate. The expression on her face was heartbreakingly sincere. Cyprin knew that expression. It was in her mirror after getting escorted out of a mall for knocking over a display of aviators, it looked up at her from the water in her bathtub after telling Moss she couldn't go to dinner because she had to wash her hair. Sometimes it felt like she got into the back seat of her brain and panicked while an asshole took control of her body. And she could recognize that in others: it was all in the eyes.

Cyprin flapped her arms in exasperation. "All right! All right. You tell me where we should go to look for Saul." Cyprin wasn't going to make Purcell confront Amanda if she didn't want to. A ticking sound started up, and Cyprin thought it was her stomach before spotting a clock on the wall of the palace foyer. She didn't have time for this, didn't have time at all. And maybe Saul didn't either.

"I know where the priestguard headquarters are. We can go there and speak to Roman," said Purcell.

That first part did not sound attractive. Cyprin moved on to the second. "Who's Roman?"

"The head of the priestguard."

Cyprin nodded, and Purcell trotted ahead, taking the lead. She was following a peach-assed prefect to see the biggest cop in Cop Town. What in twelve hells was wrong with her? A dirt sandwich or a walk across hot coals would be better. Maybe she'd even explode first; in the constant darkness she had no sense of time anymore. This brought forth a deranged fantasy about exploding all over the priestguard. The smart thing to do would be to leave Saul, leave Purcell, leave the gardens, and beg clemency from the Underground. Unfortunately, brains didn't enter the equation. Purcell was looking too heartbreakingly vulnerable for Cyprin to think about abandoning her, and Cyprin would *die* before abandoning Saul. The worst thing was, that last part wasn't bravery or compassion. It wasn't even really love. It was trauma.

"*Mama! Mama, please!*" A kid should never hear their own parent calling out for a parent. A particularly nasty strain of rat-flu had been going around the city, and Cyprin's mother had caught it. You could have cooked an egg on her forehead. Her sheets were so saturated, Cyprin had given up changing them and just brought fresh towels in to mop up what she could. She'd done the grocery shopping, hauling the bags up in two trips on the elevator. She'd done the laundry, but she always got the colors mixed. She'd even gone to a pharmacy, though the lady there had been no help, just said there was nothing to do but ride it out. Ride it out. Like this was an amusement park.

In the beginning, Cyprin's mother had been able to sit up and eat. She'd had a shower by sitting on the shower floor and could get to the toilet with an arm to lean on. But that had progressed to fainting in bed and not always recognizing Cyprin, calling out other names, or saying gibberish words.

There was a knock at the door. "Hey, kid." Cyprin's own face was reflected back in Maverick's aviators. She remembered how alarmed she'd been by her appearance. She'd looked older, a kid with all the kid sucked out of them.

"I came as soon as I heard," said Maverick. Which wasn't true. She had messaged him from her mother's phone midweek, and he'd waited for the weekend to come out.

Cyprin opened the door to him, and he stepped in, not touching anything, nose twitching at the smell of sick. He stood in the doorway of her mother's bedroom, then called an ambulance. Cyprin remembered her mother panting, eyes rolled up, chest rising and falling as fast as a rabbit's. She'd expected Maverick to sit and hold her mother's hand, put a cool cloth on her head, tell her she was going to be alright. Instead, they'd waited outside the apartment, side by side on the hallway floor, Cyprin trying not to cry and Maverick trying not to breathe in too much contaminated air.

As the hospital staff strapped Cyprin's mother into a gurney, Maverick had said, "I'm sorry, kid. You shouldn't have had to deal with that on your own. But I'm here now, I got this."

She could still remember the feeling, like a ten ton Baling press had been lifted off her bones.

"Go take a shower and get all that nasty rat-stuff off, then pack a bag for a couple of days. You can come and stay at my place." Maverick's place. In the Divine Gardens. Her mind had conjured spires of climbing ivy, beds of leaves and flowers, paths paved with mushrooms. A whole cabinet full of aviators. Maverick's strong body shielding her from everything bad in the world.

She'd been almost upset when her mother was discharged later that afternoon, after a short course of antivirals. But the warm fuzzy weightless feeling had remained—when shit hit the fan, Maverick had come through for her. He was there. He was ready to be there.

Purcell led Cyprin to the priestguard headquarters on a sub-level of the palace. It was boring and sterile. There were white double doors that looked like they ought to lead into a surgical ward. Beyond them were rows of beds, sheets tucked in with a military precision that made Cyprin mentally thrash her arms and legs. The floor was plain and white, the walls were plain and white. There wasn't so much as a window. It was currently empty of priestguard, which was good, unless that meant they were hiding under the beds.

"No wonder all the priestguard smoke," said Cyprin. "Just five minutes down here makes me want to light up."

Purcell scurried ahead. "Roman's office is just up the back."

"So, this dude—"

"The head of the priestguard," Purcell interrupted.

"Priesty Prime, gotcha. So, this dude has his office in the middle of everyone's bedroom?" Couldn't Purcell see how fucked up this was?

"Oh, he's not always here."

"But when he is, he's like, tucking them all in? Kissing them good night?"

Purcell glared back at Cyprin, who winked. "Too soon to mention kissing?" Needling Purcell eased the pressure somehow, like playing with a loose tooth. And Purcell was cute when she was angry.

"We're almost there, just . . . try to be less you for a moment."

That was too much like every playground insult Cyprin had been slapped with and she shut up. But this wasn't a good-behavior silence. No. It was a brewing silence. She was thinking about what trouble she could cause.

The office at the back of the priestguard barracks had faux windows in it, made of milky Perspex. Cyprin could nevertheless see a crowd in there, murmuring and blocking out the candlelight. Purcell knocked on the door. "Hello? Hello, excuse me?"

The people fell silent immediately. Cyprin had pretended not to be home for enough door-to-door salesmen that she was adept at doing the same thing. This was never a good sign for the knockee.

"Maybe we should come back another time," said Purcell, and she was serious. Cyprin was a honey badger, and she knew all about punching above her weight. This was something she could teach Purcell.

"No, here's what we do." Cyprin knocked hard on the door. "Open up! It's your head gardener!"

Purcell clutched Cyprin's arm. Instead of stiffening at the touch, Cyprin clutched her right back, doing an unhinged impression of Purcell's panic. If she could make Purcell angry instead of scared, that would be a start.

Purcell hissed, "I have no jurisdiction over the priestguard!"

Cyprin shook her off, knocked again, and started yelling. "I've got ten thousand gardeners wondering what the *fuck*—"

The door opened, and Cyprin shoved Purcell forward.

"I, I, I," said Purcell. "Oh, hello, Gary."

The man in the doorway amazingly didn't have the *oh no, here we go* face that Cyprin had seen several people wear when talking to Purcell. "I thought you'd gone on sabbatical," he said.

Purcell was trembling with nervous energy again. Cyprin began wondering whether she could throw her voice enough to fake a ventriloquist act with Purcell. To her relief, she didn't have to.

"I need to see Roman," said Purcell. "It's urgent."

Gary stepped out of the office, and the men behind him were leaning over a desk with a map of the city on it, drippy candles sticking the corners down. Little red markers covered it, like chess pieces pushed into groups. Gary shut the office door behind him and Cyprin pretended like she hadn't been craning her neck. What were they doing in there? Was this about the dark, or something else?

"You can't see Roman," he said. "He's dead."

"Dead?" Cyprin chimed in. Saul gone and the priestguard leader dead. She started to panic. It couldn't be a coincidence, could it? Maybe Saul did it and went on the run? Cyprin caught Purcell's eye by accident. It looked like Purcell was trying to warn her about something, but

Cyprin had no idea what. Oh, yes, that's right. Be less Cyprin. Well, to hells with that.

"What did he die of?" said Cyprin.

Gary took a step away from the door of the office. He lowered his voice. "He fell."

"Over in the bathtub? Down the stairs? In love with the wrong person?" Needling people other than Purcell helped too.

Gary didn't answer that. "We're selecting his replacement."

"Oh, replacements, yes, you'd know all about those." If Cyprin had been wearing her knuckle-dusters, this guy would've been in trouble.

Purcell stared at her in wide-eyed fear, and Cyprin felt a little responsible for that, but not enough to stop. "Who've you got up there pretending to be the Divine?"

"You two should go now," said Gary, urgently.

"Come on, Cyprin," Purcell tried to take her arm, but Cyprin pulled away. This wasn't right. They were covering something up about Saul.

"What did you do with Saul? Where is he?"

The door behind Gary tried to open and he leaned against it. "Go," he said to Purcell.

Cyprin wriggled but Purcell took her wrist in a death grip and wheeled her around back toward the exit. Damn, had she always been this strong? "Gary is one of the good ones," Purcell said under her breath.

"Oh, the good ones! The good ones!" Cyprin managed to kick a candle and a trash can over on her way out, but it was unsatisfying. She was a head and shoulders taller than Purcell; she could probably pull free if she tried, but as mad as she was, she didn't want to get piled on by priest-guard again. That one time at the flower pageant had been enough. So Cyprin let Purcell lead her away while her panic kept rising.

She was so distressed she didn't even register where they were going until her ears popped and the air grew colder. "Purcell, where are we going?"

They were heading farther down, not back up. Purcell didn't say anything, but she had the same kind of fevered purpose she'd had on the mountain. Cyprin knew better than to interrupt that. The last time had put her in a jail made of trees.

They came up to a frosted glass door that said PALACE MORGUE.

Oh.

A gothic-looking young man sat behind a desk in the front room. He shot up when he saw them enter. "Head Gardener Purcell!" he said to Purcell, and then, seeing Cyprin, "And Head Gardener Cyprin?"

The announcement hadn't been that long ago; did he have to say it like it was a question? Cyprin treated him to a premium glare.

"I need to see the body that just came in." Purcell cringed, but she added, "As head gardener, I need to see it." And Cyprin loved her a little bit for that.

The young man flipped open a kind of guest register for dead bodies and ran his finger down the line of names. "Which one?" he said. "There were two today."

Cyprin's heart, buoyed up on false hope and adrenaline, sunk to her toes.

"We'll see them both," said Purcell, and the nervous shake was back. They were way out of their league, and the kind thing might have been to tell Purcell to leave. But Cyprin did not want to face this alone.

The morgue was a hospital-smelling space that had square metal drawers all along one wall. For some reason it reminded Cyprin of a sideways version of the metal tub–bound, cloched displays of ice cream you got at some of the fancier parlors. Her stomach grumbled—or maybe it was gearing up to explode her into oblivion with the Underground's bomb—and she started thinking about what label they'd put on her drawer: STRAWBERRY SWIRL, maybe, or VERY BERRY?

Purcell elbowed her and she snapped back into the present. "You can't be laughing right now."

"Why not? None of these people are going to mind." Not ever again. Saul couldn't be here. If she didn't laugh, she was going to scream.

Their guide pulled on the handle of a drawer and slid it open, and—

That wasn't a flavor of ice cream Cyprin ever wanted to eat. She glanced away, while Purcell stepped closer, and that surprised Cyprin. Purcell was afraid of things that did not fit her narrow range of experience, but clearly this did not include dead bodies.

"How did he die?" said Purcell.

"Well, you can see his neck's broken. But there's also intracranial hemorrhaging, a broken spine, organ damage, you name it."

Cyprin risked a look, then regretted it. "That must have been some fall." Thank everything it wasn't Saul.

"He fell from the Mint Throne Room balcony."

Cyprin's heart sunk a little deeper. There was so much pressure in her chest it felt like it could hardly beat. The room tilted, and she wiggled her toes desperately because she'd heard that's what you were supposed to do to avoid passing out.

"Can we see the other body, please?" said Purcell.

Cyprin was going to die. Was it panic? Sadness? Apprehension? No, dread. This was dread.

The second drawer slid open and there was Saul. The back of his head was a bloodied mess, but his face was calm, like he was sleeping, and his hair was still neat, his skin no paler than it had been before. Cyprin tried to hold on, *ha, ha ice-cream drawers*, but she was rocketed back into the past.

Her orange juice rippled as if something was swimming under the surface. Maverick leaned against the kitchen bench, drinking his morning coffee, aviators already firmly on. "Did you see that?" she'd said.

"See what? Shark in your cereal bowl?" Maverick smirked. The morning had promise. Maverick's attention always snagged on her the longest when she was being amusing. As an adult it had taken her a long time to unpick the difference between attention and love. Maybe she still hadn't.

"No, my orange juice wobbled."

Her mother stepped out from the bedroom, adjusting her magnetic name tag and stooping to tie her shoes. "Cyprin, when I look up, you'd better have your school uniform on, because it's time to go."

She heard, much later, that a sinkhole had opened under the building. That it was nobody's fault, just a hazard of undercity layers and stormwater.

At first, there'd been a sudden feeling of weightlessness. A fling off the end of a waterslide, a jump off the playground swings. A sound like thunder rattled her bones. There wasn't even enough time to scream, but somehow Cyprin made it under the table. Scraper-collapse drills were frequent at school, and it was that muscle memory that got her there. Cyprin's home had been on one of the higher levels. Apartments were constructed out of metal cages so that the people in them wouldn't be immediately crushed when they collapsed, and all the other apartments cushioned their fall. She'd heard later that they had ended up on top of a jumble of them, tumbled together like scattered blocks. Every part of her body had been bruised, especially her lungs. As they'd fallen, she'd hit her back on the kitchen table, which was bolted to the floor, then hit her chest on the kitchen floor after that. Whole minutes passed where she hadn't been able to breathe at all, and then she managed only short, sharp little gasps. She'd thought that was it, that she was going to die of asphyxiation because her lungs wouldn't draw in enough air, but when Maverick cleared a ceiling panel away from the table and pulled Cyprin's T-shirt up over her nose and mouth like he had already done for himself, she realized not being able to breathe properly had saved her life.

One of the lenses had fallen out of Maverick's aviators and his eye behind it was a ratty kind of black. A beady little eye, half-mad, half-opportunistic like all rodents. He'd offered her a hand. "Get up, kid. It's stopped moving. We have to bust out of here so they can find us."

She'd tried to ask him where her mother was, if she was all right, but it turned into a weak coughing fit instead.

Maverick watched her trying to breathe, trying to move when it felt like every bone in her body had broken, then he shook his head and left.

Ten minutes later, or maybe an hour, or maybe several days, he'd pulled her out from under the table by her ankles and slung her over his shoulder like a sack of damaged potatoes. Maverick climbed up on the kitchen bench and pulled them both out of a hole he'd made in the ceiling, but Cyprin hadn't seen any of that, she'd just heard about it later. Her head had been face down on Maverick's lower back and all she'd seen was her mother, curled on her side on the kitchen floor, covered in white dust like she'd been rolled in icing sugar. She'd looked beautiful, an angel with snow-dusted eyelashes. But she hadn't been breathing. Cyprin tried to call out to her anyway, but Maverick pulled them both out into the blinding light of day, the dust making it seem like everything was spotlights and smoke machines.

Her mother had looked like she was sleeping.

Saul looked like he was sleeping.

It was the most nonsensical system ever. Why did dead people have to look like themselves? Why couldn't they dissolve into thin air? They were gone in every other way. It didn't seem fair to leave a reminder. She wished she could speak to the manager about that. But Saul was the Great Petaled Divine, and he was dead. God was and had always been fake. Cyprin had always known that, but Saul had held her hand, and for a moment she'd forgotten. She really had loved him. Not *love* love, but it had been something. More than she'd had before.

"Cyprin? Cyprin?" Purcell was trying to share a sad and conspiratorial look with Cyprin, but she wasn't reciprocating.

Saul was dead. The last time she'd seen him, she'd been horrible to him, and it hadn't even saved his life.

She didn't understand it.

She wouldn't understand it.

She *couldn't* understand it.

Cyprin threw up on the floor.

CHAPTER 26

PURCELL

Somehow it was less of a shock to see Saul in the morgue than it had been to see his replacement on the Mint Throne. Everybody died. Everybody. It was as natural as breathing. You fought to leave a little mark before you had to go and that was it. From what Purcell was seeing, Saul had been fighting for something too. She hoped he had done what he needed.

There had always been a Divine in these gardens, but there had always been a Whitlock too, and when you took away all the trappings of office, their jobs were more or less the same. They maintained the structures that maintained the plants.

Purcell did not serve God. She served the gardens. That had never been clearer to her than it was in this moment. It was sad that Saul was gone, yes, but death didn't break her world. Not anymore. It wasn't people coming and going from life that mattered. It was their actions while they were here. For the first time, Purcell found herself questioning her own purpose. The gardens were beautiful but were they *meaningful*?

Were they worth dying for? People died for love and freedom, but for roses? For roses that were only there to be enjoyed by God and his select few gardeners?

Saul was dead and Purcell could be next and *what was it all for?*

She cleared her throat. "How did he die?"

"He fell from the balcony of the Mint Throne Room as well," said the young man.

"What were they doing up there?" said Purcell.

"They don't pay me to ask questions like that, sorry."

"It's all right." Purcell turned to Cyprin, trying to share with her eyes all the things her mouth couldn't say in present company: *The Divine is dead, and they just replaced him; we've got to get out of these gardens right now; did you know that I am my own grandma?* But Cyprin wouldn't meet her gaze. "Cyprin? Cyprin?"

Cyprin stared fixedly at a point between her own feet and then she vomited everywhere.

Purcell stepped backward. The man who'd shown them Saul apologized—for what, Purcell didn't know—and then he darted off to get a bucket.

"Cyprin, are you all right?" asked Purcell. Cyprin was bent over, breathing hard and muttering something about strawberry-swirl ice cream. "Cyprin?"

Cyprin straightened up and wiped her mouth on the back of her hand, which was gross. She ignored Purcell entirely and took Saul's cold, slightly gray hand. Oh no, what was she—

"Wake up, Saul. We have to go," said Cyprin, and her face was totally waxen, wiped of emotion.

"Cyprin, I don't think he can come with us." Even as a little kid, Purcell had understood what had happened to her mother. She had always been raised with death as a close companion. But at the foster dorm, she'd seen other kids react like this, who didn't have a strong conception of cause and effect. They cried when they dropped food on the floor, not understanding that you can't put a shattered soft-boiled egg back together. They'd see a spectacular sunrise and ask the foster teachers to start it again, and they always acted like their parents were off on a long shopping trip that they might come back from at any moment.

Was this the same thing?

"Get up, Saul." Cyprin put her arms around Saul's shoulders and pulled him into a sitting position.

"Cyprin, he's dead." Really, what was there to misunderstand? People lived and then they died. It was simple.

Cyprin stared at Purcell over Saul's shoulders, her eyes red-rimmed but not teary. Confusion flashed across her face, genuine and all-consuming. Saul was the shattered egg, and Cyprin couldn't understand why he couldn't be put back together. She moved Saul around so that his legs flopped off the metal slab.

"Cyprin!" said Purcell, urgently. "Cyprin, stop!"

Cyprin took Saul into a bear hug and tried to lift him off the table. She was almost as tall as him, but he was twice as heavy and fell on her.

Cyprin screamed, and that was when the young man from the front desk made it back with a bucket and mop. The water in the bucket sloshed, spilling suds on the floor as he dropped it. "Oh, no, what's going on here?"

"It was an accident!" said Purcell, squeaking in fright.

Cyprin was still screaming, but there were sobs in there too. Purcell had been jealous of God before, but her heart broke for Cyprin now. The young man lifted Saul off Cyprin with Purcell's help. Cyprin rolled onto her side, crying so hard she started hiccupping. Purcell had never seen anyone react like this before. She crouched down and patted Cyprin on the back uncertainly, and that did something. The tears switched off as if a tap had been turned. Purcell was glad if she could be any comfort.

The metal drawers containing Saul's remains and Roman's remains were rolled back in again, and the morgue attendant set about cleaning Cyprin's mess off the floor. He kept glancing at them in a way that suggested his patience was running thin.

Cyprin did one more hiccup and then got to her feet, dangerously relaxed.

Purcell tried getting through to her again. "Cyprin?" Cyprin was staring at the back of the room like she could see through it. Something had gone really wrong for Saul, and Purcell had a strong feeling that they should get out of the palace. Right now. After God, the head gardener would be the next obvious target, and there were two of them. "Cyprin?"

Cyprin turned to Purcell, her face a total blank. "It's not Saul," she said, calmly.

"What?"

"It's another fake." Cyprin swayed on her feet, physically reeling.

Plenty of secrets lurked in the gardens, Purcell certainly knew that. Had someone swapped out Saul, faked a body? What would be the point? No, it made no sense. Like all scientists, Purcell believed in parsimony. Saul was dead. It was sinister and final.

"Cyprin, I don't think—"

Cyprin started pacing, rubbing her hand over the stubble on her head. She was muttering again, something about exploding—was she exploding with grief? How close had she been with Saul? The image of Cyprin doing up her bootlaces on the side of God's bed popped into Purcell's head again and Purcell's cheeks flushed. Cyprin probably didn't even like girls.

Cyprin's eyes roved around the room and then settled on Purcell. She smiled, but the smile was too sharp. "He's not dead. He must be out there somewhere."

The world had fallen into eternal night, Amanda was a traitor, the Divine was dead, the head of the priestguard was dead, and Purcell's entire family legacy was built on lies. She put her hand in her pocket and her fingers closed around the desiccated rose. There was no one left Purcell could really trust but Cyprin, and Cyprin was not at her best. The gardens were entirely lacking leadership, and Purcell should have, could have stepped into that role, but with the heads of two out of the three main powers in the gardens dead under suspicious circumstances, she couldn't stick around. Not even for her beloved roses. Sometimes you had to run to get perspective.

"We have to leave, get to the city," said Purcell. "We'll find an archaeologist. I'm telling you, this happened to my grandma. Someone will know how she fixed it!" Maybe they would find out later what happened to Saul. Maybe they would never know, but they would be alive.

Cyprin didn't agree, but she didn't resist, either, when Purcell led her away.

CHAPTER 27

CYPRIN

They quit the palace and the Divine Gardens without too much hassle, everyone distracted by the sudden dark. Now they were walking into Asperia, on some long-lost trail for Purcell's family history. Cyprin was vaguely cognizant that she might be exploding soon, but the worries were muffled, along with everything else. All she could do was put one foot in front of the other.

Saul, Saul, where was Saul? Purcell thought the worst. But Cyprin wasn't buying into that idea. Saul was in a basement somewhere, waiting to be rescued. And when she rescued him, after she'd sorted this stomach-bomb nonsense out with the Underground—well, the palace heavies would be worried for a while, but they'd settle down once they realized Saul was no longer coming for them or their institution. And of course, he wouldn't be, because she'd talk him out of taking any further risks. They'd both been too naïve. They'd thought the world was full of solvable mysteries and cartoon bad guys, when instead it had been filled with people who'd put bombs in your stomach as soon as look at you, and people who'd steal you away in the night when your friends weren't around.

Cyprin glanced back to where Purcell was scurrying to catch up, her flashlight bobbing up and down in her hurry. Purcell truly was spectacular. Spectacular and awful like a flashy storm. If they could survive long enough to see the sun again, save Saul, and get rid of the bomb in Cyprin's stomach, maybe Cyprin would do something about that. Perhaps there was a future in which they could annoy each other long-term.

All the power really had gone out. The trains weren't even running. There were no streetlights, no lit-up signs, no nothing. Just Purcell's flashlight and a little clip-on spotlight Cyprin was wearing that Purcell had found in the bottom of her bag. Cyprin was bemused thinking of the other rubbish that had been in Purcell's bag: a box of one hundred hair clips, a Tupperware containing deviled eggs, a book of plant anatomy that Purcell could probably quote from. It was so ridiculously over-the-top, unlike Cyprin, who frequently left the house forgetting important things. At least the distance from the gardens to the city was walkable. It would be a good eight-hour hike, but everything in Verdure was so densely packed, it was doable.

Doable, if she didn't explode.

Cyprin held the clip-on light at her collarbone and redirected it off the road at the buildings that surrounded them. She tried to keep the light cycling around them, like a tiny lighthouse, because otherwise there could be anything out there: thieves and murderers creeping up on them, tons and tons of rats moving like a landslide with the single-mindedness of one organism and the bloodthirstiness of thousands. At the moment there was a high concrete wall on their left side, riddled with offensive, cucumber-shaped graffiti, and on their right were warehouses. The building Cyprin was looking at had a giant tire suspended at its front in place of a sign. A deep sense somewhere between her brain stem and her spinal column was screaming that the sun should be coming up by now, heralding her demise in a wet pyrotechnic display courtesy of the Underground. It was hard to stay focused, and anytime she let her mind wander, it was filled with images of fake Saul in the morgue, dead.

"Isn't this it?" said Purcell from somewhere behind her and off to her right. "You just walked past it."

Cyprin turned and there was the Archaeology Emporium, a place she had visited once during the peak of her hyperfixation over *Lust Island*. Archaeologists doubled as historians in Asperia. Pawnbrokers too, on occasion, as they bought artifacts dredged up from the undercity by slumpers. They also kept up a long-held tradition of infusing modern history into objects that were distributed around the city, so that when Asperia built upward and the ground they now stood on was declared as a new hell, all their information would be preserved in the fossil record, as nature intended.

A candle burned in the otherwise dark window of the building, which was enough of an invitation. Cyprin followed Purcell in.

"Oh, wow," said Purcell as they walked through an entryway studded with ancient pop-culture paraphernalia. Half of it was printouts of cat memes.

"Did they really worship cats?" Purcell had soaked up this urban myth from somewhere, and Cyprin was not about to disabuse her of it.

"Yes. Cats used to be our overlords, before the AI saved us." Total lies. This was a step too far, and Cyprin wasn't really selling it properly because her heart was in a thousand pieces.

Purcell scowled back at her. "You could just say you don't know."

"I know a lot more than you," said Cyprin, which did seem true in this case.

But this prompted another nonsensical outburst. "What's the deal with the undercity, anyway?" said Purcell.

"The deal?"

"Well, I know we mine it for robots and old goods, but how did all that get into the ground in the first place?"

The city just kept building upward, packing layers onto the decay. Of course that made no sense to a divine gardener. All Purcell knew was open spaces and happy plants.

"God declares a new hell and a ton of dirt falls on everyone's heads." Cyprin's voice was dead; she couldn't even bring herself to put any effort into the hazing.

Purcell spared Cyprin only a faint nostril flare of annoyance as she knocked on the door at the end of the hall.

It was answered by a twitchy young man who seemed perturbed to see them. "Are you here to rob me?"

"What?" Purcell drew back, alarmed. "No! Of course not! What would give you that idea?"

"You're outside, in the darkness."

Cyprin noticed the energy weapon hanging loose by the man's side and bumped Purcell out of the way. She already had a bomb in her stomach, it might as well be her. "About that darkness," she said.

But Purcell clearly did not like being talked over. *She* talked over Cyprin, louder. "We're from the Divine Gardens. Here to ask about Amma—Head Gardener Amma Whitlock. Nearly a hundred and thirty years ago, she faced this same darkness and beat it. I'd like to know how."

The man ushered them in with his gun, which was not very reassuring. "Well, I don't have anything to steal. We keep the real stuff in warehouses. These are all replicas."

"I told you, we're not—" Purcell sighed and gave up, rolling her eyes at Cyprin, whose face was carefully blank. They weren't buddies, even if that was now by sheer force of will in the same way that Cyprin and Moss hadn't been real friends.

As the archaeologist rummaged with one hand in a disorganized drawer of papers marked "Divine Gardens" (his other still holding the gun), Cyprin wandered around his office. Replicas, yeah, right. He had a working Furby on a plinth in the corner, gibbering nonsense, and those things were impossible to fake—and also likely demon possessed.

"This is all I have." The archaeologist waved a single page in Purcell's face, which was an improvement on him waving his gun. "Now, go away. I'd like to lock the door and put my chair under the handle."

Purcell spent all of five seconds reading the page before thrusting it at Cyprin, and then huffing and storming out of the shop. It was a photocopy of a photocopy, so faded it looked like something spiders had written by running across a page with ink on their feet.

> With golden trowel in hand (. . .) mountain (. . .) Amma ate the darkness, and the darkness was no more (. . .) let me put this down for posterity, I said, meaning that I already had, but Amma restrained me. She had my own Golden pothos light a match, holding it to my papers (. . .) madwoman (. . .) own descendants will be cursed by this prideful folly, mark my words!

A smear of black ink could've been photocopied char. Cyprin frowned at the page.

She found Purcell loitering outside with a rime of unshed tears in her eyes.

"What did that mean to you?" Cyprin asked.

"Nothing!" spluttered Purcell. "Absolutely nothing. I—I mean Amma—never learned to share her secrets. She was all about getting ahead. I should've known that. As if she'd spare a thought for anyone but herself!"

This was clearly some heavy family-history stuff. Cyprin did not know what to say.

"My power over plants came from Amma, and so did—so did the wasting disease," said Purcell.

"The what?"

Purcell's luminous eyes turned on Cyprin, bereft. "The wasting sickness. I'll be lucky to make it to forty."

Cyprin's thoughts had to be wrenched from God dying by his forty-second birthday back into the present moment. She was perplexed. "You *inherited* your plant nonsense?" Superpowers were not some regular old recessive gene. Fuckery was afoot.

"I inherited a lot of things," said Purcell, darkly.

God dying early and Purcell expecting to die early alerted Cyprin to the panic she ought to be feeling about the bomb in her stomach. All this had to wait. She had the rose. Now she needed to find the Underground.

"Was this a waste of time?" she said, already looking around them to get her bearings. What would be the best way to get to the Underground? The bottom of a department store, maybe?

The hurt in Purcell's eyes actually stung her. "Of course. Of course! You don't even care." Purcell laughed; a deranged bark. "What's really funny is that it isn't possible for you to care less about me than my own grandma!"

Cyprin had seen this kind of despair before, and she knew it was all internally scripted. She could probably say anything, and Purcell would keep wallowing, hearing only the sad echoes in her own head. Cyprin tested it out. "Hurricane! Purple applesauce! Toothy rhododendrons!"

That did it, actually. Purcell's eyes snapped into focus. "What the fuck are you talking about?"

Cyprin stretched a hand out to her. "Your grandma was secretive and unhelpful, your powers are entirely useless to us out here, and you have a terminal illness hovering over your head. I understand, but if we don't keep moving right now, the world is gonna fall apart." *I am going to fall apart, courtesy of a bomb.* "We'll go and find the Underground. They'll know what to do."

"You don't understand anything," said Purcell, but she took Cyprin's hand.

CHAPTER 28

PURCELL

They'd left the archaeologist's building at least an hour ago, and despite Cyprin's assurances that the Underground were just five minutes away, they were still walking.

"A few more minutes in this direction and we'll be there," muttered Cyprin.

Purcell could recognize false confidence a mile away. "Are we lost?"

"Of course not! Look, there's a department store right there! There'll be an entrance to the undercity at the bottom! That's how we'll find the Underground."

They were still holding hands. Purcell's palm was quite sweaty now, but Cyprin just clutched it tighter.

The department store was entirely dark. Their flashlights shone through the glass front, lighting up mannequins in trench coats that looked way too much like real people. When the sky went dark, people must have evacuated this place. Cyprin waved her hands in front of the sensor for the autodoors, but nothing happened.

As Purcell watched, Cyprin began trying to pry the doors open with her bare hands.

"Cyprin, that's illegal," Purcell pointed out. This achieved nothing. So Purcell sat down with her back against the glass to wait for Cyprin to tire out.

Purcell's feet were sore. Her lower back was aching. She started to think about Amma.

Amma had had the records scrubbed. It wasn't that Purcell *couldn't* believe it, but she didn't *want* to believe any version of herself could be so conceited. She had confirmation now, of Amma's powers over plants, Amma's conquest against the dark, but it wasn't enough to change anything.

Amma had wanted her powers to stay hidden, passed down through the Whitlock line. This was clearly more important to her than recording how she'd beaten the dark. Or maybe she'd thought her descendants would be smart enough to figure it out. Purcell took the rose out of her pocket and twirled it in her fingers. Power over plants. Amma had power over plants, but had she cut the rose and then fixed the dark, or had something else happened in her time?

Purcell concentrated on the rose, but nothing changed.

"I've got it!" Cyprin cried out, and Purcell looked up to find her wedged halfway between the sliding doors.

She did not want to follow Cyprin into the dark, creepy department store. And she did not want to be left alone outside.

Purcell followed all the way down to the sub-basement level, where the lingerie lived. They weaved between lacy displays until Cyprin went into the changerooms and hammered on the back wall of each cubicle.

"There should be a trick panel somewhere, why isn't there a trick panel!" Cyprin's voice was guttural, half shout and half cry.

"You're lost." Purcell had known this for ages and was waiting for Cyprin to come to the same conclusion.

"We can't be!" said Cyprin, which was a step up from *we're not*.

"Let's go back outside and keep looking. Maybe we'll find someone we can ask."

"I don't have time!" Cyprin shouted, teary-eyed.

It didn't make sense. Things were dire, but not *that* dire. They had time.

Cyprin squatted down on her haunches, staring at the changeroom wall. "He's dead," she said, breathing out. She did not breathe in again.

Purcell crouched in front of her. "Cyprin?" She waved a hand in front of Cyprin's face to no reaction.

"No, no, he can't be dead." At least talking meant Cyprin was breathing again.

Purcell put a tentative hand on Cyprin's shoulder. "Shh," she said. "Everything's going to be okay."

Red-rimmed eyes snapped up to her. "Why do people always say that? It's never okay when people say that."

That was true enough. The words were said to every dying hero in the movies, to anyone with an uncertain future. Purcell said, "I think it's a way to soothe and offer hope."

"Well, it totally sucks," said Cyprin.

Purcell stared evenly at her. "Everything's going to be a complete disaster. There. Does that help?"

Cyprin smiled at her efforts. "Everything will go down the drain in screaming, burning chaos?"

"Absolutely."

Cyprin nodded and then stood up, straightening her clothing, wiping tears from her face. "Okay. We can do this. Let's keep looking for the Underground."

This time, Purcell offered Cyprin a hand.

Cyprin took it.

CHAPTER 29

CYPRIN

Cyprin cleared her throat, desperate to get away from her own thoughts. "I bet you have a poster of me on your bedroom wall."

She'd been trying to distract herself with some light goading, but Purcell stopped dead in the middle of the road, like she'd been shot. "Why do you keep doing that?" There might even have been tears in Purcell's eyes.

Cyprin's face burned at being called out. "Doing what?"

"Making fun of me! I can't help who I'm into, and neither can you—it's Saul, isn't it? It's okay, I get it, he's a lot older, but he has really nice legs! Has. Had. Sorry."

Cyprin grabbed Purcell by the shoulders and bulldozed her into the nearest defunct streetlamp. "I don't like anyone, okay? And no one likes me."

Purcell's mouth made a little O of shock, then her eyes narrowed. "That's why this all has to be a joke to you! It's not about me at all. You're scared!" Suddenly, the hardness melted off her face and she started making heart eyes, like someone who'd just spotted a kitten cowering under a couch. "You're scared," she said again. "Did Saul know?"

Oh, no, this was too much. Cyprin suddenly realized she was touching Purcell. Touching. Purcell. This wasn't like on the mountain when they'd been snapping at each other's faces. Cyprin felt all her loss and confusion on display. She pushed away and walked off into the dark, rubbing her hands on the sides of her pants.

"Cyprin!" Purcell's little flashlight nipped at her heels.

"What?" She hadn't meant to growl like that. All her sad, helpless, vulnerable insides needed to be under lock and key for everyone's safety. And why could she still smell the antiseptic of the morgue?

"If you talk to me, maybe I can help you!" squealed Purcell.

"No." Cyprin held back tears the way she had in the hospital when Maverick had abandoned her.

"Why?"

Cyprin was too overwhelmed to clam up properly. "Because there's no point. Everyone always leaves me!"

"I'm still here," said Purcell.

The shock of that fact made Cyprin stop and turn. "Yes, you hang around like a bad smell," she said, but her heart was beating superfast at the realization that Purcell, who'd had every reason to abandon her, had not.

Finally, someone had stayed.

At least for now.

Cyprin shook off the mushy feelings and put her usual hostile front back up. She kept walking, shining her borrowed light at the street. Funny, she'd been expecting all the city rats to be running about with wild abandon, but even they'd gone to ground. There wasn't a single pest. It seemed not even roaches were immune to the wrongness.

"I don't like it here," Purcell said with a whine, catching up to her.

"Don't tell me you've never left the gardens." Of course she hadn't. Purcell had always judged the world from her soft little nest.

There was silence.

"What? Did you burst forth from a flower, like the Divine?" Cyprin's voice dripped sarcasm. More silence. "Purcell, don't tell me—"

A piece of cracked concrete skipped by between Cyprin's feet, and she looked back to see Purcell kicking stones.

"It's not my fault where I was born," said Purcell, sourly.

"Did they hang a gold lanyard from the mobile above your cot? Put a trowel in your hand instead of a rattle?"

Purcell sped up, passed Cyprin, and began walking in front of her, apparently sick of looking at her back. "I went through the same interview process as the other gardeners," she called over her shoulder.

Cyprin strode faster to match her pace. This felt like the mountain all over again, but this time Purcell didn't have any trees to recruit. "Oh! Sure, you did! With exactly the same chances of success, yes!" Putting Purcell in a foul mood seemed to let some of the bad feelings out of Cyprin's head.

Purcell's shoulders hunched up. "I don't like your insinuation. I worked as hard as everybody else."

Cyprin laughed. "You have no idea how hard everybody else is working. You started at the top of the staircase, and you think just because the steps look the same, it's no big deal for people who have to start from the bottom. Come back here, you don't know where you're going!" She remembered to revolve like a lighthouse again, and this time found them crammed between a fish market and a radio station, both of which appeared to be free of looters and anything with a hairless tail.

"You don't know where you're going either!" said Purcell.

"Well, then, since you know exactly how difficult everything is, go on and lead the way."

"You don't know how lucky you are, coming from nothing," Purcell muttered, and she took the lead.

"Wow, no, of course. So lucky." Cyprin was getting so annoyed she could go whole seconds without thinking about the bomb in her stomach. And that was a good thing. Without Purcell here to get mad at, there was no telling what state she would be in. Handing Purcell with her magic plant powers and her knowledge of the gardens over to the Underground for some extra lifesaving leverage was even starting to feel like a viable option. Something she might be able to get over by just drinking herself into oblivion.

But then, Purcell had stayed.

A few hours of ugly rectangular industrialization later, they arrived in the city center, where the buildings stretched so tall the light from Purcell's flashlight didn't reach the top. There were people too. Loads of them. Milling in the street, looking bewildered.

The people were nervous, twitchy in a dangerous way. As Cyprin and Purcell passed, they whispered to each other in small, panicked groups. Cyprin even spotted a few END TIMES—REPENT! cardboard signs, though these weren't very convincing when they were cinched under someone's arm as they raided a nearby convenience market for a lifetime supply of sour candy. Candles silhouetted menacing-looking figures in the windows of glass apartment blocks, like cutout shadow puppets. Some people stood outside their homes, just looking at the black nothingness of the sky. Some were nailing boards over their windows. A few batches of priestguard went past, but they were ignoring the looters and heading in the direction of the Divine Gardens. When push came to shove, protecting the gardens was clearly their priority. But . . . they hadn't done anything to protect Saul.

I'm coming back for you, Saul, Cyprin thought to herself. *After I find the Underground and convince them not to kill me.* Refusing to believe Saul was dead was the only way she could keep going.

After that, it got worse. As the city grew more dense, they passed burning shops, and scrapers with smashed glass fronts and half-torn boards nailed over the doors. Fewer people milled about the closer in they went, and those they saw were armed and armored. An old wiry woman lurked about with a frying-pan breastplate and an illegal energy weapon at her hip, a couple of slumpers still wore their headlamps, bodies riddled with enough tech to keep them alive during a cave-in—*they* had nothing to fear out here. Who *did* have something to fear? It would have been horrible to be underground or in a giant department store when the lights went out . . . or in the apple orchard. Had Moss been at work? Were they still there, pulling double shifts, triple, trying to figure out how to keep the apples safe and well? Had they been operating heavy machinery when it went dark? Or walking down a flight of stairs?

Purcell's agonizing small talk and incessant complaining had dwindled into apprehensive silence, which Cyprin did not consider an improvement.

"Say something," said Cyprin. "Anything. Please." Her voice broke on the word *please*. She was desperate.

"So, this is Asperia? It's very . . . *synthetic* . . . here." Only Purcell could make *synthetic* sound like something she'd picked off a crime-scene floor with gloves and tweezers.

Cyprin didn't need to see Purcell's hands to know they were wringing together. "What were you expecting? Quaint little mushroom houses and people living in trees? Did you ever ponder over what you were doing up there, making a pretty garden for God? All those resources that could've been used to help people?"

"You work in the gardens too."

"Yes!" Cyprin shouted. "And the difference is, I know exactly how unfair the gardens are! How exquisite and *disgusting* it is all at the same time! If I could, I would tear it all down! What would you do? Defend every rose to your last breath while here in the city the standard apartment size halves again?"

Purcell rolled one shoulder, half shrugging and half dodging Cyprin's questions as if they were bullets. Her big eyes looked back at Cyprin. "I think that man with the broom and the books tied around his chest is following us."

Cyprin had been ready to argue till she lost her voice, but she risked a glance behind them. Purcell was right, a rangy guy was about twenty paces behind. As she stared at him, he stopped and feigned tying his shoes. Fear sawed through Cyprin's ribs, making it hard to breathe. There was always some dude. Why did there always have to be some dude? Acknowledging the guy would only get them in trouble. She looked away.

"You stay in the lead. You're doing great," she told Purcell. No matter how at odds they were, this was not the ideal time for Purcell to panic. They had to keep going.

"Okay," said Purcell. And after a moment's silence, "Cyprin, where are all the priests and law-keepers?"

"Probably hiding in one of these buildings." Cyprin scanned some of the visible high points, the skyline, the metal bracing around shop signs. No telling who might be up there in the dark, watching the streets, pointing the noses of their weapons out over it.

"Maybe they're off trying to figure out why the sky has gone dark."

"Yeah, maybe." Cyprin glanced behind them again and the man with the broom was much closer. This time, when she locked eyes with him, he didn't feign distraction. He kept on coming. "Purcell?"

"Yes?"

"No, don't turn around. Just walk faster."

Purcell made a noise like a sneeze, and—Oh. She was crying. Cyprin racked her brain for what to do about that. Soothing words were not her forte. She could manage one or two, when really pressed. She found she wanted to try. "You cry like someone out of an infomercial."

"What in twelve hells is that supposed to mean?"

Cyprin was spared the glaring scrutiny of an explanation as footsteps pounded the pavement behind them. She started running. On her way past Purcell, she grabbed hold of her elbow and forced Purcell to run too. They careened through the light of burning objects and into the fathomless spaces in between. The man behind them was close enough that they could hear his heavy breathing, but Cyprin had spotted a few familiar landmarks in the gloom: the Undersea Market and a karaoke joint. She knew where they were now.

"Purcell," she said between gulps of air. "The purple neon sign!" Of course Mama Inkburn had found a way to keep it lit up. Cyprin let go of Purcell's elbow and shoved her hard in the back. Then she turned around to face the man behind them. She couldn't let him get Purcell. No one was allowed to get Purcell except for her.

He hadn't been expecting anyone to stop. Before he realized what was happening, Cyprin took the broom out of his hands and then angled the stick out at eye height, obscuring his line of vision, making it hard for him to focus on her. He pulled up abruptly and moved left. She moved the stick with him.

"I will kick the shit out of you, man. Don't try me today." This was the extent of her self-defense skills. She hoped her bark was bad enough that he wouldn't risk her bite. She could hear Purcell behind her, running like a windmill in a hurricane. Good.

A blinding blue flash streaked overhead and grounded itself in the front window of the karaoke bar, melting glass. The man in his book-strapped armor fell over in his rush to get away. Cyprin dropped the broom and turned with her arms raised, fearing imminent vaporization. The fertility goddess shape of Mama Inkburn was silhouetted in the light that spilled from her shop door, the muzzle of her energy weapon still glowing.

"Come in," Mama Inkburn called. "We've got mushroom soup going on a portable gas burner, and tea if the generator holds up."

Cyprin didn't trust herself to form words, so she waved at Mama Inkburn instead. That was such a close call, she almost felt another Cyprin with her back against the asphalt, getting her teeth knocked out. Her heart was pounding so hard she had blocked ears and buzzing fingertips. Cyprin headed toward sanctuary.

CHAPTER 30

PURCELL

A weevil bobbed in Purcell's soup.

Beside her on the swivel-chair bar seating, Cyprin waved a spoon at it. "Oh, lucky you! You got extra protein. Looks fresh too."

A host of other people were sheltering with them at Mama Inkburn's diner. The scene almost looked normal, save for the dormant electric stoves behind the counter and the furniture they'd pushed up against the doors once Cyprin had come inside.

Purcell wrinkled her nose and leaned over her mushroom soup. The little brown thing curled listlessly in a sea of mottled gray. It was like her appetite had never been there. She pushed the bowl away, and suddenly it was sliding sideways, hooked by Cyprin's fingers. She watched, horror-stricken, as Cyprin upended the bowl. Ugh, Purcell had kissed that mouth and couldn't stop thinking about it.

Cyprin had a rheum of gray around her lips. She gestured at the empty bowl with a thumb. "You want me to get you another one? I could ask Mama Inkburn to put it through a strainer?"

"Nope, no, I'm fine, thank you. Just fine."

Cyprin gave Purcell a look of total incomprehension and then waved at Mama Inkburn, a woman whose tastes in fashion were as neon as her sign. "Mama Inkburn, what time is it?" The response set Cyprin muttering to herself, as if she had to add up all the hours on an internal abacus before they'd make sense.

Purcell was nervously toying with the rose corpse in her pocket, and Mama Inkburn spotted it, her eyes going strangely distant. "The salvation and destruction of humanity," Mama Inkburn said.

Cyprin's head snapped up. "What did you say?"

Mama Inkburn blinked rapidly. "I said it's two AM."

"Are you sure that's what you said?" Cyprin persisted.

"I am quite tired," Mama Inkburn admitted, floating over to another hungry patron. "Perhaps I had a funny turn."

"I've been thinking," said Purcell, choosing to push past everyone's eccentricities, "maybe finding the Underground is too dangerous. Maybe we could just stay right here. It seems nice, in this diner."

"We *need* to find the Underground."

"But we're safe from whatever is going on in the gardens now. Can't we just hide and regroup?"

"The Underground might be the only ones who can help us find Saul."

"Cyprin." Purcell lowered a hand to pat Cyprin on the arm. Her fingers paused a pencil-width away, when Cyprin's eyes told her she was about to touch a wild animal. She wanted—yearned—to touch Cyprin, but stopped herself. The body heat mingled between them, a kind of pseudotouch. "Cyprin, he died."

Cyprin's eyes became two shiny little peppercorns, aimed straight at a spot between Purcell's brows. Purcell felt as though her face was going to cave inward, like Silly Putty with a thumb pressed into it. The strength of Cyprin's denial was quite astounding. It was the kind of trick you'd need to steal someone else's flowers and enter a pageant with them, and Purcell wondered what else it might allow her to do. Cyprin was dangerous. Maybe you had to be dangerous to exist in this city, and Purcell felt a stab of guilt at her garden-bound privilege, at how oblivious she'd been to it.

"I hear you two talking about the Underground?" Mama Inkburn sipped one of her sodas. Her elbows came down on the bar between them and Cyprin and Purcell jumped apart. *Saved.*

"Yeah," said Cyprin. "Need to find them."

Out of the range of that blowtorch gaze, Purcell gained some fortitude. "We really don't."

Mama Inkburn laughed, and her wide-set, blue-ringed eyes took them in. "That's cute. You two got a good-cop, bad-cop thing going?"

"No," said Purcell, darkly, at the same time as Cyprin laughed and said, "Yeah."

Mama Inkburn leaned in across the counter and lowered her voice. "Right now, the Underground are somewhere under the city library. If you can get in there and ask for *A Cake Decorator's Guide to Black Holes,* I think they'll see you."

A Cake Decorator's Guide to Black Holes. What schlocky spy-code nonsense. Purcell watched Cyprin's mouth form the words silently, apparently writing them in crayon across her frontal cortex. Sweet Divine, she was so annoying. If only she wasn't so kissable as well.

"Thank you," said Purcell, who'd had politeness drilled into her as a child. "That's very helpful of you."

As soon as Mama Inkburn turned away to tend to another customer, Purcell said, "I have to go to the bathroom." And she got up and ran away.

She did not need to pee. Instead she leaned over the cool white sink, trying to breathe. The bathroom was lit with candles, and they made her reflection in the mirror look strange. She cast her eyes longingly at a half-open window and contemplated her chances of surviving on her own.

Cyprin had a point. The priests back at the palace were not known for their ability to see reason. They'd probably argue that the sun was still there, you just needed to move your head in the right way to see it, or that the Great Petaled Divine would make it rise as soon as he saw fit to. Palming this whole mess off on the Underground sounded like the only thing to do, really. Then she could rest safe in the knowledge that other people were working on the problem. As for the new Divine, well, if Purcell could convince the priestguard she wasn't going to cause any issues, they'd leave her alone, wouldn't they? She was a fixture in those gardens. Guilt followed these thoughts, that she could even think of glossing over what had happened to Saul. But they were *her* gardens too, weren't they? Boycotting them wasn't going to bring Saul back. And . . . and maybe this time she could do more than just care for the roses. Maybe she could give a little back to the people in the city, send them the overflow of spent blooms the gardeners cut every day, give away the day-old bread from the canteen that would go to waste otherwise. . . .

Purcell stood in front of the bathroom window. It was an awkward little square, but she thought she'd be able to squeeze through. Cyprin, though, what would become of Cyprin if she left? Her immediate impression was that Cyprin would curse and then go on to the Underground anyway to rat on Purcell. But that mental imagery wasn't sitting right anymore.

No, she knew what Cyprin would do. Cyprin would emotionally collapse under the weight of another abandonment. Never mind that Saul had not *meant* to abandon her, he was gone all the same, and Cyprin was plainly hanging by a thread.

Purcell couldn't do that to her.

Back in the main room of the diner, Cyprin was already standing. "Are you ready to go? The library is only ten blocks from here."

Into the concrete jungle again. It didn't bear thinking about, but someone had to look out for Cyprin. Cyprin, who was more broken and nuanced than she'd realized. Purcell nodded.

CHAPTER 31

CYPRIN

Cyprin found the library doors blown open, with piled-book bonfires outside the entrance. A few slumpers and hollow-looking citizens warmed their hands over the blaze. It was getting colder and colder out. Now and then the huddled crowd glanced nervously into the library, like children waiting for instruction.

Purcell stared at people as they went past—the exact opposite of what you should do when faced with a bunch of keyed-up mammals—and then they were in the open doorway of the library. A man in chitin-like armor held a long-nosed gun at the floor as his compatriot patted them down. They were waved through.

This was a mess. Cyprin had caught feelings for Purcell and did not want to see her harmed, but she'd do anything, anything to live another day. See another sunrise. The Underground could have what was left of the rose, take Purcell. If there was a Cyprin left to feel guilty and cry, that would be a win. Yes, that was how she ought to think about this.

"Well, I'm glad to see someone in this city is keeping calm and orderly." Purcell's voice was full of nervous fake cheer. Cyprin fought down the urge to make a crack about what a great sign burning books was. She didn't need Purcell bolting, not now that Mama Inkburn had told her she was right on the cusp of the twenty-fourth hour.

Inside, the décor was wood-on-wood. Some half-emptied shelves sat up front, but most were filled with books from floor to ceiling. The library had stained-glass windows at intervals, though some were sharp ruins now, where guards leaned the nozzles of their weapons out into the dark.

Purcell and Cyprin joined the end of a line, like they were waiting to see a bank teller. Cyprin watched the people in front of them get redirected to different parts of the library based on what they were asking for: food, shelter, emotional support.

Eventually their turn arrived. Burn marks speckled the information desk, but it was still manned, albeit by a woman in a balaclava who looked like her ideal comfort read would be something along the lines of *A Hundred Ways to Hit People Over the Head.*

Cyprin's hands were sweating. She imagined the bomb inside her as a strobing red light, growing brighter, flashing faster. If she didn't get to the Underground soon and give them something, *anything*, to sink their teeth into, she was a goner. At least she'd gotten to kiss Purcell before she had to die.

"We're looking for *A Cake Decorator's Guide to Black Holes*," she told the desk-minder. "You have that?"

The woman nodded. "Right this way, please." She was silently replaced by another nondescript figure in chitin armor.

As they followed their new guide, Purcell said, "I'd heard stories, but I hadn't realized the Underground were so organized. And look, they're handing out batteries and generators to people over there. That's nice. Isn't that nice?"

Cyprin couldn't bring herself to agree with that statement, nor did disagreeing seem a sensible venture. She settled for saying nothing. She stood close to Purcell, so close that their arms bumped against each other. Purcell's breathing and body heat made the dark city so much more bearable. Cyprin was going to keep that beautiful little meanie safe . . . right up until the moment she betrayed Purcell to the Underground.

A wiry man walked by them, a walkie-talkie held close to his mouth. "Sector forty-four is secured, we still hold the city." A static sound buzzed as the line changed, and a muffled voice replied. The man nodded, though whoever he was speaking to wouldn't hear that. Then he said, "The priestguard have pulled back to the palace. If we keep the pressure on, they'll have to keep bolstering that position. They'll be trapped."

Cyprin and Purcell's library guide gave the guy the stink eye, and he covered the walkie-talkie with a hand, as if it were indecently dressed, and moved away from them. Clearly some untoward shit was going on. Cyprin hoped Purcell wasn't going to notice that and skedaddle.

They passed through a hallway into the library's Quiet Study Rotunda, or what was left of it. All the chairs and desks had been pushed up against the walls and a literal hellhole had been sledgehammered into the floor, ringed with lanterns as if the whole thing were an elaborate setup for summoning a demon. Ladders lined its jagged sides.

"Down there," said their guide, gesturing.

Purcell leaned over the hole in the floor with very poor body awareness. It was kind of fascinating to watch. Purcell's center of gravity was going, going, gone. Cyprin grabbed hold of the loose fabric between Purcell's shoulder blades just in time to tug her back to safety. Her heart thumped as though it had been her own body about to tumble down.

To Cyprin's annoyance, the armored woman didn't seem to care that Purcell had almost cliff-dived like a lemming. She left them there and went back to her position at the info desk. Cyprin and Purcell weren't a threat to anything; they were detritus, washed up by the high tide of chaos outside. The real threat was the power outage and the persistently dark sky, and by the sounds of it, that was the real opportunity as well.

"Come on." Cyprin didn't wait to see if Purcell would follow; if she hesitated now, she'd be lost. She just picked a ladder and went down, and down, and down. The light flickered in unnerving ways that made the rungs of the ladder seem ephemeral. An updraft threatened to blast her right out, and the whole contraption shook like a bad DIY project.

Below them was the desiccated husk of a shopping mall. Cyprin's shoes squeaked on the tiles as she dropped off the ladder. She didn't have to ask anyone where to go—a trail of lanterns, battery-powered white ones like Purcell's flashlights, spread out at inconvenient intervals, leading off into the subterranean nightmare world. A nice breadcrumb trail all the way to the witch's house.

A good way back up the ladder, Purcell's bottom wobbled as first one shaking foot and then the other made it down to the next thin metal rung. Cyprin stopped dead and just looked up at her, wondering how such an awkward nerd had lasted so long. Purcell was too precious for this world. Cyprin considered yelling for her to hurry or maybe clapping and cheering instead.

The ladder rattled against the edge of the hole in the library floor. Purcell froze until the rattling stopped and then slowly, painstakingly started descending again. In Cyprin's mind's eye a hundred Purcells startled, slipped, and fell, and the thought of losing Purcell like that was terrifying. She decided against making any kind of distracting noise. There was a glass wall nearby. Cyprin picked up the nearest lantern and wandered over to press her nose against the ancient filmy surface. *Oh! Ohhhhh.* Perfect.

By the time Purcell arrived, Cyprin had nearly finished beating the dust out of an ancient leather jacket. It was a deep burgundy, with sharp metal studs at the high points. The way it fit made Cyprin wonder if everybody used to have massive shoulders. She fluffed out the sleeves and checked over the cuffs. A song was emerging, as always seemed to happen to her in the undercity. She hummed a few bars.

"Hey, what do you think?" she asked Purcell. "You want one? There's a whole store full of them." She hoped Purcell would want one. The thought of Purcell in leather was quite delectable.

Purcell blanched at the jacket, or her experience on the ladder, maybe both. "Eww, put it down, Cyprin! You don't know where it's been!"

"Sure I do, it's been right here."

"And why did it get left here? Why are there shops full of stuff under the city? What happened here?" Purcell was so animated when she was distressed.

Cyprin shrugged and bit the plastic tag off her sleeve to deflect. That didn't go quite as planned, and she spat dust. "I don't know. Whatever always happens. This is one of the top layers, so some of the stuff is still good. Farther down it gets gross."

"*Farther* down? How far does it go?" Purcell's eyes shone artificial silver in the lamplight, and it was hard to look away from them.

Cyprin scratched the back of her neck. The leather was mostly well-kept, but it was cracked and itchy around the neckline and at the elbows. "Well, there's this layer. We're at, like, the sky level of that. Some of the scrapers and malls run pretty deep. It gets ugly at around street level. Then, under this, there's another one. The architecture is all different there, and there's writing but it isn't readable. That's as far as I've been, but I've heard from some of the slumpers that below that is a shorter layer, with crystals growing in some of the houses and petrified trees, and—Purcell, are you listening?"

Purcell almost looked like she was in a trance. "And under that?"

"I've never heard of anyone going down that deep. If they do, they don't come back, or don't talk about it." It was spooky, talking about this down here, with Purcell's giant owl eyes reflecting her face back in shades of specter white. Cyprin hummed a few bars again.

"You've never asked yourself what happened to these other cities?" Purcell ventured closer to Cyprin and wound a tentative hand around her arm, which Cyprin should have dislodged immediately . . . but didn't.

"Other cities?" Cyprin felt a shift and spreading heat in her stomach, like a microwave meal overheating, getting ready to . . . explode. Though maybe it was just nerves. With an effort, she shook Purcell off and continued down the corridor, following the trail of lamps and hoping the Underground weren't set up too far away.

"There aren't any other cities." Cyprin talked as she walked. It was easier to talk if she wasn't looking directly at Purcell. "It's all Asperia. You know, roads get patched, the street level gets higher, and suddenly it's cheaper to build on top of existing buildings than to knock them down first. All that twelve-hells nonsense about the undercity isn't real, it's just myth, you know, more colorful than saying if you go farther down your toes will freeze off and your brain will implode."

The ensuing silence lasted so long Cyprin had to check to make sure Purcell was still there. There she was, scuffing along, looking like an indoor-only cat that had seen the sky for the first time.

Cyprin hated how jumpy she always got down here. The song rose in her mind again, and this time she let it out in full. "*Who's a happy fellow, Mallow, Mallow, Marshhh Mallow! Lucky, happy fellow, Mallow, Mallow, Marshhh Mallow!*" With any luck that outburst would be enough to change the subject.

Purcell missed her footing and almost fell over. "Is that—Are you singing about a breakfast cereal?"

"Yes?"

"Could you not?"

The nerve of her. Cyprin almost didn't feel like a human dung heap for leading her down here just to hand her over to the Underground. Just to save her own sorry ass. Almost. "Fine. Fun police."

A frozen escalator yawned into a chasm. Stalactites hung from the ceiling and teen stores full of moldering fast fashion lurked on the floor. Cyprin took a tentative step. The escalator stairs were barely illuminated, slick with condensation and slime. "Hold onto the railing when you come down, it's slippery," she said. She didn't want Purcell to fall.

The descent was slow going. Purcell squeaked a few times, but didn't freeze up the way she had done on the ladder. Purcell might have been as shiny and unmarked as a toy fresh out of the box, but she always, always rose to the occasion.

When they were both safely down, Cyprin followed the lantern trail again, leading off past a mushroomy stretch of bench seating between old sporting-equipment stores.

"But," said Purcell, picking up the thread again, "that doesn't explain why there are shops full of stuff down here. You're telling me it made sense to abandon this mall and build a library on top of it, but not to empty out the shops and close the mall down properly beforehand? And it's not just this place, is it? The slumpers come down here for salvage, right? They wouldn't do that if there was nothing to salvage. None of this makes sense."

"Are you still on that?" Cyprin found she needed to temper her voice, so she didn't sound as spooked as she was. "Look, there's no skeletons, right? At least, there's only the usual amount. Normal stuff happened down here. Normal, normal."

Purcell laughed, an edge of hysteria to it. "The *usual amount* of skeletons?"

"I mean, they're here, but they're all in graves and stuff. Most of them, anyway. I've heard of one or two—you know what, let's talk about something else." The smell of the morgue was back again, like some of the air there had never left her.

"Fine, whatever. Are you sure the Underground are going to do the right thing with this flower?" Without leaving space for an answer to her question, Purcell continued. "It's just, it doesn't sound like the darkness is working out badly for them. I'm having doubts. Aren't you having doubts?"

Not quite the level of agreement Cyprin had been hoping for. They stopped outside a shop full of tennis-racket skeletons and turned to face each other.

Purcell looked at Cyprin.

Cyprin looked at Purcell.

And just like that, despite and maybe because of the perilous situation they were in, Cyprin knew she'd prefer to let all this drop, even if just for a moment, and throw herself at Purcell. Purcell who was her mean little equal. Purcell who was still here. She tried to pack all that feeling into the look she gave Purcell. All the longing. All the undeniable romantic tension. Ooh, they could be so bad for each other, and like a B-grade horror film, maybe they'd be so bad they'd be good.

Suddenly, Cyprin's eye was drawn downward to where, beside Purcell's left shoe, a bunch of mushrooms popped upward like umbrellas on a windy day. Cyprin waved a hand at them. "Did you do that?"

When she looked back up, Purcell's chin wobbled. "Grandma Amma would have known what to do."

She'd been on the verge of jumping Purcell's bones. How did grandma come into this? "Wait, what just happened?"

Purcell sniffled. "You'll make fun of me."

Uncomfortable recollections surfaced, of Cyprin crying as Maverick laughed uproariously at her latest attempt at pancakes, Maverick laughing at her still needing Velcro shoes in the eighth grade because she couldn't tie laces, Maverick laughing at her first smudgy attempts at makeup. Oh, she got it. Purcell's granny was *that* kind of thing.

"I'm sorry, I'm an asshat. Please, just try me," she said. "Please."

Purcell's grandma had been hailed as a hero, just as Maverick was. Cyprin bet hardly anyone would be willing to listen to Purcell bitch about the hero of the whole damned gardens. But she was here for it. She knew how to be here for that.

Purcell gave Cyprin a guarded look that was watery with tears. "I'm a clone. Of my famous grandmother. And I'm still not as smart as her."

"Excuse me?" Behind the shock a hundred jokes got into formation and begged to be let out. Purcell was her own grandma? This was comedy gold. But if you made fun of someone else's pain for too long, that person might wind up afraid to feel anything at all.

Purcell sat down, and as her tears watered the ground, more little mushrooms appeared and stretched up toward her. "I don't know why I'm telling you this."

Cyprin ran a hand over her scalp stubble and squatted in front of Purcell. She didn't always want to be playing the too-cool asshole role that she'd copied from Maverick. Being mean was more comfortable than revealing anything of herself and being rejected for that. But it was lonely. Maybe if she'd let her guard down more with Saul, he never would have . . . vanished. Or at least he would have known how much she cared about him before he . . . disappeared. The chance to let Saul know what he meant to her was gone, but Purcell was still here and it was time to embrace that.

"I had this sort of father figure—Maverick Trelowny. He was a divine gardener. When my mother died, he was supposed to take care of me. But he never did. So I know what it's like to have a fucked-up family," said Cyprin.

Purcell's tears stopped. "Maverick? I know him. He used to come over for tea sometimes when my mother was still alive. He works in the greenhouses now."

What? "He's still alive?"

Holy dancing rats. She could've asked Purcell this whole time. But she hadn't thought to because Saul had told her Maverick was dead. Saul had lied to her and now he was gone and it was dark and they were in the undercity and she had a bomb in her stomach and she may have entirely missed the opportunity to confront Maverick.

Saul had lied to her. Why? Cyprin's vision got a bit liquidy and she studied her nails with great intent. Had Maverick looked for her? Did he try to reply to her letters only to be thwarted by terrible hand cramps? She had to know. "What's he like?"

"I never liked him. He used to complain about having a kid back in the city like it was some kind of social disease—Oh." Purcell put her hand over her mouth, but it was far too late.

He used to complain about having a kid.

The tears dried up, as if they'd soaked into Cyprin. Maverick didn't deserve her tears. He never had. "Right. Of course. Thanks for telling me."

Purcell shrugged. "No problem." There was a flat honesty about her; she'd dropped the air of superiority and perfection that she'd always seemed to wear like a crown.

Cyprin said, "You know, a lot of plants are clonal. Willows, fig, crocus." She was offering Purcell an olive branch. Their families were equally fucked up, which was something Cyprin hadn't expected they'd have in common.

"That's true," said Purcell.

"They have redundant genes that switch on and off, a higher rate of somatic mutations—plant one in a different plot, hells, just at a different time point and you'll get a completely different plant." Cyprin was attempting to make Purcell feel better. If clonal plants could each be very individual, then Purcell could be her own person too.

"That's very kind of you," said Purcell, despondently, but it seemed she'd got what Cyprin was trying to do. "Humans are different, though."

Cyprin's knees cracked as she stood. She offered Purcell a hand. "I'm sorry your grandma was a mad scientist."

Purcell's sweaty little fingers entwined with her own and they stood, waaayy too close together. "I'm sorry your dad was an asshole."

Hearing Purcell refer to Maverick as her dad was an electric shock to the heart. Her dad. She supposed he was that. To a child there was no difference between a father figure and a father.

All this time Maverick had been alive in the gardens, ignoring her. She could've walked past him or even handed him a bag of turnips. It'd been so long since she'd seen him, would she even have known? Would *he* have? Now she was miles away, in the undercity, about to explode. She'd never get the chance to change his shampoo out for pink hair dye or hide a dead rat under his mattress. Hells, as head gardener she could've had him buried up to his neck in steaming mulch or reassigned him to the mail room and forced him to write responses to all three hundred of kid Cyprin's letters.

"I wish I'd had time to confront him," said Cyprin. She took in a lungful of Purcell's marshmallow scent quite by accident and then stumbled backward a little, hot in the face. They had just shared something vulnerable, and there had been no biting comments, no slapstick humor to undo the moment. This was real. It was too real.

Fuck it. Cyprin took Purcell's soft face in her fingertips, savoring Purcell's involuntary gulp of nerves. Cyprin leaned in and kissed her.

Purcell's mouth was soft and warm, she made a little snort of panic, and her eyelids fluttered like she was forcing them shut when Cyprin sneaked a look.

It was a selfish, borrowed moment of happiness. Purcell was still a stuck-up generational gardener, and Cyprin was still going to hand her over to the Underground. There was no choice, they were going to explode Cyprin if she didn't.

Cyprin pulled away, and Purcell kissed air for a moment.

"You're not your grandma." Cyprin could give Purcell this much. "For one, I wouldn't kiss a grandma. But also, it sounds like your granny was a mean, uptight perfectionist, and that's nothing compared to your epic villainy."

Purcell's lips trembled. "You just—does this mean that you—"

"Yes, I like you, Purcell," said Cyprin. She grinned meanly. "But not as much as you like me."

Purcell spent a second glaring and then clicked back into gear. "You're confident in the Underground, aren't you? We couldn't trust anyone in the Divine Gardens to act in our best interest. How can you be sure the Underground are trustworthy? Perhaps you and I should—"

Oh no, this was not the right time for Purcell to develop a social conscience, even if Cyprin did love to hear it.

"Oh, the Underground are definitely good," Cyprin lied. "Besides, we're already in the undercity." After all the kissing, the sharing secrets, and the kissing again, she was still about to massively screw Purcell over. She really was a city rat. She'd step on anyone just to live another day. She wondered which one of the twelve hells she was going to end up in. Maybe she'd spend quality time in each one of them, as holiday homes.

As they set off, deeper into the darkness, Purcell took her hand.

They found the Underground on the lowest level of the mall, set up in a dungeon-themed game store. Cyprin went through a fake stone doorway and saw a group of about a hundred people dressed in black, balaclava-clad. Shelves holding putrefying board games, some of which were little more than sludge, had been pushed to the sides of the room, and a big, lantern-lit table had been set up in the center. Everyone milled around it, talking urgently. A few balaclava clones looked up at Cyprin and Purcell. Most ignored them. On the table, a giant map of Asperia had several blinking lights on it. It was an eerie echo of what Cyprin had seen in the priestguard headquarters. Cyprin breathed in cold carrots, held it, let it out slowly. She'd been imagining subtlety, tact, guile. But faced with the people who'd turned her life into the last five minutes of a math exam, she felt differently.

"Which of you fuckers put this bomb in my stomach?"

A rustle of movement happened as a hundred heads turned to face her, Purcell's included, her mouth a little round circle of horror.

Cyprin ignored the gut punch of Purcell's look as she grinned and went to sit on the map. "Wanna set it off *now*?"

CHAPTER 32

PURCELL

While all eyes were on Cyprin, Purcell moved slowly backward. She'd already been betrayed nine ways to Sunday, and she knew she was looking at betrayal again.

Cyprin made a snow angel on the table, sending people's notes flying. "Go on and explode me, right now!" she cried, deranged.

Rather than scrambling to get away, the nearest Underground operative leaned closer. "Did you find it? The terraforming object on the mountain?"

Purcell heard it clearly.

In Purcell's mind, a scene played out, of Cyprin being compromised by the Underground, Cyprin being sent to follow Purcell up the mountain to the rose, Cyprin taking both Purcell and what was left of the rose back to the Underground. It didn't look good. Purcell had walked right into a trap. She'd been blinded by her feelings; she'd wanted Cyprin to be good. But wanting didn't make it true.

"Excuse me, I—uh, think I'm in the wrong place." Her only thought was to back away. Purcell edged past a balaclava'd man who was leaning in the doorway. He didn't even look at her. Everyone was busy watching Cyprin. One of Cyprin's legs was stuck up in the air now like a cabaret dancer leaning back on a piano. Purcell slipped out the door.

Outside the dilapidated games shop, Purcell's eyes wavered over the possible exit points of the undercity mall. She had to get out. Long, cylindrical lights hung from the ceiling like broken fingers. Panels of corkboard, holed by age and damp, seemed ready to drop at any moment. It was oppressive. She was starting to develop the wild feeling of an animal in a trap, wondering if it could do with one less leg.

A bomb in Cyprin's stomach! A bomb in her stomach? What would they do to Purcell? Extort her to gain a foothold in the palace, most likely. She'd heard the conversations in the library, read the war-room vibe. This was a battle, and she'd been led right into the middle of it. Perhaps it had even been the Underground's idea to cut down the flower and create the darkness, and Purcell just happened to unknowingly achieve this for them. Perhaps that's what Cyprin had been on the mountain to do. The Underground certainly seemed prepared for it, and Cyprin appeared to be in trouble with them.

Before Cyprin had come along, the extent of "peril" had been a worm among the lettuce leaves, or a particularly bad hair day. Now Purcell was in the dark under the city, with a person who'd betrayed her and a group of dangerous rebels.

Panic engulfed the last rational thought and Purcell ran. Not back up toward the library where a bunch of other Underground operatives might nab her, but farther into the depths of the undercity. She was aware of wet, cold, dark, sideways, down, a lantern swinging at the end of her arm.

Her last coherent thought was of Cyprin's kisses and snarls.

When her thoughts returned, they said, *How far down are we?*

Purcell dropped the lantern she'd stolen from outside the Underground's lair and massaged her stiff hand. She leaned against a wall, catching her breath, and as she did so, something not quite algae and not quite mold shifted politely out of her way so that it didn't get on her clothes. She was in a tiled cavern. One side of it dipped down onto what looked like train tracks.

How had she gotten here? There'd been a couple of stairwells and (she shuddered) an empty elevator shaft. She'd climbed down there the way she'd climbed up hallway walls as a child, with hands and feet braced on one surface and her back pressing against the opposite wall, the lantern clutched in her teeth. Then there was an ill-advised swim across a sump, because why not get wet *again*? Somehow her glasses had managed to cling onto her face through the whole ordeal, which was a relief. She had to hand it to herself, she was *good* at running away. No one in any state of mind would be able to find her. Not even Purcell knew where Purcell was.

Huh, she thought, *this might just be the one thing that's worse than getting caught by the Underground.*

If not worse, certainly slower.

She was afraid. She was afraid, but she was practical. Purcell pushed off the wall and the black sludge that had ringed her like a chalk outline slowly moved back into place. Stay put and wait for help only seemed to apply in cases where the help didn't want to kidnap or potentially murder you. She needed to come up with a logical plan. Her job in the gardens had not been worth dying over, and neither was this. It shocked her to think Amma may have experienced the same revelation somehow, before retiring to the seaside. Were any of her thoughts her own?

Subway tracks glinted below. Tracks had to lead somewhere, didn't they?

Purcell sat down on the little ledge before the tracks and looked left and right. Both directions ran away into pitch-black tunnels. She had the bright idea of picking up a broken tile and throwing it down on the tracks to see if there was any difference in the echo. If one side sounded congested, maybe that would indicate a cave-in?

Louder than any echo came a squeal of metal, and a contraption emerged from the left tunnel. It looked like a child's drawing of a robot. A cracked plastic hard hat sat atop an oblong head. Two red headlights stood in for eyes and a smile was drawn below them with lacquered paint. Its body was the rough size and shape of a briefcase; segmented arms not much more sophisticated than twigs stuck out from its sides. A single wheel propelled it from underneath, worn down and throwing sparks. Purcell pulled her knees up into her chest as the robot passed below her on the tracks, but it didn't seem hostile.

It zigzagged a bit, then headed down the right-hand tunnel. She dropped onto the tracks and followed.

CHAPTER 33

CYPRIN

A balaclava just like all the others stepped forward. *Ah, yes, there's always a leader, even when they try to pretend there's not.* "There is no bomb."

What?

No bomb?

No fucking bomb??

Cyprin sat up and gripped the edge of the table like she was trying to break it, giving them her best death glare. "So it was you!" The little light globes marking out points of interest on the map dug into her bottom unpleasantly, only serving to deepen her anger.

"It doesn't matter who it was. It's just a tactic we use. We would never harm a civilian." The sounds coming out of the balaclava'd maniac were calm, reassuring, but the gun in their shoulder holster, and the black fabric covering every inch, were not doing much to convince her.

Just a tactic. Cyprin smiled and shook her head to herself. Then she launched off the table in a flurry of rage and flailing arms. She was almost quick enough to land a punch before several other balaclava-clad creatures wrestled her into stillness.

Cyprin sagged, panting, held at the elbows by two Underground operatives. Their ringleader came closer. They'd been rattled a little, which was satisfying. A tuft of orange hair stuck out of their balaclava, reminiscent of a tabby cat with a cowlick. "You've been up the mountain. Do you have the terraforming object?"

"Depends on what you mean by—" Cyprin managed to elbow whoever held her right side, and they staggered but didn't let go.

Tabby waved a hand. "Show her what it looks like outside of the city. Then she'll be more cooperative."

Cyprin went back to thrashing around. A chunky, battery-run tablet was brought in front of her face, so close the light from it nearly blinded her. Slowly, the haloed brightness resolved into shapes.

She stopped. "What am I looking at?"

"The eastern road into Asperia."

It was daytime in the video feed, which gave Cyprin an immediate sense of relief. The sky was blue, green grass studded the side of a road on which people in hazmat suits milled around with clipboards. Around the edges of the screen was the dumpy little mountain range that hemmed Verdure's eastern border, stippled with trees. A road sign for Asperia pointed to where the asphalt cut off into darkness. The city should have been there, in glittering anthills of scrapers, but instead, darkness domed like a black snow globe. A big machine that looked like a cross between a scorpion and a squid had rolled up to the end of the road and was shining a laser beam onto the black mirror surface, which rippled at the insult. Now and then, sparks flew where the laser met the dark. But nothing else happened.

"Are you telling me we're trapped?" said Cyprin. Was this worse than the whole world going dark? It shouldn't have been. But somehow, somehow it felt worse. At least if it was the whole world, they'd have all been in it together.

"Yes. Nothing goes in or out. We have operatives outside Verdure. We've tried from both sides and all angles of the dome."

The tablet was removed from under Cyprin's nose, but the image of the black tar dome wouldn't go away. Night-blind, the space before her resolved slowly into Balaclava Tabby.

"When we met before, we let you go," Tabby said. "You were supposed to bring the Divine to us, but our sources say he was replaced, so you went up the mountain, didn't you? You went after the terraforming object. You caused this. What did you do with it?"

Cyprin struggled again in the arms of the operatives holding her. People who planted fake bombs in you were maybe better than people who planted real bombs, but not by much. She was not feeling very cooperative. Although . . . it was very, very dark outside. "We didn't mean to—there was a flower, Purcell cut it—" Nearby, one of the balaclava clones lit up a battery-powered screen and began leafing through Purcell's bank records, medical records, TV-watching habits, everything. "Don't look at me like that! You wanted this to happen. You're out there playing soldiers and thanks to us you get to pretend that there was some other, more peaceful way that you wanted this to go!"

Cowlick crossed their arms. "You messed with the terraforming object. There will be casualties. And then crop failures, famine, disease. This was always the nuclear option. We never would have taken it. But the situation has arisen independently of us, and so we must react. Just tell me where the object is."

The other balaclava clones crowded in, intent on Cyprin, listening.

She'd been perfectly fine with dishing the dirt when she'd thought it was necessary to save her ass—well, maybe not perfectly fine. But she'd been going to do it. Now this had become about more than Cyprin.

Knowing the right thing to do in a situation had never been in her wheelhouse. Even just knowing the right thing to do for Cyprin was a crapshoot, at best. She squeezed her eyes shut for a moment to block out the Tabby nonsense.

Tabby was right.

Saul was missing because of her. Saul was somewhere out there, and the city was in danger, and all Cyprin ever did was break things. She could never seem to put them back together. Trusting the Underground was ludicrous, but when the forest is on fire, all the animals forget to eat each other in their rush to get out. She could put her trust in something like that.

Cyprin's shoulders fell, defeated. The people who held her tentatively relaxed their grip. "All right. Purcell has it. Purcell!" She turned her head to the doorway and there was no one there. Cyprin suffered a jolt of stomach-dropping apprehension. "Purcell?"

CHAPTER 34

PURCELL

Purcell took stock of her surroundings, keeping close to the safety of a nearby wall. She'd wandered through the subway tunnel until it had opened out into a plaza, where a corrugated-iron ceiling held back the weight of unfathomable tons of dirt. From there, she'd found a building, unlocked and imposing, and she'd gone in. It offered a sense of purpose where there currently was none. Raising the lantern over her head made the light stretch farther, though it also thinned it out. Cracked tiles that had once been shiny and white made up the big oblong of a swimming pool. A layer of black in the bottom could have been water or just muck. She moved away from the wall and walked, leaving the pool deck and pushing open a glass door that led into an adjoining building. After all, she couldn't possibly get any more lost.

Through the door, the rusted husks of exercise machines stood posed like a museum dinosaur exhibit. It almost felt as though she might catch tetanus just by looking. And worse than that was an underlying sense of dread, like an invisible mist coating her skin, getting deep down into her lungs. Ten thousand showers would not be enough. Something was *wrong* with this city. She'd slipped under its skin and found nothing but cancer all the way down.

She didn't know what she was looking for until she found it. A large, curved concierge desk and desk chair, plastic wheels crumbling, fabric rotted off, so that it looked like a very nasty torture device. Purcell pushed aside her squeamishness and opened the desk drawer. Inside was a lot of moldering paper, some skeletal pens, and something in a thin, see-through plastic briefcase. She took that out and opened it.

Smiley-face stickers littered the top of an attendance sheet. Behind that was a printed schedule, with classes like *Septuagenarian Swing!*, *Paddle-tastic!*, and *Bubble Club!*, each with the requisite exclamation mark. From what she knew of Asperia, it seemed in character. Maybe Cyprin had been right about this place, and it *was* the same old Asperia, all the way down. Still . . .

At the bottom of the case, Purcell found and opened a little diary. Perfectly preserved. At least the language was the same. The pages were refreshingly free of eldritch warnings or scribbled screams that ended in a trail of blood. The appointments simply grew more sparse as she flipped through. No "last day of work!" No "a portal into another reality opened up, think we might all walk through it," no "monster rose from Lake Pensive, I better call it a day." Just a half-filled schedule, trailing off, waiting to be picked up later.

Something terrible had happened here, a long time ago. Purcell was sure of it. Had the lights turned off for them too? Was there a mass evacuation? Was that why everything had been left as it was? Purcell knew what she'd take with her in an emergency, and despite how attached she was to the gardens, it wouldn't be anything from work. She needed to see what the houses looked like, and what was left in them.

She exited the rec center via an undercover walkway strewn with debris. An unexpected pang, like a blinking light in a disused call center, made her worry what the Underground were doing to Cyprin. Cyprin the would-be traitor wasn't all to blame. If the Underground had caught Purcell instead, she doubted she would have put up much of a fight. Cyprin was flawed, but understandable. Understandable and alluring in an angry, broken way.

The next passage connected to a lobby area. Lopsided chandeliers threatened sudden sparkling death from above. Floor-to-ceiling curtains that once must have been very plush now resembled the fur of bad taxidermy animals. HAPPY HOMES, said tarnished lettering, positioned like a sculpture across the lobby floor, each letter taller than Purcell. Her lantern spotlighted bits and pieces but never the whole picture, horror-movie style.

Purcell touched the plastic-wrapped rose corpse in her pocket. Her whole world had come crashing down over a plant. But not this plant. It had started much earlier than that. It had started at conception, thanks to Amma.

Amma's decision to leave the position of head gardener and retire by the sea with Ceely didn't seem so wild now. Perhaps Amma truly had faced the dark. And perhaps, like Amma, Purcell could find a way through it as well.

Purcell went up the stairs.

The first apartment she went into was quaintly decorated and contained a perfectly regular setup of bed and bedside table, kitchen, and dining area. That at least took care of the fear that monsters had called this place home; there were no eight-armed cardigans, no tail holes in the seats, no human-sized ovens. And everything seemed real enough, which meant this wasn't all some giant organism engaged in sick mimicry of the city above, waiting for people to come down and nest in its—Anyway, enough.

Purcell pushed farther into the apartment.

Ancient carpet displayed an unfortunate diamond pattern. Sad cats in matching teacups stared back at her out of a picture frame on the wall. It looked like someone had fired a mold-cannon over the whole thing. The spores were so thick in the air, you could see them.

Purcell covered her mouth with a sleeve. Her shoulder hurt from carrying the lantern. She put it down, wishing she didn't have to sit the lantern in so much mold. As the thought arrived, the mold moved politely out of the way. Something occurred to her. She lowered her sleeve to speak. The mold in the room listened to her proposal, then began to coalesce. To her alarm, some of it came out of her mouth.

The growing pile gathered into a little deformed snowman on the floor. A knobbly arm or tendril reached out and grabbed the handle of the lantern. The light wobbled and swung for a moment, not quite clearing the floor. From under the door behind her, more mold poured into the room, joining with the pile to lift the lantern more surely. The resulting one-armed version of a leaf heap swung the lamp high and then back down again. It glopped in a little circle around the room, then settled at Purcell's feet.

"Right," she said, trying not to show how disturbed she was that this had worked. "Thank you."

Her new helper followed as she rummaged around the room. Everything seemed as staged as a doll's house. A frieze depicting life in motion. All that was missing were the people. There was a cup on the bedside table, holding the crystalized remnants of some liquid. Drawers full of clothes. One of those music-box jewelery things, but the ballerina was too rusted to twirl, and the jewelery tangled in an oxidized heap. There were no signs that anyone had been hurriedly packing. No signs that anyone had met an untimely death, unless they had found a way to explode into a film of grime. Purcell moved back out to the landing and on to the next house, the lantern-swinging mold hanging close behind her.

In the neighboring apartment, colored blocks littered the floor, along with a chalkboard and a teddy bear. The fossil record of a young family, sans bones. A scrunched juice box lay sideways on a coffee table, a fashion magazine was open to a page that showed jackets like Cyprin's being worn by people who had their eyebrows shaved off. Though none of them wore their jackets with quite the same charisma as Cyprin. Cyprin, who had betrayed Purcell but who might have acted differently if Purcell had been given the chance to show her safety and love.

The colors of the room came to life as more mold left the walls and joined the pile beside Purcell. Out of the corner of her eye she could see it had grown to the size of a small child. And what had she discovered, apart from a newfound ability to animate mold? Candles. Candles and flashlights. Which wasn't unusual. Didn't everybody own candles and flashlights? Especially ye olde worlde people. It wasn't anything to draw conclusions from. Purcell drew conclusions anyway. A whole lot of candles and flashlights were being brought out in the city above too, to combat the sudden total dark. Maybe the same thing had happened to these people.

She moved on to the next place, and then the place after that, and found the same Still Life with Candles in every one of them. Yes, this had happened before. And it had happened long before Amma's time.

Ten houses later, Purcell sat on the floor of a paint-splattered artist's studio apartment. The lantern bumped beside her as the mold pile spread out to eat the wallpaper. While she rested, she imagined a million, million tiny mouths chewing, and, instead of making her feel uncomfortable, it made her feel less alone. But she was lost and thirsty and tired. Dying was not an attractive option, even with friends.

She didn't want to find her way back to the Underground in the mall or the library swarming with guards above that. She wanted to go somewhere else on the surface. Somewhere safe. She wanted to go home. To get there all she had to do was go up, right? Why hadn't that occurred to her before? It was painfully simple. Slumpers must have bored into the tops of most of these buildings. How many thousands of entry and exit points might they have left in their wake?

Purcell rubbed her sore knees and got up again. "All right. I can't just eat the wallpaper like you guys. Come on, let's get out of here."

The light careened around as the mold streamed off the walls and heaped up to carry the lantern again. Purcell let herself out onto the landing and headed along the corridor, looking for a way to go higher. She came upon a fire escape and ushered her moldy companion in before her so she didn't break her neck in the dark. It made a soft, clumpy hissing sound as it traversed the stairs.

She exited a stairwell at the top of the building into a domed garden. Dirt coated the top of the dome, and the weight of it had buckled the metal struts and broken the glass panes between them. Purcell's shoes crunched on broken glass as she surveyed the ceiling of the dome. No exits up there. No handy ladders leading down, no ropes dangling. No boreholes left by slumpers at all. The spindly trunks of ornamental trees and a collapsing park bench were the only things left intact, among sad planters full of near-fossilized sticks. Purcell perched gingerly on a corner of the bench.

The slumpers hadn't been to this building; everything in the apartments had appeared untouched. It stood to reason that if she kept going until she found somewhere that *had* been plundered, there ought to be a way out nearby. If she was lucky, maybe she'd even bump into someone who could point her to it. Purcell reached into her pocket and crackled the plastic that wrapped around what was left of the rose. So beautiful in life, now a sad, gray husk in her hand.

She found herself wondering what it would have been like in these apartments when they were still in use. The hive of light and life they must have been. Kids laughing and running in the hallways, the scent of spice and fat drifting out of a hundred kitchens. And this garden. It must have been a kind of hothouse. They could've grown anything they wanted. Perhaps there'd even been butterflies or other pollinators, and a view out over the rest of the city. Purcell shut her eyes. She could see it clearly in her mind.

She let her imagination wander down a painted pathway between planters overflowing with seasonal produce, decorative flowers. How this space must have been warm even on a cold day, the sun a golden concentrate that streamed through the glass above, the blue sky big enough to make this feel like a proper garden and not just a rooftop.

One of Purcell's fingers twitched like she was conducting a symphony. The air buzzed.

She opened her eyes in time to see green shoots pushing their way laboriously out of the dirt in the empty stone planter beside her. A twig-tree's dead wood burst apart as new growth rocketed through it. A green leaf unfurled through a crack in the old trunk.

The sentient mold pile dropped the lantern with a clatter and retreated to huddle in the stairwell. All around Purcell, green fingers burst through the dirt of their graves.

She screamed.

CHAPTER 35

CYPRIN

Balaclava Tabby ordered several minions to send drones looking for Purcell in the undercity. She had run away, and apparently not in the direction of the library. It was almost impossible to believe someone as skittish as Purcell would choose the unknowns of the undercity over facing the Underground. There wasn't even any facing particularly needed. They just wanted the rose. Or so they said—Cyprin's forehead wrinkled as she imagined the mission creep that would inevitably follow. *Give us the terraforming object, good, now give us the keys to the gardens, now we just want you to do a small job or two for us.* Still, even though fleeing seemed like a logical choice, it took gumption to actually do it. Cyprin was impressed. Well, equal parts impressed, worried, and seething that she'd been abandoned in her time of need. She had the unreasonable desire to be loved at her worst, and she'd almost got that from Purcell.

Someone sat Cyprin down in a chair and someone else stood beside it, keeping their finger hovering over the trigger of their gun. Cyprin was sweating so hard that it dripped from her cuffs onto the floor. This might still end in her demise.

Tabby walked by her, barking orders. The whites of their eyes flashed out of the holes in the balaclava as they glanced at Cyprin. "Get us two packs," Tabby yelled into a walkie-talkie. "Charged headlamps, a week's worth of supplies. Slumper equipment."

They stopped in front of Cyprin. She looked up from her chair.

"We need the terraforming object," Tabby said.

"Do you even know what to do with it?" Cyprin could hardly bring herself to care about the rose now that Purcell was gone. Her imagination had been conjuring images of Purcell falling down shafts, Purcell being eaten by rats, Purcell being smothered by a collapse somewhere. All those things would be her fault, and the little garden gnome didn't deserve any of it, not really.

They were going to ask Cyprin to go after Purcell, to find her and reason with her as a trusted face, because they needed the flower. And Cyprin was going to do it, because she needed Purcell. Ahem—Needed Purcell to forgive her.

"We'll put our best minds on it," said Tabby, with unreasonable calm. "We want the sun to rise again, Cyprin. If you're a decent person, you'll want the same."

Still, if she was going to agree to do the thing anyway, it couldn't hurt to push some boundaries. "What if I want something else?"

Tabby's balaclava bunched as they smirked underneath it. "You're bargaining for your cooperation? Go on then, name it. I'd rather not have to go out there with you in cuffs. Give me something you want more than revenge on us, and we can go forward as friends."

"I need to know what happened to the Divine."

Tabby's eyes widened almost imperceptibly. "Huh. No wonder you didn't bring him to us. Pity. You might have saved his life that way. You won't like the answers we find, Cyprin."

"Just find me answers. Proof."

"All right." Tabby extended a gloved hand toward her.

Cyprin wiped the fear-sweat off on her legs and reached out. They shook on it.

"Will you help me find the object?" said Tabby, watching her face. Their grip was a fraction too tight.

"I'll help you find Purcell. If she's dropped the flower somewhere, that's not my problem." Cyprin turned her eyes into drill holes and Tabby recoiled a little, though they held their composure well. Better than most people when faced with Cyprin's death stare.

A balaclava-clad minion hovered.

Tabby was called away and Cyprin was left waiting again. It made sense that they'd scout the area with drones instead of rushing out blindly to look for Purcell. Total sense. And if her magnificent body was just a seething pile of rats and bones by the time they got there? Well, that would be bad luck. You always take care of yourself first in an emergency, that's what every employee-induction video had taught Cyprin. You don't go rushing into trouble.

Not even when the person in trouble is objectively the best thing to happen to you in your entire life. You carefully consider the situation, bide your time . . .

A tablet was shoved under her nose again.

"Is this her?" said Tabby.

From the perspective of the gnat-sized drone, the lobby of the apartment building was obscenely scaled, the echoing hollow of an emperor's tomb. Monstrous pillared lettering stretched across the screen beyond readability. The distortion from the camera made the whole place curve. Snowy dust motes fell.

Purcell's screams reverberated off the walls, making the camera drift sideways for a second as the vibration in the air currents hit the little drone. It righted itself again and flew into an air duct, turning on its infrared scanners and heading upward. A red-warm blob seen through walls was the rough shape of Purcell, cowering. The smell of the morgue returned to her.

Cyprin shot up out of her chair, taking the tablet in both hands. Why was Purcell screaming like that? This couldn't be happening. Would Purcell look like she was sleeping too when they found her?

Tabby waved a finger to a minion behind them. "Mark that spot and plot us the best route. Bring the packs over."

The drone emerged from a vent at the top of a staircase, the red-and-gold heat blob of Purcell taking up most of its range of vision now. Soon, they'd be able to see exactly what was happening to her. Cyprin almost threw up just anticipating the horror. The drone hovered for a second to get its bearings. Before it could get going again, what looked like a mold-covered fly swatter bore down on it and the video snuffed out in a black-and-white buzz of static.

Cyprin waved the tablet in Tabby's direction. "What was that?"

"Get an extra energy weapon for Cyprin" was their answer.

Cyprin was already wrenching a pack off a nearby minion who was ferrying two of them over. She shouldered it as fast as she could. "Hurry up," she told Tabby.

What was happening to Purcell? Had the rats got her? Or something worse? Was she half trapped under rubble? Was she on the edge of some impossible precipice, about to fall? Was Cyprin never going to see her again? Some other, snarkier part of Cyprin said, *Purcell is probably screaming about the dark and the ick and being lost.* But after the day they'd had, that seemed like a best-case scenario.

Purcell pushed her and challenged her. Purcell saw her, all the pain and aspirations, the raw-meat hurt of her.

And Purcell had liked Cyprin despite all of this. That was something worth fighting for, the way she should have fought for Saul.

A weapon, nose down in a shoulder holster, was slung over Cyprin when she was already halfway out the door. No one moved to stop her or slow her down. Tabby had to jog to catch up.

Cyprin's headlamp was a size too small and gave her a tension headache. For a while, she and Tabby didn't speak. Cyprin was busy imagining all the bad things that might have been happening to Purcell. They followed the homing signal from the drone as it led them through the broken back half of the mall and past a multilevel parking lot filled with hovercars that looked almost serviceable. Tabby slowed them down a few times, covetously inspecting a couple of the old hovercars until Cyprin shot near their foot with her energy weapon and pretended it was an accident.

They went through a fissure in the concrete wall of the parking lot into an office building with a honeycomb of round cubicles. Blisters of dirt pressed in through straining plex windows.

The tablet Tabby consulted for directions wanted them to go down, so they made their way to a defunct elevator shaft in the middle of the building and gazed into the rectangular hole as cold-carrot smell came up to meet them.

"Down there?" said Cyprin, desperately hoping to be wrong.

She was handed some ropes and carabiners. Welp, she was in this now. She started descending.

An unexpected bonding experience happened in the elevator shaft. Cyprin's wayward ass made violent contact with Tabby's head, and in a desperate attempt to dispel the awkwardness, Tabby broke the silence. "So, what is Purcell to you?"

This question prompted a little montage of Purcell-related memories. Her righteous anger at the pageant. Her outfit on the mountain, her fierceness in the morgue. The way she tilted her head and narrowed her eyes when she was really pissed off. The way she twirled her hair when she thought no one was looking.

But Cyprin was mad that the Underground had already squeezed her for so much. Instead, she said, "Don't tell me you don't already know." They'd belayed themselves to very nearly the bottom of the shaft. For the most part, the threatening silver square of the elevator remained frozen above their heads, but the last few feet were accompanied by the uncomfortable sounds of metal moving.

Cyprin's boots met the dirt first. She unclipped herself and tugged on the rope. They'd planned to leave it like that for the way back, but the thought of climbing up toward tons of precariously balanced metal was not filling her with joy.

"She's head gardener, you're interim head gardener," said Tabby, with the laissez-faire attitude of a spy who'd already been found out. "So . . . you're rivals?"

"Equals," muttered Cyprin.

"I think I get it." Tabby's voice was all commiserations. "You need her around to know that you're the best," they said, completely missing the depth of it. "Your Divine was like that, for me. I never met him, of course. But I watched him from afar. Given enough time, he would have made an excellent opponent, maybe even an ally. It's too bad he didn't make it."

Tabby tried to leave the bottom of the elevator shaft, but Cyprin stood in their way. "Take that silly mask off," she said. She wanted to do harm, to cause hurt in whatever way was available.

"What?"

"I said, take your mask off, I want to see your face."

"Wearing masks is what we do. No one gets to see any other member of the Underground." Tabby crossed their arms. Cyprin crossed her arms too.

Tabby tried to sidle past her, but she stepped neatly in the way.

"Oh fine, fine. But I'm putting it back on afterward. It keeps my head warm."

As Tabby pulled the balaclava off, their hair went wild with static, like it had been rubbed against a bunch of balloons. Underneath was a person Cyprin's age, with a flip of red hair, tons of facial piercings, and rosacea cheeks.

"Moss?" said Cyprin. The immediate feeling was relief, that Moss was safe and alive.

Moss's eyes turned hurt. "You really didn't recognize my voice?"

Cyprin erupted in anger. "Would you have recognized *my* voice, if it was in an infomercial for torturing babies and cats?" That came out so loud a few rocks tumbled down from above them, but Cyprin didn't care. "Why are—Why did—*Just why!*"

"I don't have to explain myself to you," snarled Moss. "You left me high and dry. But since we're talking about explanations, what's with that outfit? My dental floss doesn't even get that far into the cracks."

"I thought about you when it went dark. I was worried you might have been trapped with the apples," said Cyprin, despite Moss's betrayal, or maybe because of it. She wanted Moss to see that she cared before she punched them in the face.

"You spared an itty-bitty moment to think of me? Why, you shouldn't have!" Moss grinned, but there was fire in their eyes.

"Moss, I'm being serious! How did you get all mixed up in this?"

"I'm being serious too. You never answered a single one of my letters. You've made it clear we are not friends. So we're not. End of story. I get my terraforming object, you get"—Moss snorted—"your new 'Moss' back, and we both go back to living in our respective chum buckets. Oh, except yours doesn't have a Divine ruling over it anymore, so we're going to come in and take that over."

What a cruel, unrepentant thing to say. Cyprin pushed Moss, but Moss caught their balance easily and laughed.

"Don't talk about the Divine like he's dead," said Cyprin. "You've probably got him tied up in a meat freezer somewhere. I wouldn't put it past you." She so desperately wanted this to be true. Deep down she knew that it wasn't.

Moss was still laughing. "I'm really not that bad. You should look into a mirror sometime if you wanna see what bad looks like."

Which was unfairly fair of them.

Somewhere out there, Purcell was getting eaten by a rat while Cyprin argued about who was the worst nonfriend. She put her hands up in surrender. "Let's go get this done and then never speak to each other again."

"Deal," said Moss.

The next section of building had collapsed into a wet sinkhole. An underwater creature clicked at them as they swam across the sump, or perhaps a remnant AI was down there, drowned, holding a drill up above its head, trying to screw nails into a ceiling that wasn't there anymore, about to reach Cyprin's feet—

"I gotta hand it to your new Moss, she really knows how to run away," Moss grumbled, shaking water off on the other side.

"That she does." Cyprin seemed to be spending a lot of her life soaked from head to toe these days, in grime, oil, water, chasing after Purcell.

Cyprin and Moss went down another broken escalator and through an empty subway tunnel, circumventing a large theater the Underground had deemed structurally unsound. Their footsteps and breathing echoed off the walls as they went. And then there was a *tick, tick, sputter* sound, like faulty reticulation. Cyprin swung her headlamp to follow the noise. She'd heard ghost stories of slumpers that went mental, sitting in the dark, tapping on the walls. But this wasn't that. The old subway stations had blocky humanoid cleaner robots. Most of them defunct, but slumpers occasionally found one that was salvageable and brought it up to sell, so she'd seen them before. This one was drawing on the walls, a metal finger ground down to the third knuckle scoring superficial marks in the concrete.

"Uh . . . hey, Moss!"

The robot had drawn a series of panels that told a kind of story, from left to right. A representation of a city, scrapers depicted like books on a shelf with little dots for windows, stick figures on the line of a road below them. Then there was a rose, jagged lines of energy radiating off it. Next was the rose again, but without its petals. The robot, with its rudimentary, childlike AI, had drawn a sad face over this. In the following panel was the same city without people. The robot was still on this one, furiously shading out the sky.

"It must have seen Purcell," said Moss, hopefully.

Purcell, sitting in the dark, blabbering theories to a creepy robot? Yeah, right. Purcell wouldn't have stayed for more than three seconds; she would have been a marshmallow-smelling blur that the robot's sensors might never even have picked up. It was hard to tear her eyes away from the mural. "You know how we were hurrying before? Let's hurry faster."

CHAPTER 36

PURCELL

Purcell shook dirt off the latest sapling she'd liberated from the planter in the garden. "Hold on, if you can."

She held it hopefully over her shoulder, and after a moment's hesitation, its roots latched on like parrot claws. It joined several others that were clutching her clothing, winding around her hair, clinging to her legs. Hunched under their weight, she felt like a kobold trying to carry all its earthly belongings on its back. In the doorway to the apartment building, the sentient slime mold raised its lantern, leaning forward in a motion that echoed curiosity.

Once she'd got over the initial shock of seeing new life rise from the dead soil of the rooftop garden, she'd tried to rationalize it as an effect of the rose in her pocket. She certainly had never raised anything from the dead. But the rose remained inert in her hand and the plants curling around her did their best to stay away from it. Purcell glared at the corpse of the rose with a sick feeling in her stomach. Amma, the darkness . . . this rose. Everything seemed to be connected.

She thought she knew which plant she'd been spliced with, though this did absolutely nothing to help anyone.

The rose was the nail that held the whole rickety kingdom together, and she had pulled it out. She really ought to be doing something about that. She imagined herself safe and sound at home, with her tools and bunny slippers, planting the rose seeds while Cyprin lounged nearby telling her all the things she was doing wrong.

It certainly wouldn't be a quick solution. Roses could take years to grow from seed to flower, and even when they were successful, they could be finicky with temperatures and humidity and nutrients. Plus, she'd be reduced to using a grow light to raise this one, with no sun. What would happen to the other plants in the Divine Gardens? There couldn't possibly be enough grow lights for all of them, not to mention the mycelial network that powered up the city was out—Would there be anything or anyone left to save by the time she grew another rose?

Purcell's eyebrow itched, and a palm that was perched on her head like a funny-looking hat trailed a leaf down to scratch it for her. She missed a step on the stairs as the weight distribution of the plants changed around her and almost went plummeting down into the lobby of Happy Homes. A quick-thinking vine lashed around the banister like a safety rope and pulled her up. Purcell broke a sweat, and an enterprising pansy moved its roots to collect the moisture.

"Ow! Hey!" Purcell resisted the maddening urge to scratch at herself and dislodge all the plants. She continued down the stairs, very slowly and carefully. The lantern-holding mold waited at the bottom, light shivering.

Now that she'd had time to stop running from the palace, from the nightmare of the city, from the Underground, she had some theories about the origins of the rose. Theory one: The Divine was a flower. This, here in her pocket, was the real Divine. People had chosen a person to worship instead, out of some misguided anthropocentric view of the universe. In Purcell's head, the Divine as a flower made so much poetic sense that once she'd considered it, she could hardly bring herself to entertain any other point of view.

But Purcell's internal world was also dedicated to science and reason, which led to theory two: The flower was a form of biotech. Like the biobot swarms that plagued the world, it might have been created for an entirely different purpose by an older civilization and had its function corrupted over a long period of time. Or perhaps its function was as had been intended, but the world was different now.

Taking the flower to the new Saul or to the Underground had been a false choice. Even taking it home to tend and grow was pure fantasy. Purcell knew now where it needed to go. It needed to go to the gardeners, who would not try to wield whatever power it had and who, as a collective, would have the right kind of brains to figure out how to fix this mess. Yes, that ten-thousand-strong brain trust would come through for her. They'd treat the thing with the right mixture of reverence and fear. This led to her imagining what else the divine gardeners might be able to solve, if their technical skills and expertise were used for the good of the city rather than making pretty flowers for a fake divine. The gardens, while a lovely place to work, had served to uphold an unfair power structure in the world. Purcell was finally beginning to understand why Cyprin had been so angry at her all the time.

But wherever she took the rose, she couldn't leave the plants that had come to life around her. They'd die without sunlight or water in the cold dead soil. For Purcell, it was like a bunch of orphaned babies had sprung out of the ground, needing love and care. They had to come with her. She staggered down the stairs under the weight of about fifty plants. The mold heap followed, shining the lamp.

She reached the lobby, calf muscles and lower back complaining, dehydrated and distressed. The potted plants there flared into life, casting off dead outer layers with the enthusiasm of nude bathers. Figs and palms that hadn't seen life in centuries unfurled like green fireworks. Purcell stood at the foot of the stairs, bracing a hand on either wall, watching the scene in dumbstruck amazement. She'd always had a more profound effect on plants when she was experiencing big emotions and not concentrating on keeping them contained in her body.

Purcell left the lobby with an armful of saplings, weaving, staggering. The more plants she had to hold, the more she freaked out, and the more she freaked out, the more plants sprang to life and needed rescuing.

Out in the street between buildings, concrete and pipes hung precariously from a dirt ceiling overhead. The pocket of air she walked through was preserved by some mysterious dirt equivalent of surface tension. She got out of there as quickly as she could.

Purcell wandered through a crushed concrete tunnel, enough of which still existed that she could hunch her way to the end. She made it into the next building, an old restaurant, and left out the back with a fistful of tulips and a creeping ivy coiled around her neck like an anxious snake. She crossed another street where the ground above bowed inward and then emerged into a sport stadium. The polished flooring was like the surface of an alien planet. It even had its own smell, a sweet tang of plastic with an overlay of old ice cube. Each footstep was lead-heavy now; gravity had quadrupled with the plants she wore like a suit. One leg buckled and she fell to her knees, forcing herself back up again. The mold pile skittered around her ankles, trying to keep close while anticipating a fall, scooting wide every now and then as Purcell wobbled.

She made it into the middle of the stadium. Above, the roof was enclosed in metal. No way up. There hadn't been for miles, there might not be for miles more. She was so far down she was probably in the twelfth hell.

Purcell couldn't carry all these plants anymore. And she couldn't leave them. She sat down—carefully—and cried. The ivy around her neck and a mandarin sapling on her shoulder competed to catch the salty drip of her tears. Waste not, want not. Desperate tendrils clung to the plastic flooring by her hips, attempting to take root. Her little mold companion ran a hectic spiral around her and then came to a stop in front of her splayed feet, its surface rippling in an imitation of Purcell's heavy breathing.

So many plants surrounded her. So many. Those who had grown leaves fluttered them in a phantom breeze of sympathy. Branches ticked and crackled. It was as good a place as any to give up. She had her own little grove. She *was* her own little grove. She wouldn't die alone.

Inevitably, Cyprin or the Underground would come looking for her. Maybe they were looking for her now. It didn't matter. She'd be hard to find, and they'd be too late. She'd lost Cyprin forever. She'd lost herself. She took the rose husk out of her pocket to make it easier for them when they came to find it. She unwrapped the little corpse carefully, so that no seeds were dislodged or lost, and then rested it in the palms of her hands. The rose lay dormant against her skin, its prickly dryness softened by the sweat of her palms.

The leaves on her back trembled. Several vines squeezed her arms in their efforts to bunch up away from the rose. Her collection of sentient mold ran away, taking the lantern with them. She watched the light dwindle down the entrance tunnel of the stadium. And then Purcell was left in the dark.

It had been quiet before, but now the silence engulfed her. She'd been working for an organization that did not help people, for a fake god—she'd wasted so many years. Even if she didn't die down in the undercity, the wasting disease would take her all too soon, and what did she have to show for her life? Her achievements were as hollow as Amma's, and she was terrified that she'd lose the chance to do better. Not the "better" of more awards and accolades, but to do better by the people who loved her. The ringing in her ears grew to a roar the same way that the sheer biomass of cicadas can make you feel small in a forest. Her feelings intensified until it was no longer hopelessness and despair but unidentifiable, overwhelming static.

This was when Purcell would usually run.

But she had no light, no energy left, and nowhere to go. The feelings expanded. Purcell was a poor suitcase for her feelings. Like a dying star eating up its solar system, she could no longer tell where the bounds of her ended and the rest of the world began. Around her, in the dark, things grew like mad. Their busy susurrus took the edge off the worst of the silence. The best greenhouse, juiciest leaf mulch, and brightest sun on the clearest morning had never been as effective a growing agent as Purcell was now. Out of sight, the stadium filled with life.

The rose corpse in her hands remained inert.

CHAPTER 37

MAMA INKBURN

Mama Inkburn's diner was a hive of light and heat in the darkness. The air was like a sauna inside, mushroom-scented steam rising constantly off a large pot that volunteers took turns stirring and serving from. As the long night went on, more and more people had been showing up at the diner, hungry and afraid. Now the space was as filled as it could be. Pretty soon they'd be spilling out onto the street. It reminded Mama Inkburn of when she'd first opened this place. She smiled as she plunged her hands into a sink full of suds and mushroom chunks to retrieve another tired bowl.

During her early days in the city, generations before any of the people sitting in her diner had existed, she'd drifted to and fro, observing how people lived. She remembered seeing unnaturally thin children learning to become slumpers by squeezing themselves through the bars of a security grille, a woman crying outside the employment office, an old man picking through bins for his next meal, and she'd thought, *Why don't all these people have somewhere to go when they're hurt, or upset, or hungry?*

She'd gone home one night and opened a hatch in the back of her skull to increase parameters on her empathy signal. Mama Inkburn was a care model, originally designed with a nanny role in mind. The empathy signal inside her was made to draw children in close, especially in cases where they were experiencing distress, but it worked just as well on adults if she dialed it up.

She'd started feeding people out of her own kitchen first. Even the ones who weren't hungry came for warmth and conversation. Word spread, and the crowds grew, and those who could donated their money, and those who couldn't donated their time. And it all grew too big for her to manage in her little kitchen, so with her savings and the donations, she bought a restaurant, and a neon purple heart to go on the wall. People kept it going with the donations and volunteer work, and Mama Inkburn left her job at the water-reclamation plant and charged her customers just enough to cover the basic costs. Some people came in because they were distressed or sad or scared, leaving a little happier; others because they needed a safe space to meet up after school, or wanted a meal without being judged, and slowly, slowly, Mama Inkburn's diner became a microcosm of the whole city—a happier, kinder version. This was her life's work, and she was proud of it.

Some sixth sense prickled her back into the present. It was like the pressure you get before a storm breaks. The air was heavy, greasy beyond the grease and humidity of the kitchen. Something was happening. Mama Inkburn wiped her hands off on a dishrag so wet it only served to move the water around. She reached under the bar for her energy weapon, primed it, and went outside. A man at the counter, finger lifted mid-order, watched her leave. A group of children, huddled with blankets and flashlights, tensed as she unlatched the door and stepped out.

All this dark was bad for business. Bad for the city. Something about it tickled like a hair in her eye, deep in her memory banks, just the same as when she'd seen that rose in Purcell's hands. But she couldn't reach it. Mama Inkburn was not the forgetful sort, so that could only be a bad sign. Was it a story she'd heard once? A vague warning that rode in the cultural memory, coded in imagery and language? The dark. Evil, death, mystery . . . mourning. Every vampire lived in it, every dark lord and their evil doings embodied it. Children wouldn't sleep in it at night. Why was that?

Outside the diner, a man wearing a balaclava and chitin armor nodded to Mama Inkburn as he walked by, keeping the peace. She tipped her head back. Not quite in thanks, but tolerance. She looked up at the sky and it was still blackest black, reflecting nothing, sucking light.

All was passably calm, but unease still gripped her.

No, really, it gripped her like magnets. A physical pull toward the sky.

Mama Inkburn lifted a hand and watched her fingertips disintegrate, atom by atom until the bare metal tips of her bones showed through. She tried to blink away the image, like a nightmare, but found her eyelids holed like cobwebs. Her first thought was that it was a personal attack: somebody trying to take her out because she was AI. But a brown mist rolled over the street, rising into the black sky, coming off everyone.

When the militia man from the Underground started screaming, she rushed back inside to send the children down through her basement and into the undercity. With half her metal skull showing, they wouldn't listen to her. She only managed to save five of them, punching a hole in the concrete floor and stepping through it with three squealing children under one arm and two under the other. Mama Inkburn blocked the hole she'd made in her basement floor with her own back and felt the ample flesh siphoning off her. They'd told her, when they'd first salvaged her from the undercity, that she'd been babbling mad. That only a full memory reset had restored her. This was it. This was why. It was happening again.

Mama Inkburn's eyelids had sloughed off completely, and she stared into the darkness. Everything smelled of dirt and children's tears and for a moment she didn't know where or when she was. She was faceless and rusted, being helped out of a tunnel and into a street by two men with thin arms and rat-tailed hairstyles, and it was a city, but it wasn't her city anymore. She would have to make it her city again. Strangers bought her nice dresses and made her a new face. She still did her makeup in the same way she'd always done, but no one else wore that style anymore. She'd been a water-reclamations worker—a math teacher . . . no, a baker . . . no, a dress-store attendant—until she'd started feeding people. They had helped her fund, had gifted her a key to—someone's uncle passed and left them a vacant shop, and Mama Inkburn had set up her diner and hung a purple, red, pink, orange neon heart on the wall.

The restaurant and the neon heart on the wall, how many times had she done that? Where had it all begun?

One of the children she'd rescued clutched her leg and she patted their head vacantly. She was a care model, but people kept dying, kept getting sucked into the sky.

An image surfaced: the earliest date stamp in her memory banks, half-corrupted. It had survived the memory wipe, had survived every wipe—bits and pieces always did, the worst and the best memories.

A hill, and on top of the hill, a blue rose. "No," Mama Inkburn said, "There's nothing wrong this time, why are you doing this?"

But the rose didn't hear her.

It had never heard her.

CHAPTER 38

AMANDA

Amanda stood in the surveillance room at the back of the admin center. *Surveillance room.* They'd never had one of those before. Never needed one. But after outside had gone dark, some of the gardeners had cleared out the storeroom with the drones and turned it into a wall full of video squares keeping tabs on everything in the gardens. They'd released the fleet of drones, which maintained a patrol pattern to keep the Divine Gardens under constant surveillance.

"Move in," she said to her walkie-talkie. It was set to a different frequency now.

The Underground aggressors appeared at the southern fence, infrared flashes of heat only visible at their wrists and ankles. Staying out of the light of the tiki torches, they swarmed across the green like shadow-creatures. The priestguard engaged, and then the dark was filled with the buzz and color of energy weapons, flashing blue, red, and white like fireworks. Amanda watched until fifty Underground soldiers and about a hundred priestguard became twenty priestguard, that sector of garden a smoking ruin. Then it started all over again in the northeastern quadrant. After the fourth skirmish, the priestguard ranks broke and retreated to defend the palace. Underground operatives in tactical armor filtered down into the admin center to regroup. Amanda shook the hand of their squadron leader and welcomed him to the gardens.

"This has been a long time coming," said the man. "What do I need to know?"

"Important assets in the palace are stored on the highest and lowest levels. There's an estimated four hundred priestguard remaining, some of them special forces. Gary has keys to all areas that you can use."

"Collateral?"

"The gardeners are loyal to the gardens, not the Divine, with few exceptions. Please do not engage them unless absolutely unavoidable."

The Underground squadron leader quaffed some water, wiped his sweaty forehead on a sleeve, and made a gesture that stopped the other tactically armed people in the admin center from lounging on things.

"One more thing," said Amanda. "Purcell Whitlock, the head gardener—she must be protected at all costs and brought back to me. Even if she tries to engage you, do not use lethal force."

The man cocked an eyebrow. "What's so special about her?"

"She has abilities. The kind that will be needed to hold this place together after we take it."

"Abilities?"

"If I explained any further you wouldn't believe me. I need her."

"Okay."

And the Underground soldiers went back out to start their assault on the palace proper.

After twelve hours or so of that, coordinating the response like a film director behind these screens with her walkie-talkie, Amanda slept, slumped in her chair in the corner of the room.

Now she was awake again.

Gary was beside her, keeping watch in her stead, bathed in silver light from screens that flickered periodically as the generator stuttered. He swiveled from the screen to Amanda and back again. Screen, Amanda, back again. "Are you seeing this?"

Amanda didn't know if it was the middle of the night or just after dawn. Her back was stuck in the shape of a chair, and her eyes were so blurry she could hardly make out what was going on. She clutched her blanket tighter around her shoulders and leaned toward the harsh light of the screens.

"What should we do?" said Gary.

On every screen in front of her, plants, flowers, fish, and biodegradable stones were evaporating into a brown mist that spiraled up under the black sky. It didn't feel real. It felt like she was watching TV. She looked down at herself in yesterday's dressing gown, topped off with her fluffy pink slippers. She'd been roused from sleep by an emergency call, and everything had been dark, and it had stayed dark, and Purcell had been out there somewhere, unreachable on her sabbatical, and Cyprin, their interim head gardener, had not been found at all. Everyone had looked at Amanda and asked, "What next?"

Amanda had told them all to go about their business as best they could, and she'd gone straight to the admin center and switched her walkie-talkie over to the frequency the Underground used. She'd said, "The time is now."

It had felt like an unbeatable opportunity to harness the chaos of darkness for a quick takeover with minimal bloodshed. But now people were dissolving.

"What can we do?" said Gary. "Should we lock the door?"

Amanda followed Gary's gaze to the top right corner of the wall of screens, where a man in priestguard robes dropped to his knees praying. They watched in silence as the top of his head sloughed off like the tip of a sand dune in a high wind. A nearby gardener ran to help, but he was worn down to the waist after a couple of steps, his legs and hips toppling over and disappearing into a snowstorm of particulates. On screen thirty-eight, the bodies of Underground soldiers were dissolving as well. Colored mist lifted out of them and rose up into the sky like reverse rain, where a brown maelstrom was forming, lit by occasional flashes of lightning.

Amanda's knee trembled until she forced it to straighten. "We leave the door unlocked. For anyone who needs help. Anyone. Not just Underground."

"What if what's killing them comes in here?"

"Then we die."

"I didn't sign on for this," said Gary.

"But you did sign on."

Amanda left Gary glued to the screens and shuffled out to stand at her desk in the main area of the admin center. Seedlings still covered the floor, their little pots forming chaotic patterns that only made sense to the endearingly pedantic mind in charge of them. And where was Purcell? Still out there on her research trip, somehow oblivious to what was going on? Dead already? It wasn't right for her to not be here, at the end of everything.

A part of her felt, absurdly, that Purcell's absence from the gardens had precipitated all of this. That there was no Divine Gardens without Purcell, and the gardens themselves were waking up and realizing that. But that was nonsense. Amanda was two years older than Purcell. There had been two years of her life where the gardens existed, and Purcell did not. Why wasn't that making her feel any better? They had parted on such poor terms. What if it was the last time she ever saw her?

Amanda leaned her elbows on the stone desk, watching the door, waiting for the first knock. For the screams and scrabbling hands. The little seedlings and fertilizer bags seemed unmoved by any sense of danger. An hour passed, and then another, and Amanda failed to dissolve. No one so much as knocked. Outside there was nothing but silence.

CHAPTER 39

CYPRIN

Patchy black tarnish spiderwebbed across giant letters that spelled out HAPPY HOMES in the lobby of the apartment building. The carpet and curtains looked like membranes, the high ceiling like the hollowed carcass of some enormous animal. Cyprin's headlamp traced dirt smears down the stairs and across the lobby floor, where the trail stopped and grew messier in an explosion of soil around each flowerpot.

"Do you think—" Moss's voice echoed and boomed across the empty space, and they self-consciously lowered it. "Do you think she lost her mind?"

Cyprin snorted and the flashlight's beam swayed in response. "No, I think a dirt monster got her." The concept of Purcell losing her mind was absurd.

Moss raised an eyebrow. "Are you kidding?"

"Yes, I'm kidding. And don't you dare look at me like that, this is not the time to tell me about all the weird and wonderful things the

Underground has found down here. Purcell's the kind of sane that irons socks and writes down the date she opens her cereal boxes. Maybe she wanted to study some old dead plants." Purcell was always studying everything so furiously, one of the best things about her.

"Hmm," said Moss, moving closer to look into a terra-cotta planter.

"That was a *very* judgmental *hmm*!" Moss needed to step off. Purcell was *hers* to insult and cast aspersions at.

"I just mean, it's a long stretch from running blindly away to having the foresight to collect specimens for work tomorrow. She must be very sure about getting out on her own, but—"

"But, what?" Cyprin put her hands on her hips.

"But the drone heard her screaming. Did that sound relaxed and confident to you?"

"Oh, relaxed and confident? That's not Purcell. But if you put an interesting plant specimen in a lion's mouth, she'd be sticking her head in there, for sure." Purcell was so eternally curious, another delightful thing about her.

"That so? Well, then, wonderful, yes, very sane, the company you keep." Moss dipped their hand into the old soil and then rubbed the dirt between their fingers like a detective at a crime scene: *Is this blood or tomato sauce?*

"On a scale of a little strange to homicidal maniac, I like to think I'm toeing the right end of the line," said Cyprin. "It gets hard to tell down here at the deep end of the pool. But seeing you wayyy over there lets me know I'm still one of the good guys."

Riling Moss up was too easy. They glared at her like she'd just pulled their tail, and it felt good. It felt like winning back a little piece of her self-respect.

"Well, the drone heard her upstairs. Shall we?" said Moss.

Cyprin waved a hand toward an ominously dark staircase. "After you."

The trail of dirt, speckled with what looked like mold, continued up the stairs. Up top, they found the Underground's drone in front of the roof-access door. It was flat, like it had been stepped on, and was sparking faintly. Moss picked it up, using their thumb and forefinger as tweezers.

"These things are expensive, you know," they complained.

"Oh, well, I guess you'll have to go extort some schoolchildren and retirees, then." Cyprin couldn't help herself. And why should she? It wasn't that long ago they'd convinced her they were going to kill her. If the Underground had asked for her life savings, she would have handed them over. Hells, she'd tried to hand Purcell over. Everything, everything was on the table when your life was on the line. The Underground were bastards. She shouldn't forget they were bastards, just because they included Moss.

Moss froze, still holding the little damaged thing in front of their face. "Was that supposed to be a joke?"

Cyprin pushed past Moss to let herself out onto the roof of the building. The stairwell felt too small. "Nope. I genuinely think you're a domestic terrorist," she said back over her shoulder. That made Moss turn satisfyingly red.

"You don't know all the injustices we fight against, the little freedoms we give our lives for, so that you and all the other citizens get to keep them," Moss said, angrily.

"What I know," said Cyprin, striding out into a rooftop garden, "is that winning at any cost isn't worth it if you're a monster by the finish line." She stopped dead, thinking of how she'd told Saul she'd like to burn the world down. If the Underground hadn't directly wronged her, would she have thought about the little people at all, or just about how pretty the flames looked? The problem with being too radical was you forgot about people and started to love ideals. Ideals could never love you back.

Moss gave her a nudge and she started walking again, through the abandoned space of the garden.

"Purcell?" Moss called out. "Purcell, are you up here?"

Purcell wasn't up here. Nothing came sniveling and complaining out of the darkness. Cyprin was so disappointed that she stumbled to a breathless halt again.

Moss didn't get the memo and crashed into her. Cyprin lost her balance, flailing. As she fell, her knees scraped on the concrete and the heels of her hands landed in an old garden bed, where ancient foliage exploded into dust, some of which went up her nose.

"Watch it!" Cyprin started, but then she sneezed, and her headlamp threw stage lights on a tiny shoot of green rising from the musty old soil. She knew only one person who could do magical things with plants, and to her greatest envy, it wasn't her.

"What's that?" Moss leaned closer.

The soil bore the pockmarks of digging, little half-finished rabbit holes made by stubby fingers. A dead garden, full of holes, and one green plant whose existence was miraculous.

Cyprin put a hand to her forehead, leaving a streak of dirt. This whole setup stunk of Purcell. "The plants started growing, and now she's trying to save them."

Moss stood up, stretching their back, and looked around. "Nothing grows in the undercity, what—Do you mean she knows how to use the terraforming object?"

Cyprin thought of Purcell using plants to trap her on the mountain before either of them had even seen the rose. "It's not the rose. She can manipulate bio bots, it's some kind of biotech."

Moss gave her a look of disbelief. "That isn't possible, or everyone would be doing it."

They stared at each other in frank disagreement for a moment too long, so Cyprin decided to bypass this sticking point.

"Well, if she's got an armful of plants, she won't have got far." Cyprin stood up, brushing the dirt off herself. "Let's follow the dirt trail." Purcell with an armful of plants would be at least ten times more awkward than regular Purcell, and that was saying something when regular Purcell was always stubbing her toes because she wasn't paying attention to where she was going, or colliding with other people because she was lost in her own thoughts.

The dirt trail took them in a loop around the rooftop atrium and then back into the stairwell. When they got to the lobby again, the dirt led out the front door like a telltale smear of blood from a murder scene. Purcell had moved on. If they weren't such bumblingly useless detectives, perhaps they would have noticed that when they first arrived. Cyprin pushed at the revolving door, which was stuck. Moss's phone rang. They took the tablet out of their pocket and answered the call with a put-upon air. "Cyprin, I have to take this. You can wait for me outside."

"Outside? There is no outside down here. Just more insides." Moss already had their back to her. She couldn't hear what was happening on the call, but from Moss's end it looked serious. They were giving it their full attention. Probably another skirmish at the palace. The Underground turning the darkness to their advantage. Cyprin did not give Moss the room. Instead, she started talking to herself, "Oh, it's all drama, drama, rush, rush, but then they have to take a phone call. Meanwhile, Purcell is out there, probably halfway through a rat's digestive system by now." The idea of pausing the search for Purcell made her bereft.

Moss looked at Cyprin over their shoulder, eyes squinting. Then they got back to ignoring her.

The call would probably only take five minutes. What could happen to Purcell in five minutes that hadn't already happened? Cyprin could take it. She drew a smiley face in the dirt with the toe of her shoe and then scrubbed it out again. Without having really tried, she gave up on waiting and walked around to stand in front of Moss, who immediately put their back to her.

"Come on, the fate of the whole city is at hand"—the fate of Purcell is at hand!—"and you wanna catch up on what Heather said to Bree about Bobby last night? Get an update on who went home on *Lust Island*? Order us a pizza with extra pepperoni?"

Moss's voice reduced to a murmur and even standing right behind them, she couldn't hear what was being said. The Underground wanted everything to go in their favor. They'd drugged Cyprin, threatened her, their leader had revealed themselves as her estranged former co-worker, and after all that, when she was *still* cooperating, they wanted to have little private conversations right under her nose? No, that wasn't going to fly. She tapped Moss on the shoulder and when they turned around, Cyprin snatched the tablet out of Moss's hands and ran for the stairs with it. Up on the third step, she held it out of their reach and used her foot at chest height to keep Moss at bay.

"Cyprin. Cyprin, give it back." To Moss's credit, they maintained composure.

Cyprin looked at her prize. It wasn't a call; it was video footage. "What?" Her legs went woozy and she half sat, half collapsed on the stairs.

"Cyprin, it's okay. I think we're safe down here." Moss held a hand toward her, not to help her up but to take their tablet back. A disembodied voice came from the screen now, saying, "Hello? Hello?" and that was a relief, that the images on there didn't come with sound.

The tablet seemed to lift almost magically out of her hands. Cyprin lay back on the stairs, staring at the mold on the ceiling, and breathing—was she breathing?—oh, yes, she was hyperventilating. The world winked out for a second, and then Moss was there, dribbling a tepid stream of water onto her face from their canteen.

"You fainted," said Moss, dispassionately.

Cyprin spluttered and sat up, rubbing her back where the stairs had bit in. "Did I really see—Were those people that—Is it—" Cyprin managed to get her head between her legs in time to throw up.

Moss's reflexes were good enough that they stepped back in time to save their boots. Cyprin's eyes watered like she'd had onions rubbed in them. She tried again. "Is it raining *people* out there? *Is it?* How are you so calm?"

"Panicking does no one any good. We don't know what we're dealing with, but we seem to be safe in the undercity for now. The Underground—" Moss's voice wavered for a moment. "We lost people, but most of them managed to retreat to a safer distance. They're setting up in that old train tunnel we walked through earlier. The effects don't seem to penetrate underground. I've had reports from other strongholds in the city. It's the same all over."

Cyprin closed her eyes, but she could still see the footage from the library, where people struggled to close the doors while their skin sloughed off like they were being attacked by invisible sandpaper. They'd closed the big double doors, upended and pushed bookcases in front of them, and hardly had ten seconds to sigh in relief before the flesh had begun siphoning off them again. Some of them had been down to the bone, writhing, before they'd gone unconscious.

"This was us; this was our fault," said Cyprin. Her skin was prickling. She wanted to believe that was just her imagination, but Moss started scratching.

"The Underground are secure for now, but I'm not sure how long that will last—if this will get worse. We still need to go after the terraforming object. We need to find it, and your friend, if she knows how to use it. That was likely the trigger, and that will be the key to stopping all this."

"Oh, great, the Underground are secured. Well, then, I can sleep easy knowing that *slightly less* than seven billion people just died."

"Come on, Cyprin." Moss did offer a hand this time. "We can do this later. Let's go find your friend."

Cyprin ignored their hand and stood up on her own. She wiped her mouth off on her sleeve. Well, this was it, she'd killed everyone with her failure to stop Purcell taking the flower and failure to stop herself from bringing Purcell to the Underground. If Saul had still been alive out there she'd probably just killed him too. She'd been an accomplice in killing everyone. Quite an achievement for someone who up until now had not so much as killed a single apple tree.

She'd thought she wanted chaos on this scale, but the reality of it was something else.

Cyprin was tempted to sit back down on the stairs and accept that it was game over, but that wouldn't be fair to all the people holed up in basements and hermetically sealed rooms, and all the people who'd fled into the undercity. Moss had said the Underground had survived that way, so there had to be others.

A thought occurred to her. "Moss, when we find my friend and she gives you what's left of the rose, what exactly are you going to do with it? What world-saving plan do you have?"

"A course of action will present itself," said Moss, stiffly, rubbing at the back of their neck.

Cyprin pawed at her tingling arms, muttering, as they stepped over some fallen concrete while dirt rained down from an unseen ceiling.

"What's that you're saying?" said Moss.

"How far does the tunnel system go back there? The subway, where the Underground are sheltering? Does it leave the kingdom?"

"I don't know. I suppose it might."

"Screw the flower, the terraforming object, whatever. We look for an exit from the kingdom that way and then come back with help." Her skin was definitely stinging now, a much more dilute version of what was happening to everyone in the overcity.

"Mmmhmmhmmhmm." It was Moss's turn to mumble.

"What was that?"

"I said, yes, let's abandon everybody to the crab bucket!"

"My plan is more realistic than saving everyone with a magic rose."

They picked through fallen metal wiring strung across an archway like pulled toffee, then emerged into a stadium filled with trees.

Trees, so deep underground that Cyprin's ears had long ago ceased to pop and now felt like they had a permanently sucked-in quality to them. It was a beautiful, magical impossibility.

An enchanted grove came right out of the plastic flooring, with an eclectic mix of basic houseplants and exotics: Venus flytraps and bananas vied for space among palms and money plants. A horticultural miracle, created by a whiny little homunculus with supernatural powers, who was lonely and lost in the dark. She had to still be here somewhere.

"Purcell!" Cyprin yelled. "Purcell?"

CHAPTER 40

PURCELL

Purcell lay down carefully onto her back and looked up at the canopy. Well, the canopy in her mind's eye. She couldn't see a thing, but when she stretched out a hand, she could feel the plants around her, trembling softly. She imagined herself decomposing, the flesh crumbling off her bones, feeding this garden. Mushrooms rising from her eye sockets. It wouldn't be long now, before the process began. She'd always known that she was going to die young, but she had hoped that when it happened, it would *mean* something.

Funny, she'd been racking up pageant wins and upgrading job titles with that in mind, but down in the belly of the city, at the end of things, all she could think about was how many times she'd said no to hanging out with Amanda in order to do more work, the wary interest in Cyprin's eyes when she'd spilled her worst secret, and how much of the world she hadn't yet experienced. She thought about Amma going to live by the sea with Ceely after her diagnosis. Purcell had lived with death hovering over her shoulder her whole life, but it had only made her cautious when it should have made her brave. The best parts of her life had gone uncelebrated: finding a sister in Amanda, catching feelings for a rival, her love of plants. A love that had twisted itself into a love of legacy.

And love—oh—she might actually be in love with Cyprin.

Her mouth was so parched breathing made her want to cough. She was so hungry it hurt. Her body was probably ravenously consuming her own fat stores.

A round thing, like a tennis ball, hit Purcell squarely in the face.

Fumbling around where she thought it had landed, her fingers closed around something waxy, with golf-ball skin. Purcell brought it to her nose and sniffed. Huh. An orange. She sat up again.

And someone called her name.

CHAPTER 41

CYPRIN

As soon as Cyprin saw Purcell, her skin stopped stinging. Purcell was in her own little soilless grove. Some of the plants even looked like they were growing on her, although it wasn't like the roots were digging into her skin and drinking her blood or anything. A little tree on top of her head had developed oranges, and they bobbed around Purcell's face like miniature planets. The remains of one she'd already eaten were scattered on the ground beside her hip.

It was so absurdly good to see her, sitting there with her legs straight out front and orange juice over her shirt. It almost felt like nothing bad could really be happening up in the city, because a reality that contained the plant-loving nerdiness of Purcell could surely not contain any great horrors. Cyprin had been such an asshole to drag her down here in the first place, *but* if Cyprin hadn't, Purcell would have been up there dying with the rest of them. Although—although, if Purcell had never picked the damn rose, maybe none of this would have happened. *Argh, not all this again.*

Cyprin kept patting Purcell down like she was expecting to find rats or contraband hidden in Purcell's clothing, perilously close to crying. She landed a couple of heavy-handed pats on Purcell's face for good measure, and Purcell finally pushed her off. "Cyprin! Cyprin, stop it, I'm okay. I'm okay."

"You could've died!" said Cyprin, and then, "I'm going to kill you." But her voice cracked a little on the last word.

"Cyprin." Purcell had this quiet pent-up air about her like she was about to impart some totally life-changing deathbed secret. *The treasure is in the—Your father was actually the king of—*

"What is it?" Cyprin leaned closer, and a waft of Purcell's marshmallow scent hit her and sent her back into the sixth grade when she used to kiss the posters of girl bands on her walls. Purcell made her remember what it had been like to be that little person, unjaded and full of hope.

"Cyprin, I've been doing it all wrong—I've been living life wrong. I want you to know that you're really special to me. That I count you as a friend. That I—I love you."

Cyprin had been desperate to hear those words from someone—anyone—for what felt like her entire life.

But now that she'd heard them, she didn't entirely trust them. And it hurt.

Goddamn, did that hurt.

Cyprin picked up a discarded husk of orange and sniffed it. "What's in these things?"

"Cyprin, I'm being serious." Purcell's big owl eyes radiated sincerity.

"After my uncle had a heart attack, he stopped eating deep-fried noodles for a whole month," said Cyprin.

Purcell frowned. "What does that mean?"

"You hang on to that feeling. Maybe if it lasts longer than a month, I'll believe you."

They both searched each other's eyes, and the moment felt unbearably tense. Cyprin wanted to pull Purcell into her arms and declare a truce. She wanted to push Purcell away and never have feelings again. That both things could be true at once was baffling.

Purcell's gaze wandered to where Moss stood.

Cyprin threw a thumb back over her shoulder. "This is Moss, from the Underground. They want the rose." Yes, right. They'd get back to business now. No more pining. No more kissing.

"Oh." A sweaty, plastic-clad dead flower was pushed into Cyprin's hand. She passed it back to Moss, half expecting to be abandoned now that they'd got what they wanted.

Purcell snorted back tears. "Cyprin, you were talking about a bomb inside you, and, and I, I thought you'd been blackmailed into taking me to these people and—"

Purcell's face had a heart-cracking vulnerability to it. Cyprin's eyes moved wildly, caught between wanting to calm Purcell down and wanting to tell her the truth. She settled for something in between. "There's no bomb, they're just assholes, Purcell. We're going to go back with them to get supplies and then we'll go off on our own, we'll get out of here."

"Back to the gardens?" said Purcell, hopefully. "I—I see now how good I had it there, and—and how shallow it all was. I want the gardens to stand for something better. I think I could do that, when we go back. I could change things so that the gardens are more meaningful, and more helpful, to the people here in the city."

Cyprin thought about how to tell Purcell what was happening up top, but words failed her. It was all too late. The world was already gone.

Moss looked the rose over, twirling it in their hands like a nervous prom date who'd just been handed a corsage. "You used it, didn't you?" they said to Purcell.

Were they thinking Purcell had caused the carnage in Asperia? *Had* she caused it? If she had, Cyprin was sure Purcell hadn't meant to.

"Oh, what? I, I don't think so, I wouldn't know how?" Purcell wrung her hands together.

Moss waved an arm. "These plants came out of nowhere, did they?"

Cyprin found herself focusing on the weapon Moss had slung over their chest, wondering if it would be possible to disarm them. She stood and put herself between Moss and Purcell. It was tense, the moment felt tense. Well, what had she thought would happen? She'd thought Moss would take what was left of the flower for the Underground, maybe leave her and Purcell there. But then Purcell had to go and bring all these plants back to life, and now it looked like she knew too much. Like she was holding something back from the Underground.

"If Purcell says she didn't do anything, then she didn't do anything," said Cyprin.

Moss raised their arms in mock surrender, the desiccated rose still clutched in their fingertips. "Hey, hey, we're just talking."

Purcell went to stand up, but she didn't do it like a normal person. Her head and neck went forward like she was about to get herself off the ground and then the plants took over. Suddenly there was a concentration of them around her, and under her, and they were lifting her gently. It was astounding. She practically *was* a plant. And Cyprin *loved* plants. Moss's mouth opened, but their hand closed around the rose.

Cyprin balled her fists. She wasn't willing to use the energy weapon the Underground had given her, but maybe she could slug Moss before they got out their gun or take Moss's tablet away before they had a chance to call for reinforcements, maybe she could—Oh. Moss had dropped to their knees before Purcell.

"Great Petaled Divine," they said.

Well, this was a development.

Purcell seemed confused. She looked at the vines and branches still cradling her, and they shied away.

But Moss still had their eyes fixed on the floor by Purcell's feet. "Your family is the longest serving in the gardens. I suppose the possibility should have occurred to us before, but—"

"The Underground believes in the Divine?" Cyprin's brain was a pretzel.

Moss glanced up at her. "We don't believe in. We allow for the possibility of."

"I'm the Divine?" Purcell's face suggested the cool kid in school had given her a compliment and she was trying to figure out whether it was a joke at her expense. As she thought things over, a vine twirled over her shoulder and did her hair. "But if I'm the Divine, what's the rose?"

Moss looked at the dead thing in their hand like they were surprised to find it still there. "Some kind of weapon, maybe. Or a remnant, like the bio bots."

Suddenly, Purcell burst into tears. "I just want to go home. I need to go home." She turned to Cyprin. "I've been blind for so long and I want to fix it; to use the resources of the gardens to help people. Maybe if we all take the rose there the gardeners could look at it, while the Underground hold off the priestguard."

A cold sweat started trickling down Cyprin's back. She didn't want to hurt Purcell, but she didn't want to lie either. Lying, as Saul had done to her, just delayed the hurt. "Show her," she said to Moss. "Please."

"There's something you should see," said Moss. They made a call to the Underground team that were settled in the empty train tunnel. "Do we have any drones still in the air? Footage of the Spring Palace and grounds? Bring it up, thanks."

The tablet screen was passed over to Purcell. Cyprin looked over

Purcell's shoulder, between the branches of the orange tree, standing by ready to catch Purcell if she fell apart.

The gardens were recognizable only by the upside-down tooth of the palace, rising out of a mound of dirt and muck. As the drone wheeled around, windshield wipers passed regularly across the screen to clear it of muck. It was still dark out, with only the drone's searchlights to light the way. The lights left the shape of the palace and bounced off dense brown storm clouds, then whirred down over a landscape the color and consistency of a freshly ploughed field.

"I don't understand." Purcell's voice was a careful monotone. She did understand. Cyprin saw that. This was the fragile denial of someone who knew the rug had been pulled out from under them but didn't want to acknowledge that in case that meant they had to look at the floor. Cyprin knew that look. She'd worn it herself when she'd seen Saul's fake—Saul's body. Denial could be protective. It could let you wrap up loose ends, get yourself somewhere safe before shit really hit the fan.

But eventually, you had to face the truth.

"Purcell, there is no Divine Gardens anymore," said Cyprin.

"What's—what's all the brown stuff?" said Purcell, her face unreadable.

A voice from the tablet answered her. "Reprocessed organic material." There was a pause. "The kind suitable for plants."

"The sky is turning people into soil?" said Cyprin.

"We'd predicted that the long dark would cause problems of famine, disease," said Moss. "But this is much worse. Great Petaled Divine, can you do something?"

Cyprin groaned. "Oh, not that again." Moss didn't really believe, did they?

"Me? I . . ." Purcell's eyes shone watery in the light of their headlamps. "What am I supposed to do?"

To Cyprin's surprise, Moss handed back the flower. "Bring it back to life, like you did with the others."

Purcell looked horrified. She had a shake to her, like a nervous Chihuahua, and she kept looking to Cyprin for help. "But the others, I don't know how I—"

"Maybe you could just give it a go, so that the Underground are happy?" Cyprin suggested.

But Purcell was already hyperventilating.

"No, no. Don't do that. Just lean over, breathe into your hands." Cyprin reached out and put a tentative hand on Purcell's shoulder, trying to comfort her.

"Everyone up there is dying, or already dead. We need you to try, Divine," said Moss.

"Shut up, you're not helping," said Cyprin.

Purcell lifted her head and took a halting breath. "I—I can try. Do you really think it's going to work? Can I put everything back the way it was before?"

"You can do anything you put your mind to," said Moss.

Cyprin rolled her eyes. That really was too rich. Moss had to be putting it on. People didn't just catch religion like that, did they? But whatever had happened with Purcell, these plants had found their way back to life. Maybe she really could do it with the rose too. She was amazing. And maybe that would be enough.

"All right, I'll try," said Purcell.

Moss nodded in respect. "Good."

Cyprin began to size Moss up again in case things went south. If they left Moss unconscious and took the screen, maybe they could use it to navigate their way out under the city. That thought churned her emotions. Moss really had been her friend. And she had been a shitty friend to have. Saving the city felt beyond her, but there had to be a way to defuse the situation so that she and Purcell could go on their merry way without the fear of pursuit from the Underground, and without hurting Moss.

As Cyprin wracked her brain, Purcell carefully unwrapped the dead rose and held it between the palms of her hands. Its plastic wrapper drifted to the floor. She wore concentration on her face. Her mouth pruned. Elevens appeared on her forehead. A vein ticked in her neck.

There was a moment of breathless silence and then a little rush of air somewhere below waist level.

The corners of Cyprin's mouth twitched despite the seriousness of the situation. "Did you—Did you just—"

"I'm sorry!" wailed Purcell. "I have no idea how to help! Do I plant it? There's nowhere to plant it. Do I destroy it? Please, I don't know what to do, I need to ask the other gardeners!"

Moss's voice cracked. "Shit is hitting the fan and there's no time and no gardeners left to ask! The city is a stomach, and it's digesting everyone! Who knows how long we'll be safe! If you don't save us, then I'll—Then it'll be up to me—All the people in the Underground—My responsibility—I—"

Oh, great, now they were both hyperventilating. The two of them were creating a perfect little feedback loop of panic. The air practically crackled with declarations of *I can't fix it,* you *fix it!* The plants nearest to Purcell began to wither in protest, their leaves curling up.

Purcell held the rose out for Moss, and Moss refused to take it. Instead of politely reasoning with each other, they were screaming now.

In Cyprin's head, the pressure gauge showed red. The glass was cracking, steam building up. Stuck in a feedback loop at the end of the world, what a way to go. And parts of the situation were definitely her fault. Large parts. But it wasn't like she could really do anything about it. She wasn't the leader of the Underground. She wasn't the head gardener, not really, not properly. And she certainly didn't have any hidden superpowers. No, all she had was an often-backfiring ability to think outside of the box, and an extremely guilty conscience.

Cyprin had a terrible idea. Call it a microsolution. Without the rose, there'd be no conflict, and no reason for Moss and the Underground to care what happened to Cyprin and Purcell. She wouldn't be saving the world, but she would be saving one small, whiny part of it. A part that liked her and hadn't left her and was, all things considered, distractingly good with plants. But how to get rid of the rose when there were no ready garbage-disposal chutes, no way to light it on fire, no acid to dissolve it into? She'd seen what havoc the rose seemed to be causing up top, it really didn't seem a safe idea to eat it, but she—She could eat it.

Oh, she knew it was an awful idea the moment she thought it. But that had never stopped her before. She was going to eat the damned thing, and she was going to do it for Purcell. Cyprin had always been on track to sacrifice herself for someone, Maverick or some echo of him encouraging her to risk her life in entertaining ways, but this time, no one was asking. This was on her own terms. For her own reasons. For Purcell.

Fuck you, Maverick.

Well, since she was already about to do something monumentally brainless—Cyprin grabbed Purcell by the waist and pulled her in for the kind of swan-neck, dippy, showy kiss they did in movies (and in *Lust Island* specials). This was it; this was probably going to be the last time. Even if nothing bad happened from eating the rose, Purcell and Moss were going to be so mad at her after this. So Cyprin gave it her all.

Purcell's heels slid on the floor, but Cyprin didn't let her fall, and when Purcell seemed to realize she wasn't about to bounce off the ground, she melted into it. Purcell's lips were so soft and almost feverishly hot, it was kind of a shock. Cyprin slipped a little tongue in to show her what she'd be missing when they inevitably went back to being enemies after this. The warm rightness of the kiss went all the way down to Cyprin's toes, and she lamented that this would be the end.

Cyprin, whose eyes had been closed up to this point, risked a look. Purcell stared back in astonishment as her glasses fogged all the way up. Her cartoonish looks when Cyprin shocked her, the solid realness of her body, her ridiculous smell—Cyprin was going to miss it all.

But it was time. Before anyone could react, Cyprin snatched the rose corpse from Purcell's hand. She turned away from Purcell, shoved it in her mouth, chewed, and swallowed. There was a moment of intense satisfaction where she thought, regardless of how many times this might have happened, how many undercities there were, how many roses there had been, *I bet no one ever thought to do that.* It would probably go on her headstone: CYPRIN ALWAYS THOUGHT OUTSIDE OF THE BOX.

Moss fell on her and forced her jaw open like she was a naughty dog who'd eaten something bad, but it was too late, and she laughed.

"Cyprin? Cyprin!" Her laugh, Purcell's concerned voice, all sound went down a long echoey tunnel, and instead of fighting Moss off, she was sinking. *Oh. Ohhh.* She'd thought something terrible might happen, but only theoretically.

Purcell knelt down, and there was a halo of light around her that Cyprin had never noticed before. She was dazzling. Maybe she really was the Great Petaled Divine. Moss was there too, looking more concerned than angry, and their hand tapping on the side of Cyprin's face felt like it was a door knock three buildings away.

Her ears were whining, her vision was going to static at the edges, and Cyprin had the horrible feeling that consciousness was going to wink out really soon. She wasn't ready to die, but if it happened, well, death was just another thing to hurtle into impulsively by the seat of her pants. She had no idea if there really might be an afterlife, if her bones would be able to feel the rats walking over them. Moss's ear was very close to her face now, as if they were leaning in to listen for breathing.

Cyprin took advantage of that. "Find Saul for me, will you?" she said, still clinging to the hope that he might be alive, even though she knew that to be patently false.

Moss pulled back and she could see her impending doom in their eyes. It was a soft shock, like realizing you've been shot only because someone's told you, the cold and the pain creeping distantly around the edges like predators at the outskirts of a campfire.

"Cyprin, I'm sorry," said Moss. "I think you might find him first."

Oh, shit. She was really gonna die. This was real. It was happening, and she was *not* prepared. Cyprin waved a weak finger at Purcell. "Purcell?"

"Anything, anything." Purcell's big, worried owl eyes blurred into view.

She could look at Purcell's luminous green eyes forever. Cyprin was not ready to say goodbye. And yet here she was, leaving anyway.

Purcell had said she loved Cyprin, and Cyprin had to . . . she had to tell Purcell she loved her back. But it didn't come out that way. "Say . . . say I'm the better gardener."

Cyprin died.

CHAPTER 42

THE ROSE

Cyprin looked down and her hands were blue petals. She was on a grassy hill—no, a mountain—and it offered her the most magnificent vantage point from which she could see gardens in every direction. Her toes were roots and they felt the soil, made microadjustments to the pH levels in a hundred different regions, tickled the right mycorrhizal fungi into the right places. Her petaled hands reached toward the sky and sampled the air, cleaning it as they did so. The sky was a violent shade of blue.

The first she sensed of the meteorite was the stink of carbon dioxide and methane as its surface ablated on contact with the atmosphere. It was a wounded streak of red and orange across the blue heavens. She lost several seconds running survival simulations at various levels of confidence, and when all the answers came up looking like tombstones there was no more time to think.

Submicroscopic bio bots were used to control the atmosphere in the gardens. She gave them one single instruction that overpowered all others and they massed together, swarming through the sky and hardening into a black dome. It was barely enough to cover the whole gardens. Cyprin pushed them, gained a couple of miles at the loss of some protective integrity, but it was never going to cover the whole world. Through the eyes of the bio bots, she watched the meteor strike the Earth and rebound, arcing into the sky, trailing debris like breadcrumbs. Without enough momentum to escape Earth's gravity it got caught just inside the orbit of the moon, and there settled into its own lazy wobble.

The initial heat and impact waves destroyed everything.

Volcanoes erupted, including the one she grew on, but she cooled the lava as it spewed up, to keep the gardens safe. She would do anything to keep the gardens safe. Tsunamis hit the dome, then even they went quiet as the bubble of Earth's atmosphere thickened with ash. When the damage settled, the world cooled down into a long ice age. Over time, everything died. Everything in the dark of the dome and everything in the frozen wasteland outside of it. Only Cyprin and the bio bots remained.

In the silent mausoleum of the dome, she sent another instruction to the bio bots, and they electrified the air, breaking down all the dead organic matter into the building blocks of life. *Make it as it was before,* she told them, and they did. But when she let the dome down so that the people and plants and animals could breathe fresh air and see the sun again, they died.

She tried a second time, starting from scratch, this time bringing back only hardy, highly adaptive creatures like humans and rats. The plants, though, she could not skimp on her precious plants. She had to have at least one of every type, even the most absurd, finicky ones like Venus flytraps and wasabi that demanded grow conditions with the specificity of divas asking for all the red candies to be removed from their rainbow mix.

The bio bots finished their construction. The dome came down. The wasabi went first, of course, as if it had a death wish. Some of the hardier creatures managed to survive for a while, but not past a generation or two. So, she made the dome again and started over.

And over.

And over again. A life without wasabi was not tolerable, so even when the rats and roaches started thriving, she had to mulch them all and begin anew. She felt bad enough about that; some of the roaches had families of thousands, but it got worse when the humans made it long enough to build buildings and create art and music, and the wasabi still wasn't growing right. People, like everything else, were just clay that she formed and mulched and formed again, but the vibrations of their screams were difficult to forget.

Her concept of what constituted a failed state changed all the time, dependent on feedback from sensors that were never designed to do more than look after the climate conditions in a garden. On some level she knew this was wrong, but there was no choice except to keep trying to save the world with whatever tools she had. Keep bailing out an ocean with a bucket. So she kept going, for a thousand years and then a thousand more. Ten thousand. Twenty. Thirty.

She will keep trying to save the world until it's saved.

The scent of marshmallows reached her from somewhere far away. For a moment it made no sense at all; marshmallows had no place in this realm of death and rebirth. As a snack they weren't even that great; the things were mostly air, and the powdered icing sugar on the outside of them got absolutely everywhere. But marshmallows conjured images of a person with curly hair, frayed nerves, and oversized glasses. Someone who had seen Cyprin for who she was and stayed around. Purcell.

Purcell had seen Cyprin for who she was. She *was* Cyprin, she was not this rose entity, but she found herself linked with it, with an ancient AI gardener who was trying to save the world by destroying it over and over.

Cyprin reached out to the bio bots that formed the black dome over Verdure and told them to stop.

CHAPTER 43

PURCELL

Purcell looked away from Cyprin's body, raw-eyed. Her plants had lifted it up off the ground and formed a bower around it. Cyprin's deathly gray skin pulsed with faint blue light, and a flower bud had pushed up out of her mouth, glowing like a tiny moon. Purcell's insides contained only utter despair.

"Did that, did it change what's happening up there?" she asked Moss. She didn't know if she wanted to hear the answer.

As Moss took their tablet out and asked the Underground to reroute more drone footage, their face fell slack with wonder. "The—the sun's out. The sun's out."

Purcell looked for herself. The footage was of the Divine Gardens. The palace was heaped in mud, patches of white marble sticking out like bone shining in the sun. The muddied lake was still there in the distance. Everything else was loose dirt, spread like a thick snowfall. And out of the still, dead landscape, a bee appeared. One of the gardeners' drones.

Cyprin had saved them all and lost herself in the process.

Purcell glanced back at Cyprin's body, conflicted with the thought that this wasn't worth it. Saving the world was not worth it if it cost Cyprin.

But this was the situation they were in. Purcell snapped back into practicality. Rescue people now, fall apart later. "We have to get up there," she said. "Someone's still alive."

"I'll talk to my people," said Moss, taking the tablet back.

"No, we have to get up there *now*." The panic that had been there all her life had distilled into purpose. Infuriating, amazing Cyprin had sacrificed herself for this, and so it had to mean something. Purcell was going to make it mean something. The plants around her agreed. And they grew.

It didn't matter that her powers were ill-gotten from her great-great-grandma. She could never really hate something that allowed her to communicate with plants.

Moss yelped in shock. Cyprin's bower started moving upward. A deep, rumbling pop sounded as vines and branches cracked layers of concrete. There was nothing like roots for finding fissures in concrete and exploiting weaknesses in the earth.

Purcell stared straight ahead. If she thought about what was happening, it would stop. It was like doing a handstand or a backflip; her mind had to hold the shape of everything, at the same time, from every angle. Cement chunks, tons of dirt, and metal wiring came down. The plants around Cyprin redirected them safely away. Sunlight spilled through the newly opened fracture. Purcell hadn't realized how red Moss's hair was, or their eyes. She tugged on their arm (surprised herself with the confidence to do that), and they followed her up the tumble of debris that now sloped out of the undercity, the length of a fallen scraper.

They emerged in the shadow of the library. Soil with the wet richness of volcanic loam covered every flat surface, on the streets, cornices of buildings, gentle slopes of roofs. Purcell stepped out onto it, aware that she was stepping on the remains of people. As soon as her shoes met the new earth, tiny green shoots sprang up around her. She looked at Moss's feet as they stepped out, expecting to see the same burst of life, but there was nothing.

She couldn't leave Cyprin. Not when there was a pulse of light under Cyprin's skin that, with a bit of wishful thinking, looked like a sign of life. Not when there might be a chance to study and undo what the rose had done to her.

Cyprin's bower had pushed up out of the crack in the ground and it towered over the street. With a little prompting, the plants that held her released her to the newly sprung plants that burst and grew around Purcell's feet as she walked, and so Cyprin's body crowd surfed down the street, following a step or two behind Purcell.

Purcell was going to the gardens, because the gardens held the resources she could harness to help people. To help Cyprin. She just had to hope there was still something left.

The hollowness of loss haunted Purcell's steps, but she wasn't giving up on Cyprin yet. She was familiar enough with the finality of death, and this didn't look like any death she'd ever seen. The flower had put the lights out in the city and dissolved people into soil. It was something she did not understand, and like any good plant scientist, that made Purcell determined to put in the sleepless nights that would help her comprehend it. This wasn't the deep denial she'd seen in Cyprin when she'd been confronted with Saul's death. This was justified hope.

They continued along the road until they stopped outside Mama Inkburn's diner. Purcell closed her eyes. A faint buzzing feeling took hold of her, like flies trapped in a jar. If she concentrated, she could just about pinpoint how many and which parts of the jar they were tapping at. She opened her eyes again. The purple neon sign was a bland white now, hanging askew. The front door was ajar, and dirt spilled through it.

"There are people trapped in there," said Purcell, pushing her weight against the door clogged with dirt.

"Oh, you want to?—Okay." Moss added their weight to hip-and-shoulder the door open.

Questing taproots infiltrated the soil at her behest, checking storerooms, feeling under tables, and finally, exploring the basement.

"Down there." Purcell pointed, and Moss reached into the soil behind the counter and wrenched up a trapdoor.

"Hello?" Moss called down. "Hello?"

On the basement floor, among shelves full of boxed drinks and noodles, was quite a lot of dirt. They stood and looked at it, solemnly.

The clank of metal on metal drew their attention to the back of the room. Some humanoid monstrosity was removing itself from a hole in the floor. Very organic-looking lidless eyeballs stared out from a stainless-steel face. There was the sound of crying children.

"Oh, thank goodness. Is it safe then?" said a familiar voice.

"Mama Inkburn?" said Moss.

"Moss, is that you? I can't see too well. My eyes are a little dry, I need to mist them."

Purcell's stomach churned and she raised a hand to her mouth.

Five grimy children poked their heads out from behind Mama Inkburn, tears cleaning runnels down their faces.

"If you can get to the library, I'll send my people up for you. They have a safe zone established in the undercity," said Moss. "It's not pretty down there, but it's somewhere to go."

Mama Inkburn's bulging eyeballs swung to Purcell. "You were here earlier with Cyprin!"

A stone of regret lodged in Purcell's throat. "Something happened to Cyprin, I'm afraid."

Mama Inkburn had nothing with which to express sadness. Her mouth maintained a dental-mannequin false-toothed grin. Her eyes stared endlessly. "Oh, I'm very, very sorry to hear that. Something happened to a lot of people, I fear."

They walked out of the diner together, and Mama Inkburn froze in front of Cyprin's glowing body for so long that Moss had to tap her on the back to see if she'd malfunctioned. Her head corkscrewed around like an owl's and Purcell took a couple of steps back, reflexively.

"There's still life there," said Mama Inkburn. "It's just not your kind of life."

"My kind of life?" said Purcell. Out in the full light of day, Mama Inkburn appeared to be the result of a high-speed collision between a person and a small bulldozer. It was hard to look at directly.

"You organics." Mama Inkburn waved a shiny hand to include Moss and the children in that statement. Then her head revolved back, and she nodded at Cyprin. "Good to see you looking well. Your friend had me worried," she told the inert body. There was no response.

Moss pointed the way to the library and radioed the Underground to expect civilian refugees in a very jargon-filled, "white eagle, this is alpha-alpha-five" style conversation. Afterward, they stood side by side, watching Mama Inkburn amble off, the children trailing her like ducklings.

Purcell took a peek at Cyprin, hardly daring to hope. Cyprin didn't move.

"How did you know they were trapped in there?" said Moss.

"I can feel . . . feel life, all over the city." Her powers, ignited by stress in the undercity, were peaking. She could reach out to all organic matter, and it answered to her.

"What, everywhere? All over Asperia? From here?"

"Yes."

"Well, that's great! We should head back to the library. I'll get someone from the Underground to bring a map of the city, and you can mark where you feel people are trapped."

"No-o." She saw sense in Moss's plan; they were forced allies now, whoever was left alive had to be, but . . . "Not yet. I have to go to the Divine Gardens. Amanda is still alive there. I can feel her. And—and I think I'm meant to go there."

Moss jogged to catch up. "All right, well, I can radio the Underground and tell them to meet us there."

Purcell stopped. "Did you really tell Cyprin you put a bomb in her stomach?"

Moss looked embarrassed. "Yes."

"For the good of the city?"

"I thought so at the time. But maybe it had a little more to do with my own quest for revenge."

Purcell nodded, her eyes prickling with tears. "She was very annoying."

"I loved her too," Moss commiserated.

"Okay."

"Okay?"

"Okay, you can bring the Underground to the Divine Gardens. We'll need a lot of people if we're going to coordinate a rescue effort for anyone who is trapped. We'll need as many sets of hands as possible."

They continued down the street. Purcell tried to keep her pace up. Anytime she walked too slowly, she felt new growth pushing insistently at the underside of her shoes, threatening to tip her over. Back behind her the trees and vines kept on growing at an accelerated rate, so that it felt like she was in a very slow chase with an old-growth forest.

At the palace gates, they found Amanda holding a tiny little washcloth and a bucket. White smears over the latticework suggested she'd been cleaning it. She wasn't anymore. She was staring at Purcell, and the plants that clung to Purcell, and then the plants that followed Purcell, and then Cyprin's body, and then Moss.

"Amanda!" Purcell waved and got Amanda's attention back. She ran to her, but Amanda put her hands out in a warding stance and started walking backward.

"What is all this?"

Oh. She was afraid of Purcell. "Amanda, I can explain—"

"All this—Was all this *you*, Purcell?"

"She's the Great Petaled Divine," said Moss, helpfully.

"She's—What? And who are *you*?"

Purcell's mind provided her with a series of possible explanations. They all felt highly incriminating. *I caused the long dark, but I didn't mean to. I thought it was just a rose. I set off a cascade of events that killed almost everyone in the city, but it's fixed now, isn't that good?*

She cleared her throat. "Cyprin saved all of us."

When Cyprin's bower entered the grounds of the Divine Gardens, the little rosebud jutting out of her mouth went into full bloom, and the power came back on.

"Oh. Oh, that feels better," said Purcell.

CHAPTER 44

THE PETALED DIVINE

Purcell sat in her old office, because, well, the chair had two divots in it in the imprint of her ass, and it was a shame to waste that. Home comforts like that came at the cost of years. "Amanda!"

Amanda appeared in the doorway. She always looked like she was about to sigh in relief whenever she saw Purcell, like the fight they'd had before Purcell left the gardens had been a bad dream. And all of that had been petty and small in comparison to what had happened to the city.

Everyone knew about Purcell's power over plants now, so there was no more bite to that secret. In the interest of airing all dirty laundry, including the bit about kissing Cyprin, Purcell had told Amanda what Amma had done to her family line.

So they were friends again. Sisters—almost. A little estranged. Amanda couldn't understand what Purcell had been through in the undercity, or what Cyprin meant to her now. And Purcell hadn't been on site to watch her precious gardens turn into dirt, her friends and co-workers and secret Underground spies atomize. They were a lot more careful with each other these days, like a couple of teacups cracked all the way through but still holding tea.

"Amanda, I'd like you to have Maverick Trelowny brought to my office." She'd been thinking about this for a while.

Amanda winced. "I'll check if he survived."

When she left, Purcell rubbed her eyes and breathed out shakily. It shouldn't be possible to forget. But she hadn't been here when everything went wrong, and sometimes, with her butt in her chair's familiar butt-grooves, it felt like nothing much had changed.

Maverick wasn't dead, and an hour later, he arrived. He stood in the doorway until he was noticed. Purcell made sure to scrutinize a few extra reports, just to make him squirm.

"Oh, it's you." She flipped down the bug-eye lens on her glasses and stared at him.

He was a slight little man, well starched and groomed, and otherwise plain in every way. He did not have an imposing presence. He did not exude charisma. He neither sucked nor excelled at his job. In short, he was exactly the kind of person who would need to milk a disaster to get fifteen minutes of fame. And he wore sunglasses indoors, which was an immediate black mark in Purcell's books.

"You're more ordinary than I thought you'd be," said Purcell. This was for Cyprin, and she was going to make it hurt.

Maverick came to life at that. "And you're all grown up. Your mother and I got on well, you know, my ties with the Whitlock line go back a long way—"

Purcell held up a hand until he blabbered into silence. "I *am* the Whitlock line. Past, present, and future."

"Well, okay. What did you call me here for?" He was getting annoyed with her like she was an uppity kid and not the acting Petaled Divine.

Purcell wasn't good at staring people down, but Cyprin had been a great teacher. She looked at the center of Maverick's forehead unblinkingly, like she was willing a third eye to pop out. "I want you to apologize to me, like I am a twelve-year-old girl, your ward, and you leveraged the worst day of my life for attention and then abandoned me completely."

"What?"

A potted monstera on the corner of Purcell's desk rattled ominously. "If you get it wrong, I'm going to do something horrible to you."

"Is this some kind of game? Playacting?" Maverick shifted from foot to foot but could not dislodge Purcell's stare.

Purcell said, "Well, now, if you don't know who I'm talking about, there's no point to this, is there? I'm thinking about bringing back the death sentence for staring at the Divine." Maverick's head went down to look at the floor immediately. She continued, "Of course, I'm just a figurehead"—nobody seemed to believe this, but she stuck to it anyway—"but I could probably manage some of the older punishments from *The Gospel of the Floral Ages*. How do you feel about having your bones become a lattice for climbing ivy? Or your living body as a bed for succulents?"

"She was never mine!" His features contorted in embarrassed rage.

Purcell cocked her head, narrowing her eyes. "Who?"

"Cyprin! Cyprin Voltag. She was never my kid. And it was fifteen years ago! This isn't fair."

"No, it isn't, is it? I'll have a general notice put out in the next bulletin that revokes your Hero of Asperia status, with full details of why I'm revoking it so that everyone will know—you still have the plaque, right? And the badge? I'll want those back." Maybe it wasn't as unhinged as the revenge Cyprin would have come up with, but this was Purcell-style revenge. Muted justice that would make Maverick's life a little grayer and colder. And Purcell knew exactly how much legacy could mean to a person.

"You can't do that."

"I can. Now go away, before I decide your skull would be better used by mushrooms." Purcell went back to signing reports. Not the usual gardener reports, but about Purcell using her powers to quick-grow vegetables from the obliterated rose plots, opening up the Divine Gardens' kitchens to everyone from the city, and staffing concerns for the admin center out of which they were now running an emergency hotline. The point of her pen bit into the paper and she imagined it was Maverick's head. But nothing she did to him would bring back Cyprin. It would only daisy-chain the hurt along. She had to remember that.

When she looked back up, Maverick was hovering in the doorway.

"What, still here?" said Purcell. At her command, a variegated ivy in a hanging pot lashed out and Maverick turned tail and ran away.

The Great Petaled Purcell looked in on the Mint Throne just to water it and trim away a couple of dead branches. No one sat there anymore, but sometimes tours came through, full of nervous daredevils willing to brave the Kingdom of Verdure a mere two months after its near-total destruction. Verdure was fully open to its neighbors now.

The world she had been a part of had helped push her to become an elitist asshole with no thought for anything outside of her own legacy.

Everything needed to change. Together with what was left of the divine gardeners and the Underground, they were going to reform the power structures of the world and then hand it over to others, ushering in a system of elected leaders who were regularly turned over.

Purcell checked her watch. She was right on schedule, as always. She let herself into Saul's bedroom down the hall. All the furniture had been moved into the Foliage Concourse as part of a museum display tribute to the old system of Divines. His collection of tea had somehow made its way into Purcell's possession, and the guilt of not using it had overcome the guilt of using it, and so Purcell had a cup each night now, imagining Saul's ghostly approval.

Saul's bedroom was bare but for some potted plants, which Purcell couldn't be without, and a big round table full of experts in various things from the Underground. In the middle of the table was a map of the city, laid out in gray vinyl, with ceramic models of the major landmarks. Strings of green lights indicated safe zones, with red lights for unstable structures and orange for unknowns. Quite a lot of the city was still orange.

"All stand for the Petaled Divine," said Acting Prime Minister Moss.

Chairs scraped as every ass in the room lifted.

Purcell shook her head at them. "It's a figurehead position," she muttered. It was ridiculous that she had to keep reminding everyone, and the way the rhododendrons in the vase at the far end of the table turned toward her every time she entered the room wasn't helping.

Purcell took a seat and flipped the telescopic lens down on her glasses. It tended to keep people honest. Right now, she was pointing it at Moss. A single drop of sweat beaded between their eyebrows and began a long arduous journey down their nose.

"How are the election plans coming?" said Purcell.

"Ah, well. It's going well. Though I wish we had a little more time to—"

The Underground's express purpose had always been to overthrow the existing system of government, and then . . . and then nothing. Left to their own devices, it was clear that they would seek to install themselves in that void. But they weren't left to their own devices. They had Purcell. Purcell, who was using the respect she still held as head gardener and her plant powers to be a thorn in their side.

And Purcell was going to hand power back to the people, like Cyprin would have wanted.

General elections were to be held next month, and former members of the Underground, the priestguard, and the Divine Gardens were not allowed to stand. Perhaps unsurprisingly, Mama Inkburn was the leading candidate. She'd chosen to leave one arm deliberately bare and robotic after her exoskin repairs, marking a new push for AI acceptance in the city.

"Good, so elections are still scheduled for eight weeks from now." Amanda was taking the meeting minutes. She was ruthlessly efficient.

"And the latest census of survivors?" Purcell prompted.

"One point two billion," said Moss.

"Do we have enough aid coming in for them?" Amanda hovered with her pointer above the trackpad.

"Yes," said a woman beside Moss. "Some convenience stores and medical centers have been able to reopen, so we've been able to dismiss a few of the aid workers from Norla and Immersea. The water lines are still broken across a lot of the city, though. We could always do with more shipments of water."

Amanda nodded. "I'll arrange it."

Moss cleared their throat. "The water lines are damaged because of root intrusions. If we were to get some arborists into the city—"

"No!" Purcell hadn't meant to say that so loudly, but the plants felt more a part of her now than ever before. She tried for a more reasonable tone. "No. I'll take care of that. Or as much of it as I can, anyway. Once everyone is talking to the plants, it won't be a problem anymore."

The streets out there were a jungle, and some of the buildings had been compromised by trees, but hopefully they'd have a fix for that soon. Amanda and some other surviving gardeners poked and prodded Purcell several times a day in an effort to understand her ability to communicate with plants. They had found that her thoughts and desires were carried to nearby plants via ambient bio bots, as Cyprin had once suspected, and they were very excited about that. There was a strong possibility that Purcell's powers, once shared and studied, might be able to domesticate the wild and dangerous bio bots outside of Verdure, and perhaps be used to make more of the world habitable.

She wondered what Amma would think. Hoped that she would hate it. They might have been made of the same DNA, but they were not the same person, Purcell was sure of that now. Her grow conditions had been different enough that she would never really be Amma, and she would never create a clone of herself as Amma had. Though a part of her still wished that she could have a conversation with her great-great-grandmother, to demand answers to the questions that still remained. How had Amma fought the darkness? How had she blended herself with the rose? Had she created the wasting disease in her own lineage by cloning herself?

"Is there anything else on the agenda?" asked Purcell.

Amanda suddenly looked nervous. "The sequencing results came back with a match today."

Her sequencing results.

"And?"

"It's that blue rose." Another silence, in which everyone stared at Purcell.

The rose that wasn't a rose but a highly advanced and ancient form of AI that seemed designed to caretake plants, or so they'd been able to glean from studying the rose that grew from Cyprin's mouth. Well, that certainly explained Purcell's powers. It also meant whatever the flower was made of was compatible with human life. Cyprin. Maybe Cyprin could survive this merging, just like Amma had. And—wait—did that mean Amma had also eaten the flower?

Amanda continued. "We haven't got the full measure of it yet, but it looks like we may be able to develop a new technology that allows everyone to talk to plants through bio bots the way you do, and . . . and we found a gene mutation in Amma's code that appears to have been responsible for her wasting disease. There might be a way to synthesize some kind of treatment before you . . ." She trailed off.

Before she died prematurely.

"And Cyprin?" asked Purcell, her eyes burning.

"I don't know," said Amanda. "The doctors still say she's in some kind of coma. They can't do anything. She'll wake up, or she won't."

After the meeting, Purcell headed out into the gardens. What she'd grown up with had been razed in so many different ways, not least of which were the people she walked on as soil now. The old co-workers feeding the new plants. It was an accelerated version of how life had always worked, but that didn't make it any nicer.

If she felt less responsibility, she might be tempted to leave. Maybe, after things were set to rights, she would. But there was so much to do. The fates of the cities underground had to be reexamined in light of what had happened to Asperia. Hidden rooms had been discovered beneath the palace, filled with obedient children all wearing replica Trellis Crowns, that needed to be investigated and explained. Right now, the kids were still housed in the palace, being cared for by gardeners and the Underground. Specialist help had been sought for them; they all seemed to believe they were the Great Petaled Divine.

Purcell went home to her old house, where her plants grew in little pots and hothouses all around the room. She brewed some of Saul's tea. Purcell's favorite mug was oversized and pink. She filled it to the brim and grabbed it with one hand and—Her fingers wouldn't close properly and slipped off the handle.

Her heart stuttered. She glared at her hand and tried again.

This time it was fine.

The flood of relief was undeniable. She had thought that—Like her mother—Like Amma. But no. It wasn't time yet. Though it would be, soon.

Purcell put on her bunny-rabbit slippers, watched *Lust Island* because Cyprin would have, and dozed dangerously with a cup of tea in her hand.

Just after midnight, Purcell's eyes opened, and she spilled cold tea all over her lap. She had a feeling like something fundamental had changed in the world. She got up, didn't bother to change her tea-stained clothes, tied her dressing gown on, and left the house.

The feeling of urgency tugged her toward the palace undercroft where Cyprin's body was lying along with about fifty barrels of wine. Even though it had been two months, Cyprin was untouched by decay, perfectly preserved in a way that made people whisper about saints and miracles and filled Purcell with hope. The rose that poked out of her mouth was still in full bloom, despite the lack of sunlight in the undercroft, and the air around Cyprin emitted a faint glow. Purcell let herself into the glass containment unit that protected Cyprin and allowed her to be studied from a safe distance. She pulled a wooden chair over—*her* chair, since she was the only person who regularly came this close—and took Cyprin's limp hand in her own. Rigor mortis had never set in, and Cyprin's pale blue glow pulsed in a ghostly rendition of blood under the skin. The rose seemed happy in her body. It had almost double the number of petals as a normal rose, and they never seemed to wilt or grow old or dull. It was spectacular. But it frightened her. It wasn't like the other plants. She got no sense of life or personality from it, no ambient electrical signals. She couldn't seem to talk to it.

She'd tried. Purcell had tried everything to bring Cyprin back. But here was Cyprin, not alive and not dead. Purcell was a long way from giving up, though. The mystery of the blue rose was like catnip to her, and she was furiously determined to solve it. When she felt the pull of the rose, she liked to believe it was Cyprin, bored and lonely, calling her out of the house. She liked to believe Cyprin could still hear her.

Purcell cleared her throat. Her heart was hammering. It was time to let it all out. "You've missed a whole season of *Lust Island*. . . ."

When Purcell got up to leave, there was a clack, and then a sputtering cough as Cyprin bit through the stem of the rose growing out of her mouth and spat it out. She rolled onto her side, coughing and gagging, fingers picking twigs and thorns off her tongue.

"Cyprin?" Purcell's knees were weak. She pinched herself to see if she was dreaming.

Cyprin held a finger up in the air to beg patience and continued coughing.

Purcell thought she ought to give Cyprin space. Instead, she rushed to her side to get annoyingly close. "Cyprin, is that really you?"

The blue glow was gone and Cyprin's skin was back to its regular tawny brown. She was smacking her lips like she still had a mouthful of rose. "Can you—" Her voice was all rasp. "Can you get me some water? Or whatever is in there will do." Cyprin made a gesture at the nearest wine barrel, and it groaned like a terrible haunting was taking place in there, the seams exploding with grapes. Cyprin glanced down at her fingers, astonished. "Did you replace these while I was out?"

Purcell's hands reached out for her, hesitated, and then withdrew. After everything, she didn't know where they stood. She felt a connection, but did Cyprin? Or had it been a case of what happens at the end of the world stays at the end of the world?

"I'll find a doctor," said Purcell.

Cyprin's hand snapped out and latched onto Purcell's wrist. "Wait." She made a funny face, then ran her tongue around her mouth and retrieved another leaf, which Purcell tried to pretend she wasn't itching to study.

"Tell me what happened first. Did I save the world by eating something weird?"

"You're a hero," Purcell told her, and noted Cyprin wincing slightly at the word. "When you ate the rose the bio bots that were dissolving people turned docile again. We—the gardeners, the Underground, everyone who is left—are doing our best to keep people alive. There's a lot that's broken. And a lot of people died. But thanks to you, not everyone." She watched Cyprin mouth the words *not everyone*, and there was a new lightness in her that Purcell had not noticed before. Purcell continued. "And Cyprin—they found out which plant Amma spliced me with. It was that rose." Her eyes indicated the bloom lying on the floor, already desiccating, petals fading like a dream.

"Huh," said Cyprin. She let go of Purcell's wrist and eased herself up into a sitting position. She made a flashy magician gesture at another wine barrel. The wood split with a crack, and vines and grapes spilled out of it. Cyprin laughed.

Purcell watched in horror as Cyprin made a series of complex gestures, and it was accompanied by a series of other barrel explosions. Grapes rolled all over the floor, vines crawled up the walls and clung onto the ceiling.

"Cyprin!" Purcell hissed, "You're going to get us in trouble! And you don't have to gesture like that, you know you can just think it and—"

Cyprin's eyes were all smiles. "If someone comes down, I'm gonna tell them you did this. I tried to stop you, but you just got so excited when I woke up, you were like a wiggly dog."

The fury rose in Purcell, but it was a familiar, friendly fury. She was so, so happy to have the chance to be annoyed at Cyprin again. Her eyes stung with emotion.

Cyprin's face fell serious. "I guess this means your granny ate the rose, which means she was just as weird as me, which means *you*—"

The embarrassment was a fire in Purcell's shoes, and she tried to shuffle it out. This was not how she'd imagined their reunion; she'd had so many fantasies about it, and in all of them she'd been cool. Suave.

Cyprin's laugh turned into a cackle. "Oh, don't be like that! Come here." She opened her arms to Purcell, kicking her legs back and forth over the edge of the bier.

Purcell shambled nervously into Cyprin's arms. She was still in her pajamas, with tea stains on the front of her shirt, and—Oh no, she hadn't even had a shower after work.

Cyprin tugged her in close, tucking her legs over Purcell's hips, wrapping fingers in her hair. "Don't worry," she whispered. "You're my kind of weird."

CHAPTER 45

CYPRIN

EIGHT WEEKS LATER

Purcell was snoring like a beast, her head in Cyprin's lap. Cyprin's leg had gone numb half an hour ago, and on the TV the credits were rolling on *Lust Island*. This was just as bad as having a cat fall asleep on you. She was jonesing to move, but she couldn't bear to disturb Purcell. Not when Purcell had her arms tucked in like little rabbit feet, her eyelashes fluttering in some intense dream that Cyprin could hardly wait to tease her about. Not when Purcell was getting hit hard by monthly gene therapy that made her exhausted but had the undeniable bonus of giving Cyprin more than just another handful of years with her.

Purcell, who loved Cyprin. Purcell, who hadn't given up on Cyprin even when she was a glowing blue corpse. Purcell, who still smelled of marshmallows even though there did not appear to be a single marshmallowy thing in her possession. Clove-scented candles, citrus body wash—Cyprin had snooped but discovered no cause. Purcell, who'd roasted Maverick on Cyprin's behalf. Cyprin still snorted over that sometimes. She'd had the chance to confront Maverick herself, but against everything they'd been through it didn't seem to matter anymore, and Cyprin had simply walked away.

Cyprin was going to tell Purcell she'd been talking in her sleep about licking delicious armpits. But in the meantime, she was victim to whatever TV program came on next. She stretched precariously without moving Purcell, pawing at the TV remote on the table, but her fingertips just knocked it farther away. She was trapped.

Cyprin sat through a mind-numbing ad about tofu burgers, in which singing and dancing cartoon rats were apparently celebrating that the burger "meat" was tofu and not rat. The image cut away to breaking news.

Mama Inkburn smiled wide, her beehive of hair dominating the screen as Moss pinned a badge of office on her lapel. The new President of Verdure. Cyprin palmed tears out of her eyes.

Purcell snorted loudly and curled in on herself, giving Cyprin the opportunity to replace her thigh with a couch cushion. She noticed Purcell was shivering and went to find a blanket. They'd moved out of the gardens a month ago, to a low-rise scraper on the coast. Purcell had wanted to smell the sea air while she recuperated, and Cyprin was never going to complain about eating more seafood. However, the recent move meant that only Purcell knew where anything was—she'd done all the organizing. Cyprin had helped with Saul's tea collection and his books, but that was it.

Cyprin stood on tiptoes and rifled through a mystery cupboard. There were towels in there, so blankets were also likely. Aha. She grabbed two fistfuls of an unseen fluffy blanket right at the top and pulled. The blanket popped out like a cork, releasing the pent-up pressure of an avalanche of snacks. Bags and bags of marshmallows fell on top of Cyprin's head.

Purcell's secret stash.

On the couch, Purcell squeaked awake. "Cyprin! Are you all right?"

"No," said Cyprin. "I'm in love with a marshmallow hoarder." She laughed.

Purcell rushed over and started picking up her hoard and stuffing them back into the cupboard, cheeks flushed with embarrassment. "As if I could trust you with these," she said.

Cyprin grabbed the next bag at the same time as Purcell and they wrestled with it.

"Leave it," said Cyprin, with a sideways grin and a sparkle in her eye.

Purcell raised her arms in surrender. "Carry me to bed?"

Cyprin's grin turned wicked, and she picked Purcell up bodily and swept her away.

Above the cloud line, on the mountain in the middle of Lake Pensive, a blue rose bloomed. Because of all the people who now shared rose genes, it had a lot of sophisticated information to draw from, and could feel the arable land expanding, things coming back to life.

Everything was going to be all right.

ACKNOWLEDGMENTS

Huge thanks first and foremost to my agent, Allegra Martschenko, for picking this book out of their slush pile, workshopping it with me at least one million times, and being supportive of my Cyprin-level chaos and Purcell-like approach to hobbies.

Thanks to my editor, Vanessa Aguirre, who went all in for Cyprin and Purcell and helped me bring them forth to the world, cheering all the way.

Thanks to the rest of the Saturday Books team: Editorial Director Sara Goodman, Associate Publisher Eileen Rothschild, Designer Devan Norman, Mechanical Designer Soleil Paz, Managing Editor Lauren Riebs, Production Editor Christine Marra, Production Manager Lena Shekhter, and Publicist Zoe Miller.

And I remain eternally obsessed with the incredible cover art thanks to the talent of Olga Grlic.

Thanks to Ash for loving and supporting a book goblin such as me. This makes two books under your pillow now; I hope you don't get neck problems. Thanks to Max and Fox for making sure writing is never lonely, but frequently bitey.

Thanks to Mum for consistently recommending great TV and books, even though it takes me ten years to recover from stuff like David Tennant no longer being Doctor Who. Thanks to Dad and Felicity for the times where I can't talk long and the other times where I need to be forcibly removed from my office.

Thanks to Mike for providing feedback on the early versions of this book—you are a force of talent, and I will forever be grateful for your existence.

And thanks to 2016 Australian Bachelor contestant Sasha Zhuravlyova for eating a rose in a moment that continues to live rent-free in my mind.

Finally, thanks to anyone who has picked up this book. I hope you had as much fun reading it as I had writing it!

I acknowledge the Wadawurrung people, who are the traditional owners of the land upon which I wrote this book.

ABOUT THE AUTHOR

Leah Hulst/T&T Agency HMUA Nisal Atapattu

Eli Snow (they/them) is a speculative fiction writer, editor, and former medical geneticist, based in rural Australia with their two cats. Their work tends to center queer and neurodivergent characters, as these are the perspectives they experience the world from. When not reading or writing, they should be checked for signs of life. Eli also writes YA fantasy under the name Elias Cold. Their YA debut, *The Duke Steals Hearts*, is available now from Page Street Kids.